UNSLOW horse. 1803

WORDS OF COMMAND

ALLAN MALLINSON

BANTAM PRESS

LONDON · TORONTO · SYDNEY · AUCKLAND · JOHANNESBURG

TRANSWORLD PUBLISHERS
61–63 Uxbridge Road, London W5 5SA
www.transworldbooks.co.uk

Transworld is part of the Penguin Random House group of companies
whose addresses can be found at global.penguinrandomhouse.com

First published in Great Britain in 2015 by Bantam Press
an imprint of Transworld Publishers

A CIP catalogue record for this book
is available from the British Library.

ISBN 9780593073223

Typeset in Times New Roman 10/15pt by Falcon Oast Graphic Art Ltd.
Printed and bound by Clays Ltd, Bungay, Suffolk

Penguin Random House is committed to a sustainable
future for our business, our readers and our planet. This book
is made from Forest Stewardship Council® certified paper.

1 3 5 7 9 10 8 6 4 2

Endpapers: *A general view of the new barracks on Hounslow Heath for the lighthorse,*
anonymous watercolour, 1803. © The British Library Board/Maps KTOP 30.3.b

To Maggie Phillips, my erstwhile agent, who
first saw potential in Cornet Matthew Hervey

CONTENTS

PART TWO: THE COCKPIT OF CHRISTENDOM

FOREWORD

And brilliant Achilles tested himself in all his gear,
Spinning on his heels to see if it fitted tightly,
To see if his shining limbs ran free within it.
And yes, it felt like buoyant wings lifting the great captain.

Homer, *The Iliad*

Command of a regiment is the desire of every ambitious officer. Command of his own regiment – that in which he was commissioned and has seen the bulk of his service – is the desire of every officer of the infantry and cavalry, the parts of the army in which the concept of the 'family regiment' remains, notwithstanding the depredations made on it of late by politicians, civil servants and, I despair to say, even some soldiers.

The regiment is an extraordinarily flexible institution. Most of all it is self-healing. Indeed it is supremely capable of regeneration. In the First World War there were countless instances when regiments (or, more strictly, battalions, for each regiment cloned itself several dozen times to produce those much-needed units, the lieutenant-colonel's command) were left with but a handful of officers and a few dozen men; yet within weeks, reconstituted, they would take to the field again with the same strength of identity, just as a river remains the same river though its water daily empties into the sea.

Field Marshal Viscount Slim of Burma, whose reputation among professional officers verges on sainthood, said in *Defeat Into*

Victory – perhaps the greatest book on soldiering ever written – that the four best commands in the service are a platoon, a battalion, a division, and an army; and explains why – in the case of the battalion 'because it is a unit with a life of its own; whether it is good or bad depends on you alone; you have at last a real command.'*

It was as true in the early nineteenth century, at the time of my cavalry tales, as it was in 1956 when 'Bill' Slim was writing of his experiences in the Second World War; and it remains so today. Two centuries ago some officers paid small fortunes for the privilege of command of the smarter (usually cavalry) regiments; and it was not entirely through vanity that they did so – rather was it the world-within-a-world, 'a unit with a life of its own', that appealed.

'Whether it is good or bad' depended – depends – on many things, but these, as Slim made clear, are ultimately the business of the commanding officer. In a unit with a life of its own nothing can be innately too trivial, for, as Lenin said, everything is connected with everything else: 'The trivial round, the common task, will furnish all we need to ask' (John Keble, *The Christian Year*, 1827). Command is not routinely exciting; much of it is about ensuring that all will be well found when suddenly it *becomes* exciting.

And so at last the hero of my cavalry tales, Matthew Hervey, is to take command of his own regiment, the regiment into which he was commissioned straight from school, in the middle of the war with Bonaparte, and with which he has served on and off for over twenty years in divers places and with mixed fortunes. He has, in Slim's words, 'at last a real command'. And this is the story of his first months, of 'a unit with a life of its own', and his determination that that unit, His Majesty's Sixth Regiment of Light Dragoons, should be good not bad.

* For platoon and battalion, in the cavalry read respectively 'troop and regiment', though in the early nineteenth century the troop was more akin to the intermediate level of command in the infantry, the company.

PROLOGUE

The Horse Guards, London, 22 January 1830

'A remarkable report, so full of good sense, and percipience – and, I may say, betokening rare judgement. It shall go to the duke with no other but a covering note.'

The commander-in-chief of His Majesty's Land Forces, General the Right Honourable Rowland, Lord Hill – Baron Hill of Almaraz and of Hawkestone in the County of Salop – took off his spectacles, laid them on the desk and moved to the window, from which he could look out on the snowy parade ground and beyond to St James's Park.

'Truly this country is fortunate in having such men as Matthew Hervey in her service. I marked him out for famous things when he galloped for me at Talavera, you know.'

'I did, my lord,' replied an officer of upright bearing in the blue undress frock coat of the Guards.

Lord John Howard, lieutenant-colonel of Grenadiers, and so permanent a fixture of the Horse Guards, the commander-in-chief's headquarters, as to be thought indispensable by a succession of holders of that appointment (including the Duke of Wellington himself, who now held the highest office of state), picked up the sheaf of papers recounting his friend's recent mission of observation with the Russian army in the war with the Turk, and waited on his *congé*.

'Has he gone to Hounslow yet?'

'Next week, General.'

Lord Hill stood silent for a while observing the ever more whitening scene outside. 'I hope he shan't become too comfortable there. I can't have an officer of his talents remain at duty with his regiment for long.'

'I think he will be greatly perturbed to have his tenure of command foreshortened, General. He's waited on his chance for many a year.'

'That's as may be, Howard, but the army's purpose is not to give satisfaction to ardent half-colonels.'

'Of course, General.'

'How do things stand on the distaff side?'

'Sir?'

'I've heard tell his wife's "retired to the country".'

'Ah; I'm not privy to the particulars, but I understand Mrs Hervey is not . . . of the strongest constitution.'

'Mm.' Lord Hill did not sound persuaded.

'Though not a great distance away – Hertfordshire,' added the upright Grenadier, as if in mitigation.

'Not good, Howard; not at all good. I've seen too many men fall at their fences that way.'

Lord Hill's predilection for hunting metaphors was always a delight, and could save a good deal of awkwardness. 'Quite, sir.'

The snowy scene without seemed wholly now to absorb the chief of men, until suddenly he returned to his former line: 'I hear he sees much of Lady Katherine Greville.'

Lord John Howard was momentarily discomfited. 'That I really cannot say, my lord,' he managed, but so perfectly pitched as to convey neither dismay nor dissent.

'Deucedest thing. I've seen too many men follow the wrong scent . . .'

The hunting metaphor continued to serve. An acknowledgement seemed all that was required. 'Sir.'

For the commander-in-chief had conveyed his meaning in the inexplicit terms of the chase, which might itself be thought analogy for the pursuit of military success – whether honours, wealth or promotion (or, indeed, all three); there was no need of exactness. Both men understood perfectly . . . though what Howard was supposed to do about it – or rather, how – was quite another matter.

'That friend of his, the halfcast . . .'

'Fairbrother, General.'

'Yes, Fairbrother – a most gentlemanlike fellow, most agreeable. That report of his – the instantaneous exploding of the mine: really most admirable. Clever fellow the Roosian, to use – what's he call it: an electric current? – to spark powder. Who'd have thought such a thing were possible.'

'Evidently not *our* engineers, sir.'

Lord Hill frowned at him in mild disapproval.

'The Ordnance intends granting Mr Fairbrother a good sum for the intelligence – and for his continued discretion in the matter. Can't be too sure with fellows such as he – not at all certain where their allegiance lies, half and half so they are – though I do say I liked him a good deal. Be happy indeed to see him exchange into the Fifty-third.'

'High praise indeed, sir.' For Lord Hill was colonel of the 53rd (Shropshire) Regiment of Foot.

The commander-in-chief fell silent again, his gaze set distant on the park. At length he turned to look directly at his most trusted of staff officers. 'Did you ever know the first Mrs Hervey?'

'I did, General. I was Colonel Hervey's supporter at their wedding – *Captain* Hervey as he then was. Indeed, too, I was his supporter at his marriage with Lady Lankester – the second Mrs Hervey.'

Lord Hill returned to his surveillance of the parade ground and the park. 'I myself did not know her, I regret to say. By all accounts she would have been an adornment to his career.'

'Without question.'

Without doubt, indeed. Lady Henrietta Lindsay, as first she was, ward of the Marquess of Bath, had been both a beauty and a wit, and a favourite at court. The marriage had been short, however, long enough only to bring forth a single child – Georgiana. Twelve years it had been since she died – a bitter death, laying her husband so low as to make those about him fear a good while for his sanity. Twelve years which, alternately, could seem to him as nothing and yet an age.

For some time Lord Hill studied the purifying whiteness – the same whiteness that had been the death of Henrietta Hervey in the tractless wastes of Upper Canada – before abruptly signalling the interview was at an end: 'Deuced weather, Howard. There'll be no hunting to speak of tomorrow.'

PART ONE

THIS BLESSED PLOT,
THIS EARTH,
THIS REALM,
THIS ENGLAND.

THE GLORIOUS ASSUMPTION

London, 25 January 1830

Lance-Corporal Johnson stood at the porter's lodge of the United Service Club with the confident bearing of an NCO of some seniority. However, if examined with the aid of a moderately strong glass, the stitching of each bar of double lace that formed the single chevron on the upper right sleeve of his jacket would have revealed the haste with which the dragoon of twenty-three years' service had been transformed into a man set in authority.

It had not been entirely 'a consummation devoutly to be wished' – not at any rate by the dragoon himself who, in the argot of the canteen, had just put up his stripe. There was many a barrack-room philosopher conversant with Mr Francis Grose's *Dictionary of the Vulgar Tongue* – able to quote from it at length, indeed – of which 'lance corporal' was a favourite entry: 'originally a man at arms or trooper, who, having broken his lance on the enemy, and lost his horse in fight, was entertained as a volunteer assistant to a captain of foot, receiving his pay as a trooper until he could remount himself; from being the companion of the captain, he was soon degraded to the assistant of the corporal, and at present does the duty of that officer, on the pay of a private soldier.'

And Grose, being an erstwhile cornet of light dragoons, was thereby an authority of Mosaic stature. Johnson himself could cite him; and 'degraded to the assistant of the corporal, and at present does the duty of that officer, on the pay of a private soldier' was one such citation. The pay was of little matter; it was that word 'degraded'.

'Private Johnson, if you are to remain my groom, you must answer to "corporal",' his new commanding officer had told him the evening before, the dozenth time at least since learning of his own appointment five days ago; 'I mayn't put aside the practice of the regiment on your account.' (Indeed, Lieutenant-Colonel Matthew Hervey had begun to wonder if *all* the devices and desires of his heart would be met with such difficulties as he took up the reins of command – at last – of the regiment into which he had been commissioned one and twenty years before.)

And so it had come to pass that the newest and most reluctant holder of rank (or rather, 'appointment', for in law the rank did not exist) in His Majesty's 6th Light Dragoons, the most junior of junior non-commissioned officers in that proud cavalry of the line, had at last – indeed, as the sand had been running out of the glass of ultimatum – complied with the desire of the lieutenant-colonel; for the desire of a superior officer must in the end be taken as an order. Yet Corporal Johnson remained unconvinced by the assurances of immunity that accompanied the lieutenant-colonel's entreaties: as a dragoon he had been of no account except to the officer for whom he did duty (the same officer for twenty years; since the Peninsula indeed), but as an NCO, even if not in law established, he would fall under the regulation of the regimental serjeant-major, and while that was no cause of disquiet to those made in the image of the RSM – men indeed whose ambition was one day to add the crown to the chevrons on their sleeve – what could such regulation bring to a dragoon such as he, who had no ambition but to do his officer's will (that is, after due disputation) and who was certainly not cast in the image of a serjeant-major? But in

Grose he did have an appeal to exception (in case of the canteen's denigrating him) – with a little licence. He was not so much the 'assistant of the corporal' but the 'companion of the colonel'.

But, having now been raised to the rank, the erstwhile Private Johnson intended playing the part, and instead of bending to the charge of transferring the assemblage of trunks, valises, portmanteaux, hatboxes and dressing cases to the fourgon outside, he now merely supervised the aproned club porters as they did so, afterwards giving them coin with the same self-possession with which he would have treated the native bearers in Bengal, or in any of the other strange parts in which from time to time he had found himself serving the King and Colonel Hervey (and before that, Major Hervey, and before that, Captain Hervey, Lieutenant Hervey, and even Cornet Hervey): the northernmost part of America, the southernmost part of Africa; the near Levant; Spain and Portugal; France; Ireland – *India*. He was glad to be done with those exotic parts for now, content to take a little ease at Hounslow – so untroubled a station.

Except that Hounslow would not be without its own vexations. Mrs Hervey – he still couldn't understand (or, more probably, *wouldn't*) how a *Lady* became a *Mrs*, especially when the first Mrs Hervey was Lady Hervey, or Lady Henrietta Hervey as everybody said she had to be called, not just *Lady* Hervey (and yet *Lady* Irvine had been good enough for Colonel Irvine's wife) – well, Mrs Hervey, who had not long before been Lady Lankester when her first husband had been commanding and got himself killed at the storming of Bhurtpore, she didn't like him much; in fact she didn't seem to like him at all really.

'And why's that, Johnno?' Wilkes the club valet had asked, when they'd sat up late in the buttery the last night, drinking to Johnson's promotion with the 'unexpended portion of the day's ration' – the claret that invariably remained in the decanters when the second bottle had been ordered.

And Johnson had shrugged, unwilling to speculate, and certainly not willing to paint any unfavourable picture of his officer's wife, even for so convivial and understanding a drinking companion as Wilkes – old soldier and occasional valet to some of the greatest of martial names. 'Colonel 'Ervey just says she won't be at 'Ounslow, not to begin with at any rate, an' 'e might 'ave to take an 'ouse-keeper for a while, but that 'e'd be sure to take on somebody they'd all get on with, and Mr Fairbrother – *Captain* Fairbrother as 'e ought rightly to be called – Colonel 'Ervey's particular friend (and right pleased I am wi' that, because Mr Fairbrother's a proper gentleman, even though 'e's a black man – although 'e's not very black at all, and a right good man with a sword and a pistol an' all): well *'e'd* said they'd all better depend on it.'

And Wilkes had just tutted, and said what rum ways the quality had.

And Johnson had silently agreed, but only up to a point. He'd seen the quality close all right in his time, but they weren't all the same. He felt sorry for Colonel Hervey. He hadn't seen his wife in more than six months, and now she didn't want to come to Hounslow – just when he needed somebody to be in charge now that he was the commanding officer. It didn't seem right. Colonel Hervey said there were social obligations that kept Mrs Hervey in Hertfordshire, and that it was his fault for coming back so un-expected from Roumelia – or wherever it was they'd just been. But it didn't seem right all the same. He'd seen the look on Colonel Hervey's face when he'd got the letter back express: he thought as though the colonel'd lay everything aside and go at once to Hertfordshire, wherever that was – nought but a day's journey, perhaps just half a day – and tell Mrs Hervey that she had to come to Hounslow; but he didn't. He just said he needed a while to recollect things, and then later he sent word by express to Hounslow, and then word had come back express towards the end of next morning.

'And tha knows, Wilkesie, Colonel 'Ervey said "good man" when 'e read it—'

6

'Read what?'

Johnson remembered that he'd not explained but merely thought it (the hour was late, and there'd been several more unexpired portions than usual). 'T'letter, from t'adjutant, Mr Malet – 'e's a good man, Mr Malet – so good they've made 'im a lord – well, 'e'd arranged a billet for us. Well, 'e didn't exactly say "billet"; 'e said "appropriate quarters". And then, I suppose, once Mrs 'Ervey's finished doing 'er social obligations in 'Ertfordshire, Colonel 'Ervey'll take the 'ouse that Lord 'Olderness'd 'ad, and she'll be t'colonel's lady – as's only proper.'

He liked the idea they were going to be staying at an inn, though; and a right good one at that – the Berkeley Arms near the heath and Cranford Park. It wasn't a post-house, so it'd be nice and quiet, and . . .

'We are ready, Corporal. Would you inform the colonel, if you please.'

Johnson woke, for an instant taken aback, for an officer he'd never before seen had just 'if-you-pleased' him, while the serjeant in charge of the fourgon was keeping his distance, as if he'd no right to speak.

He braced himself. 'I will, sir. Your name, sir, please?'

'St Alban.'

Johnson generally supposed that when an officer's name was that of a county of England, or one of its great places (and he knew about St Albans because that was where Mrs Hervey's people lived near – and Alban was just Albans without an 's'), the title 'Lord' was its likely prefix; and not wanting to let down the new lieutenant-colonel by any show of callowness in his groom (or deficiency occasioned by his orphaned upbringing in distant Yorkshire), replied, 'Thank you, Cornet St Alban, m'lord.'

Cornet St Alban made no reply (there would be time – and more appropriate opportunity – to correct the mistake), which to Johnson signalled that his surmise had been correct. With much satisfaction, therefore, Johnson turned to the porters to thank them for their exertions – not least to the bleary-eyed Wilkes, who had stayed long in the buttery after the new lance-corporal of dragoons had quit the celebratory 'ullage' and retired to his cot in the attics – and went to find the smoking-room waiter to relay the noble cornet's message to the Sixth's new commanding officer.

A few minutes later Hervey came into the hall booted and spurred, immaculate and assured in undress pelisse coat (a little shorter than its former prevalent length), with, in his hand, the peaked Prussian-style forage cap he had acquired in the Levant.

Cornet St Alban made the customary bow. 'Good morning, Colonel.'

Hervey was momentarily, if only *very* momentarily, put off his stride. He had known perfectly well that the honour 'Colonel' must now come – the privilege of all ranks when addressing the commanding officer when off-parade – but it had been so long in the coming that its matter-of-factness now sounded peculiarly . . . well, as if he had been in command a good age.

Though of course it made no difference whether he'd been in command one day or one year: the concern of both the messes and the canteen was with the orders for tomorrow, and in this the orders of yesterday were of no account. A number of the regiment had served with him from the day he'd joined, and many more since; almost everyone knew something of his reputation – as they did of any officer (justly or not) – and that was well enough; but no one could have any true notion of what the new lieutenant-colonel would be in command. And in that sense it was no better than had he been an extract – a man from another regiment, bought in, as his predecessor had been, when capability, or more likely fortune, was wanting in the regimental list. Except, of course, that those who believed they had earlier gained approval in the eyes of Captain or Major Hervey might now expect to gain favour – no, not favour . . . reward.

'Good morning,' he replied, holding out his hand.

'Cornet St Alban, Colonel,' replied the representative of the 6th

Light Dragoons, taking the hand, and with an easy smile; 'I am picket officer next-for-duty.'

'And when were you made next-for-duty?' asked Hervey, with a frown suggesting suspicion.

'Yesterday, Colonel.'

Hervey had thought as much. The adjutant evidently confided that the Honourable Edward St Alban would safely convoy the regimental equipages to Pall Mall and back (though a duty not beyond the newest joined officer, Hervey trusted), but if needs be would safely converse with the commanding officer; that is, might do so in terms that would not discompose him in the hour or so that it would take to travel the frosted road to Hounslow – which perhaps was not an undertaking to be commended to every cornet.

'Drive with me in the chaise,' he replied.

'Thank you, Colonel. With your leave, I'll have my groom run up the stirrups.'

Hervey nodded.

Johnson stepped forward with Hervey's despatch-case.

Hervey pulled on his gloves and took it. 'You'll follow as far as the Berkeley Arms?'

'Aye, sir – I mean, *Colonel.*'

He turned for the door, and then back to Johnson again. 'One thing I would know. How in the dead of night did you find corporal's stripes?'

Johnson had always been the most accomplished 'progger' in the Sixth, but chevrons – regimental-pattern chevrons . . .

'Ah went to t'stables yonder,' he replied, nodding Whitehall-wards.

'Of course,' said Hervey – the Light Horse stables at the Horse Guards, for the 'War Office party' that the Sixth furnished, the despatch orderlies who carried papers between the royal palaces. He would not ask if there were an NCO now unaccountably short of rank.

Instead he put on his cap and touched the peak to the statue of the Duke of York not long raised (and to which they had all subscribed), as custom already demanded he should, and took a final glance at Nash's handsome work all about him. This club was indeed a fine place, a 'refuge and strength, a very present help in trouble', as the Psalmist said of the Almighty Himself. And so close to Hounslow. The pictures were as yet few, and portraits only of Lord Lynedoch, the founder (Hervey had been at hand that day at Corunna, when the ball had struck Sir John Moore from the saddle, whereupon he had dashed to Lynedoch's help to bear him up – Colonel Thomas Graham, as then he had been). Yet this new place was surely more alive with the spirit of men nobly deserving the respect of their country than any other could claim: Lord Hill, tender and brave; Murray, Lowry Cole, FitzRoy Somerset, Combermere, Saltoun, Hardinge, Beresford – soldiers all who had won reputation in the cannon's mouth; and from the sea, Nelson's Hardy; and Lord Exmouth, Cockburn, Broke of the *Shannon*; and chief among them, not *primus inter pares*, but towering above all, the Iron Duke . . . What more fortune could favour a man than to be taking leave of such fellow members as these to take command of the 6th Light Dragoons (Princess Augusta's Own)?

'Thank you, Charles,' he said to the head porter as the doors were pulled wide for him; 'Thank you,' he added, nodding to the rest.

Cornet St Alban opened the door of the regimental chariot – with its 'VI LD' device newly re-emblazoned on the deep-blue gloss – and then climbed in after him. 'Leave to proceed, Colonel?'

The carriage warmer had done its job; Hervey declined a blanket, sat back and said simply, 'Very well.'

St Alban nodded to the serjeant standing to attention on the pavement, who barked something (unintelligible to the several bystanders as well as to Hervey), at which the two dragoons stand-ing either side of the pair of trace-shaved Clevelands whipped off the rugs. The postilion – Wakefield, Hervey noticed, one of the riding-master's best corporals – at once sprang into the saddle while the other bundled the rugs into the basket at rear before jumping onto the footboard between the springs; and at a quarter past nine they struck off down Pall Mall.

It was a Monday, not a dozen days shy of the new colonel's thirty-ninth birthday – by no means a late age to come to command, especially when bloody wars and sickly seasons (the black-humoured toast of the ambitious officer) were not what they had once been. And Hervey fancied himself as sound in wind and limb as any – and more than most, indeed, for of late he had not had opportunity, even if he had had the inclination, for the sort of excesses of cellar or table that afflicted many a man in his thirties who found himself in command of a troop of cavalry in a home station. The late campaign in Bulgaria and Thrace had been a business of some heat. Yet nor had the exigencies of active service taken too high a toll: his hair was still his own, and without the little threads of silver, the 'harbingers of seniority'; his eyes were clear and his face unlined save for here and there the faint trace of the battlefield, and no more weather-beaten than that of any man whose living was had out-of-doors. If he had been inclined to – if he had had the taste for – a sharper cut to his plain coat and a gayer knot in his cravat, he might even have been called a beau.

'How does Hounslow go with you, Cornet St Alban?'

'Very well, I believe, Colonel. There is perhaps too little opportunity for a field day, but I suppose that may be different when the squadrons are all of a piece once more.'

Hervey said nothing by reply, save for a non-committal 'Mm'. The regiment was, to be sure, still not wholly put back together after the late reduction and then augmentation; that much the adjutant's extensive report made clear. How quickly and completely that reconstitution would be made he would have no very clear notion until he had seen things for himself. But of one thing he was sure, that matters would be infinitely better expedited for Malet's being adjutant. For some years now the Sixth had employed 'regimental' officers rather than those commissioned from the ranks, the more usual practice, and in Lieutenant Lord Thomas Malet (as lately he was become, his father having succeeded to a cousin's marquessate), though he had but a fraction of the service normally accrued by a serjeant-major, Hervey knew they were possessed of the most diligent executive. Keeping Malet in that saddle would be his principal object as far as appointments were concerned.

'How is Mr Jenkinson?'

'Very well, I believe, Colonel,' replied St Alban again, with just a note of puzzlement at the singling out of a cornet joined not long before he.

But Hervey was unwilling to reveal his purpose, even if the cornet's reply gave him no answer. Jenkinson was the adopted son of the late Lord Liverpool, the former prime minister; that in itself was sufficient cause for enquiry. But Jenkinson had also been the particular friend of Cornet Agar, who had met his death at Hervey's side. They had been friends at Oxford – Christ Church, the same staircase. The Agar-Ellises had been all civility when he had called and told them of the circumstances, the ambush, yet he felt unease still; some nagging question of *loco parentis* . . .

And so he said nothing, and then felt curiously disobliged to say more. The Honourable Edward St Alban was the younger son of the Earl of Bicester, whose family by long tradition held the colonelcy of the 8th Dragoon Guards: there might have been diverting conversation. For Cornet St Alban had more than just a pleasing air (and the adjutant's approval); he had a singular mind and an elegant pen. Hervey had read an article of his in *The Spectator*, on the matter of Reform – the adjutant had sent him the pages along with all the other intelligence he could muster on the officers whom Hervey did not already know – and had been taken by its good sense and humanity. The war with France being long past, this was again a time when many a *bien pensant* supposed that it was the fool of the family who went into the army. And Hervey had known his share of fools – and knaves – but he was also of the opinion that 'fool' was a marque too easily applied. The common English schoolboy might not be scholarly, but he was usually very practical. If he did not care for the meanderings of *hic, haec, hoc* it was because they did not seem to lead anywhere that he wanted to go, and he was not docile. Yes, he, Hervey, had cared for *hic, haec, hoc,* having thought at one time he would take the cloth, like his father and (late) brother; but there'd been many a parson's son at Shrewsbury who had not, who sat at the bottom of the remove until he left school – and his master dubbed him a fool. Yet put him in a regiment to take command of men and get a job done, the more dangerous the better . . .

But he spoke not another word. Keep counsel, he told himself; a little distance would serve. And in this the chaise came to his aid, gathering speed at last as the Bath turnpike, the old Great West road, beyond Kensington Palace opened to allow a jogging trot, and with it the growl of the wheels where the snow was now frozen road stone. Within the hour he would be united with his command. This was no time for diversion therefore: he ought properly to be recollecting; savouring; resolving . . . and perhaps saying a prayer or two.

In all the years that Matthew Hervey had held the King's commission – from Moore's ill-starred campaign to the siege of Bhurtpore, and even of late at Hounslow – the succession to the lieutenant-colonelcy of the Sixth had as often as not been irregular. That is, the circumstances of an officer's assuming command had permitted little or no ceremony, or even intercourse between the outgoing and incoming half-colonels, being frequently a post-humous affair – and once, at least, an infamous one. Hervey's first patriarch, the unyielding but steadfast Lyndon Reynell, had blown his brains out at Corunna in some sort of derangement induced by Sir John Moore's order to despatch every one of the regiment's several hundred horses. His successor, the admirable Lord George Irvine, had been plucked from the Sixth before Waterloo to wet-nurse the young Prince of Orange-Nassau in his titular command of a corps, his place taken instead by the senior major, Hervey's former troop leader and fatherly counsellor Joseph Edmonds, who to the regiment's universal dismay then succumbed to shot from Bonaparte's grand battery. The Sixth had then come under the orders of Captain Sir Edward Lankester, but he too had fallen, so that Hervey himself, as yet a cornet, had brought them out of action that evening. And then, on the return of the regiment to England and the promotion of Lord George Irvine to general rank (and subsequently to the colonelcy of the regiment) there had followed the grim tenure of Lord Towcester, an 'extract', a man from another regiment, whom the cornets had dubbed 'Macbeth' on account of 'Those he commands move only in command, nothing in love'. And in the end his title, like Macbeth's, had hung 'loose about him, like a giant's robe upon a dwarfish thief', his tenure foreshortened by dismissal on the orders of the commander-in-chief himself, the Duke of York, though not before 'the Scottish colonel', as most every man had begun to call him, had wrought a deal of unhappiness.

All that had been set right however when the Horse Guards (the seat of the commander-in-chief) handed command to the late Sir Edward Lankester's younger brother, Ivo, who had inherited also the baronetcy. But poor Sir Ivo was to be the second Lankester to die at the head of the Sixth – seven years later, at the storming of Bhurtpore, and besides leaving a grieving regiment (he was admired by all ranks, as his brother had been, especially after so unusually long a term in command) he had left a young widow – with child – whom Hervey had taken as his wife two years later.

The Sixth had then returned to England under command of the avuncular (old-womanish, said some) Eustace Joynson, who as regimental major had succeeded to the lieutenant-colonelcy on active service 'by death', as the royal warrant allowed. However, Joynson, beset by daily trials on the distaff side (and by sick headaches), had soon sold out to the estimable Earl of Holderness, the safest hands that ever held the reins of a commanding officer's charger – safe, that is, insofar as the regiment had never been in peril of the enemy, and therefore his occasional seizures of no moment. Lieutenant-Colonel the Lord Holderness, brought in from the 4th Dragoon Guards, was so favourably connected both with the court and with the Horse Guards that nothing disturbed the routine of the Cavalry Barracks, Hounslow, where the 6th Light Dragoons (formerly 'Princess Caroline's Own', and now 'Princess Augusta's Own') enjoyed the status of well-to-do country cousins of the regiments of the Household. And then after a decent lapse of time – two years and six months – Lord Hol'ness had taken the next effortless step in his amiable stroll through military life and become a major general; not, it was true, in a very active command (in any command at all worthy of the name), but in a position to which both the government and the King were very pleased to appoint him, whose duties would not detain him at office too much, so that he might lend lustre to the court, as already did his countess as one of Princess Adelaide's ladies-in-waiting.

And so it was that in due season – though 'the harvest be over-late', said some – Lieutenant-Colonel Matthew Paulinus Hervey, younger and surviving son of the Archdeacon of Salisbury, was now come to command. And just as others had come to that appointment, it would be without ceremony, without even the shake of a hand, for Lord Hol'ness had relinquished command on 12 October, while he, Hervey, had in the eyes of the Horse Guards and those who read the *London Gazette* succeeded to command that very day.

So there would be no formality – for which, anyway, there would have been no precedent and therefore no form of parade in the regiment's drill book. And it suited him, for so bitter-cold a day hardly lent itself to ceremonial; and certainly no words from the saddle – not, at least, very many (and so what would have been the good of it?). Had he been taking command of a King's ship he would have called together some of the petty officers and senior hands and 'read in' – held before them the Admiralty orders appointing him to command, and spoken out loud the exact words of the commission, so that his assumption of command was definitely marked, and his dominion over life and limb, as well as guardianship of the vessel herself, would in turn be notified to every part of ship by those gathered apostles. This he knew from his long friendship with Captain Sir Laughton Peto RN, who some three years before had taken command of the only first-rate in commission, in which he had then been rendered an invalid in the affair at Navarino (and, oh, how he looked for an occasion soon to visit with his old friend in his Norfolk convalescence!).

And, indeed, Hervey had thought the navy's a rather admirable practice, one that was perfectly adapted to the confining space of the wooden walls, and which might even be imitated in a barracks – except that, as it was not customary, it could not serve. He was perfectly sensible that custom only proceeded from practice, but he was inclined to believe that any practice instituted with the intention of beginning a custom was certain to founder; for if it were a good practice it would already be customary. He had decided ideas about how he wished things done – indeed, he had ideas that were wholly novel – but he did not suppose that they would necessarily endure beyond the tenure of his command, however long that might be . . .

Brentford came and went with scarcely his noticing, and then Hounslow was upon them, quite prettyish in its snowy blanket – post-house after post-house, coaching inn after coaching inn – and then on towards the heath, once the place of highwaymen (and from time to time even now the gibbet), turning north by the drilling ground to the cavalry barracks. Handsome barracks, in their way – begun forty years ago, near enough, when soldiers were suddenly no longer a burden on the exchequer but fine fellows deserving of respect, the country being in dread of Robespierre and fearful the wooden walls would not be strong enough to keep out the revolution. There were three well-found buildings at right angles to each other adjoining the parade ground, the central one – forming the orderly room and the offices of the regimental staff – built of London stock and topped by a pediment, which at a distance might have been taken for a gentleman's seat, the other two being plainer, longer blocks housing both stables and barrack-rooms. In the early years the whole had been surrounded by what was no more than a park fence, but which sometime before Trafalgar had been replaced by a wall ten feet high, which, said the wags, made it more of a piece with the barracks built for the captive French on Dartmoor (closed though they'd been these past dozen years) than nearby Osterley Park, with which the pedimented headquarters might just have been compared from not too close a viewpoint. (The strangest notion came into his head: might he, like Joshua, throw down the walls – or, at least, fling wide the gates? Might he not give his men their parole? 'Thou hast ascended on high, thou hast led captivity captive' . . . He smiled balefully at his irreverence. He could imagine the face of the sar'nt-major at such a proposition.)

The gates were indeed open. The quarter guard – the 'picket', as the regiment still preferred – was already turned out in front of the guardhouse, carbines at the 'present', the picket serjeant with sabre drawn. The chaise slowed to a walk, for no one passed the guard-house at a trot, so that Hervey, on the nearside, had a moment to take in and return the compliments.

The dragoons' crossbelts were pipeclayed white as the snow on the roof, and their boots beeswaxed to a looking-glass shine. It was no common picket.

II

'SO CLEAR IN HIS GREAT OFFICE, THAT HIS VIRTUES WILL PLEAD LIKE ANGELS.'

Hounslow, later

'Good morning, Malet; I trust I see you well!'

Hervey advanced on his adjutant with hand outstretched and a look of satisfaction.

Lieutenant Malet took it with a look of equal satisfaction, and a measure of relief. He wore his best undress, hessians gleaming no less bright than the boots of the picket, whose dragoons had evidently spent the night with bone and blacking. 'Very well, Colonel. I don't know what is customary on these occasions . . . but it is good to see you.'

'The custom is that there is no custom, is it not? The regiment today is as it is every day, I trust,' replied Hervey with a wryish smile. 'No ceremony, nothing got up special?'

Malet composed himself as best he could, the game up, it seemed. 'But of course, Colonel . . . Coffee?'

'Yes, indeed. And your order book. We must make a beginning without delay.' He said it more with relish than urgent necessity.

Regiments in a state of, as it were, interregnum, were not in peril of collapse; only of a little weathering, and then perhaps of some erosion.

The door of his room was open (it was closed only when the lieutenant-colonel was at office). The room itself was greatly changed. There were some handsome prints in deep, gilded frames – Wolfe at Quebec, Clive at Plassey, and such like; whatever had hung there before could not have been of much distinction, for he had no recall. Fine damask curtains had replaced the heavy green velvet. The old leather tub-chairs were gone. So was the battle-scarred writing table that had come home from India with the regiment, and the Harlequin booty-chairs from the French wars. In their place were altogether less bellicose pieces – two fancy armchairs, a painted and gilt sofa, silk-covered in blue and gold stripes, and a mahogany pedestal library table. A fine Adam fireplace with eagle victrix moulding had replaced the heavy cast-iron stove, in which coals burned cheerily. Before, the place had resembled the business room of a ducal house; now it looked like the duke's study.

'Lady Hol'ness got up the room last spring,' said Malet. 'And Lord Hol'ness was not minded to take anything away on his leaving.'

'Deuced civil of him,' replied Hervey, glancing long at the ink-stand, which looked as if it had been polished that morning.

'That, however, came only yesterday,' explained Malet. 'And this to accompany it.' He handed Hervey a letter – or rather, an enve-lope on which was embossed the eagle with spread wings, and 'L'Ambassadeur de Russie'.

Hervey laid it down on the library table without remark. It might be anything. Since his mission of observation with the Russian army in their war with the Turks (in which he had had to draw his sword more than once – and received a handsome ribbon for it) he was well acquainted with the Imperial eagle. If this were another token of the Tsar's appreciation it was well enough, but he had a suspicion that the gilded inkstand was not from Count

Lieven but from his ambassadress, whose ways, if not serpentine, were certainly ones to be wary of. And he thought that some seclusion was therefore preferable when examining the letter's contents.

'The Bhurtpore table is in the major's office, if you would prefer its return.'

Hervey smiled. 'I am quite content. I should in truth prefer the return of the *major*.'

Malet raised his eyebrows just enough to signal that it was a matter that had not escaped note.

'How long is his furlough?'

'Until the first of July, Colonel.'

When his own majority had been topped by a brevet and temporary command of the Cape Mounted Rifles, the Sixth had been authorized a new major, and the Honourable William Staniforth had exchanged, on paper, at least, from the Fifteenth, who were warned for India (though the Fifteenth's change of station was, in the event, postponed, much vexing him, seemingly). 'Mm. Doubtless it was reasonable enough when the regiment was placed *en cadre . . .*'

Malet said nothing, but eloquently.

'Come, man; it is no use your being adjutant unless you know my mind, and that you may – must – always speak yours.'

'Quite so, Colonel. I was merely trying to discern with what delicacy I should speak. I'm afraid Major Staniforth was wont – is wont – to be rather free in his criticism of Lord Hol'ness. He made his dislike of him very plain. I could never grasp the why – although the why was scarcely the point.'

'Indeed so. But I had not heard of it. You are saying therefore that Lord Hol'ness sent him away?'

Malet raised an eyebrow again. 'Let me put it this way, Colonel: the major entered a request of absence of eleven months in the leave book, and Lord Hol'ness signed it without delay.'

Eleven months – one more and regulations required that an officer transfer to the retired-pay, and his appointment forfeit.

'Mm. We'll speak of it more anon.'

Malet acknowledged, and then nodded to the footman standing at the door.

One of the finest-looking blackamoors Hervey had ever seen – not more than an inch short of six feet, and with a bearing as upright as any on Horse-guards – advanced with a silver tray and the regimental Spode. The livery fitted like a glove, his stockings even whiter than the pipeclay of the guardhouse, and the pinchbeck on his shoes would have passed for gold anywhere – save perhaps with a Rothschild.

'Lady Hol'ness too?' asked Hervey, when he was gone.

Now Malet smiled. The Grenadiers had had Moors in their band for many a year – they made uncommonly good cymbalists – employing them also in the officers' house to lend distinction (or even exoticism), and Lord Holderness had always been close to the Household. 'It was all got up for Princess Augusta's visit.'

'Ah, the Princess Augusta. So much more favoured than her predecessor.'

Princess Caroline would certainly have liked the Moors. She had indeed taken up with one when the Prince Regent rejected her – the Dey of Algiers. And, said the wags, she was happy, as the Dey was long. Hervey smiled to himself. What frippery it all was; except that it was enjoyable frippery.

'Of Saxe-Coburg-*Gotha*,' added Malet helpfully, oblivious of the ribaldry, for there was perhaps no reason why the new lieutenant-colonel should know that title had changed. 'When Lord Holderness announced the Princess's appointment, I sought her out in the *Almanach de Gotha*, but was unable to find any such house, only that of Saxe-Coburg-Saalfeld, and Lord Hol'ness was on the point of writing to Lord George Irvine to enquire if all were as it should be, when I learned that Saxe-Coburg-Saalfeld, being one of the duchies held by the Ernestine line of the Wettin dynasty, had been re-ordered following the extinction of the Saxe-Gotha line a year or so earlier, the duchy receiving Gotha but losing Saalfeld to

Saxe-Meiningen – and the edition of the *Almanach* which I had obtained had not been amended.'

It was not a matter about which Hervey could truthfully claim great interest; nor did he regard it of real moment. But it was a matter that had to be observed correctly nevertheless, and he was only too grateful that in Malet he had someone he might rely on in that regard. But he could not resist a little chaffing. 'And you are now *au fait* with the *Staatsgrundgesetz*?'

'Indeed, Colonel. I considered it a penance for giving Lord Hol'ness a moment's doubt.'

But in truth the *Staatsgrundgesetz*, the 'house laws', which governed succession in the multitude of German states, had been to Hervey a source of fascination (and no little amusement) since his Alsatian governess had introduced him to them with pride. And he ever thanked his good fortune that she had given him excellent German (and even better French) and a toleration to the ways of the native speaker – and also that the royal visit was come and gone, for he would not have liked to foot its bill from his own pocket.

'And Abdel has a twin for whom he might be mistaken,' said Malet, still intent on the Moorish details. 'They flanked the entrance to the ante-room with consummate refinement, much admired by our colonel-in-chief's retinue. Especially Princess Lieven.'

Hervey braced, while keeping (he trusted) his countenance. Princess Dorothea Lieven had pressed him hard on behalf of the Tsar's cause against the Ottomans – she whose letter (he supposed) now awaited his attention, and whose munificence graced his writing table. Years of intriguing had evidently convinced her that all men were susceptible to her charm; that she could persuade them to undertake commissions which in the cold light of day they would surely have seen for what they were – invitations to disloyalty (or worse). Before leaving for the Levant, via St Petersburg, he had agreed to furnish her with his frank impressions of the Russian army, and likewise of the Turk. And this he had done with the knowledge of the Horse Guards. There was yet unfinished business on her account, however; business requiring some circumspection. Further to rendering his opinion in writing he had agreed then to meet with her, for (in her words) the purposes of clarification and elaboration, though he was yet to tell the Horse Guards of this. 'Princess Lieven has been here? How so?'

'She accompanied the King, who came with Princess Augusta.'

'The King?'

'Forgive me, Colonel; I had supposed you knew of it.'

'News was not too much to be had in Bulgaria. I may take it that all was as His Majesty wished?'

'Very much so, though he had to retire after the luncheon. He was very fatigued.'

'Well, well . . .' He took his chair. 'To horse, then: what would you have me know, at last?'

Malet sat the other side of the table, put on a pair of reading spectacles and took up his order book. 'You have yesterday's states, Colonel; they are not much changed. Worsley's troop – B, since the reductions – is at Maidenhead still. There were more disturbances during Sunday – two more barns burned.'

'Deuced business.' There seemed to him an especial evil in burning the summer's harvest in midwinter. 'How long will they be there?'

'Until the Oxford lieutenancy assigns its yeomanry – what's left of them. I understand the request was made on Sunday. I can't think they can be relieved before the week is out.'

'Mm. I'll wager the good freeholders of Berkshire will rue the extra pennies on the rates to pay for soldiers – first a troop of regulars, and then Lord Churchill's men. A deuced expensive economy their own yeomanry's discharge.' (The First Regiment of Berkshire Gentlemen and Yeomanry Cavalry had been disbanded three years before, in the late Mr Canning's great scheme of retrenchment.)

'And Vanneck's troop has not yet had its recall from Windsor.'

Hervey nodded. This was the everyday of light cavalry, even in the dead of the year: a troop here, another there – dispersal in penny-packets, with nothing more for the lieutenant-colonel to command than clerks and bottle-washers . . . 'Carry on.'

'It was a poor harvest, and the winter early and hard,' said Malet. 'There is notice just received of something altogether more agreeable, however. We are warned to send a troop to Brussels, for the celebrations at Waterloo. Their king will attend, Lord Wellington also and divers German nobles – and Princess Augusta, and so it seems the Horse Guards think it propitious that a troop of ours be sent, though if our King goes too, as he declared it his intention to when he paid his visit here, then I fancy there'll be his Life Guards and Blues as well.'

Hervey was at once intrigued. After the defeat of General Bonaparte in 1815 the Congress of Vienna had made a united kingdom of the Dutch Netherlands and the old Austrian (and before that the Spanish) Netherlands, under a Dutch king. There had seemed to those great statesmen redrawing the map of Europe no cause or just impediment why the Flanders of Rubens, Brueghel and van Dyck (and French-speaking Brabant and Wallonia) should not be joined together in constitutional matrimony with the old Dutch Republic – a 'buffer state' north of France. For why should not a Calvinist live in harmony with a Catholic? And why should difference of language be any obstacle to mutual understanding? Well, that was what the great statesmen of Europe had thought, so why should he, Colonel Matthew Hervey, have his doubts? These things were of no account compared with the necessity that the borders of France should not extend any further to the north, and that the Scheldt be not in French hands – pointed, as it were, like the barrel of a gun towards the Saxon shore. And so the Congress had pronounced the Dutch and the Belgics 'man and wife', one polity that no man must put asunder – without, that is, the consent of the Concert of Europe. Brussels was no longer the city it had once been (now alternating with

Amsterdam as the capital every two years, with the government remaining in The Hague), though the crown prince held court there – and the crown prince had fought at Waterloo.

'Have you warned a troop?' asked Hervey.

'No, Colonel; I imagined you might express a preference.'

'It ought rightly to be the senior.'

Malet frowned, as if the moment had come. 'Tyrwhitt's. And in this resides a difficulty. He is in arrest.'

Nothing that occurred in a regiment of cavalry was without precedent; no delinquency of the rank and file, nor of those holding His Majesty's commission, had the power to astonish – or, at least, should not have possessed that power over any who had served for a year or more. Nevertheless, somehow – perhaps by the manner of its discovery – the precedented occurrence could still come as a surprise.

'You *had* thought of informing me before the day was out – even had we not the arduous task of warning a troop for Brussels? How so is he in arrest?'

Malet raised an eyebrow, acknowledging the further chaffing. 'It seemed . . . *perverse* to include it with the first sips of your coffee, Colonel. I have as yet scant detail, but it would appear that he is detained in Dublin on charges that may amount to bigamy.'

'Oh, good God!' He'd never much cared for Tyrwhitt, not that he'd ever served with him in any sense that made for the term 'fellow officer'. 'Bigamy: better it were . . .' He was going to say 'buggery', but thought better of it. 'Better it were evading debts at the tables.'

'It is not edifying, Colonel; no.'

In this Hervey knew full well that the opinion of his mess would not be unanimous, for it was a truth universally acknowledged: what female heart could resist a red coat (or a blue one atop a cavalry mount)? It was an essential part of female education, said that clerical wit, Sydney Smith: 'As you have the rocking horse to accustom you to ride, I would have military dolls in the nursery, to harden their

25

hearts against officers and red coats.' *Caveat virgo* was the motto of many a wearer of the King's coat, red or otherwise.

'Though he must have the benefit of innocence until proven otherwise,' he said, trying to convince himself as much as Malet. 'Who is the lady – the other lady, I mean?'

'Colonel, the business is one of some convolution, and there is nothing that may be done this day. Might we suspend it until I have better intelligence, and more pressing matters are dealt with?'

Hervey was more than content to. His first cup of coffee was not yet drained. 'Very well. And is that the worst?'

'I think . . . yes.'

'Mm. Then by all means let us have things as you see fit.'

'Thank you, Colonel. Shall I warn Vanneck for Brussels instead?'

'He or Worsley . . . No, let it be Vanneck. None of them was there that day, but his sar'nt-major was.'

Malet nodded. 'Which brings me to the very question. Yesterday I received a communication from Lord Hol'ness expressing the wish that Mr Rennie join him as soon as may be. He's secured for him a commission, which in turn of course presents a vacancy . . .'

'Ah, the very question indeed, but not entirely unexpected. I'll make no remark now.'

'Of course.'

But the prospects, he knew, would be diverting to all and sundry – a new commanding officer and a new regimental serjeant-major. What sayeth Scripture? – *For the priesthood being changed, there is made of necessity a change also of the law* . . . 'Kick on.'

Malet changed the subject, as bid, much as he would have liked to speak his mind (which for the time being could perfectly well wait). 'Did you call on Lord Hill, Colonel?'

'No, I had not the opportunity. He'd lately taken leave.'

'You are requested to meet with him on Thursday seven days. I've tried to discover to what purpose, but with little success, other than, I believe, it is in connection with aid to be given the civil power in the expectation of unrest this year.'

'I wonder that the commander-in-chief himself should want to speak with me on such a matter . . .'

'I understand that others have been summoned too.'

'Most odd. Well, we shall see what we shall see, but it would be useful to know who other is to attend. What else?'

Reports, returns, reckonings, states, orders, courts of inquiry, redresses of grievance – all the administrative baggage of a regiment in peace, whose expenditure and regulation was the earnest concern of the Ordnance, the War Office and the Horse Guards: these must pass under the eye of the commanding officer. Malet himself had no wish to burden him – this was, after all, an adjutant's commonplace – yet the lieutenant-colonel's signature must ultimately attest to the sound management of the public purse and adherence to King's Regulations. He must at least apprise him of the matters on which the increasing army of clerks in Whitehall sharpened their quills for battle.

'I've warned the regimental staff to be ready for your inspection this afternoon, or tomorrow.'

The regimental staff, the not-quite-gentlemen (or not-at-all gentlemen) – the quartermaster, riding-master, paymaster, surgeon, veterinarian: these were the men on whose good artisan skill and housekeeping the regiment depended (and in great part his own reputation relied). Their ledgers were indeed bulwarks. Yes, he would see those books and their bearers presently. Besides, it was as good a way as any to acquaint himself with the latter three, who had joined only lately (the sawbones and the horse doctor since his leaving for the Levant).

He nodded.

Malet now smiled, a shade warily. 'And Mr Pearce requests an interview.'

In the Sixth, as a rule, a subaltern officer requesting an interview of the commanding officer did so for one of four reasons: to resign his commission; to exchange with an officer in another regiment; to purchase his promotion; or to marry. It was no more than a courtesy

that he should do so. To resign he merely had to send in his papers
to the regimental agent in Craig's Court, off Whitehall, and wait for
a buyer. To exchange, the same. Likewise promotion. There was
nothing that Messrs Greenwood, Cox and Hammersley could not
arrange for the appropriate fee. Marriage was quite another business. It was indeed no business of anyone's but the contracting
parties, but for a reason that no one could ever recall an officer
sought a blessing. It could scarcely have been imagined that a commanding officer might withhold it, though there had been talk once
in the mess of a colonel who took an objection to the lady . . .

'You're not inclined to tell me why?'

Malet thought for a moment. 'I'm not able to tell *all*, for I simply
don't know. But he's asked for the hand of Lincoln's daughter.'

Hervey was taken aback, for Lincoln was quartermaster. When
Tom Weymouth, heir to Henrietta's guardian, the Marquess of
Bath, eloped with the daughter of the Warminster turnpike-keeper
the Longleat heavens had fallen – and remained so still. Edward
Pearce had come to the regiment five or six years ago straight from
Eton, where his learning, looks and graceful bat had by all accounts
made him one of the most popular Oppidans of his day. He had
charmed Calcutta and the regiment alike, as well as throwing himself into the fight at Bhurtpore with commendable zeal. His future
seemed assured – as befitted the son of one of the most respected
of men. And now . . .

But Hervey had met Lucy Lincoln, in India – a girl of fifteen, her
mother not long widowed (her late husband a quartermaster of
Foot) and soon to be married to the Sixth's then regimental serjeant-major. That was five, nearly six, years ago. Yet how he
remembered the Lincolns' wedding – four hundred dragoons confounded, who had each believed that the bachelorhood of the
finest, longest-serving sar'nt-major the regiment had ever known
was somehow a condition of his service. The Lincolns had sent
Lucy to England soon afterwards to an academy for young ladies
(Mr Lincoln was not without accumulated means, and on her

mother's side Mrs Lincoln was from a respectable family of yeoman farmers, and ran a ragged school for the children of the sepoys in the neighbouring lines). Lucy Lincoln, he'd heard say, was now as pretty as the daughter of any earl, and twice as clever. Nevertheless . . .

'I wonder what says the quartermaster.'

'Lincoln says next to nothing even when he's talkative.'

Hervey smiled. 'Indeed, indeed. And what will say Pearce's father?'

Lieutenant-General Sir James Pearce was Assistant Secretary at War. There was no knowing his temper. But his younger son was intelligent and clean-limbed – Hervey had taken to him at once when he joined – and he supposed him perfectly sensible.

Malet merely inclined his head.

'Then I should see him without delay.'

'And Rennell.'

'Rennell intends committing matrimony too?'

'No, I may say that with assurance. Quite the opposite indeed.'

'Is this to be a game of guessing, Malet? Rennell was taking instruction from a priest when last I heard.'

'He was. And he is now of that persuasion; and he intends going to Rome to seek his ordination.'

'Well, what a rich tapestry of cravings is the subalterns' list. I must see him too without delay.'

The orderly trumpeter sounded 'Stables' from the middle of the parade ground – faultless quavers, middle and then treble C, carrying into the room as if nothing stood between bell and ear.

'The trumpet-major, Colonel. He was insistent that he do duty.'

Hervey smiled to himself. This was indeed no common day. But you couldn't fault a man who risked his own reputation for no need (sounding calls on a cavalry trumpet on a day so cold was a hazardous affair).

'Law?'

'Just so. He has the trumpeters in excellent fettle, mind.'

'And the band?'

The trumpeters were dragoons, 'on the strength'; the band was a more or less private affair, kept at the officers' expense – a few men who showed an aptitude for the clarionet, horn or some such, but who under a decent baton made pleasant music.

'We've not much seen them of late. They've been greatly in demand in the theatres. The new bandmaster is spirited – German again – and the band fund stands in good health. And they were re-clothed for the King's visit, in large part at Lord Hol'ness's expense.'

Hervey sighed inaudibly at yet another reminder of his predecessor's deep pockets. 'Capital. But the King: the talk at the United Service is that he will not see another year. Does he truly intend going to Brussels?'

'His very words, it seems, were that he intended once more to ride at the head of his cavalry in a charge over the battlefield again, as he had that day in June.' (Malet raised his eyebrows yet again, for the fanciful notion that the Prince Regent had been at Waterloo was rapidly becoming a subject of mirth.) 'In truth, though, I don't suppose there'd be a horse capable of carrying him, and I can't suppose, either, that the exertion would be healthful. After his visit here the surgeon observed that so great must be the excessive demand on every limb and organ that he could not hope to see another six months.'

'Well I am sorry for it, for I cannot abide the uncertainty that will hang on the new order.'

'Indeed, Colonel. The new King would have us all dressed in red.'

'What? How so?'

'I have it on the best authority that he is violently of the opinion that only sailors should wear blue.'

Hervey frowned. The Duke of Clarence had of late been Lord High Admiral, an honorific that he'd taken with excessive zeal. 'I fancy he might moderate his opinion once the estimates go before parliament.' (He most certainly hoped so, for he had just laid out a small fortune with the regiment's tailor: His Majesty clothed his soldiers at the public expense, but not his officers.) 'Incidentally, I was sorry that old Gieve had shut up shop. He made my cornet's uniform. But your assurances of Herr Meyer I thought were well found.'

'I believe that Lord George had little discretion in the matter of Herr Meyer: the King was most insistent that his tailor was without peer. I believe His Majesty would have taken the sealed patterns there himself that very afternoon had he not been indisposed.'

'Brummell's tailor too, I think.'

Malet smiled. 'Indeed, Colonel. The cornets were most reassured on hearing that.'

The coal burned low in the grate as the agreeable march through the agenda of command was reaching its end – save for the affair of Tyrwhitt's two wives – and Malet rose to pick up the scuttle.

'Not too great a blaze,' said Hervey. 'I don't intend returning after mess. I'll see the regimental staff in due course – Friday, let us say.'

'Very good, Colonel.'

'Now, Malet, your own affairs: I should deem it to be the greatest benefit were you to continue in your present position, though I know there will be a vacancy soon and you would wish for a troop.' Hervey had not intended allowing his adjutant to question that supposition, but he paused momentarily, and Malet was eager to correct him.

'I would wish for a troop, Colonel, only were the regiment more actively engaged; I am very content where I am.'

Hervey inclined his head, a little show of gratification. 'But be that as it may, I would not have you forfeit promotion. By my reckoning – and yours, if I have understood matters rightly – F Troop will be but a statement of intention for six months at least, with neither the men nor horses. We may as well have its captain in the orderly room. I've spoken of it with the Horse Guards, and they have no objection. The rank is yours for the payment of the regulation price.'

Malet was temporarily overcome. Officers of the artillery and the engineers were promoted without purchase on seniority and merit, inordinately slowly. Those of the cavalry and the infantry, with rare exceptions, purchased theirs – and, though increasingly regulated (or so the Horse Guards thought), at sometimes astonishing prices through private treaty, and with equally astonishing celerity. Only on the death of an officer on active service did a vacancy pass without purchase to the next senior.

'I am in your debt, Colonel.'

Which was, in some part indeed, Hervey's intention.

But he waved it aside. 'I think we might repair to mess now?'

Malet looked at his watch. It was past one o'clock. 'I think you'll find all the officers in barracks will have assembled, Colonel.'

'I rather thought they might have,' said Hervey, with a wry smile. 'And Monsieur Carême brought from Paris to cook?'

Malet's smile reflected Hervey's. 'So you've heard of our triumph.'

Hervey frowned: what triumph was this?

'Monsieur Carême.'

'Monsieur Carême what?'

'Ah, I thought you must have heard. Lord Hol'ness had him come for the King's visit.'

Hervey made no reply but to shake his head in despair at his ill-judged joke. Who would have thought it – Carême brought from Paris (he *supposed* from Paris) to make a culinary impression? But Lieutenant-Colonel, and now Major-General, the Lord Holderness evidently reckoned that in want of a bloody war and a sickly season to make vacancies for promotion, rich sauces and *pâtisserie beurre* would do instead. He could only congratulate the noble earl on knowing the King's mind – and stomach. For himself, he would have to trust to far plainer fare.

'Hervey, I am passing warm for the first time since leaving London – if indeed I were truly warm there. I cannot fathom why your countrymen ever return hither from sunny climes.'

Hervey's 'particular friend' stood with his back to the blazing apple-wood, to which he turned from time to time to reassure himself that its hearty crackling was but noise. Edward Fairbrother's blood was thin, of that there was no doubt, like any of his race; or rather, that half which had come originally from the tropics, Africa indeed – and none too willingly. Of his father's side Hervey knew little but that he was a planter of some wealth and refinement, though the planter families of Jamaica, he supposed, were so long established that their blood too must have thinned a good deal. But then, in the colds they'd known – he and Hervey – in the mountains of Bulgaria of late, his friend had never once remarked on it; nor had it dulled his instinct with sword and pistol. He liked to play to the gallery rather, though only, it was true, when the gallery had but the single seat.

'They return for the sport, I suppose,' replied Hervey laconically, without looking up from the writing table.

The fire spat a sudden shower of sparks, making his friend turn sharply (he was not much acquainted with apple-wood). 'Yet man is born into trouble – as the sparks. I suppose it must be so,' he said, rubbing his left arm on some account.

'Born *unto* trouble,' said Hervey, pressing his seal into the wax on the folded sheet before him.

'Did I not say that? "Yet man is born into trouble, as the sparks fly upwards." Psalms – as I recall.'

Hervey smiled indulgently. 'Job.'

'You're certain? Psalms, assuredly.'

'"Although affliction cometh not forth of the dust, neither doth trouble spring out of the ground; Yet man is born unto trouble, as the sparks fly upwards." Come, man; admit it.'

Fairbrother frowned. 'What deuced ill luck. I hadn't counted on your knowing chapter and verse, only on not being able with certainty to discount the Psalmist.'

'Then you must try humbugging other than a son of the parsonage. Countless hours in church and chapel . . . though it's

33

many moons since I read a psalm a day.' He said it almost regretfully, handing the letter to Corporal Johnson.

'First thing in the morning, Colonel?' asked his groom.

Hervey nodded. 'And you may dismiss. Thank you for your exertions today. The arrangements have all been admirable.'

The 'companion of the colonel' took his leave cheerfully. The day had indeed gone well for him: he had even been saluted by a dragoon – before the man's corporal had cuffed him for a nigmanog.

'And thank you too,' said Hervey to Fairbrother when the door was closed. 'I am most awfully obliged.'

His good friend took another full measure of the rum cordial which was doing so much to supplement the work of the fire. Their quarters were commodious by any standards, even those of the United Service Club at which they'd lodged since returning from the Levant, but he'd not spared himself in making them equally comfortable. 'Say nothing of it. I was fretful, however, at seeing you go alone this morning to your hallowing.'

Hervey frowned again. 'You are becoming arch. As I told you, taking command is a matter of no ceremony in the Sixth. And today we kept the custom admirably. You would have found little to divert you, if at all.'

He got up from the writing desk, took a cup of the cordial for himself and settled into one of the fireside chairs. Fairbrother took the other as a parlour-maid came in with a tray and began laying the table.

She was a handsome girl, as Fairbrother would observe, and with a look of sufficient wit for Hervey suddenly to become circumspect: he had no desire for his remarks to be tattled back to the barracks. The weather would therefore have to occupy them for a few minutes – and news that was general enough to be of no remark. 'Do you know the day – I mean, the Church's day?'

'I do not,' replied Fairbrother, sounding intrigued.

'The Conversion of St Paul. I recall a childhood rhyme: "If Paul's day be fair and clear / There shall be a happy year / But if it be both wind and rain / Dear will be all kinds of grain."'

'It didn't mention snow, I suppose?'

Hervey shook his head. 'I don't recall its saying anything of snow, though I'm sure there was always excess of it in Horningsham at this time.'

'There were no such rhymes in Jamaica. The weather followed a very settled design.'

Hervey took a peaceful sip of cordial.

'O for a beaker full of the warm South,' tried Fairbrother.

'What?'

Fairbrother merely raised his glass.

'Strange the things one remembers,' continued Hervey. '"Dear will be all kinds of grain." What's the end of burning barns in winter – and the worst winter in memory, it's said? A bad business, a bad business. I wonder what Worsley's making of it.'

'I fancy he'll be surprised to see you tomorrow – so soon on taking command.'

Hervey shook his head. 'I'd wager he'd expect me to come sooner than later. What else should detain me when there's a troop on active duty? But it won't trouble Worsley either way. A most even-tempered man. Besides, Malet's sending him word at first light tomorrow. It would have gone this evening, except there was no reason to hazard a man in this weather and the moon so new.'

'Quite.'

'By the bye, did I say he was now wed?'

'No.'

'A marriage of some happiness to Yorkshire, evidently – neighbouring estates. Mrs Worsley is installed at Richmond now. Richmond here, that is. I look forward to receiving them as soon as he's returned.'

They had strayed from the weather, but not into perilous country. Fairbrother smiled to himself. It was the first he'd heard his friend speak of entertaining, except that he knew he favoured Worsley highly – a quieter, more bookish sort than the usual cavalry captain, but one who'd shown his mettle in the affair at Waltham Abbey a year or so ago, when it looked as if Hervey and his party might all be blown to kingdom-come in the powder mills . . . And yet, to speak of new marriage must be bitter-sweet, given his friend's own standing in that regard. He supposed himself a poor substitute for the person who by rights ought to be sitting with Lieutenant-Colonel Matthew Hervey on this of all days – the culminating day of his good friend's – his only true friend's – service. All that had gone before, to which he, Fairbrother, had come late (but not, he trusted, too late), was but past preparation. Command of a King's regiment – and not just any regiment, but that in which his friend had been first commissioned twenty years before as an ink-fingered boy from school; and not a command bought like some piece of acreage from a dealer in these things (or for that matter like men at a slave market), but an appointment without purchase, in recognition of long merit, at the instigation of the commander-in-chief himself – *this* was the cornet's dream, not the proverbial field marshal's baton in his knapsack. And so where were the admiring eyes, the gently caressing hands, the bosom promising more intimate contentment? How could it be that with this new half-colonel of cavalry sat not his wife but a man born the wrong side of a plantation blanket?

But how *well* did his friend conceal his disappointment: his composure did him the greatest credit. It was not for him, Fairbrother, to dampen now the spirits of this man apart, on this of all evenings. On the contrary . . .

The parlour-maid was gone; he could at last engage his friend in careless banter. 'So, you are a man now set in authority, having under you soldiers, and you say unto one, "Go", and he goeth; and to another, "Come", and he cometh; and to your servant, "Do this", and he doeth it.'

Hervey frowned good-humouredly. 'You are determined to quote

Scripture at me, even if you quote it ill. I am a man set *under* authority.'

'I do not quote it *so* ill. What I would know is to whom you have said "Come" and to whom "Go".'

Hervey smiled. 'I had perfectly intended telling you, though in truth I've made no decisions – or rather, I've not made them known. The most pressing will be the new sar'nt-major. Rennie's to have a commission elsewhere, by Hol'ness's arranging.'

Fairbrother looked at him almost askant. 'Armstrong – surely?'

'Armstrong – of course. But I must tell you frankly that having supposed – hoped – for so many years that Armstrong would one day be my sar'nt-major, I am now of a mind to test that supposition.'

'*Test?*' Fairbrother was frowning as if in pain, but suddenly seemed to recollect himself. 'You don't mind my speaking in this way, do you? It really is not my business.'

'On the contrary. I value your opinion greatly, as well you should know. It's not given to every man in command to have one with whom he might speak indifferently . . . *Respica te, hominem te memento*.'*

Fairbrother inclined his head. 'I knew you not to be a sentimental man, as the saying goes – not decidedly, at least – but I'm surprised by your having doubts in Armstrong. What more might you wish of a man than he has proved these past two years alone? How do you intend testing your supposition?'

'I don't know,' said Hervey confidently. 'A little more time, perhaps.'

'That is reasonable, except that once Mr Rennie's commission becomes known, will not any delay in appointing Armstrong be an affront?'

---

* 'Look behind thee, and remember thou art but a man' – the words of the crouching slave in the chariot, that in the triumphant procession the honoured general might not forget his limits and mortality.

'Armstrong will perfectly understand: the exigencies of the service . . . But your point is well made. Indeed I should not wish to delay for one moment more than I thought entirely necessary the just deserts of such a man. We have served together since my earliest days in Spain.'

'I know it, of course. I'll not press you on who might have the better claim.'

'I'm perfectly happy to tell you. Indeed you might tell me.'

'Collins?'

'Naturally. And there's a fine man with C Troop, with whom I never served – Robertson.'

'You told me once that the custom of promotion in the Sixth is seniority tempered by rejection.'

'And so it is. But the policy merely defines the practice hitherto.'

Fairbrother sighed. 'That is a little obtuse, if I may be so bold. I meant that Armstrong being the senior – which I know him to be – he has a right to the rank unless he is unfit in some way, which unfitness cannot be because there is a better man his junior. Am I not correct?'

'You are exactly correct. I am not so much endeavouring to choose between Armstrong and Collins, only to discern whether Armstrong is truly meet. He has been through much these past five years.'

'What is it, then, that you require of your serjeant-major?'

Hervey smiled, being back on safe ground. 'That is very easily stated,' he declared, rising and taking from the writing table a small, bound volume – *The Standing Orders of His Majesty's Sixth Light Dragoons*. He turned the pages until he found the words he was looking for – the wisdom of the regiment's seventy years of peace and war: "'The Regimental Serjeant-Major, being the senior-most of the non-commissioned ranks, and forming, as he does, the link between the non-commissioned officers and the officers, and in the legitimate position for advancement, is placed in a position of great importance and responsibility; he should at all times be devotedly zealous for the reputation of the regiment, and immediately report to the adjutant when its discipline or good order is at all affected, or likely to be so by any individual; and never permit the existence of any improper familiarity towards him on the part of his inferiors."'

'"Devotedly zealous"; that's a fine thing.'

'Indeed. But let me finish: "On him, in a great measure, depends the general smartness of the regiment; he must be a perfect master of all drills, instructing every recruit most perfectly in all his exercises, et cetera, before he dismisses him; and he is never, upon any account, to pass over anything he may observe unsoldierlike in any man belonging to the regiment. He must be an example by his activity, soldierlike conduct, and dress, and must instantly correct any irregularity, want of spirit, or exertion, he may observe in the non-commissioned officers of the regiment."'

'And to all that must be added "an unfailing belief in his colonel".'

Hervey frowned. 'That cannot be required of a man. Loyalty is deserved by rank and appointment – that is sure. But respect, belief . . . that can only be earned. Besides, in adhering to that which I have just read, a sar'nt-major acts with confidence in the system of which the lieutenant-colonel is a part. The system, like the much-vaunted constitution of our American cousins, is one of checks and balances.'

Fairbrother smiled. 'I don't doubt it, though I maintain yet that there must exist some special feeling between the two, else it is otherwise merely a contractual sort of business.'

Hervey nodded conditionally. 'If I understand you correctly, you are saying that a regiment will be better found when the lieutenant-colonel and sar'nt-major enjoy a particular mutual regard. Of that there can be no doubt. It does not, however, assist in my choice of men, for each would answer – or rather, both Armstrong and Collins would.'

If Fairbrother had any further opinion on the matter it was stayed by the return of the parlour-maid, with a steaming tureen, and a second girl with a plate of warm bread.

'Soup, sir? An' Mr Ellis is coming with wine.'

Hervey smiled his thanks. She was indeed a handsome girl, and might pass for quality if she were mute and rightly got up. And she wished to please, which was ever appealing. There was something so agreeable in female company at this time, when the business of the day was done and . . . He recollected himself. 'Thank you . . . ?'

'Annie, sir.'

'Thank you, Annie. We shall serve ourselves.'

They bobbed and made to leave, and the landlord came with two bottles. 'Good evening, gentlemen. I've presumed to bring burgundy, if that's to your liking? I thought as you mayn't prefer the white with your soup and fish at this time of year.'

Hervey nodded. It was a peculiar presumption, for he had not known these things to be regulated by the seasons so, but he was not fastidious when it came to wine (Fairbrother had enough fastidiousness for both of them). 'Perhaps you'll be so good as to decant it.'

The landlord had anticipated the request, with two plain decanters brought by a potboy. 'And everything else is to your satisfaction, sir?'

'It is indeed. Your arrangements are most excellent, Mr Ellis. I think we shall be in no hurry to quit them.'

'The rooms are at your disposal, sir,' replied the landlord, backing his way to the door, and closing it behind him.

'I think he took me at first for your valet,' said Fairbrother when he was gone.

Hervey smiled. 'A very *gentlemanlike* valet.'

'I do not mean that he was in the least condescending – quite the opposite – rather that he seemed perplexed by a dark skin and a plain coat in an otherwise very military retinue.'

'You could scarcely call Johnson very "military". And besides, neither your skin is dark nor your dress very plain. I am all envy of that collar, which the landlord must have seen when you came.'

Fairbrother had acquired a swatch of curly black wool from the

Cossacks with whom they had ridden in the Levant, and had lost no time in having a coat of his trimmed with it (and a riding cloak too), though he joked that when his collar was turned up he looked like a Hottentot in want of a barber – which vexed Hervey, for it seemed to him that it was a device to claim that his friend was ever the stranger, when in truth he was more genuinely a kindred spirit than any man he knew. Fairbrother's complexion was not that of a man who had spent his years in a library at Oxford, it was true (though neither was his own); but it was no darker than that of any man who had spent his years in the sun. Neither were his features anything like the Hottentot's – only, perhaps, his hair, which tended to the tight curls of the lambskin, though it was brushed long and pomaded. No, there was nothing of the stranger, not to speak of; not to his eyes anyway. Indeed, if only Fairbrother could be induced to wear the King's coat again, there would be no occasion for doubt.

'Tomorrow I shall inspect the cellars,' said the 'Hottentot' as he began ladling the soup.

'A wise precaution. And I think I shall ask Malet to dine with us tomorrow – or the day after, if we're detained at Maidenhead.'

'Capital.'

'I'm pleased Malet's content with my scheme for keeping him at his desk for the time being. The business of the major's leave of absence will take some resolution.'

'How so?'

'I fear he is of, shall we say, the country party.'

'The "country party"?'

'Forgive me. I meant that the major was evidently not on terms with Lord Hol'ness, and is perhaps not quite ... *biddable*, as Johnson would say. In Walpole's day the country party were ever agin the court – would do all manner of things to contest the King's authority. It would be tiresome.'

Fairbrother raised his eyebrows. 'A misfortune indeed.'

'But one that might be overcome were *you* to purchase the majority from him.'

Fairbrother laid down his spoon and looked very directly at his friend. 'Hervey, I should be content to be your valet, but not your major – as I have told you more than once. Even if your captains were to welcome it.'

Hervey smiled wryly and took a sip at his soup. 'I will leave the matter for now.'

Fairbrother shrugged and picked up his spoon again. 'Tell me instead of the regimental staff. Are you pleased with what you find?'

Hervey conceded the diversion. 'In the main, yes, I am, though I met with only the paymaster today – Marciandi, come from the Maltese Regiment, who appears to have his doubts about the supper fund . . .' And Fairbrother found himself suddenly trying to follow the peculiar economy of the Sixth's institution of a third meal at public expense – an initiative of Lord Holderness's and one that had brought warnings of 'No good will come of it' from all quarters beyond Hounslow.

Of the others of the staff, whom Hervey had met in passing at mess, he gave his friend the merest of pen pictures: the surgeon, Milne – a fine Aberdeen physician who had joined the 2nd Dragoons after his wife had died; the riding-master, Kewley, lately of the 7th Hussars – full of the gospel of St John's Wood; and Lincoln of course – quartermaster *sans pareil* – of whom Fairbrother knew well already; and the veterinarian, Gaskoin – 'not of the stamp the regiment has known of late, but I suppose he will serve.'

'And you said there was a matter of distaste to you?'

Hervey sighed. 'I fear so. The senior captain, Tyrwhitt, is in arrest – in Dublin, seemingly on charges of bigamy, or something very much like. I confess I never much liked him, and notwithstanding the presumption of innocence until proved otherwise, I can't but think that the accusations are in keeping with his character. Did you meet him? I don't remember.'

'Nor, I confess, do I. You dislike him because he made easier play with the fair sex than Scripture approves?'

'No,' replied Hervey, insistently. 'Because I always thought him a stranger to the truth.'

'Ah.'

'Quite.'

Fairbrother shook his head. '"An officer may be forgiven anything but cowardice and want of candour"?'

'What else is there to be troubled with?'

Fairbrother smiled. 'You are a very contrary fellow, Hervey. You give all the impression of severity, and yet you take what I could only say is a most *reductive* view of men.'

Hervey, finishing his soup and taking a good sip of his wine, smiled too. 'I have no objection if an officer, so long as he attends to the welfare of his men, and his horses, takes his ease rather than exerting himself to further effort. Only that such a man cannot expect advancement.'

Fairbrother gave him a dry look. 'Except of course that he can, if he has the money.'

Hervey was spared a reprise of the iniquities of purchase by the reappearance of the parlour-maids with a dish of turbot.

When they had gone he returned to his subject, but at a remove. 'Tyrwhitt, it appears, has married one woman under Scotch law and then another under Irish.'

'Let me speculate,' said Fairbrother, deftly filleting his fish. 'The first is pretty but penniless, the second less comely but rich – a widow, perhaps.'

Hervey raised an eyebrow. 'I have asked for an attorney to come to explain the circumstances, and written to the Horse Guards for advice.'

'Then there is nothing more to be said of it the while. Not worth your consideration.'

'You are right.'

'And it can have no bearing on the success of your command.'

Hervey smiled again, but ruefully. 'My dear friend, I do not for once suppose that anything I do here at Hounslow – save for something scandalous – shall have any bearing on what the Horse Guards are minded next to do with me. We are a nation at peace. It is money therefore that secures notice.'

'That is uncommonly despondent of you.'

Hervey shook his head. 'Bingham buys the Seventeenth for a fortune, and there's an earl's son in the Eighth – Brudenell – who's bought his way from cornet to half-colonel in six years. No doubt he'll have a regiment soon.'

'And yet you've frequently spoken for purchase.'

'Yes, it served the country well in the late war with France. But in war there is a moderating process, a winnowing. The musket and the cannon decide these things. I fear that without such an arbiter . . .'

'And yet you have no truck with Reform!'

'What has Reform to do with it? A few more Whigs in parliament will make no difference to the prospects for advancement!'

'I fancy it is somehow all of a piece.'

'It doesn't follow in the least.'

Fairbrother had been the cynic for so many years that he might himself have supplied the answers, but he relished disputation, especially at a good table. 'You don't suppose that Reform would somehow be the progenitor of better things?'

Hervey looked at his friend with incredulity. 'Indeed I do not! For all its ills, I believe the country to be soundly governed – soundly enough governed; as soundly as may be. You may scorn the Tories for believing in the divine right of kings, but the Whigs merely believe in the divine right of noblemen. It seems to me the prospects for a man with ability but without means are greater under the Tories than under those who would control matters with their wealth. Both, I grant you, are imperfect, but so is mankind.'

'There speaks a son of the church!'

'I speak as I find.'

'Then you would go through life content with the choice always between two evils rather than trying to rid the world of both?'

'Great heavens, Fairbrother, I'm a soldier, not a . . . dreamer.'

'Well, let me opine – I may say as a dispassionate observer – that Reform will oppress your Duke of Wellington sorely. I am strange to your affairs, of course, but not so much that I cannot sense the common indignation – for all that we are only come back these few weeks. And because he freed the Catholics he will have to yield to loyal Protestants. Indeed, I have read there are some of his own party who would have Reform on just this cause – to check the advance of these very Catholics.'

No one was more surprised than he, Hervey, that the duke had become the repealing prime minister – for all the duke's famed expediency: *a good general knows when to retreat, and has the courage to do so*. It was a motto he himself had taken to heart, though it was easier said than done – especially without friends at court. 'Upon my word, you have not been idle these past weeks.'

Fairbrother inclined his head to acknowledge the compliment. 'There were plenty in the United Service who would talk if they thought they had an audience. Therefore – let us not shrink from the thought – if the duke opposes the sentiment and there is unrest, as there must be, therein lie opportunities for distinction for the soldier. Did His Grace himself not have to fight a duel last year?'

Hervey frowned. The duel was indeed an unedifying affair, but ultimately of no account – a slight by the Earl of Winchelsea during the passage of the Catholic Relief Act (though he knew no more about it than he'd read in the newspapers and heard tattled in Pall Mall – if evidently less than his friend). 'My dear Fairbrother, this is not Paris. Englishmen do not dig up the cobblestones and erect barricades – not at any rate Englishmen of the sort that seek suffrage.'

But Fairbrother would not be shaken. He had seen the lust for glass and blood – as he put it – that lurked in the breast of the lower orders, in the small affairs that passed for revolt in Jamaica. 'The mob, Hervey, the mob.'

It was folly to deny it. The mob: *mobile vulgus*, the vacillating crowd, that to which proper Tory government – in parliament the knights of the shires; in the shires themselves the gentry – must ever be alert. It could not be ordered by draconian government – certainly not alone (look at what Lord Liverpool's 'Six Acts' had wrought a dozen years before). No, the good ordering of society by those who stood high in it was worth a hundred enforcing yeomen. Compassion – not toleration of idleness, but recognition that ills came also to the deserving poor – was a principle of good government, as well as a right Christian one. But in the end there could be no pandering to the mob.

Hervey sighed. 'It will have come to a pretty pass if advancement follows on scattering the mob. It would make us no better than Fouché's policemen.'

'Then by your own reckoning you are condemned to an eternity at Hounslow!'

'Perhaps it shall do me good. Perhaps it is time to plant cabbages.'

'Pish! Plant cabbages in this frozen earth?'

'I should of course wait for more clement weather. We do speak figuratively, do we not?'

'As you will. But let me lay a wager – that you shall see action ere the year is out.'

Hervey frowned doubtfully. 'Where?'

'That would be soothsaying, whereas I was merely prophesying.'

'By "action" I couldn't count the mob.'

'Nor I – though that will come likewise soon. I mean against the French.'

'The French? How so? They've had their dice with adventure.'

'Or the Austrians, or the Prussians. Or for that matter, the Russians.'

Hervey's frown turned to a look of wry assurance. 'Then I should be taking your money as a common thief. There is not the least chance of war; Vienna put paid to that, did it not? Do we not have the Concert of Europe? Have they not abolished war?'

'I shall not rise to the bait. You do not believe that. Castlereagh's "Balance of power" will be a Moloch: it will continually require a blood sacrifice.'

Hervey had never been of a mind that in this world the lion would be caused to lie down with the lamb, though he did believe that a stout fold could be made, and that a good pack of dogs could see off the ravening beasts. It made for interesting discourse before the turbot was finished, and then with renewed vigour as the entrees were brought, and afterwards a pudding too rich for either of them to do justice to.

And when Landlord Ellis and his parlour-maids had cleared all away and brought them port, of which they drank only a very little, and that of the lightest sort, they talked some more of the 'condition of England', and then of the regiment – or *Hervey*'s regiment, as Fairbrother, with propriety, insisted – until the clocks about the inn variously began striking the final hour, and Hervey rose and made his excuses to his friend, for, he explained, there were letters yet to write, and he was unsure what time they would return from Maidenhead tomorrow. And Fairbrother was more than content to retire – with one of the decanters, for, he explained, it would warm him in his bed as he read a page or two of *The Examiner* (it had become of late his favourite reading on, as its proprietors proclaimed, 'politics, domestic economy, and theatricals') – knowing that Hervey must be about his business early and bright in the morrow, while he himself could rise at his leisure.

'I bid you, then, "good night" – Colonel.'

Hervey waved him adieu, chaffed him on the merits of rising before noon, and watched the door close.

And he was content with it thus, for he could not ask more of his friend, especially in this bleakest of midwinters, than to sup with him and hear his thoughts with sympathy and discretion – and, in due course, no doubt, with wise counsel. As for the letters that would keep him now from his own bed the while . . . Well, those to home must rightly take precedence – or rather, to Wiltshire

47

(the reply to Princess Lieven's, which Malet had presented, would wait): to the Venerable the Archdeacon of Salisbury (or *Sarum*, as his father preferred, ever mindful of the time before the Reformation); and of course to Elizabeth, a sister more devoted than any man had right to call his own; and to Miss Hervey – Georgiana, who was rising twelve (and who might thus expect something more than a childlike line or two), a daughter who had scarce spent one month true with her father, and who now bore a resemblance to her late mother that would only become more painful with the years.

In the event they did not detain him too long, being mere expressions of hope that he would see them ere too much time had passed – just as soon as duty permitted (a formula he knew was worn thin, but the only coat, so to speak, that he knew how to wear). And then he retired to his bed – a bed warmed by the pan coals and the hot-water stone, but empty.

And with the darkness, the exhilaration of command suddenly extinguished, like the candle, there came again the wretched solitude. In the year following the death of Henrietta, he now recognized, he had been merely confused, hopelessly thrown. And then when somehow he had found himself able to take up the reins once more – back in uniform, a man under authority – the true import of her loss had sapped at him more insidiously. On his passage to India, night after night he had lain sleepless in his berth – thinking about her not being there; and then thinking about his not sleeping for thinking about her. And there had seemed no way out of thinking. The futility of it all could oppress him still. Yet that had been then, and this was now; but, oh, what a further falling off was there. His solitude was made infinitely worse by self-knowledge, that he had taken a wife who was no wife, that it was his own fault, for he had done so 'unadvisedly, lightly, wantonly', as the Prayer Book warned against; and before that had taken another man's wife . . . the 'manifold sins and wickedness, which we, from time to time, most grievously have committed'. He had put Kat from his mind a year ago – almost two years ago. But she kept returning. No matter what, she kept returning. He did not rightly understand why. She had never possessed him body and soul, as Henrietta had done (at least, he did not think she had). There might be days, weeks, even perhaps whole months, when she did not return; but then, at no especial time – nothing demanding a bosom for solace – her face would come before him. It came before him now. And he wished her here beside him. Not 'to satisfy men's carnal lusts and appetites' – though that, he knew, would entail – but for the 'mutual society, help, and comfort' expressed in embrace, as the Prayer Book promised. But it could never be. He had taken another man's wife, but he could not compound the adultery by doing so while himself now bound by the vows of matrimony. He was thus condemned to the empty bed, to the darkness without embrace. There would be temptations, occasions, opportunities, and his feet were no less of clay than those of better men than he. But he would fight the temptations, for he knew too well the sickening of the soul that followed: 'Every sin that a man doeth is without the body; but he that committeth fornication sinneth against his own body' – Corinthians (how wise, now, that admonishing man of Tarsus seemed). But Paul was a saint, and he himself a mere man: might there not be some sinless comfort – some Shunammite to keep him warm, as the ageing David: 'So they sought for a fair damsel throughout all the coasts of Israel . . . and brought her to the king. And the damsel was very fair, and cherished the king, and ministered to him: but the king knew her not.'

But kindly sleep came instead, knitting up the ravelled sleeve as always in the end it did – and for which he would give thanks, as habitually he did, though knowing that sleep was but a passing balm.

III

PRINCIPLES OF MILITARY MOVEMENTS

Next morning

Shaved, dressed, booted and spurred, breakfasted on ham, buttered eggs, toasted bread and coffee exemplary in its heat, Lieutenant-Colonel Matthew Hervey put on his forage cap, fastened the chain of the cloak which Lance-Corporal Johnson had been holding to the hearty blaze in the Berkeley Arms's great fireplace, pulled on his gloves, took up his sword-scabbard, nodded to the adjutant, and stepped out into the frozen courtyard.

'Hep!'

The Sixth's peculiar executive word of command – every regiment's was in some degree different – brought the half-dozen dragoons to attention in the saddle (among them Serjeant Acton, lately corporal, Hervey's coverman in the Levant). The regimental serjeant-major, dismounted, took one step forward, halting with an emphatic crunching of snow, and saluted. 'Good morning, Colonel.'

Hervey returned the compliments. 'Good morning, Mr Rennie. We might be in Galicia, think you not?'

The RSM may have been an extract – brought in from another

regiment (the 4th Dragoon Guards, Lord Holderness's old corps) – but he had seen service as an orderly with Moore in the Peninsula, one of the few left in either mess (and fewer still in the canteen) who had charged against the French in that bitter cold, retrograde march to Corunna.

But Rennie was ever a man of formality: 'Yes, Colonel; the ground is frozen very hard.'

An Armstrong or a Collins would have found some cheery retort from his stock of regimental banter – as indeed would have Lincoln in his pomp. But it was early days, perhaps – a new command-ing officer. Hervey contented himself with a respectful 'Indeed, Sar'nt-Major', and took the reins of his temporary charger from the orderly dragoon. Perhaps Rennie's formality was anyway for the best, recalling that at the end of the march to Corunna the lieutenant-colonel had blown his brains out.

It could be a perilous business, mounting, at the best of times – perilous to the pride, at least – even with stirrup leathers long. On snow running to ice, with an untried horse, the odds on in-voluntarily dismounting (as the saying went) were reduced further. Nevertheless, Hervey waved away the mounting block – a barrel got from the Berkeley's cellarman – not trusting its capacity to remain upright, shortened the offside rein so that the charger, if it had a mind to, could only swing its quarters towards him, placed his left foot in the stirrup and sprang into the saddle with the speed of a seasoned tumbler.

'Very well, Mr Malet.'

The adjutant, who had managed to mount with no less agility but without the attention of the assembled party, gave the nod to the point-men, and the cavalcade set off. As they left the yard they were joined by Fairbrother, to Hervey's considerable surprise, atop one of the Berkeley's best hirelings. His green cloak, with its black lambswool collar, and the hat he had taken from a Cossack in exchange for a bottle of his father's rum, gave him a most alien look, needing only a couple of chickens hanging from the saddle and a lance on his shoulder to complete the impression of a free-booter from the Steppes. Hervey merely remarked that he was glad to see him.

Only as they were clear of the little crowd of onlookers gathered at the front of the Berkeley did he venture any conversation with the swaddled supernumerary. 'It is excessively obliging of you to accompany us. I fear you will see nothing to divert you, however.'

Fairbrother made some muffled reply indicating resolution rather than contentment, so that Hervey was altogether mystified as to why his friend should wish to leave the comfort of the Berkeley Arms for a perfectly humdrum visit to a troop in billets, especially having protested unceasingly at the cold since their arrival back in England – though he himself had to admit it: it was damnably chill (and there were upwards of thirty dragoons bedded down with ague brought on by the icy air). The evening before, Fairbrother had merely said that he thought he ought to – somewhat unconvincingly, for Hervey had not heard 'ought' from his friend in all the time they had been acquainted – and later that he probably wouldn't. And then the quite decided 'I shall remain here.'

But lying thoughtful in the early hours, Fairbrother had in fact resolved to be *useful*. Useful in the sense that Sir Thomas Graham had been to Sir John Moore (he trusted that he did not flatter himself too highly), and that – yes, like Boswell to Dr Johnson – he might also in due season be able to give account of his friend's tenure as lieutenant-colonel of this regiment of light dragoons, whose company he had so come to enjoy. For besides the conviction that it would be a tenure of distinction, and therefore worthy of memorializing, he believed he owed to his friend the discovery of purpose in his life. Before their meeting three years ago at the Cape that life had been a worthless affair, an indolent existence, determined in part by a sort of indifferent resentment that, like Shakespeare's tawny Moor, whatever his merits he would first be misliked for his complexion. He was an able soldier – his service with the Jamaica Militia and then the Royal Africans had been enough to assure him of that – but it was not until Hervey had roused him from his torpor among the palms (though a torpor in which, undeniably, he read constantly and extensively), and put his instincts to use on the frontier in the uniform of the Mounted Rifles, that he had abandoned resentfulness as a pretext for in-activity. No, he could not reasonably suppose that comparison with Boswell and Dr Johnson was truly apt; but he would proceed nevertheless on the assumption that it might become so. If only it weren't so deucedly cold . . .

'Plough Monday come and gone these two weeks and not a clod yet turned,' said Hervey, apparently still intent on generalism.

'Is that an affront to religion or to good husbandry?' asked Fairbrother, keen to test his own wit in such temperatures, but also genuinely uncertain of his friend's meaning.

Hervey looked at him a little warily. 'You'll recall our conversation last evening – a poor harvest, winter early and hard? The price of corn?'

Fairbrother had been expecting something suitably theological on the blessing of the plough, and he lapsed into silence, disappointed.

Hervey left him to his thoughts for a while; then, thinking there might be something amiss, asked, 'Is all well with you?'

He sat up straight in the saddle. 'But of course. I was merely contemplating.'

'What exactly?'

'I was contemplating the situation of the yeomanry, what were its prospects and all.'

'I had rather you become a regular.'

'I *am* a regular.'

'Of a colonial corps. And you are on half pay.'

'And there I choose to stay, despite your most flattering entreaties. I was interested merely in the *situation* of the yeomanry, and how it comes about that a regular troop of cavalry must be abroad in the country at the first sign of trouble.'

Hervey nodded. 'Mr Malet!'

He did not have to turn his head or raise his voice much above the usual, for the snow deadened the horses' footfall. Only creaking leather and the occasional jingle of bit and spur broke the silence. They were marching 'at ease', not 'easy', and no speaking therefore permitted in the ranks.

The adjutant closed up. 'Colonel?'

'Do you recall exactly what was the fate of the Berkshire yeomanry?'

'Very exactly, Colonel; I have a cousin who served with them – there were two regiments, the first raised in the west of the county, and the second in the east. Neither had been called out in aid of the civil power in more than ten years, which was the criterion for deciding which should be disbanded, and so the first was stood down two years ago to the month – I myself attended their last parade – and the second followed in April. I attended theirs too as it was on Upper Club.'

Fairbrother detected another obstacle to his complete under-standing of the world. 'May I?'

'What?' said Hervey.

'Upper Club?'

'A playing field at Eton,' explained Malet. 'There was a grand dinner afterwards, once they'd handed their arms to the Ordnance, and then they all rode home as if from market. A right jolly affair.'

'I should have thought it a rather unhappy occasion,' replied Fairbrother.

'The disbanding, yes,' said Hervey; 'but a yeoman likes a good party. And in truth, they were a tagrag and bobtail affair, as I recall.'

Fairbrother frowned, though swathed as he was there was no telling. There was a little of him that bridled still at the English regular's disdain of occasional soldiers. Many a time it had only been the Jamaica Militia standing against the threat of Bonaparte when the regular garrison was prostrated by yellow fever. 'Was it ever considered, do you know, that the mere existence of the yeomanry was a preventive to disorder? That the fact of their not being called out was testament to that?'

Hervey smiled ruefully. 'One of Queen Elizabeth's courtiers once said that soldiers in peace are as chimneys in summer – I don't recall who. It is only for the certainty of winter's coming that they are not stopped up.'

'And the King's peace – is it supposed that it maintains itself?'

'It is, I grant you, an imperfect simile.'

'Only the dead have seen the end of war?'

Hervey sighed. When last he'd heard that, Cornet Agar was refuting the attribution: 'I have searched Plato in vain,' he had said at table; and Hervey recalled how a wager was entered in the book, that 'Mr Treneer is not able to provide chapter and verse re said quotation in any work of Plato within a year and a day, wager to be a case of claret (6 doz bots)'.

How he missed Agar's youthful exuberance.

Yet there was no custom to determine the status of the wager if one of the parties died before its settlement. He wondered how it would proceed therefore, though it was a very little matter and not at all his concern. There were, though, still certain exequies to be performed, if not now his business then certainly of some moment to him. Agar had been buried near where he fell, at Adrianople, but, like Shelley, his heart had been brought away – *Cor Cordium* – to be presented to his people, and they had yet to say how they wished to honour it. The ivory casket he had had made bore an inscription, at Fairbrother's suggestion, from *The Tempest* – Ariel's song (which, he said, was that of Shelley's grave – his ashes – in Rome): 'Nothing of him that doth fade / But doth suffer a sea-change / Into something rich and strange'.

Agar's death could not be helped. It had come as much by his boyish impetuosity as by his – Hervey's – own failure to see the ambuscade. He himself was almost killed; and Fairbrother he had taken for dead. Yet by rights Agar should never have been there –

should never have been with him in the Levant. His company had been a delight, but at heart he was no soldier. Perhaps it was what his brother – and more so his brother's wife – had understood when they asked Hervey for his special protection. But Agar had been determined to go. There were antiquities he wished to see – the whole country of the Bulgars indeed, and the wonders of Thrace and Constantinople . . .

'Hervey?'

'Yes – *quite*; as I was saying – soldiers in peace, chimneys in summer. Just so.'

The adjutant sensed it was the moment to fall back his three lengths, but Hervey stayed him (it wouldn't do to appear preoccupied on his first parade). 'The going here on looks fair. We'll hazard a trot.'

He shortened the rein and eased the gelding into the most collected of trots, gradually allowing more as he felt the footing secure, and began rising. 'Horses are to be led in-hand for one half of one hour at the commencement of a route-march' said the Sixth's standing orders, but since they had already come from the barracks he was content to take things a little quicker, not least because they marched in light order, with neither carbines nor spare shoes.

He could never quite comprehend why it was that snow sometimes balled within the hoof, so that it was perilous to venture at more than an ambling pace, while at other times it fell away from the frog like sand. Doubtless some mechanical or man of science could explain, but he himself could see no pattern to it, and therefore reason, in spite of at least twenty winters with ample opportunity to observe. But on this occasion at least the snow was obliging, and the trot therefore good and steady.

Half of one hour, the going peculiarly silent and all talking ceased, only the jingle of bits and curb chains and here and there a horse snorting, with all attention on the road ahead, the fresh fall furrowed by the wheels of the odd coach and carrier, and roiled by its ironshod teams – four miles, give or take a furlong or two, well clear of the Heath, over the Colne in its icy trickle, and the castle at Windsor now in distant view, and soon would be the chapel at Eton. They had seen so little traffic that it might have been early of a Sunday morning – just the Oxford stage, inbound, with eight sorry-looking outside passengers, the driver daring little more than a jogging sort of walk with so much weight up, and halting as the dragoons came past, raising his whip in salute, and one or two of the heartier sorts behind him their hats (a rum lot of hats, too, thought Hervey).

But then as they came back to a walk, half a mile on, the cold air very clear, there was the distant but unmistakable figure of a dra-goon, the horse's movement steady, the rider erect.

Malet pressed forward again. 'Corporal Beevor, Colonel. He rode for B Troop at first light.'

'Well, he cannot have reached Maidenhead and returned in that space of time . . . unless he set off at midnight.'

'No, Colonel, I can vouch for his leaving at six.'

The dragoon closed at the briskest of trots, slowing only a few lengths short, then reining to one side and saluting (Hervey did not know Beevor, save by reputation – a coming man, by all accounts, his father a quartermaster in the Carabiniers).

'Good morning, Colonel. Corporal Beevor, adjutant's detail, reporting. Colonel.'

Strictly, by custom and probably regulation too, as adjutant's detail he ought to have reported to Malet rather than to him, but Hervey approved of the NCO's common sense – admired his self-assurance – and returned his salute without checking the stride. 'Proceed, Corporal Beevor.'

The dragoon brought his horse alongside. 'Colonel, while riding for Maidenhead to alert B Troop to your inspection I encountered them at ten minutes before eight o'clock on the road east of the town. I informed Captain Worsley of your intentions, Colonel, and he instructed me to present his compliments and inform you that the troop is to conduct a field day in the great park at Windsor and expressed the wish that you would approve, and inspect them instead at their evolutions, Colonel.'

Hervey's first instinct was to suspect some ploy – that having been prior-warned of the visit, Worsley had figured it better to have the troop in the field rather than in billets, and had turned them out before dawn in order to have them under tight regulation in the park by the time he himself arrived. 'What time did you set out this morning?'

'Six, by the guardhouse clock, Colonel.'

Hervey turned to Malet. 'And no other left for Maidenhead before that hour?'

'None that I know of, Colonel. I gave the order to the sar'nt-major a little before watch-setting.'

Well, thought Hervey, there was no profit in pursuing the line. Besides, it had not been his intention to take Worsley by surprise – on the contrary, which was why he had told Malet to send word. And, indeed, the great park at Windsor was a deal less far to ride. It would all work to advantage, whether a ploy or not.

'The troop's going to post a vidette at Queen Anne's Gate, Colonel, so as to lead us to them,' said Beevor.

'Admirable. You may fall in, Corporal Beevor.'

Beevor saluted, reined round and fell in behind the serjeant-major, who eyed him with the suspicion habitually reserved for the thruster, while the adjutant fell back his appointed three lengths again.

Hervey turned to Fairbrother with a look of satisfaction. 'What a fine thing it is that an NCO may speak directly to his command-ing officer so, with such address and confidence of his report. None of your red-coat stiffness.'

Fairbrother could not but agree. It was a fine thing indeed to be with a regiment of cavalry. He himself had worn a red coat – with the Jamaica Militia, and then the Royal Africans, who, he main-tained, were little more than a penal battalion – before he had put on the nobler green of the Cape Mounted Rifles. A red coat was a fine thing to give a man a martial air, but a corporal in a red coat spoke only to his serjeant, and he in turn to his lieutenant – and so on until betimes the word reached the colonel by when its import or force might be lost. If he, Fairbrother, were ever to leave the half-pay list it would be to join a regiment in blue (or green) – except, of course, that according to his friend, the Duke of Clarence would put all of the army into red the moment 'Last Post' was sounded for the King.

'How much further is the great park?'

'Well, yonder's the castle – so five miles, perhaps.' Hervey sounded surprised. 'Don't you recall our practising war in these parts: it was but two years ago?'

It was in fact the better part of three, and much water had flowed under the bridge at Dorney since, the scene of his triumph over the Grenadiers in the great mock battle – which in no small part had been thanks to his friend's address.

Beneath his swaddling Fairbrother looked rueful. 'I do, though chiefly that it seemed to take place at night and that it was a great deal warmer.'

Hervey smiled. How diverting mock war could be, the outcome determined by umpires, like a game of cricket. It was, of course, better than no battle at all, but the bullet and the sabre were the real arbiters of war – and artillery, he had to admit – and they judged without partiality, favour or affection. He wondered what scheme Worsley had devised for his troop. He hoped not simply the evolutions in the drill book.

'Fortitude, Fairbrother. Another half an hour or so and we'll see what B Troop does to keep warm. It's hard weather, I grant you, though I must tell you we had it far harder in Spain.'

'Twenty years ago, Hervey – twenty years, the blood thicker in youth, able to stand all privations!'

Hervey smiled the more. 'I would have you know that I am in no degree less hardy than in those days.'

Fairbrother made no reply, for he believed his friend truly

thought so. And he supposed it only right that he should think so, however improbable. He knew for himself his own falling away (though in fact he remained remarkably supple). Perhaps he merely let indolence blind him to what sheer effort and self-belief could work . . . No, not indolence; he would apply to the French – *ennui*. For that was his real state of mind at the Cape, before his friend had arrived to reinvigorate him.

Well, invigorated he was now – if temporarily enervated by the cold – and he must not fail to display that vigour before his friend and his friend's dragoons.

'I cannot doubt it,' he said, beginning even as he did so to believe it true.

And he related a story of one of the slaves on his father's plantation who, on his fortieth birthday or thereabout (for these things could never be precisely determined) had cut more cane than any man half his age, that his body seemed perfectly adapted to the task, that to cut the same measure of cane his machete swung only twice for the younger men's three times.

And Hervey reminded his friend that he himself was not yet forty, but that he took note, saying he had long believed that drill – discipline, practice, 'training' (as some now called it) – was everything. And Fairbrother was then moved to recall other tales from the plantation, some distinctly improbable thought Hervey (and when challenged, Fairbrother agreed, while asserting that plantation stories were not always the literal truth but rather representations of it, and therefore not without merit), until a quarter of an hour had passed and they began rising to the trot again.

Another quarter of an hour brought them to Queen Anne's Gate, where a cornet was waiting with an orderly. He made his salutations and led them apace to the exercise ground half a mile to the south.

Hervey was at once intrigued by what he found, B Troop engaged in evolutions not to be found in the drill book. Thirty dismounted dragoons, their horses tethered towards the Star Clump, played the part of a gathering of malcontents, to which twenty mounted dragoons were approaching in line at the walk, in as calm a fashion as they could in the face of jeering and fist-shaking.

There were no regulations for dealing with breaches of the peace, but after the business of St Peter's Fields eleven years before – 'Peterloo' – when the Manchester and Salford Yeomanry had got themselves into a merry mess, the practice had been to halt at a distance from the unlawful assembly, beyond the range of brick-bats, then to draw swords and observe the effect. Usually the rasp of metal on metal and the appearance of cold steel was enough to disperse the mischief-makers, but if not, an advance at the trot invariably did the trick. Almost invariably, for it had not been unknown, especially in a great assembly, for the people in the front rank to be held to their ground, if unwillingly, by the press of those behind, until the troops had closed, in which case the flat of the sword gave encouragement. At St Peter's Fields, the yeomanry, try-ing to get through a crowd of many thousands to arrest the famous 'Orator' Hunt on the platform beyond, had lost their heads and cut with the edge of the sword, and then found themselves in hopeless, bloody disorder, until the magistrates sent in the 15th Hussars to extricate them. The hussars, by all accounts, were scrupulous in using only the flat of the sword, but got no thanks for their restraint from any but the Duke of Wellington (who, in truth, had been none too concerned whether flat or edge) – though the praise of the then Master-General of the Ordnance was nothing to compare with the opprobrium of the newspapers.

Worsley, however, appeared to have devised an alternative. The dragoons still mounted were approaching at the walk in open order, and as they closed with the 'roughs' they turned the horses on the forehand, quarters right, and took three or four lateral steps – a solid barricade of horseflesh advancing slowly but deter-minedly, pushing back all before them. Then, taking the word from the serjeant-flanker on the right, they swung round to face the 'crowd' again to give them opportunity to break, before repeating the turn on the forehand and beginning the lateral march once more.

'I see his purpose right enough,' said Hervey, nodding with what passed for approval. 'A very large but peaceable gathering to be dispersed peaceably: but why should a peaceable crowd have to disperse at all?'

'A crowd may turn into a mob in an instant,' suggested Fairbrother.

'And I'd rather it were then that the military were called on, and not before. But be that as it may, I compliment the troop on its horse-mastering.'

'I think Captain Worsley would wish to acknowledge the compliment as Versailles's, for he spent the summer there,' said Malet.

'Did he indeed? What thinks the RM, I wonder.'

Malet took the question to be rhetorical. The riding-master, schooled as he was in the principles of military equitation at the 'Cavalry Riding Establishment' at St John's Wood, was first and foremost a man of strict regulation (though Hervey had seen little of him before taking command, the RM having exchanged from the 7th Hussars not two years ago); but he was, too, a man of enquiry, perfectly able to recognize advantage wherever he saw it.

'Captain Worsley was the guest at Versailles of the comte d'Aure, the *maître* of the *Grande Écurie*. Do you know him, Colonel?'

'I do not,' said Hervey, maintaining his watch on B Troop (though flattered to be thought likely to know the master of the King of France's Horse); 'except by reputation. He is, by all accounts, an advocate of the natural school of equitation. Most refreshing.'

'There's little natural about that sideways movement,' added Fairbrother, equally intent on Worsley's men. 'A deal of practice, I'd say.'

'And useful of itself therefore, whether or not it truly serves any purpose in a throng,' replied Hervey, though perfectly understanding the doubt implicit in his friend's observation.

Ten more minutes of 'Versailles drill', as he was beginning to think of it, and then Worsley signalled the troop to change – 'malcontents' into the saddle, and the 'aiders of the civil power' to take their place. Hervey continued to watch keenly. The troop was well aware that he did, but there was an easiness about them that was pleasing: the words of command were few, the harrying of the dragoons by the NCOs even less. This was show, of course – if a troop did not wish to show before its lieutenant-colonel then it must be in want of pride – but it bespoke a confident purpose, a sure discipline; and hardly in the most favourable of conditions. Hervey was content.

And with the drill having reached, so to speak, a point of balance, it was now the moment for Worsley to present his compliments in person. He trotted briskly up to the assemblage, trumpeter at his side, and halted before his erstwhile fellow troop leader. 'Good morning, Colonel,' he said brightly, with a smile of both confidence and gratification, and saluting with emphatic correctness.

Hervey smiled back warmly, returning the salute with no less exactness. They were indeed old friends – certainly in terms of late years. He leaned forward and offered his hand. 'Heartiest congratulations on your marriage, Worsley. You must both come and dine with us – with me – at my quarters presently.'

If the momentary confusion of the plural – and indeed, *which* plural – registered at all with B Troop's captain, he did not show it. 'Delighted, Colonel.'

'And now perhaps you will explain your scheme of things?'

'Of course. I spent some time last summer in France and was much taken by their new methods.'

'Yes; Malet has told me.'

'In particular their exercises in yielding from the leg, and it occurred to me that there was some practical application to be had in dealing peaceably with a gathering, such as we've had occasion once or twice to do – one which was threatening no great violence. Versailles used the exercises solely as a means of increasing suppleness.'

'Admirable,' replied Hervey, keeping his doubts to himself for the time being (why *would* a magistrate read the riot act, the customary prelude to calling on the military for assistance, if the crowd were peaceable?). 'How did they correct the tendency to lean towards the leg?'

'By insisting the rider looked to where he was yielding. Or occasionally an apple on the head.'

'Perhaps we should have the RM devise some programme of comparison. It would be a fine thing for the officers to think on it. A very proper diversion. Your sar'nt-major: he took to it keenly enough?'

Worsley returned the smile with equal wryness. 'Yes indeed, Colonel, as I'm sure you may imagine.'

Hervey turned again to observe the object of their unspoken admiration – Collins. It was good to see him restored to his rightful troop after secondment to his – Hervey's – own at the Cape when Armstrong's wife had died. He now had – what? – twenty years' service? As a serjeant-major his authority appeared effortless, his resource limitless and his judgement unfailing, though somehow, to Hervey's mind, he would remain still the Corporal Collins of that last battle at Toulouse, the year before Waterloo . . .

No, it was more than twenty years, for Collins had been at Campo Mayor – had cut down the French colonel of dragoons in single combat – and he'd worn a corporal's stripe then, had he not?

But Armstrong had been a corporal at Sahagun too . . . The years had passed, and their promotion had slowed with them, just as had his own. 'Soldiers in peace were like chimneys in summer' – what an apt saying it was. Yet where had been the peace, truly, since Waterloo? There'd scarcely been a year – if at all – that he himself had not bloodied his sabre.

He realized – and, strangely, for the first time, for he had always thought of Armstrong as the man of mature rank and Collins as the coming young NCO – that the passing years had been the same for the two of them; and that there would not be years enough remaining for both Armstrong and Collins to wear a crown atop their four chevrons. To be *the* sar'nt-major – not of a troop but of the regiment.

They chatted the while, until, roles reversed, the second half troop practised its peaceable dispersal of a peaceable assembly.

It was all done really rather well. Practical or not, Hervey saw nothing but usefulness in having men so handy and troopers so supple.

Eventually Collins and the lieutenant seemed satisfied too, and ordered the troop to rest and make much.

It was now Worsley's opportunity again. 'Leave to present the officers, Colonel?'

Hervey nodded. 'By all means.'

Worsley signalled them forward – his lieutenant and two cornets, and Collins, who came up at the trot and reined to a sharp halt in line.

'Hep!'

Up went four hands as one in salute.

Hervey acknowledged with a touch to the peak of his forage hat, and a smile. 'Good morning, gentlemen. Noble work, and smartly done.' He paused just long enough: 'Would it beat the French though, Sar'nt-Major?'

The subalterns smiled, and Collins even broader. Being singled out first was a compliment – and it was a good joke too.

'Might well, Colonel, now that Bonaparte's dead.'

Hervey nodded approvingly. A good NCO was never in want of an apt riposte. 'Well said, Sar'nt-Major.'

He was indeed the image of a serjeant-major, as the shine on his leather, despite the exertions of the day, suggested. And beyond that he had the makings of a quartermaster who would not stint himself in all that was necessary to the comfort of all ranks. No, Hervey corrected himself: not merely the makings, Collins had the present qualities. But he could hardly be quartermaster without first holding the foremost non-commissioned rank.

He turned to the unfamiliar face. 'Cornet James, I presume.'

'Colonel.'

'Your father had a troop when I joined as a cornet,' he said, as James pressed his mount forward to take the extended hand. 'I've not seen him these twenty years. He's well, I trust.'

'He is very well, Colonel, yes, thank you.'

'And Mr Kennett, it is good to see you again too.'

The lieutenant in turn came forward to shake hands.

He was far from being Hervey's favourite sort of officer. There was about him a certain expression of superiority, something faintly disapproving, an aloofness. Hervey could not suppose that dragoons warmed to him, though he was competent enough – that much was evident merely by watching him this morning. How far he could truly be trusted was a matter for conjecture, but in truth it was perhaps of no great moment to him what was the character of B Troop's lieutenant, especially with a man like Worsley as captain, and Collins to keep an eye on things from the ranks.

'And Cornet Jenkinson, Colonel.'

The last of the officers rode forward to shake hands.

It was not the easiest of moments, as Hervey had anticipated, Jenkinson with Agar at Oxford . . .

'Your people are well?'

So vague an enquiry was meant purely as a courtesy, Hervey expecting a mere 'Very well', like James's, but the Honourable Charles Jenkinson was somewhat more literal – more curate than cornet, if entirely well-meaning. 'My sisters are all well, Colonel. My eldest is now out and her younger sister is out this year. My father hopes to be offered a place in the cabinet soon.'

Hervey made an effort to be matter of fact. 'Indeed? Then we must hope that it is a place in which he may be of assistance to us in the Sixth. And your sisters: I hope we may see them at Hounslow ere long.'

Again, he had imagined the expression to be purely rhetorical, but . . .

'In point of fact, Colonel, my elder sister, Catherine, has dined at Hounslow several times, though it was as Cornet Agar's guest rather than mine.'

Hervey hoped he did not wince. 'Agar's loss will be felt by a great many.' He was about to add a word or so about his dying well, but thought better of it. It was not his to explain these things: he had done so in a letter to the Horse Guards, commending his conduct, and it was for the commander-in-chief to determine if any recognition should be given, at which point the entire army would be made privy to the despatch.

He turned back to Worsley. It was close to noon. 'What arrangements are there for the rest of the day?'

'Rations and then pivot drill, Colonel.'

'Then I'll take a turn of the park and afterwards watch a little more.'

He said it with, he hoped, more enthusiasm than in truth he could muster, for the day that the regiment – every regiment – was able to manoeuvre freely, without a pivot, would indeed truly be a red-letter day. So much time was wasted turning a line on a fixed point that it astonished him that no better system had been found – or rather, approved. It was all the fault of old 'Pivot' Dundas – dead these past ten years, pensioned a good dozen before then, and yet his *Principles of Military Movements* still held as great a sway with the Horse Guards as those of Frederick the Great, whom he had sought to emulate, still held in Prussia. General Sir David Dundas, a crabbed old Scot, had done fine things in his day, not least two years as commander-in-chief during the Duke of York's penitential absence after the scandal of his mistress's selling commissions, but the 'tide in the affairs of men' had left his pivot drill high and dry –

or ought to have. Someone in the Sixth, many years ago, had composed a rhyme in mock-heroic, aping *The Iliad* ('Come Heavenly Muse, Great David's wrath disclose . . .'), and with it appropriate illustrations in the mess's lines book, which had afforded much amusement to the more subversive officers in the regiment – which in the case of Dundas was practically everyone:

> *This is the Scotch commander of men,*
> *Who in spite of his years three score and ten,*
> *Delights every morn to get up with the lark*
> *To pester His Majesty's troops in the Park . . .*

(and so on for a dozen verses).

But that was all an age ago, and Hervey was thankful of it (and trusted that he himself did not pester B Troop in *this* park). The present commander-in-chief, Lord Hill, he held of course in the highest regard – most affectionate regard; but 'Daddy' Hill's days were spent in the business of retrenchment, so he understood, doing battle every bit as bitter with the Treasury as that he had done with the French. What the army – what Lord Hill – needed now therefore, reckoned Hervey, was a quartermaster-general with the wisdom of Sir John Moore, and one whose opinion counted. Then the cavalry would see a change – and (who knew?) even the red-coated Line, for there were enough men in green to show them how . . .

'Have you seen the great plinth that is built for the statue of His late Majesty, atop Snow Hill?' asked Worsley.

'I have not,' replied Hervey, recollecting himself. 'What statue is this? I have not heard of it.'

'Oh, a very fine one – an equestrian statue, all of copper. I've seen the clay model it's to be cast from – Marcus Aurelius on the Capitoline.'

'Indeed? I'd have thought His late Majesty more likely to prefer the image of a ploughman.'

There was the polite laughter customary for a superior officer's jest, but in truth the notion of the poor old King – 'Farmer George' – mounted in triumph as a Roman emperor seemed incongruous to say the least. Yes, he had gained a few spice islands and the Cape of Good Hope in the war with France, but he had lost the American colonies twenty years before, and to the mind of many that was all there was to be said.

'But we'll take a look at Windsor's new Capitoline, by all means. Carry on, then, please, Captain Worsley – but ride with us if you will.'

The officer commanding B Troop saluted and turned away to give his orders, while Hervey reined about to give him the privacy to do so in the manner he saw fit, for it was Worsley's parade not his.

'Did not Marcus Aurelius see himself as the bringer of peace rather than as conqueror?' asked Fairbrother when they were out of earshot. 'I've never been to Rome, of course, but I've read of the statue and seen images of it. He bears no sword, if I recall it rightly. Perhaps it's more apt than at first seems.'

Hervey had both seen the statue and listened carefully in his lessons at Shrewsbury. And he did now recall that his friend might be right. 'We need Agar to tell us definitively, of course, though I suspect Jenkinson could offer an opinion. Indeed, I am rather surprised he didn't . . . But you are the most valuable fellow. What error I might fall into without your counsel!'

'I liked the way Jenkinson spoke freely,' said Fairbrother, tightening his girth strap again in anticipation of a gallop, having eased it while they stood watching. 'It pays you a compliment – and, of course, Worsley.'

'Just so. By the bye, I'll be interested to see what post the duke does give the new Liverpool, Jenkinson *père*, for he was conspicuously without one throughout his brother's time.'

Fairbrother inclined his head in a knowing way. 'Ah, the sibling rival, the stock trade of drama – and sibling loyalty too: "Is there no voice more worthy than my own / To sound more sweetly in great

Caesar's ear / For the repealing of my banished brother?"'

'I think that is enough of the Ancients, Fairbrother. Let us get ourselves across the bourne yonder and then give these horses their head up Snow Hill.'

Fairbrother gave him a somewhat rueful look. 'A hill aptly called. A gallop on snow will be entirely novel to me. I may well be down the other side faster than the grand old Duke of York.'

IV

AN EYE LIKE MARS

Later

The chimneys of Windsor in winter, and all about, were at their labours. In the still, cold air the smoke rose but a few feet before spreading edgewise, joining with that of adjacent chimneys in a great, grey canopy. But one column rose higher – far higher; bigger too, and darker.

From the top of Snow Hill they could see for miles.

'Something well alight to the west,' said Hervey, pulling off a glove to get his telescope from its holster.

Worsley was doing the same. 'Towards Winkfield, I reckon,' he replied, getting the glass to his eye; 'and flames, distinctly.'

'Well, no smoke without the proverbial fire, but what's the cause of it? And a prodigious blaze, by the look of it. I think it worth your inquiry.'

'I was about to ask leave to explore, Colonel. Innocent or not they'll have need of hands to extinguish it. I'll save the pivot drill for another day and take the troop whole, for it's on route back to Maidenhead. They'll enjoy the gallop.'

'Go to it, then,' said Hervey, lowering his 'scope. 'And write me word of what you find. And my compliments on your field day. Dine with me when you're returned.'

'Very good, Colonel.'

Worsley saluted, visibly encouraged, then, reining round, set off down the slope at a bold pace.

Words of praise; words of encouragement, and an invitation to hospitality – words of command. Hervey was ever mindful of those his own captain had spoken when first he had joined: some officers need driving, most need encouraging, very few need restraining. Words in command were mightier than the sword.

Fairbrother smiled to himself. '"An eye like Mars to threaten and command, / A station like the herald Mercury / New-lighted on a heaven-kissing hill".'

Hervey turned. 'What is that you say? Speak plainly, for my ears are as numb as my toes.'

Fairbrother shook his head. 'I was merely recalling something I read.'

Hervey frowned; his friend could be extraordinarily arch. He turned instead to the adjutant. 'Well, Malet, what think you now: shall we pay a call on the orderlies at the castle? We might at least find a cup of something hot.'

Windsor Castle was the furthest of the War Office party's stations, with an NCO and two dragoons. There was not the least necessity of inspecting them, their being under such constant supervision as obtained at the Crown's principal residence, but Malet agreed it would be diverting, especially on so cold a day.

'Capital idea, Colonel.' He turned to the serjeant-major. 'D Troop furnishes the War Office party: who will be the NCO there at the present, Mr Rennie? Would you know?'

'I believe it will be Corporal Fagan, sir.'

It was not the business of the RSM to know every last detail of a troop's duty roster. Rennie's recall was impressive, and Hervey's nod said as much. 'Then let us go and see him.'

As they turned north to descend to the Long Walk, Hervey thought it apt to draw in his friend again, who was so evidently weary of mock battle. 'The straightest two and a half miles, I'd venture, this side of the Appian Way. Is it not a fair prospect, the castle?'

'It is,' replied Fairbrother. He had been contemplating it for some minutes.

'Charles the Second began it, and then William of Orange planted the elms, and the Georges added to it. The late King had a good many stones brought from Leptis Magna, though I don't recall—'

He pulled up suddenly, as if someone had plucked at his coat. He looked again towards the ever-darkening column of smoke. 'Damn it, it can't be a hapless thing. Not on such a day . . . Come, Malet!' he snapped, reining sharp about and spurring his charger awake: 'Let's pay B Troop a second visit.'

The little party sprang to life like the field after a bolting fox, swinging as one west down the hill in pursuit, though the RSM kept a stricter hold on his followers than any field master. They steadied at the bottom to a canter across the parkland towards the Battle Bourne ponds, and then a straight line through the South Forest, putting deer to flight in all directions before bursting onto the Windsor road, narrowly missing the Ascot stage bowling south, then scrambling across the ditches alongside, and back into a gallop due west across the parkland of Cranbourne Court.

Hervey was relishing it – like a fast run with the Duke of Beaufort's hounds on a good scenting day. He'd been so much abroad of late that he'd forgotten the pleasure of an English chase. 'I've rarely hunted a cleaner line,' he called to Fairbrother, checking just an instant to cross the Hatchett lane at the far end of the park, his gelding responding admirably to the merest flexing of the reins – and tiring almost not at all. They'd galloped true on the smoke even through the forest (though 'forest' did always seem to him overwrought) and strayed not fifty yards either side of dead straight. The park itself was not unlike the country of the Zulu, but without the thorn – except he was sure no Zulu ever saw the snow.

What a life was this: India, the Cape, the western Levant, and all in the space of four years – only the time it took (decently) to back a foal. Would that it could be ever thus!

Ten minutes, and only a few furlongs to run – yet no sign of B Troop. How could they be so far behind Worsley's men?

Back now into a hand-gallop across empty pasture, skirting the frozen fishponds, taking the hedges apace – and with not a faller – on up a steady rise, across the Winkfield road . . . and then, atop, with just a furlong more, a clear view at last of the blaze.

'Is that B Troop?' he called to Malet. He could scarce believe they'd got there before him without his crossing their line.

'I think it must be, Colonel. There are no other.'

They galloped on.

Down the slope, uneven old plough, one more hedge and a half-hidden ditch, across some empty pasture – and they were at the fiery barn.

Worsley saw them and cantered over. 'A dozen men, by all accounts, Colonel, and rough with it too. They set about the farmer, and his men, broke up a threshing machine and set light to the barn. He reckons they made off northwards and west, not half an hour ago. I've sent the sar'nt-major to look for tracks, and Kennett with the rest of the troop towards Maiden's Green to head them off – and a couple of NCOs to ride the roads either side. Unless these devils have horses I can't see how they can have got very far by any route.'

'No indeed. They'll be more footpad than highwayman, though if they've gone to earth they'll take some finding here – so many coverts, though I suppose there'll be tracks in the snow. Did the farmer see pistols?'

'No.'

'It doesn't mean they're *not* armed, of course. There's every reason to conceal them . . . But tell me, how did you come here so quickly?'

'I took a line through Cranbourne Park to the Winkfield road and turned south – I know it well. The troop had just begun moving towards the park and I sent my trumpeter to have them do the same.'

'Action is eloquence,' said Fairbrother, just audibly enough for Hervey to wish he'd used the words himself.

Instead he contented himself (and Worsley) with another 'admirable', and then: 'We may well have gained a march on them. They *must* be in the bag hereabouts. The trick now is to close it.'

'That I'm sure of, Colonel, but it'll be dark in a couple of hours, and rummaging in the bag will be deuced difficult. Another troop would make all the difference.'

Hervey looked at Malet.

'C's the only one not at London duties, Colonel, but their parade state this morning was fewer than fifty.'

'And we couldn't get them here before last light,' Hervey replied. And then a thought occurred. 'The battalion at Windsor . . . We'd not be able to get them much before dark, but they could search through the night.'

'Better, I think, in daylight, Colonel. So many cottages and field barns,' said Worsley.

'You'd have a damned cold picket of it the while.'

Worsley did not answer, for the proposition was irrefutable.

'But it would have the merit of allowing us an hour or so to secure the bag, so to speak, before calling out the Guards. Then at least I might have some purchase with their commanding officer. What may we do to assist you?'

'Feed and rations, I think, Colonel.'

Hervey turned in the saddle. 'Mr Rennie?'

'At once, Colonel,' and the RSM had saluted and reined about before Hervey could say more – not that it was in the least necessary to say more.

Hervey surveyed the farm and the nearby cottages. 'I suppose there's nothing to be done to put out the flames. There's no wind, which is a mercy, so it ought to burn itself out without further harm. I think you had better carry on, Worsley. Let's meet at the church in an hour . . . which minds me: I wonder if there's aught to be seen from the tower?'

'Jenkinson's taking a look.'

'Capital. Then we'll take a turn for ourselves towards Maiden's Green. There may be a sign or two.'

The day was already darkening. Spirits were not lowered, however; not in the least. Indeed, Hervey himself was thoroughly brightened by the gallop and the prospect of apprehending such brutish breachers of the King's peace.

Warmed by the blaze and enlivened by the task, they made a line south to the Ascot road at the trot, turning west onto it and keeping the same pace for half a mile or so before reaching the church, where they found Jenkinson on the battlemented tower but with nothing to report, so continued on, up the road but seeing next to no one save Worsley's videttes, despite the hue and cry, until they came on Lieutenant Kennett at the junction with the road that was to be the line of the cordon.

'The troop is posted, Colonel,' said Kennett, with no very great enthusiasm.

Hervey found himself irritated. 'What do they have to eat?' he asked abruptly (and not entirely reasonably, for Kennett might have been allowed that his only thought to this time had been how to dispose his men).

'I . . . I don't yet know, Colonel.'

'Do they have biscuit issued?'

'I'm afraid I can't say, Colonel.'

'But you yourself will be feeling the pinch of appetite?'

Kennett failed to see to what the question tended. 'Oh, no, thank you, Colonel, for I brought with me some chicken and a veal pie.'

'Did you indeed,' was all that he heard by reply, as Hervey moved off in pointed silence.

Malet's voice followed. 'Mr Kennett, the favour of your attention if you will . . .'

The adjutant's 'if you will' – admonition cloaked with civility. Hervey kicked into a trot; there was no need to hear Malet's precise 'words of advice'.

'I fancy the veal pie has suddenly become less appetizing,' said Fairbrother when they were out of earshot.

'You know, Worsley's a man of ten times Kennett's consequence but I'll warrant he'll be the last to eat today.'

'I don't doubt it.'

'Mind, between Rennie and Collins, none of them shall starve for long.'

Malet rejoined them a few minutes later. Hervey knew it was beneath his dignity to enquire of the 'interview', but couldn't resist the raising of an eyebrow.

'Whether or not a true penitent, I can't rightly say, Colonel; but at this moment he's pondering on the miracle of the loaves and fishes. The troop shall taste veal pie, if but a very little.'

Hervey smiled to himself. Subtlety was much to be prized in an adjutant when the lash was no option.

They stopped at each vidette in turn for a few words: Kennett had at least posted them soundly, a furlong apart, patrolling left to right, and they seemed to know what they were about – twelve in all, half an hour to ride the length of the cordon.

As they neared the junction with the lane that ran north-west to south-east, forming the right-hand boundary of the 'bag' (which was patrolled with economy rather than picketed, for the intelligence suggested the miscreants had made off west towards Ascot), Serjeant-Major Collins came up from the south-west.

'Drawn blank, Sar'nt-Major?'

'Aye, Colonel, but handily I'd say – maybe. The snow's turned over a good deal all over the place, awkward to follow any track, but there's nothing at all towards yon cordon save for the odd deer. They haven't got west of Maiden's Green, not across the fields at any rate.'

'I suppose they might have come in the first place along the road, which would account for the virgin snow. There'd be nothing to stop them if their faces weren't known hereabout . . .'

'The farmer was very exact about them making west, Colonel. He said he watched them as far as the wood beyond his home pasture. But he has sheep all over that way, and I couldn't pick up anything. They're not in the wood still, I'm sure of that. But they won't be short of cover, and they can try and slip away once it's dark and they know where the patrols are.'

Hervey nodded. If they were going to get a company of infantry from Windsor, the bag had better be tight-drawn during the night. 'Come, let's find your captain.'

They cantered down the lane to the Winkfield road and on to the rendezvous at St Mary's church. Smoke from the barn was settling in the hollows, and one or two braver village souls were going about their last-light business, none of them giving the remotest impression of complicity with the incendiarists, though there was no knowing – there was no time to know – in what regard they held the farmer.

Worsley was there already, coming down the tower on seeing them approach, and with a resolute if frustrated look. 'We can't have been thirty minutes behind them, at most; yet not a sign.'

''Cept Sar'nt-Major Collins says they haven't crossed the road west, for sure.'

'Ah, then you do think it worth fetching infantry from Windsor?'

Hervey nodded decidedly. 'I do. I'll go there directly.'

'In that case I'll put the cordon on a longer footing – with your leave?'

'By all means. Where will you plant your pennon?'

'Here, Colonel. There's a beer-house yonder I've had Serjeant Bancroft look to. It has a good copper, if Mr Rennie can bring us any meat. There's corn at the farm which seems to have escaped the flames.'

'Depend on it. But have Jenkinson call on the manor too. They're bound to have hay. Has the parson come by? He ought to have useful intelligence.'

'He's abroad. There's a curate. He's gone to fetch the parish map.'

'Very well. I'll return, if I'm favoured, by midnight. The moon's young, but it's bright – or it was last night.'

'Indeed. We may try a little earth-stopping,' said Worsley, with a wry smile.

'Capital. Come, then, Malet; let's see how many guardsmen the King will spare us.'

Malet was only pleased he was not asked his opinion.

Five miles, perhaps six, horses now tiring and the night descending rapidly – Hervey took it at a trot, but even so, his charger lost a shoe (it was as well there'd be farriers and new horses at Windsor). An hour, just under – in these conditions, a forced march.

He went straight to the barracks in Sheet Street, which was neither a salubrious quarter nor in any way a pleasing example of the builder's art (he silently gave thanks for his own situation at Hounslow), and was surprised to be told that the commanding officer was at orderly room, even at the late hour of five o'clock.

But then, Lieutenant-Colonel Ralph Calthorp, commanding the Grenadier battalion, was no mere 'court guardee', and was at once animated by the appearance of the lieutenant-colonel of light dragoons come in from the snow with a call to arms. He likened it indeed to the alarm before Waterloo – if to Hervey's puzzlement, for Waterloo was hardly yesterday, though on learning that they had both slept on that sodden ridge before the battle, he was all sureness, and the lieutenant-colonel of Grenadiers all impatience to assist.

'But I cannot move a single man from his post without the authority of the King himself,' explained Calthorp, seizing up his hat and greatcoat. 'Come with me to the castle. We'll seek out the King's secretary.'

They went on foot – and a dreary, slushy, unedifying march

it was, the gaslight illumining many a sight that was better unlit. But it was a short march at least, and there was no challenge from the succession of sentries as they proceeded up the bailey past St George's Chapel to the state apartments, only the presenting of arms as the orderly serjeant scurried ahead with 'Colonel coming!'

A plain, unguarded door admitted them to a crypt-like space through which they marched unhindered to a stone staircase which ascended to a vaulted chamber devoid of any furniture or ornament, and on through featureless passages ill-lit by oil lamps, and then a further unremarkable door which suddenly admitted them – quite to Hervey's surprise – into a suite of well-appointed rooms that looked bathed in limelight, occupied by what he took to be clerks.

'Sir William,' commanded Colonel Calthorp tersely, without checking his stride.

A footman sitting by a gilded door sprang to his feet and opened it.

The colonel continued the motion into the room beyond. 'Knighton, have you the ear of His Majesty at this moment? I wish to remove a company of my guards to apprehend a party of felons – nay, insurrectionaries – in the park.'

Sir William Knighton, His Majesty's private secretary, looked up as if it were the most regular of requests. 'His Majesty at this time gives audience to the prime minister.'

Calthorp frowned. 'I didn't expect an audience myself, Knighton. I fancy a scrip from you will be sufficient for the Lord Chief Justice, if it comes to law. Oh, this is Colonel Hervey of the light dragoons at Hounslow. It's his men who've run the miscreants to earth.'

Sir William, who bore a passing resemblance to his principal in the days before the pleasures of the table had wrought such destruction with the royal figure, rose and offered his hand.

Hervey took it and explained the events of the afternoon.

Before the crown secretary could make reply, however, the door to the audience room opened and the King himself appeared, and behind him the Duke of Wellington.

'Your Majesty,' cued Sir William.

They all bowed.

The King seemed alarmed. 'Colonel Calthorp, is the time come?'

'Your Majesty?'

'Is it the time? Is the guard ready for inspection?'

A faintly consolatory look came to Colonel Calthorp's face. 'Presently, sir.'

'Your Majesty, may I present Colonel Hervey of the light dragoons at Hounslow,' tried Sir William, concerned to pass over the apparent misunderstanding.

'Yes, yes, I dined with him there not a month ago.'

Hervey could not but observe his sovereign with pitying horror – a florid, bloated figure in a lurid dressing gown, his hair awry, his eyes agog, his mouth dribbling; a man of no great age but dilapidated beyond his years. He was never more relieved to see the duke than now, for so abject a ruler must be in need of the wisest of counsel.

'Your Majesty, if I may,' he replied, 'I am just returned from Constantinople.'

The King turned to his prime minister. 'Arthur, do you know this man? An excellent fellow. He keeps the finest table of all my Guards.'

'I do indeed know Colonel Hervey, sire. An officer of commendable zeal.'

'Were you at Waterloo, Colonel?' asked the King, becoming animated once more.

'I was, sir.'

'Did you see me lead the charge of the cavalry? Was it not the greatest of affairs?'

Hervey, bewildered, glanced at the duke for some sign, but saw none. 'For the most part I was on the left flank, sir, until later in the day, by which time the heavies had made their charge.'

'Ah,' said the King, dejectedly. 'But you saw it, Arthur. I led them straight at the French, did I not?'

'I have often heard Your Majesty tell me so.'

'Well, well . . . Shall you dine with us, Colonel?'

'Sir, I am come to ask release of a company of Your Majesty's Guards to search an area to the south of your park where I believe my dragoons have cornered a party of incendiaries.'

His Majesty's countenance changed. He was at once fearful, but yet defiant. 'They have set fire to my farms?'

'Not to Your Majesty's farms, sir, but to a barn of a yeoman farmer at Winkfield.'

'Alarum! What, ho! – no watch? no passage? Murder! Murder!'

'Sir?'

The King was now exceedingly agitated. 'You must by all means have my Guards – all of them, and my Horse Guards too. Hunt out these devils. Strike them down! Spare them not. No quarter! You understand, Hervey? Every one of them put to the sword!'

Hervey stood awkwardly, at a loss for words.

'Your Majesty,' said the duke, kindly but firmly, 'you may trust that Colonel Hervey will do his duty.'

'I shall depend on it, Arthur. And I shall reward him well for it too. And these miscreants, these base fellows who would burn barns within sight of my own castle, they shall be executed and their heads placed on poles on London Bridge.'

'I am sure the justices will do their duty too, sir,' said the duke, calmly. 'But, with Your Majesty's leave, I would have a word with Colonel Hervey before he goes to his.'

'Of course, Arthur, of course. You must give your orders for the coming battle, make your dispositions and so forth. I myself shall tour the line when it is daylight. But no cheering, Hervey; I'll have no cheering. Damned Jacobin thing. They cheered Bonaparte before Waterloo. I heard their beastly roar.'

'Indeed, Your Majesty,' replied Hervey, bowing as the King turned and took his leave.

'I bid you good night, Arthur. You will avail yourself of sleep, mind. A near-run thing it may be tomorrow.'

'Indeed, Your Majesty. Good night.'

When the door was closed, the duke turned his gaze on Hervey. 'His Majesty is not himself today. I hardly need tell you, I trust, that his exhortation to slaughter must go unheeded. Transportation will serve as well, if the death penalty is commuted.'

'Quite so, sir.'

'But your reply to the King – the charge and all: it was nicely done.'

Hervey bowed.

The duke now turned to the crown secretary. 'Well, Knighton, I must return sharp to Whitehall. I shall come again on Friday.'

'Very well, Prime Minister. I'm sure His Majesty will be much recovered then.'

'Physicking him, are you?'

Sir William Knighton had formerly been the King's physician, when he was the Prince of Wales, and was thought by many to administer powders still, as well as advice. 'No, duke, I no longer practise. Sir Wathen Waller attends His Majesty.'

'Mm.' The Duke of Wellington nodded his farewells, picked up his cloak and stalked out to his chariot.

Sir William sat down, looking decidedly troubled. 'Gentlemen, I perhaps hardly need say that I must rely on your absolute discretion. His Majesty has been unwell, and in consequence of his medicaments can become . . . excited.'

'Of course, Knighton,' said Colonel Calthorp. 'We are all His Majesty's loyal servants.'

Hervey nodded.

'Very well. You have His Majesty's leave to search for this gallows-fodder with a company of Foot Guards, or indeed with as many as may be expedient. I shall make a formal minute of it if you wish.'

Calthorp looked at Hervey for a reply.

'I think it unnecessary, in the circumstances.'

'Very well. May I offer you some hospitality?'

'For my part, I thank you, but no,' said Hervey, much as it would have pleased him to say 'yes'. 'We must see to matters and then return to Winkfield.'

Sir William bowed. 'I believe His Majesty would appreciate an account of events, when the work is done. You may render that in writing, Colonel Hervey, but I believe it would greatly please His Majesty if you were to make your report in person.'

Hervey nodded. 'I shall do my utmost to comply with the latter.'

And they left the castle with as little ceremony as they had come.

'I would have given a deal to witness it,' said Fairbrother, pulling up his collar as they turned from Sheet Street onto the King's Road, 'though I was most hospitably diverted by the Grenadiers.'

Hervey's charger, reshod and with a good measure of oats inside him, champed at the bit as if it were first parade. 'It's better that you didn't,' he replied unhappily. 'It was not an edifying encounter.'

'But you have your beaters at least.'

Indeed he did. A hundred Grenadiers would march out of barracks at four o'clock and take this same road, and at fifteen minutes before sunrise they would form line along the Winkfield road to advance in open order and drive the 'firebirds' onto the guns. Every house and cot, every hut and barn, every stable and byre, every copse and hedge – every hiding place of every kind – would be searched. There would be no escape. Not if B Troop kept its ground well in the meantime.

'You know, Fairbrother, once for a while I was on quite intimate terms with the poet Shelley – you've heard me speak of it – and though I found him in himself a most engaging man, I couldn't abide his politics. And yet something he once wrote came to me most forcefully as we left the castle.'

'Now you are a little inclined to be a republican.'

Hervey did not rise to the bait. 'It was a poem about England after "Peterloo", about the King's being mad and parliament corrupt . . .'

But Fairbrother had spent long hours on the *stoep* beneath the palms reading everything that was sent him by his bookseller in London. He could quote Shelley at almost the length that he could Shakespeare: '"An old, mad, blind, despised, and dying King; / Princes, the dregs of their dull race, who flow / Through public scorn, – mud from a muddy spring".'

'Upon my word, you have a powerful recall.'

'It is a poem of some power – or should I say anger? – and therefore commanding recall. And only but a dozen or so lines. But I should have thought it repugnant to your Tory principles: "An army, whom liberticide and prey / Makes as a two-edged sword to all who wield." Is that not seditious stuff?'

'He wrote it after "Peterloo", as I said, not long after I met him, in Rome. I liked him a good deal, but he misrepresents the army in the business that day at Peter's-fields. It was the yeomanry that gave the sword, not the regulars.'

'It is perhaps of some comfort to be cut by a volunteer's blade rather than a regular's?'

Hervey frowned. 'As I said, I liked Shelley – very much – but I don't subscribe to his England then or now. These things must be weighed in the balance. The senate unreformed is as may be, but I don't believe reform would bring improvement, as I've told you before, though I dare say the call for it is about to become clamorous. But I do say this – and I tell you most privily – those words describing the late King: they were not fair, by no means fair. He was not despised – pitied, but not despised. But the words might well apply now to his son. It was a most unhappy encounter this evening . . . And when he's gone, as the tattle has it he soon will, and the evidence of my own eyes could hardly dispute it, we'll hear nothing but "reform", and in no small part on account of this king.'

Fairbrother did not reply at once, as if weighing his friend's words . . . and then, "'A senate, Time's worst statute, *unrepealed*". I wonder if mere *reform* will satisfy.'

"'Unrepealed". Quite so.'

'But this political circumspection has not dulled your ardour for the business at hand?'

Hervey braced, as if cold water was thrown at him – perturbed by the notion that he somehow perceived his duty otherwise. 'Not in the least. Violence to law-abiding citizens, and arson – a barn in *winter*! – I'll have not the least regret if they go to the gallows.' And as if to emphasize his determination to see them taken up the scaffold, he pressed into a fast trot.

Fairbrother fell silent. He knew when it was better to be so: his friend would already be ruing, no doubt, his lifting the mask, speaking his inner thoughts – thoughts not conducive (he would no doubt believe) to good order and military discipline . . .

The moon was obliging, however – not yet into its first quarter, but bright nevertheless in the cold, clear sky, with the snow to reflect its light – and the road was clear too, so that the silence lasted barely an hour. When they reached Winkfield the church clock was striking ten.

'Colonel, sir, the captain's doing his rounds,' said the picket corporal in a voice from the valleys as they came up to the crossroads. 'Serjeant-major's over yonder at the tithe barn, Colonel.'

'The troop serjeant-major or Mr Rennie, Corp'l Parry?' (Hervey surmised that it was Parry, though he couldn't see him, for there was but one Welshman of rank in the regiment.) And it was indeed an occasional point of confusion: *the* serjeant-major was always Rennie, but there again a dragoon looked first to his own troop.

'Serjeant-Major Collins, Colonel,' came the reply.

'Thank you,' replied Hervey, dismounting and holding out his hands to warm at the picket's fire. 'Stand easy. Is there anything to report?'

'There is nothing to report, Colonel. Everything is as quiet as the chapel on market day.'

Hervey had once ventured into Wales from Shrewsbury and found it a gloomy place, but acknowledged it bred a hardy sort of man for a soldier; and Parry's turn of phrase was never without colour. 'Very well. What feed and rations have you had issued?'

'Oh, ample corn, Colonel, and hay – good hay, too, mind. And best beef and bread, and a nice measure of brandy. And we've potatoes in the fire, and a good brew. No, Colonel, we's very well provided for. Thank you for asking.'

Rennie had evidently risen to the occasion, thought Hervey, wondering by what means of credit. But he was glad the sar'nt-major wasn't by his side now, for Parry would be receiving words in his ear – 'As you were, Corporal! The colonel is *never* thanked – except at orderly room, and then only for his lenient punishment!'

'How are the reliefs rostered?' he asked instead, tolerantly.

'I and my three stand duty until midnight, Colonel, and then we are relieved by Corporal Harris, and then all we stand-to-arms at six o'clock.'

'And then?'

'And then, Colonel, we are to take prisoner those who did this wicked thing.'

'Very well,' replied Hervey, satisfied he had the measure of B Troop's temper, and confident they would maintain a cordon tight enough to pen the firebirds until morning. 'I bid you good night, Corp'l Parry.'

The NCO of the valleys braced to attention again, and answered with an earnestness that might have rung false had it not been characteristic. 'Good night to you, too, Colonel, sir, and to you, Mr Malet, sir.'

Hervey turned away with an inclination to smile. It was good to speak with such an NCO – any NCO – off-parade, in the silent hours, by the fire; nature was revealed more truly, and although a regiment was nothing if it did not, when required, act as one body, that body was made of many parts, and it was well always to recollect it.

And he had asked questions enough; this was Worsley's troop after all, and Worsley was perfectly capable of mounting a night watch. He needed only now to tell him what was afoot for the morning, and so they marched without ado to the tithe barn.

It was remarkably well lit – he supposed by every candle the church could render. Serjeant-Major Collins was writing up the evening states at a makeshift table.

'Good evening, Colonel,' he snapped, springing to attention.

'Stand easy, Sar'nt-Major. What's to report?'

'Colonel, the troop is disposed as it was when you left for Windsor, but on half-sentry. Captain Worsley is doing his rounds at this time with the orderly serjeant. Mr Rennie has just gone up to the manor again to get more corn for the morning. There's not been sight nor sound of the incendiaries, Colonel.'

'Mm.'

'The troop has dined well, Colonel. Have you had aught to eat yourself?'

Only now, given leave to think of it, did Hervey realize how hungry he was. 'As a matter of fact, I haven't.'

Collins called into the shadows, 'Corp'l Tinker, a plate for the colonel. And tea.'

Where a plate was to be found was intriguing but in the circumstances not the stuff of enquiry. He could only hope it wasn't hallowed. 'Thank you,' said Hervey simply.

'And the adjutant and the rest of your party, Colonel?'

Hervey glanced at Malet and Fairbrother, and smiled ironically. 'They dined well off the Guards, though I'm sure tea would be welcome – as ever.'

'And will the Guards be coming to assist us, Colonel?'

'They will. At dawn. And if we've been able to confine those devils the while, I've no doubt they'll be in irons by midday.'

'A fuller moon would have served, Colonel, but even so, they'll have a job moving without being seen. Their only chance'd be to follow their tracks back east, but Captain Worsley put a patrol on the Cranbourne road too. Oh, one more thing, Colonel: the gentle-man at the manor says the officers are assured of his hospitality. He's the magistrate too.'

'Is he, indeed? I think the sheriff himself has been sent for, but a magistrate could be a boon. Be that as may, I'll be glad of a few hours' sleep while we wait. And stabling.' He turned to Malet with an enquiring look.

'I'll go myself at once, Colonel.'

V

'STAND UP, GUARDS!'

Next day

'Rouse, Hervey. Past five o'clock, on a cold and frosty morning.'

Fairbrother was unusually hearty; indeed, it was unusual for him to be awake at all at such an hour.

Hervey sat up. He had slept for four – enough, but scarcely satisfying. Hot tea, the kind that as a rule Johnson brought him whether in quarters or bivouac, would have been welcome and reviving; instead he took the proffered glass of brandy.

He had lain atop the blankets under his cloak having removed his boots and sword but little else. Malet had first woken Fairbrother in the room adjoining – though in truth Fairbrother had been awake a good while on account of the cold – and taken his assurance that he would wake his friend in a timely fashion for the breakfast that Winkfield's magistrate had ordered for five-thirty.

It had been past midnight when they had at last accepted the hospitality of the manor. Worsley had returned to the tithe barn at eleven, and Hervey had spoken with him at some length about the arrangements for the morning. He had checked the instinct to visit all the videttes in person, for that might have suggested he lacked confidence in B Troop's captain – and this was hardly Waterloo, or even Bhurtpore.

He dismissed Fairbrother and the second glass, and after pulling on his boots, fastening on his sword and gathering up his cloak and cap, descended to a breakfast worthy of a Melton hunting box.

The magistrate had said he would open his court in the manor house to remand any captives at once to the crown court in the custody of the parish constable, who would of course call on the Guards to escort them to Windsor, whence the sheriff's men would convey them to Reading gaol. 'I'll brook no riot in *my* jurisdiction, Colonel,' he'd said, and as Hervey watched him do battle now with knife and fork to fortify himself with the roast beef of old England, fowling piece by his side as if summary execution were within his powers, he could not doubt that here was a doughty warrior for the King's peace. It was all he could do to persuade him to remain in waiting at the manor rather than dispensing justice from the saddle.

'Have you read Fielding?' asked Fairbrother, as they left the house, much intrigued by his first encounter – other than on the page – with the Tory squirearchy in the exercise of rustic justice.

'No, but since you ask me at this time I think I may have an idea of his subject.'

'I was minded of Squire Western, but for the latter's West Country vowels and curses.'

'But thank God for him, no doubt, and Winkfield's magistrate too, and not a Fouché. His justice'll be tempered by good country sense. But see, we haven't time for this. It's good that you're with us still. I'd like you to take a note of what transpires this morning. Malet would do it as a rule, but he'll be much occupied.'

Fairbrother pulled his collar up and adjusted his hat. 'By all means. A life of Colonel Hervey might one day be my fortune!'

'You are uncommonly droll. For my part, with business to be about I fear I shall be poor company.'

Fairbrother said nothing. It was when there was business to be about that his friend was *incomparable* company – albeit single-minded; and it amused him always that his friend never perceived it thus.

But as the clock was striking the quarter after six, and the party mounted and left the stable yard, Hervey, warmed by strong-roasted coffee and good meat, was suddenly inclined to be hale (as perhaps was his duty). 'Mr Rennie, your provisioning was worthy of a Bengal sutler. I never heard such satisfaction expressed as last night.'

But the RSM was constitutionally inclined to be taciturn. 'Thank you, Colonel. The market at Ascot was most obliging.'

Hervey would not be put off. 'Sar'nt Acton, the stables were commodious?'

'Oh, aye, Colonel,' replied his coverman. 'Good standing stalls, and a couple of loose boxes for us to bed down in, and plenty of clean straw. Warm as wool we were.'

'What remarkable alliteration.'

'Aye, Colonel: *deep*-litter-ation!'

Hervey laughed. Quick wit was born of intelligence (and besides, it was good to be kept amused of a cold morning). 'Well I trust you won't see the same bedding tonight except in a palliasse. If the Guards set to with address we should have cleared the ground by midday.' He turned to the adjutant. 'Have you ever seen the Guards at a field day, Mr Malet?'

'Only at a review, Colonel.'

'Then today will be of some novelty, if not so pretty as a review . . . Ah, good morning, Worsley.'

B Troop's captain was waiting at the picket post by the church as arranged, with just his trumpeter.

'Good morning, Colonel. I believe we may have them – half a dozen at least. Sar'nt-Major Collins and Corporal Lynch were doing poacher drill in the early hours and saw them doubling back from the vidette line – evidently they'd been too wary to cross, for we'd lit torches the length of the road to confuse them as to our strength – and they went to earth in a hut. They passed very close to the sar'nt-major, which is why he was able to count six with such surety. But he didn't want to bolt them.'

'Smart work indeed.'

'I shall commend him, Colonel. And skirmishers from the Grenadiers have just come into the Winkfield road.'

Hervey quickened the more. 'Then let's go and see the company in.'

It was still the hour when no one was abroad, and the party could move boldly. The moon had set two hours before, but against the snow they could see their way, and the first intimations of dawn were adding their light.

Fairbrother rode up alongside his friend, intent on a word, but Hervey anticipated him.

'"A cold coming they had of it",' he declaimed cheerily. '"The ways deep, the weather sharp, the days short, the sun farthest off *in solstitio brumali*, the very dead of winter". What eloquence is that!'

'Eloquence indeed: your father's sermon each Christmas, I believe you've told me a good few times?'

'Though not his words – not his own words, that is.' He fell silent for a moment . . . 'When I have the reins properly in hand, so to speak, we shall go down to Wiltshire, you and I, and pay our respects.'

He did not add 'for I am sorely missing Georgiana', but Fairbrother knew well enough that the separation must pain him. Not in any cloying way (for besides, his friend had never had true opportunity to form any deep affection), but as a duty not rightly discharged. Nor was this frozen hour the time to be entering on a discussion of the obligations of paternity . . .

A cock crew, the first of the day.

Fairbrother was delighted by the gift, to deflect their thoughts with Latin of his own: '"*Gallo canente, spes redit*"!'

Hervey brightened again. '"At the cock's chaunting, hope returns" – my God, Fairbrother, I've known that many a time, I tell you . . . But there'll be no hope for those felons yonder, no matter how loud the cock crows. Not if Worsley's troop have done their duty, and the Guards do theirs. Upon my word, Collins has done a fine thing last night, smelling them out.'

They turned onto the Winkfield road as the half-hour was striking, and were just able to make out a mounted party preceding what he took to be the head of the Grenadier column.

'Hervey?' came the clipped voice from the *prima luce*.

'Is that you, Calthorp?'

'It is. Good morning to you.'

'And to you. I'm glad to see you. You come most carefully upon your hour.'

'Let it not be said that the Guards do not keep strict time, though yonder striking clock is by Windsor time ten minutes in retard.'

'Fortunately the sun keeps its own time. I reckon in twenty more it will be light enough to begin, would you think? And we know exactly where are six of the fugitives.'

'Admirable. But first I would introduce Mr Freely, who is a deputy sheriff of the county, resident at Windsor . . . and a Justice of the Peace.'

Hervey nodded and acknowledged the justice's salutation with a brisk 'Freely.'

'And Captain Jessope, who commands the Left Flank Company.'

Again he nodded; 'Jessope,' then added, 'I knew a Jessope in the Second Guards. He was killed at Waterloo.'

'A cousin, Colonel Hervey.'

He had been greatly fond of d'Arcey Jessope. The fleeting memory saddened and then warmed him. 'Very well. Gentlemen, may I present Captain Worsley, who commands B Troop, and whose dragoons since dusk have been picketing the square mile or so which shall be our country, and who has the whereabouts of half a dozen of the blackguards. And Lord Thomas Malet, my adjutant, and Captain Fairbrother, on detachment from the Cape Mounted Rifles.'

There was general nodding, and repetition of surnames, and evident interest on mention of the Cape Rifles.

'Mr Freely, your presence is assuring, though I trust ours is but a straightforward business this morning: there is no doubt that a felony has been committed. I would have you know it. I would wish no later ill consequences.'

'Indeed so, Colonel Hervey. We are indebted to you for the prompt action of your regiment. Do I understand correctly, however, that you allude to the vexations of civil disorder?'

Hervey was not without experience of those exact vexations, and replied with some dryness, 'You do, sir. An officer has but one decision to make, a simple choice of whether to be shot for his forbearances by a court martial, or hanged for his over-zeal by a jury. An odious business, the dispersing of a mob, though of course it must be done.'

'I am a barrister-at-law also, Colonel, and much in sympathy with the difficulty you describe, but a decision made in the fair and honest execution of an officer's duty cannot be doubted by a jury – and if it be so, then the justices of appeal would not hesitate to overturn the judgment.'

A Berkshire lane on such a morning seemed to Hervey to be ill suited to debating the practice of the law, and he was inclined therefore to concede to the sheriff and take his ease . . . except, as often, there was an antagonistic scruple at work in him, a troublesome companion, as sometimes he saw it. 'That is as may be, Sheriff, but I am minded too of the fate of Captain Porteous.'

'A wretched business, Colonel, I am agreed, though I venture to say that an *English* jury might not have acquitted in such a case in the first instance, the force being manifestly excessive.'

'Judged from the peace of a jury bench, perhaps, but who is to tell? Temporization on such occasions might be said to be a dangerous and even cruel policy.' But Hervey was content to have made his point, and besides, the Guards were in want of orders.

'Let us adjourn, gentlemen,' agreed Colonel Calthorp, turning to the commander of the Left Flank Company. 'To your duties, then,

Captain Jessope. Let the guardsmen take their ease for a quarter of an hour.'

'Sir!' snapped the captain, who then relayed his commanding officer's wish to the company serjeant-major, and there followed what seemed to Hervey like the yapping of an irate terrier, which went on intermittently for the best part of a minute. But soon the guardsmen were evidently taking their ease, pipes lit the length of the column. They had formed line in two ranks from column of threes, ordered arms, stood at ease and then easy, piled arms and fallen out, but in place, and all without a single word of command that made sense to any but one practised in hearing it. The darkness might hide a multitude of sins, of course – not least the violence of the NCOs – but Hervey was impressed nonetheless by the handiness of this column of a hundred. Drawing the covert should at least be a prompt and easy affair.

'One thing more, Hervey,' said Colonel Calthorp when the words of command had ceased: 'with the consent of the sheriff's deputy, the non-commissioned officers will load muskets ere we begin. The guardsmen themselves will proceed with fixed bayonets.'

Hervey imagined he might himself have given the same order to Worsley – substituting sabres for bayonets – except that the troop had no cartridge with them (and bone in the firelocks instead of flint). 'Eminently practical, Calthorp. Men who would set light to a barn in daylight would not hesitate to carry a firearm.' He turned to Worsley: 'I suggest Corporal Lynch accompanies the Guards and that you ride with Jessope.' (Suggesting how B Troop's captain make his dispositions, and thereby the Grenadiers, was hardly proper, but it saved Worsley the business of doing so himself.) 'You would be in agreement, Calthorp?'

'Indeed so,' he replied, turning to the deputy sheriff, with whom he was determined there should be no misunderstanding. 'But let me be rightly understood, Freely: I've no desire for blood. My non-commissioned officers have ball-cartridge for the preservation of life, not its extinction. Clean barrels and twelve captives would constitute the greatest success – *any* captives, in truth, for doubtless they'll sing like canaries.'

'Your sentiment is noted, Colonel Calthorp. I understand the order perfectly, and, insofar as it is not impertinent for me to say, entirely approve of it.'

'We are of one accord, then, Calthorp,' said Hervey. 'Captains Jessope and Worsley to ride together, and you and I the same, I think?'

It was a shrewd and necessary move, for Calthorp was his senior (it was ever so with an officer of foot guards, whatever his date of promotion), and if Hervey was to exercise any influence on the pro-ceedings it must be by suggestion – and suggestion, in his experience, was made all the more compelling by intimacy.

The lieutenant-colonel of Grenadiers was himself content: if there were to be any honours in the wretched business of appre-hending incendiaries, he had no objection to sharing them. 'Very well, Hervey. Allow me a moment to confer with Jessope, and then I propose we take post in the centre when the line advances.'

Hervey nodded and pulled away a little.

Fairbrother moved alongside him again. 'A fine job of work, that – Collins's poaching drill, as Worsley calls it.'

Hervey smiled, if unseen still. 'I rather fancy he may have learned that from you at the Cape – the stuff of the veld?'

Fairbrother was ready enough to admit his superiority in 'veld-craft', as the Cape Rifles were wont to call it, but he'd seen enough of Hervey's troop there – especially Collins – not to claim it exclu-sively. 'You are too modest. No one could crawl unobserved into Shaka's kraal, as you did, and be without resource in these things.'

Hervey frowned. In truth it was something he would be glad never to recall again. 'I could not commend what I did that day to anyone. On reflection, it was imprudent. But in point of fact the observing officers in Spain were playing the poacher's game long before. Collins showed exemplary address, however, and at his own instancing.'

Fairbrother now cut to the point. 'Neither is he a man to do so out of any desire for the notice of his commanding officer.'

Hervey smiled again. 'You are a worthy advocate. I confess it *had* occurred to me.'

'Then I shall desist from further advocacy. Tell me, by the way, what was the affair of Captain Porteous that so presses on tender consciences?'

Hervey explained.

Indeed, the case of Captain John Porteous, though a century gone, was a cautionary tale for any man wearing the King's coat. A smuggler by the name of Wilson was hanged in Edinburgh for robbing a customs officer. A riot ensued – whipped up, no doubt, by fellow villains – and Porteous, captain of the guard, ordered his men to fire on the crowd, killing or wounding several dozen of them. At the sessions that followed he was sentenced to death but then reprieved, whereupon the 'mob' dragged him from prison and hanged him from a dyer's pole.

'Ah, then I read of it in Scott. I hadn't thought it was a true business. But his defence was that he'd never given the order, was it not?'

'It was. The court did not believe it – but, more's the point, neither did the mob.'

Fairbrother shook his head. 'The rule of the mob: we are, I suppose, ever but a judicious cut of the sabre from its terrible prospect.'

'That is uncommonly well put,' replied Hervey, reaching into his pocket for the flask of brandy that his host the magistrate had so generously provided. '*Judicious* – most apt. An *injudicious* cut and a street gallows beckons.'

Fairbrother took a draw on the flask and handed it back. 'And you say your parliament had long opposed a standing constabulary, preferring the cut of the sabre, however injudicious – or indeed, unjudicial?'

Colonel Calthorp was evidently taking much care in his conference with Captain Jessope; a discourse on aid to the civil power was the last thing Hervey would have chosen at such a time, but as there was nothing else to do . . . 'I told you: they equated a police force with Fouché's spies. But let's not trouble over it now, for mine and three other regiments were spared for the sole purpose of securing the King's peace. And I mean to justify that decision.'

Besides, like any Tory – as a son of the gentry, even the minor gentry, must be – his first instinct was for order. He had long observed, from the violent inclination of so many in his native county of Wiltshire, that no one and nothing could prosper while in fear of the mob.

But first there were the matters at hand. The sun had seemed more sluggard this morning, but it was at last turning night into something that passed for day. Worsley's trumpeter's horse could now be discerned as grey, and the guardsmen's greatcoats a bluish colour rather than black. Another quarter of an hour, he reckoned, and 'types and shadows' would have their ending. But men immobile in this frosty lane would be finding it a trial . . .

Moments later – to his relief – Colonel Calthorp rejoined them. 'Light enough now for our purposes, Hervey? If we bolt any, your men should have ample sight of 'em – yes?'

Hervey was as sure as may be. 'Depend on't.'

'Very well,' said Calthorp, distinctly warming to his task. 'It ain't Waterloo, that's certain, but it ain't every day that His Majesty's Grenadiers take to the field.' He braced. 'Stand up, Guards!'

The order would be found in no drill book, but it was hallowed by precedent, for the Duke of Wellington had brought his Guards Brigade to its feet at Waterloo with the same words. They had lain concealed behind the ridge – 'in the alien corn' – and the duke had sprung them in the face of the *Garde Impériale* just as they were about to force the line. That, indeed, was how His Majesty's 1st Regiment of Guards had won their name (and bearskins) – throwing back the *Grenadiers-à-Pied*.

However, Colonel Calthorp's intention could no more carry the length of Left Flank Company than could the duke's have carried to the whole brigade at Waterloo. And so it would be translated into the terminology of the drill book and executed by degrees, the business of the non-commissioned officers – once the captain had given the word.

'Left Flank to stand up, please, Com'ny Sar'-Major.'

'Sah!' The snow was unable entirely to deaden the stamp of his boot as he came to attention.

Then, stentor-like, came the word: 'Company: Fall in!'

A hundred guardsmen rose from what comfort they'd managed, tapping out pipes, re-fitting equipment, adjusting chin-straps, getting into line in open order to a chorus of yapping corporals.

'Stand properly at ease!'

The two ranks steadied and then braced. They were now under the canon of the drill book.

'Company, att–e–en . . . *shun!*'

The earth seemed to tremble.

The company serjeant-major turned to his captain and saluted. 'Sah, the company is on parade and awaiting your order, sah!'

'Thank you, Com'ny Sar'-Major.'

Captain Jessope drew his sword, the signal – if only to himself in this half light – that he now took back formal command. Then he put his weight into the stirrups and braced to the task.

'Officers: take post!'

The lieutenants and three ensigns drew swords and found their place as best they could.

'Left Flank Company: stand fast the non-commissioned officers; remainder will fix bayonets; fix . . . *bayonets!*'

The clatter was like a mill-full of flying shuttles.

'*Shun!*'

Eighty guardsmen snapped back to attention, their muskets topped with sharpened steel.

'Non-commissioned officers: with ball-cartridge . . . *load!*'

More clattering – twenty-odd ramrods tamping down the charges.

Had it been full company drill the business would have required six further commands – *Handle Cartridge, Prime, Cast About, Draw Ramrods, Ram Down Cartridge, Return Ramrods* – but an NCO of Grenadiers might be relied upon to load his musket in his own time.

'Left Flank Company: shoulde–e–r . . . *arms!*'

Hervey turned to Fairbrother. 'Mark well, for I wager you'll not see its like again in many a year.' He said it in a voice just low enough to conceal the admiration, for it didn't do to praise these fellows too much – especially in the hearing of his own.

Fairbrother replied that he could not discern if he spoke merely in fact or in sorrow. 'Recall our wager at dinner, Hervey – action ere the year is out. Perhaps not with red coats, but . . .'

'Rear rank will move to the right; ri–i–ght . . . *turn!*'

There was another earth tremble.

'Rear rank will extend the front rank to the right: *quick march!*'

By what means this unusual movement was accomplished Hervey could not quite see, but the continued yapping of the corporals, and then '*On,* sah!' told him that it was. More words of command turned the former rear rank to the front, brought their muskets to the order, and then dressed the whole line as if on the Horse-guards.

'Can't have them going off crooked,' said Colonel Calthorp; 'even if they do have to scramble across that ditch. Wouldn't serve.'

Captain Jessope had taken post in front of the company. He now looked left and then right, ordered muskets to the port, and then 'Advance!'

His horse took the ditch in one easy movement, landing cleanly and encouraging the guardsmen to try the same. When they were all across, Worsley put his to the ditch, Corporal Lynch alongside.

'They'll extend left and right the more to cover the ground,' explained Calthorp. 'A cricket pitch between each man, with a few non-commissioned officers as flankers. A mile-long skirmish line, in truth.'

'The cover's not too close,' said Hervey. 'They shouldn't have a deal of trouble. Good hunting.'

Indeed, although the cover was next to nothing for the greater part of the first furlong, the guardsmen went to it with a will. Any half-likely-looking bush or burrow – and in went the bayonet. Here was fine sport for all.

Captain Jessope had decided not to send a party directly to the lair, believing it better to keep the line as a whole advancing at an even pace, for he wanted to spring or capture every one of them, wherever they'd gone to earth. But it was now a struggle to keep that dressing, for the ground was increasingly broken by ditches filled deceptively with snow, fences in various states of repair, and evil thorn hedges. Still, by half past seven, the light all but full day, they had managed to advance a quarter of a mile, with the ground swept clean in commendable silence (no beat of drum, and the voices of the NCOs having given way to hand signals), and at last Corporal Lynch could point out the fugitives' hut – in clear sight another furlong ahead.

Jessope trotted behind the line of 'beaters' to the ensign nearest the objective. Supposing the occupants would have a lookout, he reckoned there was scant chance of surrounding it by stealth, hoping instead the appearance of so many troops would persuade them that flight was futile.

Another hundred yards and he told the ensign to have some NCOs close in – such a cramped affair the hut looked now – in case one of the fugitives should be so desperate as to discharge a firearm.

Three corporals doubled forward – skirmishing drill – the ensign just behind them, sword drawn.

Fifty yards to the hut and still not a sight or sound of anything but the beasts of the field.

The ensign signalled them on.

Thirty yards, and the muskets came to the aim, ready.

Twenty yards . . . ten . . .

The ensign signalled one of them to the back of the hut and the other two to halt. Then he motioned them to cover him as he went forward, sword lowered to the engage.

The door burst open. Out dashed six men as one.

The first almost impaled himself on the sword but sidestepped in time, only to be caught by a swinging butt from the covering guardsman.

The flat of the sword felled the next, and the third went down to another savage butt.

Fourth and fifth met with the same fate – the fifth with both blade and butt – but the sixth, a ferret of a man, leapt the ditch at the side of the hut and took off west. Guardsmen scrambled after him, unable to clear the ditch in one. He'd gained fifty yards before they found their feet.

'Stand fast!' shouted the ensign. There was more cover to beat, and the man was running on to the line of dragoons: let the cavalry have their sport.

Hervey, seeing the bolting fox, could only trust that they would. The Guards had certainly had excellent sport themselves.

He need not have worried. Worsley had told Lieutenant Kennett to keep the dragoons in the lane, rather than try to get the longer view. There was a hedge running its length: better to make the fugitives, rather than his own men, tackle its thorns. He turned to his trumpeter. 'Sound "Alarm"!'

C's and E's, the simplest of calls (and the quavers shortened) – as thrilling to a dragoon and his horse as 'Gone Away' to a hunting man.

The 'fox' had slipped into dead ground, however. Kennett's men would just have to wait for him to break cover in the lane.

Hervey was glad that Worsley had sent Collins to keep an eye.

'Draw swords!' Kennett's voice travelled well in the still air.

Nevertheless, NCOs repeated the order the length of the line, until a mile of steel stood ready for the next command.

The interval between dragoons was perhaps too great to allow the fox to be chopped at once, but none could slip across the lane unseen; and once through the hedge on the other side – shorter, thinner – in the open pasture beyond, it would be nothing to take him at a canter.

Meanwhile a dozen guardsmen were herding the bloody and fearful captives back towards the Winkfield road at the point of the bayonet. Hervey and Calthorp congratulated each other: even if the other birds had flown, the authorities should soon discover who they were.

In the lane, dragoons were now braced like lurchers waiting for the slip, Kennett taking post half-way along, where the hedge thinned and lowered a little to give a view of sorts.

Serjeant-Major Collins had come up too, from the far end of the line. He drew his sabre and stood in the stirrups to see where the Guards had reached . . .

And it was as sudden as any venery – a figure darting, fox from lair, hare from form. Across the lane before any could turn. Into the hedge – to cover once more.

But the hedge, though nothing to that he'd just worked through, was yet too thick to let him pass without struggle. Kennett saw and dug in his spurs, Collins likewise.

The brown-clothed figure thrashed frantically, but Kennett was too quick. Out from a pocket came his 'man stopper' and into the aim.

'No, sir!'

Collins's sabre flashed, driving down the pistol with the flat. It fired into the ground, startling Kennett's charger, so that it was all he could do to keep his seat.

'What the deuce do you mean, man?' he yelled, with swearing worthy of the army in Flanders.

Two dragoons galloped up. Collins shot them angry looks. 'Get back to your posts! Look to your front!'

He grabbed hold of Kennett's reins. 'Sir, that was murder but for a split second.'

'Unhand me, Serjeant-Major. You have no knowing that I was to fire, only to threaten.'

But Collins was having none of it. He cursed, sprang from his horse and launched at the blackthorn captive, dragging him out roughly and demanding he say where the rest of the band was. 'Or you'll feel the touch of cold steel.'

Kennett turned away and called back the two dragoons, and an NCO who had come up, saying calmly, 'This felon's for the magistrate, Corporal, when he's told us where his accomplices are. Make ready to take him to the court – the manor in yonder place.'

'Sir!'

Collins pushed the man towards them. 'He's neither armed nor does he have any notion where the others are, only that they struck off northwards after dark. Doubtless he'll be able to recall who and what their dwelling, once the JP's told him his fate otherwise.'

'Sir!'

The dragoons returned swords and grabbed the man by the shoulders, kicking off down the lane at a brisk trot, half dragging him between the horses to the encouragement of the corporal's 'Step sharper, you gallows-fodder, you!'

Hervey now came up having heard the shot and breasted the hedge further down the lane, Malet, Fairbrother and Serjeant Acton close on his heels.

'Good morning, Colonel,' piped the escorts in a greatly satisfied unison.

Seeing the man was evidently without injury, Hervey merely acknowledged and cantered on to where Kennett was standing in his stirrups speaking with the Guards ensign on the other side of the hedge.

'Good morning, Colonel,' chirped the lieutenant as he came up, saluting sharply. 'We have taken a prisoner.'

Hervey acknowledged the salute, and that of Collins standing a length or two away. 'Yes, I saw him. Well done, Mr Kennett. What was the shot?'

'The man was half-way through the hedge, Colonel. I fired at the ground and he gave up the struggle to escape.'

Hervey looked at him keenly. Collins said nothing. 'A warning shot?'

'I did not fire to hit him, Colonel.'

That much was the truth, but by no means the whole truth, and there was just something in his way of speaking that suggested it thus. 'Then it was fortunate the man was not between the bullet and the ground,' replied Hervey cautiously. 'Well, there are six of them now for the bench. The others, it seems, have made clean their escape.'

'The prisoner said they'd taken off northwards during the night, Colonel.'

'Indeed? Did he say how they had become separated?'

Kennett looked at Collins.

'Colonel, he said they'd split into two parties to make it easier to evade the constables they thought had come. His lot headed west but reckoned they couldn't get across the lane here because of all the torches, so they went back to lie up till they were sure the coast was clear.'

'You spoke to him yourself?'

'I did, Colonel.'

'And he said no more?'

'No, Colonel. He said he couldn't peach on his friends. We reckoned the magistrate'd be able to explain his best interests to him.'

'Just so, Sar'nt-Major,' he replied, quietly confident in Collins's judgement. He turned to Malet, who had been very pointedly silent. 'I think our work here is done.'

VI

RENDERING IN WRITING

Later that day

On return to Hounslow, Hervey had gone at once to the orderly room to write an account of 'the affair at Windsor-park' – just as the Duke of Wellington had himself sat down after the battle at Waterloo to write a despatch to Earl Bathurst, the Secretary for War. The duke's example – doing the business of the day *in* the day – had never been lost on him. That the duke's despatch, written in the most tumultuous of circumstances, had contained errors – and, said many, apportioned praise unequally, even unfairly – mattered less than its promptness, and as Hervey would have to send a copy in his own hand to the general officer commanding the Home District, and the clerks would have to make copies for the record, all other business of the day was suspended. It was, in truth, a trifling affair in comparison with the many in which he had been engaged since that day in 1815, but a command by his sovereign had to be addressed with proper diligence and ceremony – and there was always the question of the Law: who knew what trouble a pettifogger might stir up?

When it was done, he gave Malet the Windsor copy – 'by hand of officer' – and that for the general officer commanding the Home

District also, which was to be delivered by one of the orderlies of the War Office party. And then, his immediate task complete, as darkness fell and one of the clerks put more coal on the fire, he asked if Lieutenant Rennell were in barracks, and if so, for him to attend presently.

In fact it took less than a quarter of an hour for Rennell to report to the orderly room, for unlike most of the officers of an afternoon when there was no field day he was indeed in barracks. 'I have a very great deal of Latin to acquire – reacquire,' he explained, as Hervey chaffed him amiably.

'Let us sit in these comfortable tubs, for I've had nothing but the saddle and the writing chair since before the break of day. And coffee?'

'Thank you, Colonel.'

'You've heard of the business at Windsor, with Worsley's troop?'

'I have, Colonel. I wished I had been there.'

'Well, the business is concluded, save for the justices – the Assize court, I suppose – and I wished for the diversion of speaking with you on the matter of your resignation. Thank you for the courtesy of requesting an interview.'

Rennell bowed.

'I shan't press you on the matter; I neither stand *in loco parentis*, nor can I claim that the exigencies of the service require you to reconsider; we are, after all, in an army of retrenchment. I merely wanted to ask what will be the course of things after your leaving. But first, I might ask . . . your people – they are quiescent in this?'

An orderly came with coffee, which eased the course of the comradely enquiry.

'They are, Colonel. I have two brothers and a sister – and already two nephews and a niece.'

Hervey smiled to himself. Rennell had chosen to address the lesser question of geniture (though doubtless it was of much moment to his mother); the greater question was of religion, for his father was dean of Winchester. But if Rennell chose apostasy (not a word he liked, but . . .), then it was not for him to question. Besides, he would in due course learn from his own father what was the dean's opinion, for the two had received their ordination at the same time and place, and remained correspondents ever since.

'And you will go to Rome.'

'I shall – to the English College, and in five years or so will be ordained priest there.'

'I have seen the college, a place of great peace. The city itself is not without its vexations, however.'

Rennell smiled. 'I have been told so, Colonel, though I fancy that in five years one becomes accustomed to the vexations.'

'Indeed. I was there but a month.'

'Where you met with Shelley, I understand?'

'I did,' replied Hervey, faintly intrigued as to who might have done the telling. 'I liked him, too, for all his reputation – and occasionally his manner. But it was a short acquaintance. You will not be in want of good company in Rome, I'm sure – English company, I mean. There's a whole street of English – I forget its name – and constant visitors, of course. And not *too* intolerant of your religion, I think. "A paradise of exiles" did not Shelley call it? But I hope you will remember with advantages your fellows here.'

'Oh, indeed I shall. They are fine men, all. Well, almost all.'

Hervey would have liked to enquire of the exceptions, though it was impossible that he should, or Rennell reply. Instead they chatted, not entirely inconsequentially, until Hervey thought better of it and rose to suggest he had work to attend to. 'So, I shall enter in the officers' book your intention to write to the colonel and to send in your papers to the agents.'

'I'm obliged, Colonel.'

'We shall shake hands on your leaving, but I give you mine now, and my good wishes. Yours is a noble endeavour, if I might say it. Will you write to me from Rome from time to time?'

Rennell looked mildly surprised. 'By all means, Colonel. With great pleasure.'

They shook hands, and Hervey watched him out with a powerful sense of having beheld a man – and a man scarcely a dozen years his junior – possessed of a rare and singular conviction of purpose. He found it strangely disquieting.

Malet came in. 'You were not able to change his mind, Colonel?'

'I didn't try. Did you expect me to?'

Malet smiled. 'I knew it would do no good – begging your pardon, Colonel: I meant not to suggest that you had no powers of persuasion!'

'That is understood,' said Hervey, smiling too and warming his hands at the fire. 'As I can offer him no inducement – and damnation is not open to me – what line of persuasion is there left? By the bye, Rennell is, I suppose, on good terms with his fellow officers?'

Malet frowned slightly. 'As far as I can observe, yes – very well, I should say. Though I don't suppose he would number Kennett among his closest friends. He's cursed him as a papist more than once.'

'Has he, indeed?'

'It's never come to pistols, but I can't think it goes without annoyance with him. It would not with me. And Kennett's haughtiness is so marked on occasions that I wonder he *isn't* called out by someone or other.'

'Mm. What do you make of his firing – on reflection now?'

'Oh, sheer arrogance. And – I scarcely dare say it – pleasure in putting a ball so close to a man. Mark, Colonel, I hold no brief for any of that gang of felons.'

'That is understood . . . Well, I think my time at office is done for today. Those despatches will reach their destination this evening, I trust?'

'They will. St Alban has that for the King in his hand as we speak.'

'Very well. I shall go to my quarters. Would you have any papers I might see got up for me?'

'Of course, Colonel.'

When he asked for papers to be got up for him, he had not expected there to be quite so many. They filled a small dressing case, which Malet had somehow found and adapted for the purpose – the 'business of the day' in the body of the case, and, in the pocket of the closure, a number of letters addressed to him personally. Resisting the natural inclination to read these first, Hervey sat down at the writing table in his rooms at the Berkeley Arms, without changing, and worked his way through the documents that so minutely regulated an army in peace, the very same as had detained him only two days earlier – reports and returns, reckonings, states, orders both routine and particular. Each demanded his careful attention before at last (for the most part) revealing their lack of consequence. Each he duly signed, as required by the appropriate sub-branch of the War Office, or the Commissariat (in its turn, a subordinate of the Treasury), or else the Board of Ordnance. In several cases he certified – as he knew must countless other commanding officers – returns that he could have no expectation of verifying even if he were to give his entire day to the matter. There was, of course, a daily round of counting and checking at the hands of the officer of the day – the picket officer – and, monthly, a more thorough examination of specific accounts by the captain of the week; and indeed, annually, an entire audit by a board of officers – but ultimately the lieutenant-colonel must confide in men who had been raised in regimental ways straight and narrow (though not too narrow as to preclude the procurement of necessaries denied by the letter of the regulations). In Lincoln he had a quartermaster he might trust with his own last penny; the others he simply did not know well enough. Malversation was a constant – and very proper, and even necessary – concern for the commissioners of public accounts; but to a man set under authority, having soldiers under him, its prevention could not become an all-consuming business. And obsessive scrutiny started with the smallest thing – like a corn on a hoof. Corns, untreated, grew, suppurated, and at length rendered the animal lame. For as the saying ran, 'No foot, no horse'.

No foot, no horse. He laid down the veterinarian's casting list. He had no certain recollection of the number of horses routinely cast – and he had appended a note asking to see the figures for past years, inasmuch as they remained in the regiment's records (he realized that he did not know the policy for the retention of any records, but supposed there must be a regulation, whether War Office, Treasury or Board of Ordnance, and had also asked Malet in the note for advice), but his sense, from the experience of his own troop these past years, was that the figure was unduly high. Perhaps if he had formed a higher regard for the veterinarian he might not be so ... uncertain; the veterinarian's manners and appearance were not those of a gentleman, which was only to be expected, for the occupation of veterinary surgeon was not one that commended itself to a gentleman; except that of late years the Sixth had been fortunate in having veterinarians who had acquired the attributes (and even, at times, the appearance) of gentlemen, whereas Thomas Gaskoin had the air of the ostler's yard, or the corn-market; indeed, he looked more like an old-fashioned farrier than a modern practitioner of the 'science' imparted at the college in Camden whence he was licensed. Hervey sighed as he pushed the figures away; he could, he supposed, reconcile himself to the unbecoming appearance of one of his officers, if only he could be sure of his capability – but he could not help deploring that he might have to do so.

He sighed again, and took a long measure of claret. The remaining papers were but routine orders, easily read – indeed, some affording wry amusement – and then at length he was free to attend to his letters.

As was his rule, he read first those that were evidently of the nature of business – from the regimental agents, his bank, his tailor and so on – and then those that bore a more personal seal. Of these latter, two were in a female hand – but neither one from Hertfordshire – and only when he had read the others (a dozen or so of felicitation on learning of his return &c), did he turn to them.

His sister's looping hand was unmistakable:

Heytesbury,
25th January

My dearest brother,
I received your letter only yesterday on return from Lyme Regis and on going to Horningsham, which events I shall try to explain, though I scarce know how to begin. I am wed at last, and so very happily I cannot but daily count God's blessings upon us. Heinrici is the best of husbands, and our house is full of laughter and merriment from breakfast until the last candles are put out. Heinrici's children are a constant delight to me, and they call me Mama *without the least formality or abashment, for they called their true mother* Mutti*.*
We are living at Heytesbury, where Heinrici took a long lease on the park, and Georgiana is with us. Indeed she has been with us since our marriage in September and accompanied us to Lyme, though as a rule she attends Miss Havelock's school in Warminster. She is very well and daily grows in everything that is admirable in a child. I am so glad that you are returned, and safe returned, and that we might see you presently. It grieved me that you were not here to witness that joyous day in September, but such are the constraints of your life that I could never bear on them for such a selfish purpose. There is so much to speak of when you visit, but you may rest easy that it is all of the most agreeable nature. Indeed, one of the most agreeable pieces of news is the preferment of our father to a canonry in the Close. We are all to go to Salisbury these seven days to see the house and to make the arrangements. Our father has already engaged Mr Williams to be curate at Horningsham, for he is to keep the living as well, but all this news and other should rightly keep for your

113

visiting us, by which time the arrangements will be more definite,
though it is probable that Mama and Papa will move to Salisbury in
the latter weeks of March to be lodged by Easter, for our father is to
have charge of some of the worship of the Passion Week, so it would
be for the best, I think, if you were to stay here at Heytesbury unless
you are to come very soon.
    Your ever affectionate sister,
    Elizabeth Heinrici zu Gehrden

Hervey put down the letter and smiled. He had been so thoroughly inclined against the marriage – until meeting the *Freiherr*, the baron. For Heinrici had been with Dornberg's brigade at Waterloo – in the Duke of Wellington's army, not the Prussian, in a hussar regiment of the King's German Legion. He was, in truth, as much an Englishman as was the King, only that he was of the first generation, and consequently spoke with the accent of Hanover, the King's German realm ... And so now his sister was Baroness – *Freifrau* Heinrici, 'von und zu'. What could he say but echo her thanks for God's blessings? And Georgiana so evidently happy too. Far happier, no doubt, than had she gone to Hertfordshire, as first he had supposed she would. Perhaps, indeed, far happier than if she were to come to Hounslow, even if he were able to have a proper establishment.

These, though, were matters for his visit home; there was nothing he could do now – except later to pen a letter by return, a letter of congratulations (of exaggerated congratulations, indeed, to make up for his past churlishness) and some indication of when he might journey to Wiltshire. And, of course, compliments to his father and mother on their good news in exchanging a modest (in truth, dilapidated) country parsonage for a well-found canonry in the handsomest close in England.

The hand of the remaining letter was less familiar, but recognizable enough, and he hesitated before breaking the distinctive seal, certain of finding mischief – if of the most artful kind:

Dover-street,
26th January

My dear Colonel Hervey,
I thank you for your letter of the twentieth inst. I hope to have
opportunity ere long to question you on its contents, for there is much
that is of interest to me to which you rightly allude. You will have
received the ambassador's invitation to the levee on the twenty-fourth
of next month, but there will scarce be opportunity on that occasion
to speak frankly, and I would beg that you call upon me at an earlier
date. Furthermore I am to give a supper, very small, on Thursday
seven days for Lady Katherine Greville, who returns to London, and
were you able to attend I should deem it a great favour.
I remain your most humble servant,
Dorothea Lieven

Hervey's stomach tightened as if before an affair of the sword:
Lady Katherine Greville returned to London. If, as the letter
implied, it was her first return, then she could not have been at
Holland Park in . . . eighteen months – twenty perhaps (he had lost
count). Why now did she come? Did she know of his own return?
Surely not so soon. But why not: the posts to Ireland, now that
there was steam, were but a couple of days . . . And there was no
mention of Sir Peregrine. Would Princess Lieven's party be for both
of them if he were returned too? She could not know the truth,
surely? Kat had vowed she would tell no one, not even her sister.
And yet what had he expected – that she would remain in that
savage place for ever, and Sir Peregrine on Alderney, an absentee
'father', just as he'd been an absentee husband? But what did she
mean by returning now? And what did the princess mean by this
invitation? He could not of course accept. It was insupportable. He
could not make Kat's reacquaintance in a drawing room – if he
could make her reacquaintance at all. Not now that . . . Except, in
point of fact, he did not know what was her precise situation.

He sat back in his chair, unable quite to see straight, until at last the words came to him – a duke's words again, but this time Marlborough's: 'No war can ever be conducted without good and early intelligence.' He could scarcely compare his predicament with war, though it might prostrate him just as finally. But so much depended on knowing Kat's situation; and that of her husband. This latter he could discover easily enough, and with discretion. It was merely a matter of consulting the pages of the *London Gazette*, beginning with the most recent edition, until it was found what appointment Lieutenant-General Sir Peregrine Greville now held. No, it was not even as cumbrous a business as that: all he would need to consult were the *Gazette*s as far back as the beginning of the year past, when he had left for the Levant, when he knew Sir Peregrine to be lieutenant-governor of Alderney and Sark. He could even avoid the tediousness of that, he supposed, by asking his friend at the Horse Guards, Lord John Howard: he would know at once the appointment of every general not on the half-pay . . . But it would be shameful to ask such a thing while concealing his purpose. Which was also true of his clerks, for why should they occupy themselves with such work, for the benefit not of the service but of himself (and he had equilibrium enough, still, to discern the difference). No, he must read for himself.

How to discover Kat's situation, though? And even then, after he had acquired his 'good and early intelligence', what was he to do?

But that, however, he could with advantage put from his mind for the time being, for it entirely depended on the precise nature of the intelligence.

He could – must – however write to Princess Lieven declining the invitation. On what pretext he was uncertain – and pretext there must be, to allay suspicion (if the princess were disposed towards suspicion, which he thought she was). Perhaps it might not be too early for him to travel to Wiltshire instead? He must in any case thank her for the present of the silver, and assure her also that he would call to elaborate on his letter – his report of what he saw of her countrymen in the war in the east – at an early date. Beyond that he felt obliged to write nothing more; indeed he thought it imperative to write nothing out of the ordinary that might suggest the least disquiet. He took another glass of claret, then looked in his writing case for the piece of paper on which he had written his intelligence of Princess Lieven before their first meeting a year ago:

Dorothea (Darja) Christorovna Benckendorff. Born 17 December 1785, Riga. Father genl of inf, mil commandt Riga. (Branch of family of Markgrafschaft of Brandenburg had settled in Esthonia and entered Russian svce). Genl Benckendorff m. Baroness Charlotte Schilling of Cannstadt, confidante of Princess Maria of Wirtemberg, who afterwards became wife of Tsar Paul I. On Charlotte B's death (1797) 4 children commended to Tsarina's care. M. (at 14) Maj-genl Count Christopher von Lieven (25 yrs) in Russian svc. L. promoted lieut-genl 1807. 1809 L. represented Tsar at Prussian court. When B.parte prepared to invade Russia, L. appointed to London.
Received title Prince 1826 when mother created first Princess of Lieven.

These were the material facts, to which might be added the rumour – scandalous, scurrilous, perhaps unfounded (who knew but the other subjects of the rumour?). Her lovers numbered, it was said, Count Metternich, Prince Nesselrode, François Guizot, His Majesty the King, Lord Palmerston, and even the Duke himself. Could any woman be so assiduous? It was one thing – like Kat – to have an aged and distant husband who showed neither interest nor capability, and to seek instead the consolation of the arms of a man more attentive (of whatever age); but it was surely fanciful to imagine seduction (if that word were appropriate) on the basis of system. She was certainly handsome – now, even at forty-four (though that was unremarkable, for Kat was but a few years her junior) – and at the Congress of Vienna, when her star shone irresistibly bright, she must have appeared as the Medici Venus; if bosomless. He half wished he had never met her (but only half, for

117

he had found her hospitality at Dover Street agreeable and profitable, and his mission in the Levant had undoubtedly been made easier by her 'meddling'). What was it that she wanted from him? It was well known that her paramount interest was the well-being of Russia – the wellbeing exactly as perceived by the Tsar. But he, Hervey, had done all that he might in this cause (not that this had been his intention, rather the result of circumstance). What use could he be now that he was returned to England? He possessed few advantages, beyond the ineffable delight of commanding a regiment of cavalry.

He sighed, took another sheet of paper, opened the inkwell and dipped in his pen.

'You asked me to 'ave a bath drawn for you at seven o'clock, sir,' said Corporal Johnson, who had come into the room without his noticing. 'I mean, "Colonel".'

Hervey was just dripping wax onto his letter – trying with particular precision for a neat seal, addressed as it was to so high a personage as the ambassadress of the *Imperator* of All the Russias. 'Thank you, Corp'l Johnson. I had no notion of the time. Rather a bagful of papers. Has Mr Fairbrother left?'

'Aye, sir – Colonel. 'E said 'e wanted to catch the coach at 'alf past six.'

'Did he say what time he would return?'

'No 'e didn't.'

Hervey pressed his stamp into the wax, but left it a fraction late, so that too much came away as he lifted it. 'Damn!' He picked up the stick to begin again. 'What was it he said he was to see?'

'*Robert the Devil.*'

'I never heard of it. Where did he say it was?'

'T'Theatre Royal.'

'Which one?'

'I didn't know as there was more than one. 'E didn't say. But 'e did say it were in Covent Garden.'

'Ah.'

'Is that good, then, sir – Colonel?'

'The Theatre Royal in Covent Garden? Why yes.'

'Cap'n Fairbrother said 'e knew some of the actresses.'

Hervey dripped wax on the edge of the letter. 'Damn!'

'You mean 'e doesn't?'

'No,' said Hervey, shaking his head resignedly. 'I mean that this wax has a malign tendency.'

'Oh.'

But it might not have had if its handler had been less put out by the discovery of his friend's assignation. He could hardly begrudge him the company of a pretty girl, though, no matter how painted she was.

He pressed his stamp into the new seal, and this time removed it clean to make a good impression. 'Capital,' he said, taking up the penknife to remove the excess wax.

'That's what I thought, Colonel. I thought "what a nice thing for Captain Fairbrother to go by 'imself to London".'

'No, I didn't mean that I thought it was a nice thing – though I do – I was referring . . . It is of no moment. Would you hand me the boot jack?'

Johnson set it up for him, and fetched the slippers from his dressing room, talking the while. 'That were a good thing that Serjeant-Major Collins did this morning, weren't it?'

'Discovering their hiding place, you mean?' replied Hervey, pulling off a boot with a deal of straining. 'You should have seen it. B Troop did uncommonly well.'

'No – I mean stopping Mr Kennett shooting the man as was getting away.'

'But he didn't. Mr Kennett fired into the ground to force the man to come out of the hedge.'

Johnson raised an eyebrow.

In the many years – twenty and more – of their happy connection, Hervey had become finely attuned to the various

119

expressions of (rendered verbally) 'please yourself'. 'What?'

'I've 'eard different.'

'How different? And from whom?'

'Wouldn't be right to say from who, Colonel.'

Hervey was of a mind to acquaint him with the Mutiny Act, in which, as far as he recalled, there were no provisions for anonymity. But he had to concede that in this first instance of the unique privilege (and benefit) of his groom's being able to impart intelligence direct from the barrack room to the commanding officer, it did not do to stand on the letter of the law. 'Very well,' he said, with just enough testiness to make his point. 'What is it you've learned different?'

Johnson handed him the slippers and picked up the second boot. 'Mr Kennett was intent on shooting the man, and the serjeant-major knocked 'is pistol down with 'is sword, and that's when it went off.'

Hervey's brow furrowed. 'Was it, indeed.'

'Saved 'im a deal o' trouble, I'd think, the serjeant-major did.'

Hervey looked at him intently. 'You're assured of this?'

'I 'eard it from one as saw it, an' 'e told me there was somebody else who'd seen it, an' I went an' asked 'em, an' they said t'same an' all.'

'Mm. Well, well. How general is this knowledge?'

Johnson looked at him as much as to ask what knowledge was not general in the canteen.

'Quite,' said Hervey. But then, suddenly cautious, 'You weren't told this on the understanding that it would be passed to me?' Useful as the intelligence was, it wouldn't do for there to be a 'speaking pipe' from canteen to commanding officer. That way all discipline would be up-ended – and, indeed, the reliability of the intelligence would diminish.

'No, Colonel. It came out matter o' fact. An' none of 'em'll ever know what I says to you.'

Hervey felt rather chastened. 'No, of course not. I hadn't meant to suggest . . . But a difficult thing, discerning the aim of a pistol, unless you're looking straight into it.'

But this was something Johnson didn't feel obliged to give opinion on. 'I've laid out yer towelling, Colonel,' he replied, nodding to the dressing room.

Hervey sighed to himself. 'Thank you. Would you ask the innkeeper to send up my dinner in one hour?'

VII

GOOD AND EARLY INTELLIGENCE

Next day

At office the following morning, Hervey pondered once more on the veterinary returns, and at length called Malet in.

'I think I shall make a formal inspection of Tyrwhitt's stables tomorrow.'

'Very well, Colonel,' replied the adjutant, writing in his order book. 'Tyrwhitt's especially?'

'I want to see what is the general state of things, and Tyrwhitt's is the senior troop.'

'Very good, Colonel.'

Hervey nodded, pleased to have resolved on a clear course of action. 'By the bye, have you warned Vanneck for Brussels yet?'

'I have, Colonel – on the day you instructed me to.'

'Ah.'

'Do you wish to rescind the warning?'

Hervey hesitated. 'I don't much care of warning for such a thing and then reversing the decision, especially for something that I imagine will be pleasing to all, but I had thought last night to send Worsley's troop instead. But it is done now, and should stand.'

'Is there anything else, Colonel?'

Again Hervey thought for a moment. 'I ought rightly to have told you this on the morning I took command, though I believe I said that it was no use your being adjutant unless you know my mind, and that you may speak yours.'

'You did, Colonel.'

'But I must have you know – must have you perfectly understand – that we speak with absolute candour.'

'Yes, indeed, Colonel. I believe I had perfectly understood that. Is there some cause for doubting it?'

Hervey shook his head. 'I only doubted that I had made myself clear. I infer therefore that you have not heard rumour of Kennett's true intention with his pistol yesterday.'

'No-o.'

He related what Johnson had told him.

Malet shook his head. 'It surprises me not at all, though I don't suppose the two dragoons would be able to swear upon oath that the pistol was pointed at the man.'

'My thoughts exactly.'

'What do you wish me to do, Colonel?'

'What would you advise?'

Now Malet paused for thought. 'I think Captain Worsley should be apprised.'

'His troop's now all returned, are they not?'

'They are. The yeomanry arrived at Maidenhead yesterday morning. And of course I shall speak with him.'

'And Collins.'

'Of course, Colonel. And unless they can throw light on the matter, I believe it best to let sleeping dogs lie.'

'For they may rise and bite you?'

'I would not fear any bite of Kennett's, Colonel, but we should have a great to-do and the evidence would not be strong – though I am no lawyer.'

'It occurs to me that a magistrate might lay a charge of attempted murder – or intent to murder, if there be such a crime. You do not consider that we are complicit in such a thing if we do not report the facts to the authorities?'

'I believe that our responsibility as far as the law goes is to investigate the evidence, and if it is considered to be demanding of an answer should then, and only then, bring it before the civil authorities.'

'So we may not, indeed, let sleeping dogs lie.'

'I don't think we're obliged to question any witness directly, Colonel, for an attempt was not actually made – by their account – the shot following Collins's intervention; and it would be deuced difficult to find evidence of *intent*.'

'This much I'd concluded last night. The difficulty seems to me, however, to be one of unhappy alternatives. On the one hand, Collins's action, if unjustified, is an assault on an officer, whereas on the other, if his action *is* justified, Kennett is guilty of a felony, *ipso facto*. And there will be no shortage of "legal opinion" in the canteen.'

Malet sighed. 'There is ever conjecture in the canteen, Colonel, as I hardly need tell you. I rather think that you have perfectly stated the case for letting hounds sleep. Is it not a matter for what I believe is called "prudential judgement"?'

Hervey had all but made a study of it: fine words, a fine notion – the judgement of Solomon &c . . . yet so difficult to accomplish. He had certainly not been able – not with consistency – to discern the right course in his own affairs.

He nodded slowly. 'I suppose we may presume that such conjecture will reach the ears of Mr Rennie, if it has not already done so.'

Malet was puzzled by Hervey's hesitation. The Sixth – *any* regiment – were not Unitarians: the commanding officer was the undoubted god-head, and the adjutant high-priest, but not least of the trinity was the serjeant-major, the apotheosis of the rank and file. They were of one substance – 'three in one'. It was they who set the tone, regulated the routine, chose the NCOs, the apostles of the regiment's creed. Did

Hervey not entirely confide in Rennie, because he was not raised in the same ranks? Was he somehow trying to guard Collins against the stern application of unprejudiced military justice? And what was his, Malet's, duty in the circumstances?

'Shall I inform the sar'nt-major, Colonel, or will you?'

'I'll speak with him myself. And then, as you say, we shall let hounds sleep.'

Malet rose.

'Damn.'

'Colonel?'

'Oh ... it's nothing. Only that I've just recalled Lord Hill's summons today week.'

'You have another appointment?'

'One that I had wished to avoid ... But no matter; I must think of something else.'

'There is one more thing, Colonel. Captain Tyrwhitt's attorney will pay a call tomorrow. I shall then be able to apprise you of the situation ... Unless you yourself wish to hear him directly.'

Hervey shook his head. 'I have no great fondness for lawyers, Malet. You may see him yourself,' he replied, before adding, a trifle pained, 'unless that seems unduly unsympathetic to Tyrwhitt.'

Malet's look suggested that sympathy for Tyrwhitt should be measured.

'Very well. I'll await your report ... And now, would you dine with me this evening? I've sent a note to Worsley asking the same – with his wife, also. It is a very short notice, but I hope it will serve.'

'I should be delighted, Colonel. Thank you. At what hour?'

'Eight. I shouldn't wish it too late for Worsley to get back to Richmond.'

Meanwhile there was yet more paper to attend to.

But Fairbrother evidently dined elsewhere – as the day previous. He had the acquaintance of two of the Theatre Royal's company – female company – whom he had met at supper a year before with one of the Covent Garden *entrepreneuses*, a pretty, Italian-looking flower girl who had intercepted him and Hervey when they were making their way to a gunsmith in Leicester Street prior to leaving for the Levant, and with whom he had lost no time in reacquainting himself on return.

The flower girl had liked 'the Captain', who treated her well and demanded nothing untoward by return, and the actresses were of the same opinion, not least because Fairbrother, as they, had the complexion of warmer climes and the easy manners that went with them – and an air that was somehow protective, like a brother or a cousin, perhaps. They had arranged a box for him last evening, and when the play was over he had taken them to supper; and after a couple of hours' conviviality had engaged a hackney to take them home across the river, before making his own way to the Strand for the night coach to Hounslow.

But as he turned into Bull Inn Court, darker-lit than the streets about, there was a scream.

He at once put his back to the wall and reached in a pocket for his Deringer pistol.

'Help! Help! Murder!'

He could see but a few yards – a split second to decide: a lure or a female in distress?

He took off his hat and held it out as a foil, edging down the passage.

A dozen yards from the Strand – outside the Nell Gwyn tavern, darkened and barred – was a woman crying, kneeling by a man who lay on his side.

'What's to do? What's to do?'

He could get no answer.

'What's to do, woman?' he demanded, stepping past to see if there was anyone skulking.

'They've killed him,' she sobbed. 'Murder.'

Fairbrother knelt to see if the man were indeed dead.

There was a groan as he tried to move him, and blood.

'What has happened?' he asked again.

'They stabbed him, stabbed him . . . without a word.'

'With a knife? A sword?'

She just sobbed, shaking her head.

'Didn't you see?'

Still no answer.

'I must get a cab, get a surgeon.'

'No,' she howled. 'They'll murder me when you're gone.'

'Who will?'

No answer.

'There's nothing for it but to get him out of this alley. Here,' he said, giving her his hat and struggling to lift the man so as to drag him the dozen yards into the gaslight of the Strand.

There were no groans this time – or if there were, he didn't hear them, the effort to move the dead-weight prodigious.

The safety of the gaslight quieted the woman, who he now saw was both handsome and young – younger than her gentleman-friend – and dressed as quality. He found the wound, not without difficulty, for the shirt was blood-soaked, took off his necktie and began to staunch the flow as best he could.

None of the pedestrians showed the instincts of the Samaritan.

'Hail a cab,' he barked at one of them. 'A man here's sorely wounded.'

It took a compliant passer-by several attempts, for cabmen were not fond of inebriates, as they fancied the fare to be, but after some minutes a hackney did pull up, driven by a man in an old military greatcoat.

He was inclined to be helpful. 'There's the infirm'ry in Vill'ers Street, but they don't take the likes of this as a rule. Guy's is the place, I reckon – London Bridge.'

Fairbrother and the hesitant Samaritan got the man into the cab, but only with difficulty, the door not being wide. Then he handed up the woman, thanked the passer-by, waved to the driver and closed the door behind them.

The woman had stopped sobbing, but pressed herself into the corner of her seat, with a handkerchief to her mouth, and gazed out of the window fearfully.

'The gentleman was escorting you to a carriage, ma'am, I fancy,' said Fairbrother, himself sitting back, there being nothing more he could do for the insensible figure at his feet.

She looked at him as if to ask what or how he knew, then nodded.

'Did you have far to travel?'

She shook her head.

There was no knowing whether the man intended travelling with her. Nor did he feel it proper to enquire. 'We must inform the police,' he said after a little way more. 'They will wish to hear your account – and mine.'

She nodded again, as if resigned.

'Did they rob him of anything?'

She shook her head.

Her unwillingness to speak was perhaps understandable, but frustrating too.

'I am Captain Edward Fairbrother, ma'am.' He gave his rank to reassure, though he did not use it, as a rule.

She nodded appreciatively, but nothing more.

'You are not, I am to suppose then, the wife of the gentleman?'

She looked at him anxiously, but said nothing.

'I recognize the gentleman, ma'am. It is General Gifford, is it not?'

She nodded.

'I'm afraid a coroner's court, if it comes to that, will demand more answers than I. Why was he attacked?'

She shook her head again. 'I don't know. I saw just the one, but I think there were more. I believe they may have mistaken him for another. The man I saw said, "Laidlaw, you have ruined me", and then he thrust with a knife – or some such.'

'Forgive me, ma'am, you are a married woman?'

She looked away.

'And this, therefore, will ruin you.'

She nodded again.

Fairbrother fell silent. And then, as the carriage turned for Southwark Bridge, he decided on their course of action. 'I shall have to give evidence on oath, perhaps, so it is better that I know nothing more. If you were to slip away when we reach the hospital, might your identity remain concealed?'

'It would, sir.'

'And you would take the risk of doing so – the streets unknown to you?'

She nodded.

'Then it is resolved.'

His dinner guests gone an hour and more, Hervey put a late shovel of coal on the fire, and poured another glass of claret for his friend. 'What an extraordinary affair. And she merely disappeared into the night like . . . like Eurydice.'

'Aye. I wondered if it were right to let her, on that account, for it was a beastly place, all turnings and windings, but she showed no terror. And it was not so very far from the bridge, which was well lit.'

'And it was most definitely Gifford?'

'Unquestionably. I saw him so many times in the United Service that I could scarce mistake his features.'

'No, indeed. And what did you do next?'

'When the orderlies at the hospital – which, I must say, is not like any that I have seen; an admirably efficient place – when they had taken him in and I'd given such details as I could, I went to Bow Street by the same carriage – whose driver I took details of, that I could call him as witness if need be – and there I made a deposition to a serjeant of police. After that, being almost three o'clock, I set off to walk to the United Service to see if they would admit me, by way of the new market, where I found a cup or two of very service-able coffee, and brandy, the market-men most hospitable. And then at about four o'clock I thought better of the United Service and went instead to Piccadilly and got a bed at Hatchett's, where I slept long . . . And then I rose and breakfasted in the afternoon before going thence to see a notary to transact a little business, and thence to the hospital for word of the general – and he was by no means dead. So you see, it is not at all amiss that I should return so late, though I am very sorry to have missed evidently so convivial an evening.'

Hervey shook his head, discomfited by the apology. 'No, not at all amiss. You are on the half-pay; your time is your own.'

'I meant that I ought to have sent word.'

'It seems to me that you scarce had opportunity. It has indeed been a most convivial evening, though. Mrs Worsley is the most excellent of her sex, and the two are plainly the happiest of couples. Worsley's quite transformed in her presence.'

Fairbrother sipped at his wine with unusual moderation. 'Perhaps I would have intruded.'

'Intruded? How so?'

'Alligator lay egg, but him no fowl,' he replied, in the accent of the plantation.

Hervey grimaced. 'I do wish you'd put that nonsense from your mind.'

'I have no true place here. There's nothing I can be about in the barracks, and – strange as you may think it – I am now afeard of being idle.'

'Then this is progress indeed! Here, have a little more claret.'

Fairbrother took the point, and the wine. 'You know, those market-men were a decidedly rough sort, some of them. The sort you found in the Royal Africans. Yet tractable.'

'You tipped them well, no doubt.'

'I did. And to scour the passageway when it was light for any sign of the affair. I'll meet with them again in a day or two.'

Hervey nodded approvingly . . . 'And Eurydice's identity shall be protected.'

'I trust so.'

He nodded approvingly again. 'You are the most gallant of fellows, Fairbrother. I count myself the most fortunate of men to have your acquaintance. And Gifford shall, too, if he recovers.'

'If he doesn't go the way of Eurydice's lover.'

Hervey smiled. 'Yes, indeed. The comparison was more apt than I'd supposed. But Gifford, I should think, is made of sterner stuff.'

VIII

NO FOOT, NO HORSE

Next day

There was a formula to an inspection of stables, one that Hervey was well acquainted with from many years of inspecting and being inspected – though never before had he entered the stables of a troop other than his own to that end. It was something of a stately dance, indeed, for its purpose was not so much to discover the state of affairs in the horse lines – that much would largely be known by the daily returns and the appearance of the horses on parade – but to assist in the maintaining of that state of affairs by exhibiting to the dragoons the standards that were required; and in the case of the commanding officer inspecting a troop, to hold its captain to those standards, which in turn assisted him in his own scrutiny. (And, indeed, the same principle was applied in the annual inspection of a regiment by the general officer.) There must therefore be occasion to praise, to encourage and to warn, but not, in the case of a commanding officer's inspection (or indeed a general's), of finding material fault, for that was to reflect ill on the routine within the troop as a whole – on the non-commissioned officers, the farriers, and the troop officers, and in the case of a general's inspection of the regiment, on the commanding officer and his staff. And so in this game of questing acknowledgement of efficiency, it was usual that the NCOs' horses were placed at the nearest and furthest ends of the stable, making the best impression on the inspecting officer as he entered and left. New straw would be laid immediately before he arrived, and the smell of Stockholum tar would pleasantly fill his nostrils instead of ammonia. But it was also necessary for there to be opportunity for the display of displeasure that might ensue from the discovery of actual, though trivial, neglect (however theoretically impossible that neglect might be). A lantern, or some such, a part of which had escaped ferocious burnishing, usually served.

The purpose of Hervey's inspection was different, however. He was not intent on playing the admirable game of show so much as making a covert inquiry into the business of casting. He had no idea what he was looking for, only a sense that if there were truly something amiss with the practice and procedure of the regiment it would be manifest in the stable. Tyrwhitt's troop could have no idea of this purpose, of course, and they had therefore made all the customary preparations. The lieutenant, Mordaunt, on whom command had devolved these past two months, was a capable man, exchanged from the Thirteenth in India when the climate there had begun to make depredations on his constitution, but whose taciturnity had not so far allowed him to become endeared to the mess. The serjeant-major, Prickett, was newly made up, but a sound enough NCO who had risen by the principle of seniority tempered by rejection. Hervey had never served in the same troop as he, but had always known of his solid reputation. The three cornets were the not unusual mixture of idleness, variable competence and unlimited charm.

At two minutes to ten by the barracks clock, Hervey, the adjutant and the regimental serjeant-major stepped from the orderly room. Waiting outside were the veterinary surgeon and farrier-major, and two orderly corporals. They marched off briskly, past (this being a Friday) the assembled trumpeters on the parade ground, who sounded the 'Flourish of trumpets' when the clock struck ten, just as the inspecting party reached the doors of D Troop stables.

'Att-e-en-*shun!*'

The stamp of boots and the ringing of spurs echoed impressively in the confined space of the stables, accompanied by whinnying and grunting from those troop horses not yet accustomed to the disturbance of formal inspections.

Hervey returned the lieutenant's salute. 'Good morning, Mr Mordaunt.'

'Good morning, Colonel. Four officers, fifty-two dragoons and forty-seven horses on parade. Fourteen dragoons and horses on detachment.'

One of the orderly corporals made note.

'Thank you,' said Hervey, taking the whip from under his arm into his right hand, and acknowledging the troop serjeant-major's salute in turn. 'At ease, please.'

Serjeant-Major Prickett barked the words of command, to a repeat of the whinnying and grunting.

Hervey took a pleasing breath of Stockholum tar as he entered, the NCO closest to the doors coming to attention again as he approached.

'Good morning, Corp'l Farmar.'

'Good morning, Colonel.'

With his own troop Hervey would have been able to exchange some pleasantry – or, if he were feeling grave, ask some appropriate question – but with another, even though he knew of Corporal Farmar as one of the best rough-riders in the regiment, he was not yet able to do so. He had yet to establish his 'proprietary position' rather than mere authority. Besides, on such a mission as today's he did not wish to be distracted by banter.

He studied Farmar's horse, a sleek chestnut mare, from beside the stall-end. Somehow Lord Holderness, doubtless by the expenditure of a good deal of his own money, had been able to maintain the old custom of troop colours – to revive it, even, for in India it had been impossible. So that A Troop was once more wholly bay, B was entirely black, as was C; D had light chestnuts, E was meant to be brown (though E, his former troop, returning now from the Cape, had left their troopers behind), and F – when it began to muster – would have blacks too. And, disdaining the regulations still, all the trumpeters' mounts were grey.

'How long has she been yours, Corp'l Farmar?'

'A year just gone, Colonel.'

'And gone well?'

'Very well, Colonel.'

'"Four white feet, go well without her"?' (He relaxed his guard – he knew – but it was good to be back in the world of the troop: *One white foot, buy him; Two white feet, try him; Three white feet, look well about him; Four white feet, go well without him.*)

'Me, I wouldn't go without 'er, Colonel; never a day lame,' replied Farmar, smiling.

Hervey bent to pick up the off-hind.

'Why is it oiled? Since when is a hoof oiled for inspection?'

The disposition of the stable changed in an instant.

Farmar could answer only awkwardly, 'Orders, Colonel.'

Hervey turned to Lieutenant Mordaunt.

'I . . . understood . . .'

'With permission, Colonel,' said the veterinary surgeon.

Hervey looked at him, but said nothing.

'In this fierce weather, Colonel, I have advised it is best to protect the foot with an application of oil to the enamel, and of Stockholum tar to the horn.'

Even the horses were silent.

Hervey angered, yet to disparage his veterinarian – whose authority with the farriers was always precarious (and with the officers even more so) – in front of such an assemblage as this would be to the detriment . . .

'I do not question that advice, Mr Gaskoin,' (though in truth he would) 'but it has ever been the practice in the regiment that for inspection the foot should be perfectly clean. How else is it to be examined?'

'I beg your pardon, Colonel,' replied Gaskoin, judging it prudent to offer no other answer.

Lieutenant Mordaunt added his voice: 'I must beg pardon also, Colonel. I failed to draw a proper distinction.'

There was nothing more disarming than a man who freely admitted his error, and Hervey now had to acknowledge it for the sake of Mordaunt's own standing – not least because the man who should have been answering for his troop was in arrest in Dublin.

'Mr Malet, please be good enough to make the practice clear once more.'

'Colonel,' replied Malet simply, already having shot Mordaunt a look that required him to attend on orderly room when the inspection was over (Mr Rennie had summoned the troop serjeant-major in like manner).

Hervey moved several stalls on, without a word, ignoring the remaining NCOs and their exemplary mounts, till he caught the eye of a young-looking dragoon. 'What is this man's name, Mr Mordaunt?'

'Parr, Colonel,' replied the lieutenant, as the dragoon came to attention.

Hervey nodded, pleased (relieved) that Mordaunt at least knew his troop. 'How long have you been enlisted, Parr?'

'One year and one half, sir.'

'One year and one half, *Colonel!*' barked the troop serjeant-major, dismayed that in spite of a whole hour's extra drill and instruction there was still a dragoon who had failed to heed, and already feeling the pain of the interview with Rennie that was to follow.

'Sir,' replied the dragoon, shaking.

'*Colonel!*' barked the serjeant-major even louder, and approaching despair ('Sir' was ordinarily correct in addressing the serjeant-major, but the commanding officer was on parade, and so any voice was deemed to be his, no matter who the speaker).

'Colonel,' stammered the dragoon.

Hervey began to wonder if this were not a performance for his own benefit (such things were not unknown), but Parr's ashen face looked real enough, and he felt a sudden urge to say 'It matters not' – though he very determinedly resisted it.

'When were you assigned this horse?'

The dragoon hesitated, and then said, 'When I passed riding school, Colonel. Last May, Colonel.'

Hervey nodded. 'When was he shod?'

'On Monday, Colonel.'

Hervey turned to the lieutenant. 'Mr Mordaunt, have the hoofs cleaned so that I might examine them.'

Private Parr's stall was at once all industry.

Hervey, meanwhile, turned about to speak to the dragoon opposite. 'What is your name?'

'Twentyman, Colonel.'

'How long have you been enlisted, Twentyman?'

'Five years, Colonel.'

'You were in India, then?'

'No, Colonel; I joined from Maidstone when the regiment returned. Colonel.'

'When was your horse shod?'

'Three weeks ago, Colonel.'

The gelding stood obligingly without trying to turn its head as Hervey stepped into the stall and ran his fingers along its back. There was no sign of saddle galls. He lifted the tail; there was no nick. 'How old is he?'

'Five, Colonel.'

Twentyman was probably the first to be assigned the horse since it was brought in as a rough; and he kept it well – inasmuch as he could tell without looking at the feet.

He returned to Private Parr's horse, its hoofs now divested of oil and tar, and picked up the near- and then the off-fore, looking at each for a matter of seconds only – it took no longer to see the work of the rasp – before rounding on the veterinarian. 'Attend to this, if you please, Mr Gaskoin,' he said, with as much asperity as he could manage without raising his voice.

The farrier-major and the troop farrier braced for what they knew was to follow.

Hervey turned to Mordaunt. 'There is no purpose in my continuing the inspection with every foot caked in grease and the first that is not bearing the evidence of poor shoeing. I had thought never to find such a thing in D Troop – or in any troop, for that matter. Be so good as to have them ready for reinspection tomorrow morning.'

And with that he turned on his heel and stalked out of the stables – behind him a crescendo of recrimination.

It did not serve for the commanding officer to be discomposed on any matter. A cloud of unease settled over a regiment, which somehow dimmed the light in the otherwise brightest of corners – places free of any taint or blemish, paragons of good order, perfect discipline and attentiveness to the King's Regulations. All alike awaited the next visitation of displeasure.

And – as Heaven knew – it was by no wish of Hervey's that the cloud of displeased colonelcy sat over the cavalry barracks. His intention had been to leave the stables, unbeknown to any, in possession of some clear indication as to what he must do in regard to the question of unwarranted casting (if, indeed, there were unwarranted casting). But all he had succeeded in doing was discovering that D Troop's farriery was deficient (he discounted the possibility that he had exposed but a single, exceptional, example), and, perhaps, that efforts had been made to conceal the fact by ordering hoofs to be oiled.

Yet that itself was no small matter; and so began his mental commination. Evidently Mordaunt was not *au fait* with all that occurred in his stables. Worse, in a way, neither was the troop serjeant-major – or, worse still, he connived at its concealment. Evidently, too, the farrier-major had no command of his farriers, and the veterinarian no notion what evils they concealed by their oleaginous tricks. Or perhaps he did. Perhaps he sought to conceal his own incapability with the spurious justification of science – 'In this fierce weather . . . best to protect the foot with an application of oil to the enamel, and of Stockholum tar to the horn'. Who knew what thick layers of filth were rotting the horn of every foot in the Sixth? And what about the RM? Did he not observe anything amiss? Nor, for that matter, the adjutant . . .

He sat at his desk, hands clasped, brooding on the parlous state of the regiment he had aspired to command these twenty years.

Malet came in with coffee, unbidden. 'Colonel?'

'Take a seat,' said Hervey, peacefully.

He did so, and for once without his order book.

'Not a good beginning,' continued Hervey, after taking a sip from the regimental Spode.

'No, indeed.'

'Was it not Lord Hol'ness's practice to inspect a troop periodically?'

'It was, and I never knew it to be the case that feet were oiled. Though I have to say that it has been many months since there was such an inspection, with all the distraction of the King's visit, and Lord Hol'ness's absence on leave, and then his new appointment.'

'And there being no major.'

'Quite.'

'You are thinking that Gaskoin's advice to oil and tar in this weather might be justified, and that the dumped foot might be but an aberration?'

Malet looked surprised. 'Not at all, Colonel. But I'd wager that an inspection of Worsley's troop, or Vanneck's, or any other for that matter, would not have gone thus.'

Hervey looked at him intently. 'But D Troop otherwise.'

'Mordaunt ought to've known better, even though he's not long been lieutenant, and an extract. But he had two months' furlough before Christmas to attend to the affairs of his late father,

139

and *that* while Tyrwhitt was absent. If any troop was in want of its officers it was his. In truth, though, I'm disheartened by Prickett's dereliction.'

'We may take consolation in knowing that Mr Rennie is at this very moment making him aware of the extent of it. Think if it had been Lincoln!'

But in saying that, Hervey raised in his mind once again the question he had just been pondering: would it have happened if Lincoln *had* still been the sar'nt-major? Yet the question was ultimately to no end, for Rennie was soon to depart – though it did once more raise the question he was almost hourly mindful of: who was to replace him?

Malet spoke softly. 'Gaskoin, I believe, has the confidence of the captains, though not to the same degree as his predecessor.'

Hervey nodded. 'You think I was too hard on him?'

'No, but it wouldn't serve, I think, to be so now.'

Hervey said nothing for the moment, looking towards the window instead; and then, 'In this fierce weather . . .' (it was snowing again).

Malet shook his head. 'Weather or no, he can't have supposed it to be right . . . But we shall see tomorrow.'

'Indeed. A little more coffee, if you will . . .'

Malet obliged, and refilled his own cup. 'Ten o'clock again?'

Hervey inclined his head. 'What otherwise was to be the routine?'

'Sar'nt-major's parade. Mr Rennie will have to begin it later.'

'It is hard on the others just because D Troop is in default, but it can't be helped. Tell Mr Rennie he has a free hand. And Sunday?'

'No parades, Colonel.'

'No chaplain, no parades. In truth I'm glad of it, though it cannot persist. Men like to see the parson who'll read the burial service over them, if nothing else. When did you say the new one comes?'

'June.'

'Well, doubtless there's an impecunious curate hereabout who'll take a service for a shilling or two meanwhile.'

'I'll attend to it.'

'Make haste slowly, though,' said Hervey, with the first suggestion of a smile that morning.

Malet rose, his mission complete. 'Will you be at office this afternoon, Colonel?'

Hervey at last closed his mind to the business of D Troop's stables. 'No, I must go to London. Will you have the chaise come in an hour?'

The snow was not troublesome. Indeed, it was welcome, for the regimental chariot bowled along at a brisk trot without the jarring when wheels ran on bare-metalled turnpike. And so silently: Hervey and Fairbrother could talk freely without effort (had the driver held the reins from the box instead of postilion they would even have had to lower their voices). By the time they were nearing the Hammersmith bar, Hervey was all but restored in spirits. Malet had applied a balm – how *well* he had dealt with him after stables – but Fairbrother administered proper medicine: a true draught of equability.

And so now he could attend to the business that brought him from Hounslow, and without agitation (nor scrupling that he did so, for in the aftermath of the 'untoward affair of D Troop stables' his absence from barracks was a distinct advantage). Or rather, he could attend to it with no more agitation than the business itself occasioned, for its execution would be faintly distasteful and its results likely even more so.

Before the clocks in Whitehall had struck two, the chariot was pulling up at the United Service Club. 'I trust you'll not find your charge of two nights past a corpse,' said Hervey as he got down.

Fairbrother grimaced. 'I must depend on it, or else the coroner's court'll put me under oath.'

'No doubt I'll hear a thing or two inside. Let us meet at seven for dinner. Let Corporal Wakefield be away sharp from the hospital to rest the horses across the way,' said Hervey, nodding towards the Horse Guards, and then to Wakefield to drive on.

Fairbrother acknowledged and bid him adieu.

Inside the United Service he learned the latest soon enough. 'Good afternoon, Colonel Hervey,' said the porter. 'Dreadful news. Gen'ral Gifford was assaulted in the Strand two nights ago and they says he might not live.'

Hervey took off his hat and affected an unconnected air. 'Dreadful indeed, Robert. What is known of his assailants?'

'Oh, a murderous gang, new-come – Albanians, Moldavians, Bulgarians by all accounts.'

'Indeed? Whence exactly – how – are they new-come?'

The porter looked puzzled. 'I know not, sir. They's gypsies, aren't they?'

Hervey nodded. 'Of course. Do you know why it was they tried to murder the general?'

The porter lowered his voice conspiratorially. 'Well, sir,' he began, looking about, 'they *says* as 'e was on 'is way to a secret rendezvous connected with the war, and they cut 'im out.'

'The war?'

'Yes, sir – the war that yourself has lately come back from.'

'Upon my word!'

'And when we in the servants' 'all 'eard, we reckoned as you must know something of it yourself, sir.'

'Well, Robert,' he began, trying to measure his words so as not to appear dismissive, while at the same time scotching the notion, 'I never heard of such a thing.'

But the porter was a man long schooled in confidentiality – or rather in the judicious sharing of confidences. He nodded knowingly. 'Of course, sir.'

Hervey gave his hat and travelling coat to the under-porter and went at once to the library. It was deserted, but a fire burned cheerily, for which he was grateful: reading a year's worth of the *London Gazette* would be an affair of several hours. They were, at least, admirably ordered by date, and easily to hand, so that he was able to make a brisk beginning – after first ringing the bell and ordering coffee.

He had read three *Gazette*s by the time the waiter brought it.

'Have you heard the news of Gen'ral Gifford, sir?'

As a rule the library was a place of silence, but these were pressing times, and Hervey was inclined to be tolerant despite the task before him.

'I did, James. Dreadful business.'

'And 'e was dining 'ere only the night afore.'

'Was he, indeed.'

The reply was meant as an expression of acknowledgement, but the waiter took it as a genuine enquiry.

'Oh, yes, sir. 'E dined with Gen'ral Greville.'

'General Greville?'

'Yes, sir – the one who's guv'nor in the Channel.'

Hervey composed himself. 'That is very . . . ingenious of you – to know who is General Greville.'

The waiter did his best to affect indifference, while patently the word 'ingenious' gave him much satisfaction. 'Gen'ral Greville gave a big dinner when he joined the club last year, sir. We all remember it because Mr Peel came.'

This was disquieting news – General Greville a member.

'Indeed? When was this?'

'The beginning of December, sir. And the other night 'e gave a party before 'e left for the Channel again, the one that Gen'ral Gifford came to. Do you know Gen'ral Greville, sir?'

'I am not acquainted with him . . . But he's returned to the Channel Islands, you say?'

'Yes, sir.'

'You're sure of it?'

'Yes, sir. We 'ad to load all 'is boxes into 'is carriage for Portsmouth.'

Hervey brightened; at a stroke he had discovered what he would otherwise have laboured at with the *Gazette*s – and the intelligence was much to his liking. 'Thank you, James,' he said, placing more coin on the tray than was customary.

And then after his coffee, with three – probably even four – hours now unexpectedly in hand, he began contemplating his next assignment. It had been his intention to go to the regimental agents, Messrs Greenwood, Cox and Hammersly in nearby Craig's Court, and there arrange for a notary's clerk to be summoned, who would undertake, with the greatest discretion, a search of the notices in *The Times* pertaining to Kat's situation. However, discretion was a precarious commodity, he knew full well, and he had been troubled about the plan. Why should the commanding officer of His Majesty's 6th Light Dragoons wish to know if Lady Katherine Greville, the wife of Lieutenant-General Sir Peregrine Greville, had given birth? What if the clerk, for all the profession's legendary confidentiality, were to ask that question of another? And what if he in turn were to ask it of yet another – and so on until it reached the ears of a clerk in the office of Sir Peregrine's agents, or even of his attorney? What then might two and two make? He cursed himself for having gone to the Levant without first discovering . . .

But now was opportunity to dispense with the perils of an intermediary and go to the offices of that very newspaper to read the notices for himself.

He had tipped the cabman and asked him to make special haste, and the man had well earned his shilling, turning into Printing House Square – named not for its current printer but that for the King – after but half an hour. Pall Mall to Blackfriars – two miles; even had he known the way he could not have walked it in less.

The offices of *The Times* were smaller than he'd supposed, but more given to his inquiry than he'd expected. At the corner of the square was the 'Advertising Office', which he found most businesslike, and perfectly ready to make available to him there and then for a simple fee past copies of the newspaper – and, indeed, to assist his search.

'Which dates are you desirous of examining, sir?' asked the minor official of the newspaper of record, a very respectable-looking man.

'The month of March last.'

'The entire month, sir?'

'Well, that would depend on my finding what I am looking for. And if not March, then April, or perhaps February.'

'I see,' replied the clerk, although his look said that he did not exactly. 'An item of news, perhaps, or an editorial notice?'

Hervey was hesitant. 'No, rather it would be a private notice.'

'And, sir, you wish to read each edition of the newspaper to discover a particular notice?' The clerk sounded faintly disbelieving.

'Does that present a problem?'

'No, sir, not at all; not, at least, for the newspaper. But, sir, there are a great many private notices, as you will know. Is there, perhaps, some detail that might better lead us to the page?'

Hervey remained measured. 'That is uncommonly obliging, but I don't know if there be such a detail.'

The clerk now looked solicitous. 'May I, sir, suppose that it is the notice of a death you seek?'

Hervey smiled. 'No, no – not a death. Quite the opposite . . . But if it *were* a death, how might you discover the page?'

'The name would be entered in our account book, sir, with the date of publication of the notice.'

'Ah, yes, of course. I hadn't somehow . . . And it is the same for a birth?'

'Exactly the same, sir.'

'Well, in which case, I am seeking the notice of the birth of a child . . . of Lieutenant-General Sir Peregrine Greville.'

'Greville, not Grenville?' replied the clerk.

Hervey nodded.

'Would you wait a moment, sir.'

While he did so, Hervey read the news of the war in the Levant, lately concluded – notably of the unhappy situation of the hospitals in Adrianople, and, indeed, of the insanitary condition of the city as a whole. It had been a fine prospect when first they'd come on that ancient place after their long march from the Danube and through the formidable mountains of the Balkans – and the terrible battle at Kulewtscha. What escapes they'd had on the way; and how wretched that young Agar should have perished when all was won, and to such brigands – so swarthy, murderous a band . . .

'Sir?'

He banished the memories and turned to the counter behind which the clerk now stood with a ledger and a look of satisfaction.

'I have it, sir. The edition you are seeking is that of the thirtieth of March. Shall I fetch you a copy?'

'Do you have the notice entered in the book?'

'Oh, indeed, sir.'

'Then I should be content with that.'

The clerk put on his spectacles again. '"The twelfth of March at Rocksavage, County Roscommon, to Lady Katherine Greville, a son and heir." That is, of course, presuming that the said Lady Katherine is the wife of General Sir Peregrine Greville.'

'Indeed.'

'And therefore,' he added, with excessive pedantry but evident pleasure in the happy event, 'that the said heir is that of General Sir Peregrine Greville.'

Hervey swallowed. 'Indeed so.'

Though it or something very much its like was what he had expected to hear, the words of the notice were nevertheless over-powering.

'Sir?'

He snapped to. 'Yes?'

'Is there anything else, sir?'

Hervey shook his head. And then he brightened, for the sake of appearance. 'No, nothing. That is most admirable. Capital. Capital.' And then, almost absently, 'Would a half-crown suffice?'

'A half-crown, sir? The newspaper is but sevenpence.'

He gave him a half-crown in any case, and said he was much obliged, and left the office in search of a hackney.

But having found none at once he decided to walk. Time was no longer at a premium, and the air would be welcome – suffused even as it was with the smoke of ten thousand coal fires.

It was a walk in which he saw nothing and heard nothing, however, the dread in his breast rising with every step, until he wondered if it would overwhelm him. Kat's 'situation' was beyond anything his twenty years a soldier had prepared him for. 'He who leads men must be able to quell his own terror to tolerable levels in order to take action' – the counsel of his first commanding officer. In the end, it was not solely a matter of practice but of the will. He could let his imagination run riot with the awful possibilities that his news portended, or he could quell the gathering storm of his mind and do his duty until forcibly relieved of it – quell it if not by practice then by the will.

And by that will, slowly at first, and then with increasing resolution, he did indeed begin to raise his head, pull his shoulders back, and step out. *For I also am a man set under authority* . . . He had a regiment to command.

At seven o'clock Fairbrother found him in good spirits, and no sign of the terrible discovery – the deferred discovery – he had made in Printing House Square.

'Let us go in at once, and then return early to Hounslow,' said Hervey as his friend came into the smoking room. 'There's much I have to do. How was General Gifford?'

'He was quite remarkably well. '

Hervey checked his stride. 'How so? You said he lay in the coach as good as dead.'

'Indeed he did, but I'm no doctor – and I've seen stranger things. As have you.'

'"And he that was dead came forth, bound hand and foot with grave-clothes"?'

'Gifford was not even grave-like. He spoke as if he had merely taken excess of bad liquor.'

'Well, I am very glad of it, though I have a mind that the porters will consider themselves robbed of a good line in tattle. They're full of stories of Balkan brigands, though – strange to relate – they failed to mention your driving them off and rescuing him.'

Fairbrother raised an eyebrow, and lowered his voice. 'That is as well, in the circumstances. There was therefore no mention of the lady, I take it?'

'None.'

'The general spoke of her with some distress.'

'I'm not surprised.'

'I told him I didn't wish to know her name – for the reasons you understand – but he told me her husband is one of the government.'

Hervey became rather more circumspect as they entered the coffee room. 'Gifford's a good man. His wife died in India some years ago. I recall it well.'

They took a table by a window at the far end of the room. The curtains were not drawn, Waterloo Place with its snow and its gaslights and the handsome Athenaeum a more than usually fair sight.

'I like this city,' said Fairbrother decidedly. 'Even in weather so strange to me.'

Hervey was at something of a loss for words, for at this moment he equated London only with his misfortunes, yet he had no desire either to disclose these or to take away from his friend's innocent contentment.

A waiter brought a decanter of club claret, and the list. 'The venison is very good, sir.'

'Thank you, Alfred. We'll think on it.'

But Fairbrother already had, looking only for which soup to begin with – the red or the white? 'I take it that you concluded your business,' he said, putting down the card.

Hervey nodded, taking a sip of his wine. 'I did.'

Fairbrother sensed it was not a profitable line of enquiry. 'I took a sweating bath at the Hummums in Covent Garden. Most invigorating.'

Hervey looked at him, curious. 'You are a very exploratory fellow. I'm excessively in awe of it.'

Fairbrother sat back in his chair, with a quizzical look. 'But I, of course, am not bound by King's Regulations. Nor, indeed, by *Manners and Tone of Polite Society*. Nor do I have soldiers under me.'

'Alligator lay eggs again?'

'Exactly so.'

'Pish!'

They had now known each other for three years, or the better part of. Or rather, they had first made each other's acquaintance three years ago. It had taken rather more than that for their acquaintance to turn into mutual respect and affection, though three years was by no means long for the forming of friendships among military men (Fairbrother would have balked at the adjective 'military'). They had seen much service in that time – owed much to each other in that service – and spent much time in each other's company even when not in the field. And yet when it came to those things that oppressed him greatest, Hervey could not confide in his friend. And he did not know why. Indeed there was no man he could – would – confide in. He believed most devoutly in the principle that had animated the Romans (*Respica te, hominem te memento*), and although his command was hardly that of a legion, he wished earnestly to apply it. But in his own mind, in the silent hours – and moments – he knew all too well of his human failings, for he lived daily, and alone, with their consequences. He could not reveal to another – not another man – the extent of his mask, for in so doing he might discover that it was greater than he himself had thought. And what then? In truth he did not wish to look behind him – *Respica te* – because, seeing what he would, he might not have the strength to look forward again and proceed.

IX

DEFAULTERS

Next day

'Well,' said Hervey decidedly as they strode from D Troop's stables for the second time, the 'show again' inspection; 'I had not thought to see so thoroughgoing a transformation. Not even a dirty lantern.'

'Indeed, Colonel,' said Malet, not adding that the lanterns had burned late into the night to work the transformation – for why should such effort be of remark?

'What say you, Sar'nt-Major?'

'Very commendable, Colonel.'

The veterinary surgeon remained silent, reckoning that he'd not been given leave to speak.

Nor did Hervey invite him to, for the moment. 'Would you have Mr Mordaunt come at midday?' he said to Malet.

'Colonel.'

'I fancy you will speak with the troop serjeant-major, Mr Rennie?'

'I shall, Colonel.'

Without checking his stride Hervey acknowledged the salute as the trumpeters came to attention on the square. 'Carry on, please, Trumpet-Major!'

'Colonel!'

Only then did he address the veterinarian. 'Mr Gaskoin: Corporal Figgis – his farrier-pay to be stopped until he is certified once more as competent?'

The trumpeters began sounding the customary fanfare for Saturday, making the veterinarian's reply something of a strain (which afforded Hervey some amusement). 'Yes ... indeed, Colonel. It shall be.'

'And who shall stand duty during his re-apprenticeship?'

Gaskoin was quicker with an answer than expected. 'Weeks, Colonel, who was assigned to E Troop.'

Such details were beyond, rightly, what a commanding officer ought to concern himself with, and Hervey knew it; but they were details of which the veterinarian must be master, and he wished to determine if it were so. In truth, nothing would please him more than to hold the loosest set of reins in his hands, for he might then be free to contemplate higher matters.

But if he were to have a handy regiment, then just as a handy charger he would have to be sure of its schooling. And he'd made a good start: it was particularly satisfying – auguring well – to dismiss the little party outside the orderly room with a cheerful salute and a 'Thank you, gentlemen.'

'Coffee for the colonel, if you please,' said Malet as they swept up the corridor, wondering, as Hervey, if it were Abdel he addressed or his brother.

Hervey took off his forage cap and half tossed it onto his writing table, the atmosphere in the orderly room transformed by the satisfactory inspection of the D Troop stables.

The coffee was brought at once, for the orderly room serjeant had his spies at the stables. It made Hervey even cheerier.

And Malet would have given a great deal to be able to leave him to his enjoyment of the bean, but matters were pressing, and they would not be made any less disagreeable by delay.

First, however, Hervey insisted on better – at least, routine –

things. 'I called on the Horse Guards yesterday. We're to place a troop at the Royal Hospital to reinforce the Household Cavalry, and a second at short notice here to replace them if called out. On account of the parliamentary debates.'

'I didn't know you intended calling, Colonel, else I would have given you the latest *Gazette*.'

'I hadn't intended to, only that I found myself rather unexpectedly with time in hand.'

'I'll make the arrangements.'

'Worsley's to the hospital, I think, and D at notice here.'

Malet looked pained. 'I think it better, Colonel, to withhold any decision till I've made you aware of certain other matters.'

Hervey frowned. 'Tyrwhitt?'

'The situation with Tyrwhitt is not propitious, but the greater problem is with B Troop. Kennett has laid charges against Serjeant-Major Collins. Worsley informed me after first parade.'

Hervey darkened. 'What charges?'

'Striking a superior officer, and insubordination – along the lines you spoke of on Thursday.'

'This is very ill. Very ill indeed.'

Malet needed no telling. Nor was it merely the fall from grace of one of the Sixth's best – some said *the* best – serjeant-majors: under the Mutiny Act, striking a superior officer could carry the penalty of death, remote though that sanction might be. 'Worsley's sent Kennett from barracks for the time being.'

'That's wise . . .' said Hervey, calming a little, and then after thinking blackly for an age, 'There's nothing for it but for Kennett to be made to withdraw the charges.'

Malet shifted in his seat. 'Captain Worsley informed me that he had spent an hour trying to do so. But . . . Colonel, with respect, can you be entirely sure that Collins did not strike Kennett?'

Hervey looked at him in disbelief.

'Colonel, I must be scrupulous in the matter.'

The voice was of gentle insistence, not pettifogging. It took but a moment for Hervey to reconsider. 'You must, of course, be scrupulous. I pre-judge things, no doubt. But I tell you, I can conceive of no evidence that would make me change my mind.'

'Nor mine, in truth, Colonel. I shall see Kennett and question him.'

'Where is Collins now?'

'The sar'nt-major was to summon him as soon as the inspection was finished.'

Hervey nodded again, slowly. 'Very well . . . What other business is there?'

'Tyrwhitt. I spoke at length with his attorney yesterday—'

'Is this pleasing, and if it is not, can it wait for another day?'

Malet raised his eyebrows. 'It isn't pleasing – not at all – but, yes, it can wait for another day.'

'Monday. I'll consider it then.'

'I thought you were to go to Wiltshire that day, Colonel?'

'My mind is changed. There's too much to be about for the moment. And I've calls to make. What are the arrangements for worship tomorrow?'

'None, Colonel. There are no parades.'

'Of course; so you informed me.' He reached for a pencil to make a note. And then – but as if his mind were not wholly on the matter – added, 'We must make some arrangement soon. Church parade on Sunday seven days. Any minister'll do.'

Malet made a note too, but said nothing. He would leave it till Monday, along with Tyrwhitt and any other intractable evils.

But Hervey was not yet finished. 'Do you have the list of today's defaulters?' (It had always been the custom in the Sixth to hold regimental courts martial each Saturday, this being the day of the adjutant's and RSM's parades.)

Malet opened his order book. 'There are five dragoons, Colonel. No NCOs. A private of A Troop, deficient, in part, of uniform; one of C Troop, attempting to deceive his inspecting officer;

another of C Troop, in possession of peas for which he cannot honestly account and for making improper use of the barrack bedding; one of D Troop, drunk before dinner although confined to barracks, and another of quitting barracks without leave after last post.'

'A remarkably light bill.'

'Indeed. Three hundred lashes the lot,' suggested Malet in an attempt at therapeutic levity.

Hervey huffed, and raised his eyebrows. In any battalion of infantry – and even some regiments of cavalry – the lash was the corrective of first choice. But the Sixth did not flog; it never had, not even in the sternest days of the Peninsula (or rather, the lash had at some time out of mind been put away, and its absence scarcely noticed). The one deviation from this rule at the hands of a commanding officer come in from another regiment – Lord Towcester – who would ultimately be deprived of command by order of the Duke of York himself, was remembered even now with repugnance, so that, perversely, the fear of another such lapse of custom acted as a sort of preventive. Nor was there any lack of alternative correction. Stoppages of pay – in effect, stoppages of grog – was harsh punishment, the sting lasting longer than that of the lash. Restriction of privileges – when privileges were few – had their effect also. Detention in the guardhouse and a ferocious regimen of fatigues was enough to recall all but those unredeemably possessed of devils. And for those who broke not just the peculiar law of soldiers under authority but the law of the land, there was prison and the gallows. When the regiment was at war, the saying went, the NCOs showed the men how to fight, and the officers showed them how to die. In barracks, on the other hand, the principal occupation of the NCOs was to bully the men out of vice, whereas that of the officers was to flatter them into virtue. And Hervey had long been of the opinion that virtue would be so much easier to advocate were it to carry some pecuniary advantage. Indeed, he had resolved some time ago that he would at the first auspicious moment lay before the commander-in-chief just such a scheme.

He leaned back in his chair, his former spirits all but restored. 'I was told at the Horse Guards yesterday that one man in seven on the home establishment is in a prison.'

Malet nodded. He did not add (for he had sent the numbers to him with all the others) that the Sixth's penitentiary muster was but five dragoons – four for desertion and just one for violence to a superior. Nor had there been a man hanged since the return from India.

The numbers then prompted a happier thought. 'I did not ask before: how do things stand with the men's reading room?'

'Very well, Colonel. Corporal Tenty has charge of it, and Jenkinson the supervision.'

Hervey was about to ask what newspapers were provided when the orderly room serjeant appeared at the door. 'Colonel, with permission, sir.'

'What is it?' asked Malet.

'A despatch from Windsor Castle, Colonel, brought by one of the War Office party.'

Malet took it from him. 'He's waiting on any reply, I trust.'

'He is, sir.'

'Very well.'

The serjeant withdrew.

'Better read it at once,' said Hervey.

'It's addressed to you in person, Colonel.'

'I have no secrets at Windsor,' said Hervey, with a smile.

Malet broke the seal and began to read. 'His Majesty commands the presence of Colonel Hervey of His Majesty's 6th Light Dragoons at a levee at Windsor Castle at 7 o'clock p.m. on the 1st Proximo.'

'Monday? What good fortune I'd not left for Wiltshire,' said Hervey, delighted by the honour the invitation did him, if not by the inconvenience it might have occasioned.

'I'll make the arrangements, Colonel. Who will attend you?'

He needed but a second to consider it. 'St Alban.'

'Very well.'

'Is there anything else – any more business to discuss?'

'No, Colonel,' replied Malet, in some relief now that equilibrium was returned.

'Then I'll attend to memoranda, and then see Mordaunt.'

'Twelve o'clock?'

'Twelve o'clock . . . And Malet . . .'

'Colonel?'

'You'll get Kennett to withdraw these preposterous charges? The sooner the better – for all.'

'I shall do everything in my power, Colonel – once I've discovered exactly what that may be.'

Fairbrother was in a hale and at the same time contrary mood that evening. He stood with his back to the fire in Hervey's state room, as he had taken to calling it, extolling the delights of London while declaring that he did not think he could bear the cold much longer. 'I've a mind to seek a warmer clime for a month or so.'

'I thought you said last night you were pleased with London, even in this weather,' replied Hervey, not looking up from his writing desk. 'I should miss your company, but I couldn't deny you comfort simply on that account.'

'I did say that, yes, but today is today.'

'And the glass has fallen again, I grant you.'

'But where to go? I had thought Portugal, but the place is in turmoil.'

'Peto was always attached to the Canaries,' said Hervey, continuing to write. 'Perhaps you might consult *The Times* to see what sailings there are.'

Fairbrother threw another apple-wood log on the fire. 'But if I were to go away I should then be but a swallow.'

'My favourite of birds.'

'Truly? How can you have a favourite that's not here for half the time?'

'I was too hasty; *one* of my favourite of birds. I can't but include the robin. And the hoopoe.'

'Upon my word, you are a soldier through and through!'

Hervey laid down his pen and looked at his friend, bemused. 'How so?'

'On the one hand a red coat – if only a red breast – and on the other a crest to make your dragoon's plume look dull.'

'Very droll. But do you know why the swallow can't abide an English winter? It's not that the cold chills him – for his feathers are as warm as the robin's – but because he subsists on insects that fly, and when the weather is cold there are none. Or so I read.'

Fairbrother picked up another log, thoughtfully. 'A rather elegant analogy.'

'I thought so too,' said Hervey, smiling and picking up the sealing wax. 'And now that I have finished this we shall have our dinner, for there's much I would tell you.'

'Is the letter to Hertfordshire?' asked Fairbrother casually, adding the log to the blaze.

Hervey sat for a moment as if in thought. 'No. There shall be no letters to Hertfordshire.'

Fairbrother turned to look at his friend directly. 'I really think that—'

'There shall be no letters.' Hervey put down the sealing wax and poured a glass of claret. 'And that is an end to it. And I have weighty matters to discuss with you.'

'Is not Hertfordshire a weighty matter?'

Hervey kept his countenance, but was emphatic. 'I must deal with what I can, and with what is worthy of being dealt with . . .'

Fairbrother made no reply. He had pressed as far as he might. It puzzled rather than troubled him that his friend could not find the words – or was it the inclination? – to discuss the affairs of the heart. There might of course be another with whom he did, which would be for the better, but he had no knowledge of anyone; and he rather thought he would, for they'd spent such time together these past three years that . . .

There was a knock, and the door opened. 'Beg pardon, sir, but may's bring your dinner now?'

Hervey smiled warmly. 'Yes, Annie; do.'

He rose and took the decanter to refill Fairbrother's glass. 'Your mentioning the robin minds me of something. Do you know how much is a cornet's uniform – in the Sixth, I mean? Esterhase, who's just joined, laid out a hundred and thirty pounds with his tailor. Malet told me at office this morning. His pay won't cover it in a full ten years – though that'll scarcely trouble him: by all accounts he has three thousand a year, and a good deal more when he's of age. But there are others who'll find any change to red more than merely *chromatically* objectionable.'

'Perhaps if you were to plead their case at Windsor on Monday, when you meet the Duke of Clarence?'

'If he were there I might well, but I can't suppose he will be.'

'There was much talk at the theatre and afterwards as to who will succeed Clarence in due season.'

'I dare say there was,' said Hervey, glancing at the parlour-maids, whose ears were pricked. 'But it is settled, is it not? The Princess of Kent?'

'There is, it seems, a question as to paternity.'

Hervey frowned. 'We had better talk by and by. How was your sport this morning?'

Fairbrother smiled to himself: *Manners and Tone of Good Society* – speak as you will in front of indoor servants, but not those of a public house. 'Sport? Very indifferent. Cranford Park has few birds, it would seem, though its squire is most hospitable. I shot a hare but regretted it, for it was not running fast; and that line of Keats rebuked me – *the hare limped trembling through the frozen grass.*'

'Upon my word, the cold does indeed steal in on you!'

The parlour-maids, having laid the table, now withdrew to fetch the dishes.

'You don't suppose, do you, that they are in the pay of the Princess Lieven?' asked Fairbrother, nodding to the door.

Hervey chortled. 'Touché.'

'As I was saying, the talk at the theatre was of the Duchess of Kent's private secretary, Captain Conroy. He was much younger than the duke – twenty years, by all accounts – and . . . well, the way of the flesh, you might say.'

Hervey shifted uncomfortably. Sir Peregrine Greville was twenty years Kat's senior – more, indeed. 'You might say that. But twenty years is not so great a difference. There is no . . . inexorableness in such a matter.'

'The duchess is, by all accounts, a very handsome woman, and Conroy a fair-looking man. You knew him, I suppose?'

'No, I never had occasion to meet him. I know of him, of course.'

'Strange; I understood him to be of your seniority, or there-about.'

'He served neither in the Peninsula nor at Waterloo, nor in America, and never in India,' replied Hervey, dismissively.

'I beg your pardon,' said Fairbrother, feigning indignation.

The parlour-maids returned with their tureens.

'Thank you, Annie – and . . .'

'Susan, sir.'

'Mr Ellis said that you asked for no fish, sir,' explained Annie; 'so there's soup, and a frigize, sir – rabbit – and there's roasts as well if you'd like.'

'We shall call, thank you.'

When they were gone, Hervey returned to his charge. 'I was unduly severe. Conroy served in Ireland . . . on the staff – of his father-in-law.'

The intelligence was more damning than if he had said nothing.

'Lord, you know a deal about him.'

'His distance from the battlefield was long a matter of remark.

And his intimacy with the duchess likewise, but if they are lovers now it is not to say they were lovers when the duke was alive. I do think it ill that a woman might not enjoy the company of a confidant without her virtue being at once suspect. Nor that a man might pay his respects without his intentions being taken for the worst.'

'I believe you have said as much on another occasion. I stand rebuked.'

Hervey knew precisely the occasion, and that Fairbrother made connections. He was in no mind to entertain them, however. 'Furthermore, I know there's not any way of proof of such things . . . and I think it a treason, very probably, to speak thus.'

Fairbrother looked pained. 'Hervey, it is I you speak to.'

Such an intimate rebuke he had not heard in many a year. He put down his spoon, looked at his plate and then at his friend. 'My dear fellow, I beg your pardon.'

His friend would not have him excessively discomfited, however. 'I know there's much on your mind. I spoke without due thought.'

Hervey smiled. 'I hope you'll continue to do so.'

And then his look became solemn again.

'Now, I fear I must tell you of an unpleasant turn of events regarding Collins . . .'

Unpleasant indeed – and the more so as Collins had been the most faithful, resourceful of supports to both of them at the Cape. Fairbrother listened in silence as Hervey recounted the various conversations with Malet, Worsley and the regimental serjeant-major, and told him his thoughts on the affair – what he had authorized Malet to do, and the courses he believed open to him.

Fairbrother said nothing at once by reply, as if still trying to comprehend. When he did it was with a look of *Your ways are strange to me*: 'In the Royal Africans things would not have come to this pass.'

The words sank in only by degrees. As a rule Fairbrother never spoke of his time with that notorious corps. On the occasions he did, usually on finding something to his liking in contrast with his own experience, it was in tones of dismay. And Hervey was hardly surprised: at the turn of the century the Royal African Corps had been raised for the defence of Goree Island off Senegal, captured from the French, and became at once a 'condemned battalion', its ranks filled from the hulks and with black recruits from the West Indies. The officers, he understood, though in truth he had never known any, were no more than might be supposed in such a regiment. But his friend had obtained a commission on transfer from the Jamaica Militia, a perfectly respectable corps, and as the son of a very gentlemanlike planter (albeit a son born the wrong side of the blanket) he had, he knew, at once found the entire corps as incomprehensible as it was disagreeable – the officers no less than the rank and file. This late discovery of a superior aspect of interior economy was therefore intriguing indeed.

'How so? How could it not have come to this pass? The discipline was ferocious, was it not?'

'It was very ferocious, but matters were almost invariably dealt with summarily, without due process of law. Somehow a case such as this would have been settled without formal charges and court martial. Pistol, very possibly.'

Hervey cocked his head. 'Pistols? Between an officer and an NCO?'

Fairbrother nodded. 'Oh, I don't say that it would have been an affair of honour, of pistols in the plural.'

'Ah, I see. Straightforward murder, of the one or the other.'

'Or chastisement – a horsewhip, perhaps.'

Hervey shook his head. 'What an altogether unhealthy place Goree must have been.'

'Indeed it was,' said Fairbrother, pouring his fourth glass of claret with the satisfaction of knowing he would now seal his point: 'But it was never lost to the French, though they tried to take it back more than once.'

Few things his friend had ever said quite set Hervey's mind so awry as the present-day notion of trial by combat. Not even combat – simply the application of force. It was one thing for an NCO to chastise a dragoon, the justice swift and sparing him the torment of 'due process', but quite another to subject an officer to an indignity which would in turn undermine his authority. Truly things in the Royal Africans must have been beyond his comprehension. And he sought to put it from his mind, though as their dinner proceeded the image of the horsewhip returned from time to time – the cad's scold.

The frigize was wholesome, and plenty, but they called too for the roasts, and more claret, and there was a sweet pudding of sorts, and they made the best of their evening, not speaking any more of events and affairs of business. At half past ten, the decanter empty and the candles beginning to gutter, Fairbrother suddenly announced that he was more fatigued than he'd supposed, and would retire – which he did promptly but with assurances that he would be up betimes to attend whatever divine service were ordered (gratified then to learn that there was none at Hounslow). Hervey, just as suddenly feeling the call of his bed, bid him good night, drained his glass and went to his writing desk to pen one last letter.

It took longer to compose than he'd imagined, however. Perhaps it should have come as no surprise, for to tell Wiltshire – once more – that duty was detaining him longer than expected (when he had not seen his people for the better part of a year) was a matter of some delicacy. But at least he was moderately satisfied with his effort, and was sealing it as the clock struck the hour and the parlour-maids returned.

'Thank you, Annie; it was all very good.'

'I'll tell cook, sir. She's awful proud of her rabbit things. Can I bring you some coffee, sir, or tea?'

Hervey shook his head. 'But you may bring a bottle more of the claret, or of port if that's to be had.'

'I'm sure it is, sir,' she answered obligingly, nodding to Susan to clear the table while she went to find the cellarman.

He turned back to the desk to address his letter: *Baroness Heinrici, Heytesbury, Wiltshire* – a fine title, a fine address . . .

And then on an impulse he took another sheet of paper and began writing the same lines, more or less, to Georgiana.

Annie was some time returning. 'Beg pardon, sir, but the first bottle was hard to draw the cork, and then Mr Ellis said it was tainted.' She advanced to the writing desk with a salver and the new bottle. 'I'm afraid I don't know how to decant it, sir.'

'It will do very well, I'm sure,' said Hervey, taking the bottle while still intent on his letter – then seeing that it was indeed port, and looked admirably fortified.

Susan had by now filled the trays with all that had to be removed, and Annie motioned her to take the smaller one away.

'Shall I put more wood on the fire, sir?'

Hervey looked up from his letter, touched by the solicitude. 'Thank you, Annie. You are very good. Just a small piece to make a flame for a few minutes more. I shall be retiring soon.'

She put on a well-split piece and poked the coals until it took light.

'It's awful cold, sir; shall I bring a warming pan?'

He turned again. 'You know, Annie, that would be a true comfort. I'm most obliged to you.'

'That's nothing, sir.'

She returned in ten minutes with a copper warmer, took it to his bedroom, and ran it the length of the bed – a dozen times at least.

She finished as Hervey was sealing the second letter. 'Thank you, Annie. Would you take this for your trouble this evening?'

He gave her sixpence.

'Oh thank you, sir. Would there be anything else?'

He shook his head.

'Beg pardon, sir, but will you be staying here long – at the inn, I mean? I know you are at the barracks but we was wondering for how long. If you don't mind me asking, sir.'

Hervey smiled. 'No, I don't mind your asking, Annie. I expect to be at the barracks for some time – some years, I trust. As for the Berkeley Arms, I cannot say; but I can assure you that were I to leave it would not be on account of its being uncomfortable in any regard.'

Annie looked pleased to learn it. 'My brother's gone for a soldier, sir,' she said, shifting the weight of the warming pan in her hands, anxious that she might now be speaking out of turn.

'Has he indeed? Most admirable.' He checked his instinct to pick up the pen, needing to add his initials below the seal.

'Yes, sir. He went six months ago to London.'

Hervey could not but be a little charmed. All he ever saw of a dragoon was the man that stood before him, nothing of what lay behind – the family left for good or ill, a sweetheart abandoned perhaps. He wondered to which corps this brother of so fine a girl – of whom she was evidently so proud – had gone, to which serjeant's shilling-blandishments he had succumbed. So steady and obliging a girl – a brother whose qualities encompassed these would be an asset. He hoped he'd gone somewhere worthy.

'I think it must be very hard, sir, being a soldier.'

The candles flickered, but the light was kind. Annie was unread, unfinished, yet her looks and air would carry her. There was nothing more he wished for at this hour than companionship, the companionship of the pillow, the willing embrace – a few hours' consolation, and warmth on waking. And Annie stood before him demurely, not as a lady of pleasure, yet seemingly at his bidding. Perhaps she too wished for companionship. All he had to do was rise, give the sign – assent. Or did he entirely misread her innocence?

He braced. 'It's not so hard to do one's duty, Annie. Your brother will learn that.'

And he looked down long at the letter, until at length she said simply and softly, 'Will that be all, sir?'

He turned and smiled with all the warmth he had for a moment contemplated sharing. 'Yes, Annie. That will be all. Good night. And thank you.'

And when she was gone he poured a glass of the port and sat back, and pondered on his misshapen virtue. He had not dismissed her on account of Scripture, or even fidelity to his marriage vows, but for a notion of propriety – that she was the sister of an enlisted man. 'It's not so hard to do one's duty,' he'd said. But it was, and he wished he'd been able to tell her so.

X

HEIRS APPARENT AND PRESUMPTIVE

Monday

Hervey had not worn court dress for some time. Corporal Johnson had taken care to preserve his best uniform before leaving for the Levant, however, and had just had new white hose sent from Wall Street in St James's. It was now all got up spick and span, with the silver and gilt showing well in the candlelight, and Johnson stood ready to assist with the vesting.

'I must say that if the new king would do away with these breeches it would dispose me more towards his red tunics.'

'I think they're very smart, and just the thing,' replied Johnson, taking the trees from his court shoes as Hervey pulled on the stockings.

'Damnably cold in weather such as this.'

'Corp'ral Wakefield'll 'ave t'carriage warmed up right enough.'

'I'm sure he will. No doubt I make too much of it.'

He took a while to straighten the hose to his satisfaction, and then Johnson handed him the button-hook.

'But this new king, 'e won't be king for a bit, will 'e?'

'No,' said Hervey, managing to fasten the top two buttons of his knee-breeches more deftly than he'd expected. 'I'm not at all sure the talk is correct. The King, though excitable, and fatter even than Corp'l Stray, didn't look *quite* next to death's door.'

'But why is it 'is brother who's going to be t'king? What about all 'is children? I thought them 'ad to be king first.'

'All bastards, Corp'l Johnson. The first marriage was not deemed legal. And his only child by our late royal colonel Princess Caroline, as you'll recall, died giving birth.'

'So that's why t'Duke o' Clarence is t'heir?'

'Yes,' (the struggle to fasten the remaining two buttons was rather greater than he'd expected, but he eventually managed to pull them through the button holes without detaching either of them, then handing back the button-hook and taking the shoe-horn) 'but strictly speaking he's called the heir presumptive, which means that if the King were to produce an heir, the duke would become second in line not first.'

'But 'e's not going to do that, is 'e – produce an heir? Not now.'

'It strikes me as highly improbable,' said Hervey, with a wry smile as he eased his left foot into the shiny buckled-patent.

'And does t'Duke of Clarence 'ave any heirs?'

'A man has only *one* heir, and, as it happens, the duke has none, though he too has a good many bastards. And if he were to become king and Princess Adelaide were to produce no heir, the throne would pass to the daughter of his younger brother, the late Duke of Kent.'

'That's who we saw a couple of years ago when we were on that scheme at Windsor, and Princess Augusta were there?'

Hervey slipped in his right foot and handed back the horn. 'Your memory is very exact – Victoria, yes.'

'That'll be queer, a woman.'

'We have not been ill-served in the past.'

'How was that, Colonel?' asked Johnson, handing him a silk stock doubtfully.

'Queen Elizabeth? The Spanish Armada?'

'Ah, Good Queen Bess. But that were a long time ago, weren't it? Things were diff'rent then.'

Hervey looked at him, puzzled, but thought better of seeking clarification. 'There are two things of difficulty in a woman's acceding to the throne, one of which was Queen Elizabeth's difficulty too – who shall be her husband? And the other is that she may not be Queen of Hanover, because by their law a woman can't succeed to the throne.'

'Ah, so who'd be in charge of 'Anover then?'

'The Duke of Cumberland, the youngest of the old King's sons. And in turn *his* son.'

'Well, that's all right then, isn't it?'

'Except that Hanover would no longer be in personal union, as it's called, with the British throne.'

'An' that isn't good for us?' Johnson held up the coat for him.

'Well, I don't suppose it'll be the least concern to us during my command. What happens thereafter's another matter, though having a sister who's now a subject of the King of Hanover it might be of greater moment to me.'

Johnson frowned. 'How's that, Colonel?'

Hervey explained as he finished dressing.

Johnson had known all about the marriage with the baron, but had not thought that it would make Hervey's sister German. He liked 'Miss Hervey'; she wasn't like *Mrs* Hervey at all – well, she was like the *first* Mrs Hervey. But it *was* queer marrying a German, even if you got a castle and became a baroness. He'd never met a baroness before (he didn't think). He supposed you could just say 'Ma'am' to them all the same. And Miss Hervey wouldn't mind anyway if he got it wrong. Not like *Mrs* Hervey. If you got anything wrong with *her* it would be like being checked for something on guard mounting . . .

Outside – five minutes to five o'clock exactly – the regimental chariot was drawn up. It was twelve miles to the castle, and there was a good half-moon (these things were always arranged with

168

close attention, Hervey marked). It ought to be a comfortable drive.

A minute later his orderly officer, Cornet St Alban, presented himself, and in three more they were under way.

Two dragoons accompanied them (Hervey had said it was not necessary, but Malet countered that changing a wheel in levee dress would hardly be edifying, and in any case, it would serve to relieve the dragoons on the War Office party) – and their progress was remarkably unhindered. Hervey first scrutinized the *Gazette* which Malet had put into the coach, and then talked very agreeably with his temporary aide-de-camp about Reform, the matter on which St Alban had written in *The Spectator* with, to his mind, singular dispassion and clarity. But where did the eminently reasonable arguments St Alban advanced have end? If popular – indeed turbulent – clamour was to be rewarded with such tinkering as was proposed by the radicals, would that not encourage yet more clamour? It was all very well for high-minded Whigs secure in their broad acres to advocate improvement of what was at times an undeniably sorry affair (the House of Commons), but what manner of man would it be that emerged to sit there in place of those with so solid a stake in the country? These were the men, were they not, with a true understanding of the general wellbeing, rooted as it was in the solid earth of the shires and the good sense of the church established? And then, when the Whig nobility had secured their 'reforms', what would be the fate of that other affront to rationalism, the House of Peers? Would that not go the way of their forebears in Cromwell's day? Indeed, was not 'Reform' but a specious cloak for the introduction of republicanism? He declared that although in the peculiar circumstances that was his military service (peripatetic) and his father's profession (pecuniary) he had no vote, he was perfectly content to allow such an indignity as the price of the English peace – which was the envy of Europe, if not the world. And St Alban countered that such an affront was insupportable – he himself having two votes (one in his father's borough, one at Oxford) while his commanding officer, much decorated in the service of his country, had none.

'Hard cases make bad law, it is said,' Hervey had countered, thoroughly warming to his subject, as if polishing his credentials before joining the stoutly Tory assembly at Windsor.

'Indeed, Colonel, but bad law makes hard cases too,' replied St Alban, with disarming forthrightness. 'And perhaps solely for want of effort. I'm not a thoroughgoing Whig. I find much sense in what Mr Burke said, that when it is not necessary to change, it is necessary not to change, but he wrote also that a state without the means of some change is without the means of its conservation.'

Hervey nodded. He had no objection to change – far from it: but it should be brought about gradually and naturally, as the seasons changed. 'That is surely so. But tell me, for I've scarcely been in England these three years, and you were better placed to know: is there truly a mood here – in the country parts, I mean – that the authorities are so exercised by it? The affair in the park was vexing enough, but was it really a harbinger of worse to come?'

St Alban considered his answer for a moment. 'I believe, Colonel, that there is a mood – yes, but that it is in truth a mood of many parts. I am, though, much taken by something Mr Cobbett wrote lately,' (Hervey took note of the dignity 'Mr' accorded to that inveterate radical – and former NCO) 'that it is scarcely possible to agitate a fellow with a full stomach.'

And that much Hervey found unanswerable, suffused as it was with both humanity and his own experience. The chaise had slowed to a walk on coming into Windsor, as if the gravity of the matters under discussion required it, and he was glad of the change of speed, which seemed to give him leave to consider the matter more fully, but the horses were now bending to the sharp incline of Castle Hill in a trot once more, which belied their twelve-mile approach march. Horseshoes rang on the cobblestones where the guardsmen had cleared the latest snowfall.

'Thank you for your candour, St Alban,' said Hervey at length, with (to his own ear at least) a faint note of surprise. 'You have given me much to ponder – and indeed to argue this evening if I'm bearded by "Ultras",' he added wryly.

As they turned onto the bridge over the old moat the pair came back to a walk for King Henry's Gate, where the sentries presented arms and a colour-serjeant saluted extravagantly – a considerably more auspicious entry than his last, said Hervey to himself, and wondering if he would find the King in any better state of mind.

An avenue of Grenadiers at the 'present' lined their way up the bailey, past the lower ward lit uncommonly brightly by gas, where carriages were already parked, past St George's Chapel, and the motte, and Great Round tower, on through the Norman Gate and into the upper ward, where at last the chaise drew up before the canopied entrance of the state apartments.

Hervey got down briskly, took off his cloak, hitched up his sword, acknowledged the salutes of more Grenadiers and footmen, and marched into St George's Hall with as much self-possession as he judged reasonable. He had no doubt that a lieutenant-colonel of light dragoons would be of little consequence to many – perhaps even all – of the assembled grandees of the court and the men of moment in parliament, but he had no intention of submitting to their opinion. How many were to be at the levee he had no idea – he supposed several hundred, for the castle was a vast place, by all accounts – but he had at least the assurance that in St Alban he would have diverting company if no other were forthcoming.

There was an orchestra playing at the top of the grand staircase – Grenadiers again, with some strings. Even to Hervey's ear it was pleasing.

'I did not ask: do you know the castle?'

'I have not been here since I was a page, Colonel,' replied St Alban, gazing up in some awe at the soaring vaulting. 'It's vastly changed, I think. The King has done much with it, and of late too.'

Hervey abandoned his somewhat forced insouciance to gaze at the decorator's art – the suits of armour, swords, shields, pikes, halberds, and the lifelike equestrians at the top of the stairs.

'Those suits are uncommonly small, are they not? Or a miniature, do you suppose?'

'That I do remember, Colonel. They were made for Prince Henry when he was a youth, the Prince of Wales, soon after James the first ascended the throne. One, I recall, was a present of the French king. We pages were allowed to try them.'

Hervey stood in appreciation before them for some time. 'How history might have been different had their prince lived to fill a man's suit.' Better, though he did not say, than with his brother, Charles.

'Indeed, Colonel. "He is dead who while he lived was a perpetual Paradise; every season that he showed himself in a perpetual spring, every exercise wherein he was seen a special felicity . . ."'

Hervey nodded. 'Well spoken. My father used that sermon on two occasions that I know of, and when I asked him whence the words came he told me from the King's chaplain, but that he had taken them from Donne, so that he himself had no compunction in appropriating them in turn.'

'We pages were made to recite them before putting on the armour. I don't recall why. I suppose a mark of worthiness, perhaps.'

Hervey looked at him with approval. He was glad, now, to have come here, for he'd not expected to be. 'We had better proceed.'

Footmen bowed and held out hands to usher them towards the place of the audience, but Hervey was perplexed that the guests seemed so few in this stately progress, for it was his experience always to queue – though he supposed the castle was so great as to make the largest of assemblies seem small. He was certain that they arrived in good time.

The guiding hands led them to the Grand Reception Room, a

Rococo confection of gold leaf, looking glass and tapestries, where another orchestra played, and the earliest arrivals made their introductions and glanced uneasily (some at least) at their reflections. Hervey took in the room with as little movement of his head as he could manage, and then turned to his aide-de-camp. 'Is there anyone of your acquaintance?'

Cornet St Alban looked about the room, his brow furrowing slightly. 'None that I can see, Colonel. Those with their backs to us I can't vouch for. I recognize the Marquess of Framlingham, but I'm not acquainted with him. His interest, I understand, is entirely with cattle improvement.'

Hervey smiled. 'And that is his marchioness, I take it – with the feathers to outdo an hussar?'

St Alban smiled too. 'I can't rightly say, Colonel. The feathers are magnificent, though.'

Hervey felt no great inclination to present himself to anyone. Nor could he see any uniforms, to which he might have been obliged to do so.

'Ah, but I see over there, now that he's turned, is Rowly Fane,' said St Alban happily. 'He was page here, too.'

'Not a son of General Harry's, I suppose?'

'Yes, indeed – his youngest. He came up to Oxford in my year. I wonder what he does here?'

'Well, in due course you must discover.'

After ten minutes or so of more intense scrutiny, the room began to fill steadily. The King had commanded their presence at seven, which by custom allowed half an hour more, whereupon he would make his appearance, take a turn about the assemblage, nod here and there, stop to talk to no one, then retire to a low dais and receive those singled out by his gentlemen-ushers, leaving the room half an hour later to dine in semi-state with a further chosen few, while the rest were shown to a buffet of legendary indulgence. So said the equerries.

'Hervey!'

He looked round. 'Upon my word, Howard!'

'I saw your name on the list just this evening. You didn't say on Friday that you were to be here.'

'That's because it was only on Saturday that I was commanded to be here. And you? This is all part of your duty, I suppose.'

'I was made an additional usher last year.'

'Of course. This is Cornet St Alban.'

St Alban bowed.

Lord John Howard returned the compliment. 'The Earl of Bicester's son?'

'I am, sir.'

Howard smiled. 'Your father writes the best letters of any lord lieutenant. Lord Hill circulates them at the Horse Guards, with "Read, mark, learn and inwardly digest".'

Hervey allowed them a word or two more before pressing Howard on another matter, knowing that his old friend would soon have to excuse himself to his ushering duties. 'I'm summoned to the Horse Guards on Thursday and I'm damned if I can discover the why. I'd thought of asking you on Friday but you were called away before I had opportunity.'

Howard glanced at St Alban, who bowed and retired out of hearing.

'So confidential?' asked Hervey.

'So confidential that I myself know little but that it concerns precautionary measures in the event of further civil violence. Lord Hill himself is to speak.'

'"The secret things belong unto the Lord"?'

Howard frowned. 'Quite. And for what purpose I don't know, but ten lieutenant-colonels of cavalry in all have been summoned.'

'*Ten* colonels: I hadn't supposed there were so many on the home list.'

'I think some may be from the half-pay, but you might therefore conclude that it is a business of some moment. "Those things which are revealed belong unto us, that we may do all the words of this law" – as you're evidently of a Scriptural mind this evening.'

Hervey inclined his head.

'By the bye, your friend, Fairbrother – I understand he's to be offered a rather handsome bounty for the information he provided to the Master-General. I saw a letter this morning with a testimonial from the Royal Society. They wish to meet with him.'

'That I'm very glad of. He is not without means, but he is some-what without purpose at present.'

Howard nodded. 'But not a word till the eggs are in the pudding . . . But see, I must go and attend on Sir Henry Hardinge,' he said, indicating the little knot of beaux in the middle of the room.

Hervey saw – and approved. 'What a man is Hardinge. There was never a brigadier greater admired in the Peninsula.'

Henry Hardinge was but a few years his senior, but had commanded a brigade of Portuguese, and was at Ligny with the Prussians, where he lost the better part of an arm. The duke had made him Secretary at War eighteen months ago when Lord Palmerston resigned.

'He's at his desk by eight of a morning, by all accounts, and there still when the hour-hand touches it again.'

'The smaller the army, the greater the work.'

'I suppose it is so . . . but you'll forgive me, Hervey – until next week?'

They bowed, and Lord John Howard took his leave.

Cornet St Alban rejoined him. 'The King has just come in the room, Colonel.'

The band ceased its merry airs and struck up *God Save the King*. Hervey strained for a glimpse of the royal progress without giving that impression. 'It cannot be but a trial for him – he has such an embarrassment of breathing, and his legs so terribly swollen. I wonder he puts himself to the ordeal.'

'The equerries say he's dosed heavily, but he will insist on it.'

Footmen in the finest livery he'd seen preceded the sad figure –

the tallest too, and ramrod-straight, giving the occasion all the majesty that the poor old, dropsied King might otherwise have been unable to conjure.

There was no seeing him for the cloud of attendants and those paying court, so instead Hervey observed the onlookers in the outer circles of the room. They appeared rather disconsolate, if respectfully attentive to the unseen progress. Although he had never sought such company, nor even wanted to be here this evening, he found himself wishing he had seen a levee in the days of the King's pomp.

Ten, perhaps fifteen minutes, and the procession had reached the dais. The band returned to its merry airs, and conversations were once again taken up. Hervey acknowledged the bows of several who supposed they might be acquainted, and spoke with two officers of the Coldstream who were lately returned from Portugal, until at length a gentleman-usher came up.

'Colonel Hervey?'

'Yes?'

'Lascelles, Colonel. His Majesty commands your attention.'

Hervey bowed to the Coldstreamers and took the usher's lead to the dais.

The King was speaking to a prince of the church, and then an ambassador, during which time Hervey could observe him keenly. He was most exquisitely got up, but his sad bulk, clothed in so much blue satin, gave him the appearance of an eiderdown, his bloated legs, so finely stockinged, and his feet so elegantly shod, hanging like those of a marionette whose strings had been loosed. And yet he seemed to be listening intently and speaking with awareness – and with none of the excitability of the time before.

When the ambassador withdrew, the usher took a step forward. 'Colonel Hervey, Your Majesty.'

The King nodded, and Hervey approached.

'Your Majesty,' he said quietly, bowing.

'Matthew,' began the King; 'it is so very good you are come.'

Hervey was taken aback on hearing his name. 'Sire.'

There was a moment or two in which the King said nothing, seeming to struggle for breath a little. Then he smiled ever so slightly, almost resignedly. 'So very good of you. I was most grateful for your letter. I might have been there, with you – would have, you know, were it not for ... It is so damnably ill for men to do as they did – burn barns, offer violence. And you, your dragoons, apprehending them – admirable, admirable. You shall have some recognition.'

'Sire, I did my duty, as any man. I merit no recognition.'

'You will be so good as to allow me to be the judge of that.'

The regal rebuke was nicely done. 'Sire.'

The King shook his head slowly. 'I am grievously saddened that my subjects think so ill of their sovereign as to scorn him in his own park.'

This was not the occasion to discourse on the condition of England, troubled or otherwise. Besides, Hervey felt compassion – a surprisingly profound compassion – for this unhappy ruler, who knew, surely, his time of judgement was near (and not merely in the reckoning of his subjects). He put the carriage priming aside, though not quite completely. 'It is infamous, sire, no matter from what grievances the action springs.'

'You think their grievances just, do you?'

Hervey felt emboldened enough to speak what might be thought only obvious. 'England is indeed a blessèd plot, sire, but a *demi*-paradise only.'

The King seemed to smile. 'You have wit, Matthew. It is most apt.'

'Sire.'

'But you do your duty unflinchingly, and are in no doubt what is that duty.'

'As all my dragoons, sire.'

The King seemed to smile again. 'I wish ... I wish you had come earlier to court – before ...' He held out a hand as if to indicate a body that was not his own. 'Ichabod, Matthew: the glory has departed.'

'Your Majesty's enemies have much detained me abroad, sire.'

177

The King appeared to chuckle. 'Well, well, it is all for the best, I suppose. You will come again?'

Hervey was surprised at the note of request. 'Sire, I am at your command.'

'Well, well.' The King turned to his chamberlain. 'I shall retire now to dine.'

Hervey stepped back.

'Good night, Matthew.'

'Good night, Your Majesty.'

He bowed, very formally, as the King rose unsteadily and began his withdrawal.

Cornet St Alban returned to his side. 'Colonel, Sir Henry Hardinge asks to see you.'

Hervey nodded absently, his mind still with the King. 'He wore the look of death, St Alban.'

And the death of a king – even this despised king – was not to be contemplated without disquiet. Shelley might well write of 'graves' – the 'princes' (among England's other corruptions), 'the dregs of their dull race' – from which 'a glorious Phantom may Burst, to illumine our tempestuous day'; but what emerged from the sepulchre was not always luminous. Far from it.

'Colonel?'

He woke. 'Yes, of course. Sir Henry Hardinge.'

They made their way to the further corner, where the Secretary at War stood talking with Lord Rosslyn, Privy Seal.

Hardinge beckoned him, the Privy Seal taking his leave with an exchange of nods that seemed to settle a matter of some moment.

'Colonel Hervey, I am very glad we meet at last. Indeed, I'm astonished we never met before. I've heard much of you of late, and will do so in future I've no doubt.' He let go of his left arm, which his right had been supporting, and offered his hand.

'Thank you, Sir Henry. I saw your "fighting cocks" charge at Orthez.'

The duke himself had given them their name – the little army of Portugal, dressed by London and led by some of his best officers.

The Secretary at War smiled fondly. 'Devil of a man to manage, the Portugais, but once under discipline he's a deuced fine soldier.'

'Indeed.' Hervey did not speak of his own, more recent, experience, which had confirmed his opinion of many years – sad as it was that Portugais should be set against Portugais in the present war of the two brothers contending for the throne.

'But I must be brief, Hervey, for the King has retired and we're summoned to his table. Your action last week over the incendiarists: admirable, admirable – its promptitude and resolve, and not least its restraint; especially its restraint. We're in for a hard season of this sort. And it'll be the very devil if there's too great a repression – and even worse if there's insufficient. Lord Hill is to see you, I know, next week. Your capability in this will be most prized. And now I must bid you goodbye, but I hope we shall meet with more leisure ere too long.'

Hervey turned to St Alban when he was gone. 'He wishes to commend us for the affair in the park last week, as did His Majesty. Who would have thought such a little thing would command the attention of the King and his ministers? There is patently intelligence of which we are wholly unaware . . . But come; we must go have our supper before the hungry "civilians" take our rations.'

The room had now become two slow-moving streams, the lesser one towards the furthest door and the semi-state apartments where the King would preside, and the far greater stream towards the Waterloo Room, as it was to be known when the King had finished with its decoration. Here and there, like rocks dividing the waters, stood two or three individuals intent still on their tête-à-tête, so that there was no very great hurry in the general progress, though Hervey was determined not to allow his uniformed advance to be checked by ambling gents in plain clothes, and their equally unhurried ladies.

But then he himself checked. Indeed, stock still.

There stood Kat, one of the 'rocks' close on the dais – as arresting as the first time he saw her.

For what seemed an age he could not move. Or could not determine which way. Flight was instinctive but insupportable; evasion unmanly.

'St Alban, you will excuse me for a moment,' he said softly – so softly indeed that the cornet was at first solicitous.

'May I be of help, Colonel?'

'No ... thank you. Take your place at the tables. Speak with young Fane, or who you will. I'll join you presently.'

He stood a while longer, observing at a distance, trying to gauge Kat's disposition.

She looked happy – if not playful, as before, still with that power of attraction which, even now as the tables summoned, was adding numbers to her little court.

But how should he approach? He must not discomfit her in front of those who might notice. But if he stood at a distance until he caught her eye, how might that serve?

And then came the consideration – he saw now too well – that ought to have been his first: would she welcome seeing him at all?

That, however, was a question he could not answer now; nor perhaps at any time unless directly by Kat herself. And of the other two considerations, each seemed as bad as the other – save that presenting himself was more gentlemanlike than havering at a remove.

He threw his shoulders back and strode resolutely to where she stood.

Kat saw, and looked square at him as he halted before her (had she seen him earlier, before he had seen her?), and with not the slightest symptom of dismay held out her hand.

Hervey kissed it with (he trusted) appropriate decorum.

'Colonel Hervey, it is so very good to see you. You are well, I hope?'

'Very well, ma'am. And you?'

'As you see, I trust, Colonel,' she replied, with the smile that had first beguiled him. 'You know Lords Warrender and Tullamore, and Sir Hugh Alvanley,' (she indicated each, and he bowed); 'this is Colonel Matthew Hervey, who commands the Sixth Light Dragoons.'

They in turn bowed.

'Now, if you would excuse me, gentlemen, I would have a word with the Colonel concerning a mutual acquaintance, and I must not delay before dinner.'

The two peers and the knight of the shires bowed again and took their leave, with looks of curiosity as to who was this lieutenant-colonel of cavalry whose name was unknown to them – save, perhaps, some collateral line of the Bristols – but who displaced them in the attention of Lady Katherine Greville, still one of the brightest ornaments of the London drawing room.

'Well, Matthew,' she began, lifting her head to meet his gaze.

And Hervey could say nothing, her ease towards him so unexpected.

'Well?' she pressed him, but gently.

'I . . . I did not expect to see you here. I had no idea . . . I . . . You look quite remarkably well.'

She smiled. 'I have not been ill, Matthew.'

'No, no . . . of course.'

She looked, indeed, just as she had when he had last seen her – not in the least reduced by motherhood (as she had so feared she would be). Her figure was not an inch altered, her eyes shone as bright as ever, and her complexion remained that of a woman half her age – her blush, if anything, yet more tempting.

'And you too are well, Matthew?'

'Yes . . . yes, I am very well.'

'And all else is well?'

'All else? Yes . . . I think . . . very well.'

'You sound unsure, Matthew. Your regiment is well found?'

'Ah, oh . . . the regiment . . . yes, indeed; very well found, thank

181

you.' He glanced somewhat anxiously towards the furthest door. 'But are you not summoned to the King?'

She smiled again. 'The King will wait, Matthew. Do you yourself stay?'

'I? Oh, I shall take a little to eat with my orderly officer and then drive to Hounslow, not late.'

'Will you visit with me, Matthew – when you are able?'

'Kat, I . . . that is . . .'

'Soon, for there is much that it would be pleasant to speak of.'

He swallowed. 'I will, yes.'

There were but a few left in the room now, who may have been studying them or not, but Kat was indifferent to their interest. She smiled at him with a warmth he'd not felt since leaving her eighteen months ago.

'I shall go now, Matthew, but I'm glad you'll visit with me. And soon.'

And she kissed him – and none too fleetingly – then turned and walked from the room with the greatest self-possession.

He ate little and spoke even less, and on the drive home was all but silent. At the Berkeley Arms he thanked Corporal Wakefield, acknowledged the salutes of the two dragoons who had returned on relief from Windsor, bade St Alban good night and climbed the stairs to his solitary quarters. He thought perhaps that he had never quite known his true feelings for Kat, but that now he did. Yet she would for ever be disunited with him, and he with her. He knew now, therefore, exactly to what he was condemned. The regiment of dragoons at his command could not suspend that sentence; but, for the time being at least – for the next three, four or even five years – they must wholly preoccupy him. There was no other way.

XI

THE SECRET THINGS

Three days later

'And he will not withdraw his accusation – not on any account?'

Malet shook his head. 'No, Colonel. He is in an altogether recalcitrant frame of mind.'

'Do you believe he truly considers he is in the right?'

Malet raised his eyebrows. 'Kennett is of the frame of mind that considers it his right to do much as he pleases.'

Hervey turned to the RSM. 'Mr Rennie?'

'For my part, Colonel, I have interrogated Serjeant-Major Collins and am of the opinion that his testimony is entirely truthful.'

'Solomon, were he to examine this affair, might conclude that since this is a matter of intent and perception, both may be entirely truthful – which I am prepared to believe; indeed, it would be infamous to suggest that an officer or a serjeant-major would speak other than the truth.' (He knew he said it more for effect than with conviction.) 'But Solomon was his own lawmaker; I myself cannot order that the baby be cut in two.'

Rennie stood impassively, Malet less so. 'There's now talk in the officers' house, Colonel.'

Hervey looked at Rennie.

'And in my mess, too, Colonel – I'm sorry to say.'

Hervey was unsurprised; it could only have been a matter of time. 'And Kennett does duty now at St James's?'

'Yes, Colonel. I sent him there – or rather, Captain Worsley did – to do duty with Harrison and the War Office party.'

'Much the best way. And Collins, Mr Rennie?'

'He remains at duty, Colonel, which I believe is the proper way – as well as being best for the troop.'

Hervey nodded. It was not the RSM's to remove any NCO from duty, but his opinion was – or very nearly – all. 'Much for the best, in both cases. Very well, Malet: you had better have everything rendered in writing, on oath. That at least ought to buy a month's peace. And who knows what will happen in that time – though the auguries aren't good. I might speak with Lord George Irvine.'

The serjeant-major braced. 'Carry on, Colonel, please?'

'Carry on, Mr Rennie. And thank you.'

He turned to Malet when the door was closed.

'For a guilder I'd . . .' He shook his head. 'I'm damned if Collins will be subjected to court martial. There must be another way. I'll speak with the Adjutant-General's office at the Horse Guards this afternoon, after the conference.'

Malet nodded. 'Indeed, Colonel, you'd better start out at once. The sky looks heavy again.'

Hervey agreed, and after a few more words on regimental routine, and several signatures, he put down his coffee cup, gathered up the papers on his desk, took his cloak and cap, and swept out of the orderly room.

'I shan't suppose I'll be returned before watch-setting,' he told Malet as he got into the chaise, 'but if there's anything to be acted on in advance of that I'll send word via the War Office party. Lord Hill's perfectly capable of springing a surprise.'

An hour and three-quarters later he got down at the Horse Guards in the arcade beneath the commander-in-chief's office – the only road-metal free of snow he'd seen since leaving Hounslow. Fairbrother had travelled with him, intending on going to Guy's hospital to see General Gifford again – and thence to the theatre, and the night coach back to Hounslow after supper.

'Give my respects to the general if it seems appropriate,' said Hervey as he bid him goodbye. (He might perhaps have gone in person to pay his respects, though he was not closely acquainted with Gifford; but a drive the other side of the river would not help his return at a decent hour.)

A sentry of the Blues came to attention as he made for the peculiarly unceremonious entrance to the headquarters of His Majesty's Land Forces.

Inside he announced himself and was taken to a meeting room overlooking the empty parade-ground, where half a dozen officers were already gathered. Three he knew, and the other three he knew *of* – six lieutenant-colonels of cavalry, two of them commanding. Five more arrived in the course of the next quarter of an hour, and two staff officers from the headquarters and a clerk from the Home department. Coffee, chocolate and madeira kept them entertained the while, as well as reminiscences – occasionally even of Waterloo.

At eleven o'clock precisely Lord Hill appeared.

The room bowed as one.

'Good morning, gentlemen.'

His geniality was undiminished by the cares of office, though his coat had become undeniably tighter, and his pate shinier yet. Hervey swelled with the pride of his acquaintance.

He went round the room shaking hands and passing remark, until everyone was greeted by name. 'Well, well – please be seated. I shall not detain you long, though I shall ask of you a good deal.'

They took their places round a large, oval table covered in green baize.

'Gentlemen, the Home department, it seems, is in possession of intelligence that would suggest an increase in violent disorder

will follow when winter is finished, on account of a general suscep-
tibility to treasonable acts, and also the depressed state of
agricultural wages.'

Hervey heard this with a degree of misgiving. He had suffered the
Home department's alarms before, though if Lord Hill spoke in
these terms it could not be without foundation. The prospect of a
summer campaign against a new 'peasants' revolt' was not a happy
one.

'The prime minister has been considering a scheme of dividing
the country into districts of about ten thousand persons, each
under the control of a half-pay military or naval officer who would
be responsible for the prevention of crime and the maintenance of
order . . .'

This he heard with grave misgiving too. Cromwell's 'rule of the
major-generals' would be no more palatable to the country for the
martial lawyers being demoted to colonel and commodore.

But he was not alone. 'So far, however, it appears that the scheme
has not found favour with the cabinet,' continued Lord Hill, giving
away nothing yet of his own estimation. 'Therefore, *rebus sic
stantibus*, the responsibility for order remains with the lieutenancies
and their magistrates, who as you are aware may call on the assistance of the military.'

And always did so, reckoned Hervey – and either too readily,
when instead a decent parish constable or two would have done the
job, or else too late and the military were obliged then to use
uncommon force ('a switch in time saves nine').

'The duke is of the opinion that cavalry are the only effectual
troops for the maintenance of order – in terms of celerity and, shall
we say, reliability – in the country districts especially, and also that
the yeomanry are superior too in this respect.'

Hervey blinked. He had long stopped calling yeomen 'cat
shooters', but he was in no doubt that their discipline and
capability stood in markedly poor relation to the regulars.

Lord Hill's thoughts had, as before, anticipated the same. 'That,

I'm sure, will run counter to your instincts or even experience. But the duke is of the opinion that calling out the yeomanry shows to the disaffected that the loyal are both willing and able to put them down if they resort to physical force.'

Undeniably it did, Hervey would concede, but fairly or unfairly the yeomanry's local connections also gave them the character of parties to a dispute. Besides, at harvest time a large number of officers and men were occupied in gathering in their crops.

'However, in more exigent circumstances support to the yeomanry may become necessary, and the duke wishes, with a view to that support being given expeditiously, to set in hand a contingent scheme of rapid reinforcement, which is the reason for your forgathering.'

Hervey groaned inwardly. He had quite enough on his plate without making contingent schemes.

'The Home department and the War Office, with my headquarters, will compile the schedule of support, but it is first necessary to have a thoroughgoing appraisal of the yeomanry and their country. This appraisal has already begun with the scrutiny of routine reports and returns, but I consider your *coup d'oeil* to be indispensable. In short, gentlemen, I wish to receive from you your assessment of those commanding the yeomanry, and the evils particular to their counties, and the most effectual way in which support might therefore be given.'

Hervey groaned again. This was not the work of a few days.

'My staff here' (he indicated the officers from the Horse Guards) 'will give you your individual assignments and make the necessary arrangements. It is my hope – my intention – that this schedule be complete by the first day of April, and I should be obliged therefore if your appreciations are severally received by the last day of March, though in the case of the far distant yeomanries there may be some stay. I might add that not every yeomanry is to be examined, only those adjudged to be in the shires most susceptible. And that the survey is to be conducted with the greatest discretion.'

Hervey was glad at least of the need for urgency. He must trust that fortune and good sense assigned him the Oxford – or, better yet, the Wiltshire – yeomanry.

'I think I have made myself clear, gentlemen, but if you have questions of me then I am content to hear them.'

There were none (probably because it would imply either that Lord Hill had *not* made himself clear, or that the questioner was a fool).

'Very well, gentlemen, I thank you and bid you good day,' adding as he turned to leave, 'Colonel Hervey, a word if you please.'

Hervey followed him from the room, conscious (and by no means unappreciatively) that eyes were cast in his direction.

Snow swirled over the parade-ground, a pretty enough sight this side of the great Venetian window in the commander-in-chief's office, but a decided hindrance to the early completion of their mission.

'Sit you down.'

Hervey took one of the two upright chairs in front of the commander-in-chief's desk, and Lord Hill the other.

'That was a deuced-smart little affair of yours at Windsor. You saw the duke in the course of it, did you not?'

'I did, General, when I was at the castle seeking the Grenadiers' help.'

'Well, as you might suppose, he thinks highly of your address. He is in a most sanguinary state of mind at present.'

'You don't concur in this, sir?'

'In acting with address? I do most certainly, as well you should expect.'

Hervey's instinct was to beg pardon for implying otherwise, but he said nothing; it was Lord Hill who had made for equivocation with his 'sanguinary'.

'I confess that I am, however, exercised by the state of incipient disorder, and our own incapacity to stem it by the immediate application of force. The duke places much importance on this survey of the yeomanry. I believe he's set his mind against all further concessions to the radicals; the affair of the Catholics was a most bruising one and put him out of favour with the King for a while, to the detriment of much business.'

For all his Tory principles, Hervey had never been able to share the duke's antipathy to some further measure of relief for the Catholics, though he had to admit that he had but a poor measure of experience of Ireland compared with its former chief secretary. It seemed to him that too many of his fellow-countrymen – those that had not served (served, that is, in the Peninsula) – conflated the religion of the Pope with, at best, a drag anchor on the ship of progress, a force that would permanently dim the Enlightenment (extinguish it if it could), or else, at worst, a plague-like thing spread by priestly black rats, that would enervate the nation to the point that its enemies might take possession without a fight. Yes, in the Peninsula he had seen much that was akin to superstition – *was* superstition – but it had been harmless enough. And at times he had seen its beneficial effect. He did not give these matters great thought, it was true (not any longer), but it seemed to him that the stern avoidance of sin, as defined with such chilling completeness in the Prayer Book's *Commination*, so often the mainstay of his own church, was alone too arid a doctrine. But the Catholic relief measure was now carried, and the country was neither benighted nor plagued – and so perhaps might it also be with Reform? What terrible things it risked, though. But, he reckoned, the duke must know his business – if, that is, command of the country were anything like command of an army . . .

'It seems the cruellest of things, sir, that having fought so long against the Great Disturber we should now face disturbance as great at home.'

'Quite, Hervey. And there's no doubt – I speak very plainly with you – that the late retrenchment leaves us in a most perilous position were the country to fall into general tumult. Disbanding so many of the yeomanry was a short-sighted expedient which we're paying for already – I hardly need tell you.'

No indeed, thought Hervey; Worsley's troop might as well have been renamed 'Berkshire Yeomanry'.

'The duke himself has also formed, I believe, a greater notion of their worth.'

Hervey began wondering to what this was all tending, and whether its purpose might not be solely to allow the commander-in-chief to speak his thoughts with someone other than his staff (and who was not therefore obliged to give them expression in orders to the army), or one who might relate them elsewhere. That Lord Hill chose to do so with a former galloper of his was perhaps not so astounding, but it nevertheless demanded some consideration.

'When you are returned, Hervey, you are to come and speak with me about all that you find, in addition to rendering the specific intelligence in writing.'

'With pleasure, General.'

'I think Norfolk the very place to gauge things.'

Hervey's heart sank: Norfolk – distant and broad, not a task of a few days.

'You're not pleased at the prospect?'

'In truth, General, I'd expected – hoped – to be assigned Berkshire, or Wiltshire . . . Oxford, perhaps.'

Lord Hill's expression was suddenly turned wry. 'Well, there ain't any yeomanry in Berkshire, as you know too well, and your letter contained all that there's need of for the schedule there; and Wiltshire's the one place where I'm confident the yeomanry's well found and the arrangements on a sure footing. Norfolk, on the other hand, is a deuced difficult county; if trouble were to become widespread there the call on regular troops would be prodigious. We must make the most expeditious, the most economical, provisions. Norfolk's a weather vane.'

'I understand, General.'

Lord Hill rose. 'Besides, is there not someone there who is overdue a call? Is not that admirable fellow Peto in want of company?'

Hervey smiled. Surely this man was the most genial, the most amiable of generals? Not for nothing had his nickname with the troops been 'Daddy', such was his solicitude. 'Indeed, sir.'

And then the countenance became grave again. 'You'll have heard of the Gifford business? Infamous.'

'I have, sir.'

'The Home department believes it may be all of a piece with that of which we've been speaking.' He shook his head. 'Assaults on military officers in the street . . . Unspeakable.'

Hervey frowned. 'I'm doubtful of that, General. It was my good friend Captain Fairbrother who came on him directly afterwards. According to a witness the assailant had called out a different name, seeming to mistake him for another.'

'Indeed? I had not heard it . . . Your friend came upon him in the street, you say?'

'And took him to Guy's hospital.'

''Pon my word. Then it's from him that my information shall come in this matter. Did he say how Gifford came to be in such an insalubrious place at such an hour? That damned rookery close by.'

'Is it really so insalubrious a place, m'lord? I don't think Fairbrother would be given to it were it so. I understand it to be a regular short cut between the Theatre Royal and the Strand.'

Lord Hill made no reply to the particular, sensing perhaps the difficulty in suggesting that his friend had somehow descended to the nether regions. 'A deuced mysterious business, be what may. A general officer cut down in the street . . . I call it a matter for the closest study.'

Hervey took his cue to leave, bowing and assuring the commander-in-chief that he would lose no time in setting out for Norfolk, and returning as promptly to relate his findings.

'And my compliments to your friend Fairbrother in his address that evening. I should have been bereft had Gifford died. His work on the estimates is invaluable.'

191

'With pleasure, my lord.'

'A most useful sort of man.'

'General Gifford?'

'Fairbrother – *fidus Achates*.'

Hervey smiled. 'Yes, yes indeed.'

'The electrical exploder – that was he, was it not?'

'It was.'

'Mm. Well, I might send for him about Gifford.'

'I'll inform him, my lord.'

Hervey left the Horse Guards with the most elegant of portfolios – all chased leather, red, with the royal cipher embossed in gold – and within a sheaf of instructions, letters of introduction, authorizations, money orders and requisition forms. He supposed he ought to return it when his assignment was over, but it would make a fine present for Georgiana when at length he was able to see her . . .

It was not yet one o'clock, but matters were pressing. He sent word to Corporal Wakefield at the light horse stables to bring the chaise to the United Service at four, where in the meantime he would write letters – letters arising from his (frankly) unwelcome assignment; and then pay what calls he could – that is to say, felt able to – before returning to Hounslow.

One letter he would write with the greatest of pleasure. The sole consolation of his wintry sojourn to that most singular of counties – where, like the King, the true glory had departed, leaving but melancholy fragments of what had been (though he had to admit that he visited but the once, and very briefly, after Waterloo) – would be to see his old and most excellent friend, most admirable of men, Captain Sir Laughton Peto RN, late of the command of His Majesty's Ship *Prince Rupert*, wounded most grievously at Navarino two years before, and now 'beached' most terribly in his native county, albeit in the care of that most patriotic of men, the Marquess of Cholmondeley . . .

But he knew he would have to curtail his calls that evening, sparing only those of business – the agents, and his bank. In any event, he had thought better of troubling Lord George Irvine again so soon after taking command, for the unpleasant details of Tyrwhitt, and now Kennett (there was little, if anything, the colonel could do in either regard), would suffice in writing. And Kat ... well, he trusted he was not evading his promise at Windsor by writing that circumstances now prevented his paying her a call at an early date (he would explain with as much candour as possible that duties took him with little notice to Norfolk, and that he thought he might be detained there a month, perhaps more, though he certainly hoped not to be). Though he would evade, and prudently, he considered, any particular promise on return, for their encounter at Windsor had left a corner of his mind in little short of turmoil. As for Princess Lieven's supper, he could now send word – even at so late an hour – that by the command of Lord Hill he must make haste on an assignment of the utmost importance (it amused him to think how she would at once set her mind to discovering what occupied Lord Hill). It would vex her, he knew full well, but it was undoubtedly for the best. He ought also to send word for Fairbrother, but he had no very clear notion of where to send word to, for he would surely by now have left Guy's hospital – and Covent Garden was a large place to scour. But first things first – or rather, and for once, family affairs first. He owed his people a longer missive than he'd so far managed, and Georgiana deserved more than a pretty piece of leather; he would devote the rest of the afternoon to making amends.

And so when the regimental chariot drew up just as the bells of St Martin's church were carrying the hour along Pall Mall, he was ready to return alone to Hounslow to put in hand the arrangements for his expedition to the country of Boadicea, whose deeds had thrilled him as an ink-fingered boy at Shrewsbury – difficult as it now was to imagine the blood of the Iceni flowing in the veins of the North-folk. And well it were so: for with the whole of the yeomanry disbanded the length and breadth of East Anglia, none to call on from Suffolk or Cambridge, nor even Lincolnshire (more regulars stationed in Gibraltar than in all of those counties put together), what a perilous state of affairs Canning's government had bequeathed the duke with their retrenchment. 'When you are returned you are to come and speak with me about all that you find', Lord Hill had said. And it was a fine thing to have the confidence of the commander-in-chief so, and a compliment that he should have been singled out for the most perplexing of the reconnaissances. In so short a time, though, might he even begin to make sense of what Nelson's county needed? Better not to ponder on the responsibility too greatly.

Besides, all this was nothing compared with the immediate exigencies of the regiment (as well as his own). Nothing could happen in respect of Collins during his absence, for without a major at regimental duty, he could not anyway delegate his full powers of command. The delay in taking statements of evidence, all of it on oath, would be helpful; he expected to return before the ink was dry. And in that time, as he'd expressed to Malet, cooler counsels might prevail with Kennett. That said, he must at least consider the worst case, and therefore what more direct action he might take. It was the very devil, and he knew of no precedent to guide him. As for the minutiae of command, which in aggregate made the difference between a good and an indifferent regiment, all he could do was give general orders and directives, then trust to the good sense of Malet, Mr Rennie and such others of the Sixth as were to exercise their executive authority in his absence. It need not concern him overmuch. It was the deucedest thing, though, to be detached from command within a fortnight of assuming it – even allowing that his assignment was of the utmost importance to the King's peace. He must simply make of it what he could. After all, he would at long last see Peto, and if there were ever a man to talk with about the vicissitudes of command it was he.

XII

NELSON'S COUNTY

Next day

Despise Bonaparte as he did, Hervey had always embraced the
Great Disturber's caution to his generals – 'Ask of me anything but
time'. The whole of the day after his meeting with Lord Hill he
spent at office – from dawn until late in the evening – while arrangements were made for the journey. Much of what he attended to was
in its way routine, but things would be so much more to his liking
thereby on return. And he was determined to leave on Saturday
morning as soon as the sun was up.

Matters at office proceeded smoothly save in one respect:
Fairbrother was not inclined to accompany him, and resisted all
attempts to be persuaded otherwise. He claimed incipient malady,
pressing affairs of business, undertakings given to General Gifford,
an aversion to 'tractless paths of boundless void' (as he understood
Norfolk to be at this time), and a desire to visit with several
acquaintances for reasons varied and unrelenting – though he conceded that in a month or so if Hervey's duties detained him in the
north he would be glad to come to his assistance.

And indeed, after Hervey's initial disappointment – dismay – at
not having the company of one with whom he might converse freely

and whose opinion he valued so highly, he saw that in truth Fairbrother might be more of help to him where he lay than in Nelson's county. He therefore put a number of affairs of his own into the hands of his friend (how apt was Lord Hill's appellation *fidus Achates* – the faithful Trojan, companion of Aeneas, who was the favourite of Apollo), and urged him also, when his particular business had been completed, and his visits made and his incipient malady overcome, to travel to Wiltshire to see his people – a *voerloper* as the Cape Dutch had it, telling all that he could in anticipation of the eventual, keenly looked-to return of the ever-absent son, brother, and father.

But although he, Hervey, was – and always had been – content enough with his own company, the mission on which he was to embark seemed to him to demand some interlocutor of sorts. There was a deal of evidence to be gathered and 'rendered in writing', there would be supplementary particulars to follow up once the day's collecting had been assessed; and the sheer size of the county . . . He would need the properties of St Anthony of Padua to be in two places at once.

And he allowed himself a smile unexpectedly, such that Malet remarked on it and asked if all was well.

'Not St Anthony,' he replied, 'but St Alban.'

'Colonel, I would share your amusement if you would share your joke.'

'I shan't try your devotion, Malet; I was merely amused by the process by which I'd arrived at the answer.'

'The answer to . . . ?'

'Who shall accompany me. I need an adjutant, and since I cannot spare you – since it is you who will be exercising command for me – I must choose another. St Alban has the capability, and very possibly too a useful standing with the families of the county.'

And so St Alban was duly warned for duty.

The Horse Guards' arrangements were generous, providing for the hire of a hack post chaise, but Hervey had decided to post as well with the regimental chariot and Corporal Wakefield, with Johnson and another, and the two vehicles proceeding in convoy. Malet argued that it would be prudent to have Serjeant Acton accompany them, but Hervey countered that it was hardly a hazardous assignment and he did not want an *entourage* – just a second dragoon for the hack chaise to ride postilion, a man capable with harness and the like. All was therefore settled for the little party to leave the Berkeley Arms at nine o'clock the following morning, and at ten o'clock that evening Hervey at last left the barracks as confident as might be that he had left no 'i' undotted and no 't' uncrossed, and that any unforeseen dots and crosses would be placed precisely where he would wish them.

'Only keep Collins from a court martial until my return,' he said to Malet on leaving. 'The regimental inquiry can be spun out a month, and then there will be legal opinion to seek, which ought well to take another month, especially if paid for by the day. And on no account are he and Kennett to do duty at one and the same time. Indeed it would be best for Kennett to be kept at some duty agreeable to him in London, or wherever can be.'

'You may be sure I will arrange it, Colonel.'

'And if there should be anything untoward, I have written to Lord George with an explanation of my absence and the circumstances, so he would be of assistance.'

Malet nodded, though he felt equally sure that he would not need to call on the assistance of the colonel.

'Well, I bid you good night then. Don't trouble to come out to see me off tomorrow. You have your parade and all.'

'I do, Colonel. I wish you a calm sea and a prosperous voyage – and a speedy return.'

'Aptly put for so salty a county,' said Hervey, with at last an easy smile; 'but I may assure you that the roughest of seas will not detain me there.'

*

By the time he returned to the Berkeley Arms the fires and the candles had burned low. Johnson had put a plate of cold chicken on the writing table, and a bottle of port, and Hervey sat down in front of the embers to eat his supper – with more duty than appetite, but pleased at last to be relieved of the work of the day.

But though content that at office he had done everything that duty and devotion could possibly expect of him, he could not be content that he had treated with Kat entirely honourably – a letter only, and not a very intimate one at that. Could he not have spared but one hour last evening? Except that it would not have been but an hour – though that was a matter for him, not the force of destiny, possessed as he was of free will. And he could hardly claim fear of prolongation as just excuse. Rightly, he could not claim fear of anything at any time, as a soldier, and as a gentleman. And for a moment or two he contemplated – wildly – riding now to Holland Park to put right his ill judgement (or whatever it was), only recalling himself to his senses on imagining the mortification that his knocking on the door in the early hours would occasion (Kat's establishment were the very models of loyalty and discretion, but there was no cause to try them so sorely). Instead, eased by the port and sobered by tomorrow's call of duty, he took to his bed.

They were away sharp at nine. It was his birthday, which he had only lately remembered, rather after the fashion of most years. Indeed, the last time he had marked the day had been in the icy fastness of Fort York, in Canada – a dozen years before, when Henrietta had got up a party, though heavy with child (or had it been when Georgiana was born, for he had been elsewhere on patrol in the weeks before her time was come?). Well, it mattered not; not in the least. There would never again be such a marking, he felt sure. Nor was it worth his regrets. This day was as yesterday or tomorrow; no more, no less. And there was business to be about.

They posted by way of Harrow to the Great North Road, changing again at Hatfield and Stevenage (passing close to Walden Park, where he supposed Kezia must be in residence yet – and with little more sentiment than mere recognition); and all the time keeping a steady trot, and with never more than two horses, in tandem, so that he was able to talk to St Alban without effort, while Johnson and Private Gilbee, St Alban's groom, enjoyed the comfort of the hack chaise, apprising him of the task in hand, how he intended going about it, and what difficulties might arise, until as the light was beginning to fail they reached Royston, and there spent the night at the Old Bull. And then, on the second day's posting, when St Alban had taken his place in the hack, and Johnson and Gilbee theirs in the respective baskets, he had been able to browse Pigot's *Directory of Norfolk, Leicestershire and Rutland*, make a beginning on Stacy's new *A Norfolk Tour* and study the maps which the Horse Guards had with commendable foresight procured for him – Bryant's newly issued sheets, 'Respectfully Dedicated to the Nobility, Clergy and Gentry of the County', 12¼ inches to 10 miles, from an 'actual survey' very lately, consisting in the most admirable and well-defined detail (though the Board of Ordnance had completed their own survey, their maps were still in draft). All in all, he trusted, Pigot, Stacy and Bryant presented him with a very fair portrait of the county.

The snow lay deep in the fields yet, but the ways were tolerable going, even after leaving the Great North Road, for the turnpike companies had set parties to work with the shovel, not wanting undue loss of revenue, and there had been no fresh falls for two days. When they resumed their journey, therefore, on the Newmarket turnpike, even though the country became more undulating their steady pace of the first day continued unchecked. They changed horses at Sawston and then Newmarket Heath, and again at Mildenhall, where they ate a fine venison stew, and then at Thetford before the lonely run to Attleborough, changing there for the last stretch to Wymondham, where with creaking leather and stiffening joints they at last pulled up for the night at the White Hart. Fresh horses were got at once for the hack chaise, however, for Hervey wanted St Alban to go that evening to Kimberley Park nearby (the moon was full and one of the White Hart's postboys knew the road well) to see if the lord lieutenant were at home, for he lived also beyond Norwich, and if he would receive him next day; otherwise he would drive to Norwich in the morning to see the Royals, the 1st Dragoons, the only regular troops in the county, save Marines, and thence to his seat at Witton. St Alban had returned by eight, however, with the news that the lord lieutenant would be glad to receive him at Kimberley at ten in the morning.

Kimberley Park, three miles north-west of Wymondham (which only now did Hervey learn was pronounced with a short 'y', and the 'm' and 'o' entirely silent), was the ancient seat of the Wodehouses, Tories among broad acres of Whigs. The hall was set amid some of the greatest oaks he could ever recollect, with a fine stream and lakes, and a park whose nobility – thanks to 'Capability' Brown – was evident even under its snowy blanket, with pleasances he would have wished to explore had it not been for duty. The carriages came to a halt on the hour, and servants were at once on hand to attend them.

The Honourable John Wodehouse, Lord Lieutenant of Norfolk, Custos Rotulorum, Vice Admiral of the County and Lord Steward of Norwich Cathedral, received them in the library before a good fire. He was a big, active-looking man of about sixty, with grey hair brushed forward covering his temples, kind eyes and a general expression of amiability. He began by saying that he feared Hervey's journey was 'somewhat otiose', for on receiving a letter from the Home department last month he had at once instigated measures for the re-raising of the yeomanry: 'I have only yesterday written to Mr Peel informing him that I have placed matters in hand to re-form four troops each with a strength of – to begin with – fifty officers and yeomen, and that these will be accoutred by sub-ventions from the Militia vote and armed with the sabres which were placed in Norwich castle on their disbandment, requesting also the necessary letters patent and the firelocks, powder and shot, and instructions as to pay.'

Hervey thought it all very admirable, but rather in advance of what he understood the Home department was intending – except, of course, that at the time of disbanding, His Majesty's Government had only been anxious to avoid the expense of keeping in being such of the yeomanry as had not been called out for some time, leaving it for the gentlemen of the corps to decide if they would continue in being entirely at their own expense. But it was no part of his remit to argue the Home Secretary's case; if the lord lieutenant were placing certain matters in hand then all he had need to do was judge their efficacy against what he knew to be the War Office's intentions.

'So you'll see, Colonel Hervey, that events have, as it were, overtaken your purpose in coming here. Within a month or so we shall have a troop once more at Downham, and at Dereham, Yarmouth and Halesworth.'

Hervey put him right regarding his mission, in particular the regular reinforcements that he was to judge expedient.

'Of course,' the lord lieutenant conceded affably, 'the regulars aren't my business, but I'm at a loss to understand how you are to decide matters before an application is made by the civil power. Do not mistake me, Colonel; I am heartened by this evidence of the authorities' forethought – the Horse Guards' forethought – which must proceed from the impulse of government; I detect the duke's hand in this for sure, and I'm glad of it – overdue as it may be.'

Hervey assured him that the Horse Guards' purpose was to be more 'anticipatory' than merely answering to the civil power, some degree of 'deterrent' effect perhaps – while, of course, the authority of the magistrates and the other officers of the law was in all things absolute: a regiment sent from London, say, might replace the Royals at Norwich, who in turn might disperse to support the troops of yeomanry, or they might disperse themselves throughout the county to give that support instead, or even in addition to, but also to act independently if the need arose – but be able to combine rapidly that they might scour the roads, for example, by day and by night, relay information, 'master' the country. His own assessment, from study of his maps and the census returns, had led him, he explained, to the same conclusions, broadly, as the lord lieutenant – that Yarmouth, Dereham and Downham were the appropriate towns in which to place the major elements of any reinforcement, but also Thetford, rather than Halesworth; and he wondered, too, about the influence the Royals – or whoever were the regular cavalry – would be able to retain in Norwich if there were a general tumult elsewhere in the county and their squadrons dispersed; for a city of sixty thousand could not be left to a mere depot troop.

And the lord lieutenant, seeing the evidence of the War Office's earnest and the address of the Horse Guards, told him that he placed himself at Hervey's disposal in the coming days – indeed, that his party should stay at Kimberley Park until he felt their work was done. And at a stroke Hervey perceived that his work thus changed from inquiry to confirmation – more exact, immeasurably easier and greatly quicker; and, indeed, altogether more agreeable.

So it proved. For a fortnight he travelled the county, though Halesworth he left to St Alban, and the northernmost parts he was assured were under the best regulation by the great families, and not therefore needing his personal attention. Everywhere he was received hospitably and with intelligence, so that he not only completed the assignment ahead of his best expectations but also formed a considerable attachment to the county – which he freely admitted was not that of his imaginings; at least, the 'slowness' of the people he instead began to see as more a worthy instinct for the better ways of times past than innate dullness – of times before, as one of the recusant gentry put it to him, 'the stripping of the altars'.

And what altars – what churches. He was compelled so many times to stop and gaze, or to enter and be astonished. It was as if he travelled in foreign parts, on some grand tour. What manner of place must this county have been five centuries ago, when these pinnacles, buttresses, clerestories, fan vaultings and hammer beams were fashioned – the people more numerous, the wealth much greater. And the towers – solid-square, as a keep, or round, like a turret; and reaching so high above land so plane that it seemed every prospect encompassed a dozen half-castles framed against a vast sky.

But his true instincts were never long repressed by mere sight-seeing. Was there ever such opportunity to master a country, to place it, as the French said, *sous surveillance*, as here? From the top of each tower, square or round, a corporal with a telescope might see everything that passed between him and the next. And, with but a little extemporization, some system of signalling might be devised to summon help rapidly in the case of mischief. He began relishing the possibility, the trial – pitting his regiment over such a distance against the dark forces of riot, mutiny, rebellion. And he put St Alban to work for a morning in the library at Kimberley to make a survey – the result heartening; indeed he thought it so promising that even had his survey of the yeomanry yielded nothing auspicious he could assure the Horse Guards they need have no fear of Norfolk. There were, outside the towns, a little short of five hundred churches. If half of these were to be made videttes it would render the better part of the whole county under the eye of authority – the work of but one battalion of Rifles, or, indeed, of any battalion of the Line practised in outpost duties. It was, he felt sure, a proposal that itself justified the entire wintry exercise, even had he not been able to make so expedient a report on the yeomanry.

And so after his grand tour of the county, during which the spring's thaw set in – which, though it made some of the roads heavy going, allowed him to observe how much of the country was under the plough rather than pasture – he visited the Royals once more to talk with their commanding officer, and then spent three days before the fire in the library at Kimberley compiling the report for the War Office, making a copy for the lord lieutenant and a second for himself, so that he could send his findings at once to the Horse Guards.

It was on the last day of the month, therefore, that with the greatest sense of satisfaction as well as of anticipation he at last felt able to visit his old and very dear friend Laughton Peto.

XIII

THE COMMODORE

1 March 1830

'I will tell you about Captain Peto,' he said, as they bid farewell to Kimberley Park and set off on the thirty miles to Houghton Hall in the north of the county. 'I met him when he was a frigate captain, almost fifteen years ago, and I was taking passage to India. And then again ten years on when he was commodore of the flotilla which attacked Rangoon, though we'd seen each other in the years between. And for Rangoon he was knighted, and very properly, for the business was done with great despatch. And then, with the reductions in the navy, he was for some time without a ship, until summoned to command of the *Prince Rupert*, the only first-rate in commission, and to take her to join Admiral Codrington's squadron in the Mediterranean.'

'Ah – Navarino.'

'Indeed – the "untoward event".'

Poor Codrington: told to cooperate with the French and the Russians to compel the Turks to leave Greek waters – but without resort to force – he had sought to overawe the Ottoman fleet in the bay at Navarino, in the Peloponnese, but it had come to a fight and the Turk had been sent to the bottom. London was furious: 'I send you the ribbon of the Garter,' the King wrote to Codrington; 'I should be sending you the rope.' But Peto was most grievously wounded in the battle.

'Indeed he is a cripple, a chair-bound invalid,' said Hervey, shaking his head. 'When I saw him last, two years ago or thereabout, it was the most pitiable sight, for he had lived for the sea ... But there's evidently much fellowship in the county, and Peto's being a Norfolk man – his late father a parson, like Nelson's – the Marquess of Cholmondeley took him in at Houghton.'

He did not say that Kat had made the arrangements, though he remembered her words as if yesterday – 'And George has most eagerly contracted to attend to all dear Captain Peto's needs until such time as he is able to return to his own house.'

She had never met Peto but knew of her lover's strong affection for him. Indeed, Hervey had wondered at her efforts on his old friend's behalf, so close to his wedding with Kezia, but had promptly dismissed his worst thoughts as unworthy. Besides, what did it matter what motive had secured for his friend such a comfortable convalescence?

But Peto had not yet returned to his own house. That much he knew. How might he ever return, indeed, needing the ministry of nursemaids? And where were the nursemaids to live – and the cook and the housemaids and the valet and all the others who would needs attend on him, for his house, he had always protested, was very small ('good only for a curate', he used to say)?

'I was William Cholmondeley's fag at Eton – the marquess's brother. He was not a hard taskmaster.'

Hervey, still contemplating his old friend's abject condition, scarcely heard. He pinched himself. 'Indeed?'

'Now he's member for Castle Rising, a stone's throw from Houghton – a rotten borough!'

Hervey frowned. 'St Alban, you try me.'

But St Alban was not going to allow the opportunity to pass.

'Truly, Colonel, how can it serve that another green mound, like Old Sarum, returns a member – two members indeed – and Birmingham none?'

Hervey sighed indulgently. 'I suppose you might argue that if our forefathers, who strove so manfully to make a parliament, chose to dispose the seats in this way, who now should gainsay them?'

'Colonel, are not members of parliament meant to be lawmakers, not antiquarians?'

Hervey smiled. 'Castle Rising is, I grant you, from what I observed when we came out of Linn Regis, a place that might not justify returning two members – or, I grant you, even one. But hard cases make bad laws, as I've said before. So how does a good Whig square his conscience and accept a rotten borough?'

St Alban smiled by return. 'Cholmondeley is a Tory, Colonel. Perhaps in the circumstances – our going to Houghton and all – it is better that I do not speak of Reform.'

'I think so too. We are here, after all, for the preservation of the peace, not to excite tumult. Besides, I shouldn't want to be denied the best port.'

They went by way of Dereham, which they'd visited earlier and knew there were good post-horses to be got, and Fakenham, which they'd not seen, and where they rested the Dereham hirelings – excellent clean-limbed trotters – and ate a hearty stew of mutton. Their progress had been slow on account of the roads – cross roads not turnpikes – which would have been better going before the thaw; and also to spare the horses, for they were unsure if they'd find a change at Fakenham (which in the event, they did not, the place keeping changes only for 'The Hero' plying between Linn and Cromer). So on they drove for Houghton with the tiring roadsters and the no less wearying Corporal Wakefield and his fellow postilion.

The Linn road, fortunately, was flat, turnpiked and in good repair, but they took it at just a jogging trot, and stretches walking, for Hervey had told Corporal Wakefield that they'd be out again in the morning and he didn't wish to beg fresh horses. It was a full two hours after leaving the Red Lion in Fakenham, therefore, that they turned off for New Houghton – 'new' not because, like so many villages in the county, the Black Death had carried off the old, but because a century before, the prime minister – the *first* prime minister, Sir Robert Walpole – had uprooted the old (save the church) to make way for his great new house and its park. But Sir Robert had done his tenants well, reckoned Hervey, seeing how good and large were the cottages – profit too of the public purse.

And what profit: the drive from lodge to house was as splendid as any he'd seen – ancient oaks, sweet chestnut, so many deer as to be uncountable, and the house itself greater than Longleat, perhaps even Wilton. What a piece of work this Walpole must have been, who 'judged of men's worth by the weight of their fee'. And then an earldom . . . Yet, as in Adam, all die; and Walpole had been dust these many years. Was all this a monument to anything worthy? He began to grow restless. He was uncertain whether he could like this present *châtelain*, for all his hospitality to Peto.

And then he shook himself. He had a strange disposition to resentment – 'strange' because, as a steadfast Tory, he believed essentially in the old order of things. 'Are you well acquainted with the family, would you say, St Alban?'

After so prolonged a silence his travelling companion was a little taken aback. 'I . . . I am acquainted, Colonel, yes. But I cannot claim intimacy.'

'Mm.'

'Is there anything you wish to know? I—'

Hervey waved a hand. 'No matter. We shall see what we shall see.'

But if St Alban would have known more, and Hervey, their thoughts were diverted now by the appearance of several footmen, who beckoned Corporal Wakefield towards an arch beneath the *piano nobile*, like that at the Horse Guards.

'My dear friend!'

The voice boomed in the arcade as if through a speaking-trumpet.

Hervey saw and was astonished: Peto, standing. A stick, yes, and his right sleeve tucked in a pocket – but upright, and . . . *hale*.

'I spied you half a mile distant. On watch since four bells!' He advanced determinedly, and none too stiffly, thrusting out his left hand.

Hervey took it and tried to summon words adequate for the miraculous transformation of the man he had called an *invalide*. 'My dear, dear Peto – I'm . . . all astonishment. I . . .'

'Salt baths, Hervey. Every day for a year. And walks in yonder park. And the deucedest fine nursing a man ever had.'

Hervey shook his head in disbelief, still clutching the hand. 'The nation owes Lord Cholmondeley a debt it can never repay!'

Peto nodded decidedly. 'The best of men, Hervey; the best of men. I'm only sorry he's not at home . . . But there's other company – but now, who's your friend?'

The 'friend' took a step forward and bowed. 'Cornet St Alban, Sir Laughton.'

'St Alban? There was a St Alban at Lissa – Hoste's flag lieutenant.'

'A cousin, Sir Laughton. Later captain of *Niobe*.'

'Indeed he was. Well, well.' He turned to Hervey with the look of the quarterdeck. 'And what was the signal Hoste raised before the action?'

Hervey looked bemused. 'I confess I know but the one – "England expects . . .".'

'Not so very far adrift, Hervey. Do *you* know, Mr St Alban?'

'"Remember Nelson", Sir Laughton.'

'By heavens, sir – exactly so! And you should've heard the cheering! Norfolk man, y'know, Hervey. Father was parson over at Ingol'thorpe. My God, how the parsonages of Norfolk have served this country! Married county, too – a Walpole. Fine woman. An' he died but fifteen months ago. What loss, what loss . . .'

Hervey was so moved by his old friend's animation that he

felt as if the lump in his throat would grow to choke him. Tears welled up.

'And— 'Pon my soul, is that you, Johnson?'

Johnson had got down from the second chaise, looking to make good his escape to the servants' hall. He braced. 'It is, sir. Very good to see you looking so well, if I might say so, sir.'

'You may. You may indeed.'

'Except that it is Corporal Johnson now,' said Hervey.

'Corporal, eh? Then I'll order grog for all hands.'

'Thank you, sir. Thank you very much,' chirped the half-frozen groom.

Peto's smile was ever broader. 'Now, Hervey, your dragoons and your horses will be given every comfort, and I shall seek the same for you and Cornet St Alban.' He turned and waved his stick in the air like a huntsman rallying hounds.

Footmen and grooms swarmed on the carriages. St Alban excused himself on the pretext of seeing up the papers.

Peto clasped Hervey's shoulder. 'Shall you first look over the house, or have some refreshment – tea, to restore; coffee, to rouse; or brandy, to invigorate perhaps?'

Hervey smiled. It was as if they were aboard *Nisus* again, when first they'd met – warily, to be sure, at first; and forged the firmest friendship on the long passage to India. 'It's already darkening too quickly to appreciate the house's evident superiority, and, besides, I came to see you, my dear friend, not Mr Kent.'

'Ah, so you are acquainted with the house?'

'Only from the directory with which I've been travelling. Houghton and a good many others. Tea?'

'Capital! Tea it is. And we shall take it like Christians. Besides, the family sold off the best pictures years ago.'

Nevertheless they passed along marbled corridors hung with paintings that, to Hervey's mind, were of the first quality. He supposed he had not seen *so* many great houses, but he had seen Blenheim; and here was display of that same order. They came eventually, however, to a drawing room that was imposing in its proportion and decoration yet comfortable in its furnishing. And a fire burned brightly, for which he was grateful.

'Yes, I had it built up with good Houghton lumber,' said Peto, tugging heartily on the bell-pull. 'And I threw on some tarred flotsam picked up on my rounds. It's been damnably cold without, but in here I might fancy myself in the Canaries of a winter. Here I spend a good part of every day on my manuscript – the affair at Navarino – my publisher awaits it eagerly – and where I take my refreshment too unless we dine in state – as we do this evening.'

Hervey shook his head in disbelief at what the Almighty – and his friend's own nature – had worked. 'I am just so very glad to see you restored so in both body and spirit.'

Peto looked pained suddenly. 'My dear Hervey, I assure you I was never deprived of spirit. I did my duty at Navarino, and that's everything to a man who wears the King's coat – as well you know.'

But what Hervey had been minded of, at least in part, was his sister: withdrawing her acceptance of Peto's offer of marriage had been the cruellest of things; as if – in what he supposed might be his friend's own words – a man-of-war had first been dismasted, and then raked from astern. It was not a thing he could have spoken of with St Alban, but it had preoccupied him during the drive – how he might broach the matter when he was come here.

His disquiet was at once proved unwarranted. Peto straightway made sail for close action, and with the greatest breeziness. 'Now tell me: how is your sister? Is she wed yet? Is she "Baroness", or whatever the rank may be?'

Hervey, quite taken aback, confessed that on all three counts the answer was in the positive. They were not the answers his old friend wished to hear – that he knew only too painfully – for he was no doubt ready to renew his offer, without prejudice so to speak, had Elizabeth's circumstances changed. And yet he detected no sign of disappointment – which he could only take as even more evidence of the resolution and courage that was characteristic of this most estimable of men.

The door opened and footmen appeared to begin the ceremony of tea. And with them came a woman of, by Hervey's rapid reckoning, eighteen or nineteen years – certainly not yet one and twenty.

Peto's face lit up as he advanced on their visitor and took her hand. 'Miss Rebecca, you are come most perfectly. May I present Colonel Hervey . . . Hervey, Miss Rebecca Codrington.'

Hervey bowed, though momentarily arrested by the name (he couldn't suppose she would be a Codrington of any other than the great admiral's family, the 'victor' of the 'Untoward Event'); and Rebecca Codrington curtsied.

'I have heard much about you, Colonel, in the past few days especially,' she said, with an openness and self-possession that belied her evident youth.

Peto felt he must explain. 'Miss Rebecca was taking passage on my ship to join her father at Malta, but a storm carried us beyond, and so it was that she – and, I might add, a good number of other women who'd managed to keep themselves aboard – found herself in the eye of the second storm, at Navarino I mean. And did marvellous work with the surgeon on the orlop – all of them did. And she came here last summer, when she was returned with her father, and prolonged her stay; and her company, her ministrations – I'm not afraid to admit it – have wrought miracles.'

Hervey was at a loss for words. Before him was a tall, slender young woman possessed of a fine figure, pretty in a way that also suggested intelligence, and with the patent accomplishment of one who was the daughter of a vice admiral of the red and grand cross of the Bath. Why had she detained herself here? Why was she not out in society? Were the Codringtons Norfolk too? Perhaps she was an intimate of the Cholmondeleys?

But it was hardly opportune to try to ask, and so he was pleased instead to pass the time of day – indeed, to speak with some candour of his purpose in the county – as well as of old times (such as he thought appropriate for a young woman of her station – though he had to concede that she had seen battle; or, at least, the bloody consequences of it).

And then after an hour or so, when the light outside was gone, she rose and took her leave, saying she must have word with the housekeeper and the butler, and see that all was well for the party's stay, and for their dinner this evening.

When she was gone, Peto sat back in happy contemplation, before announcing suddenly, 'I'm resolved to return to the service, Hervey!'

'You are? That is . . . splendid news,' though he wondered how likely could be the prospect.

'And it will be that girl's doing if I succeed.'

Hervey began a little more to understand. But was it quite right – quite prudent – to seek the influence of a father through his daughter? In any case, was not Codrington's star in the descendant? 'How so, exactly?' he tried.

'The Duke of Clarence is no longer High Admiral, and George Cockburn is first naval lord. And while poor Rebecca's father is made to hoist the quarantine flag, so to speak, his captains at least are regarded favourably, who were, after all, following only the orders of the commander-in-chief. Cockburn's a most excellent fellow. I served under him in the West Indies.'

Hervey was now puzzled. If Admiral Codrington could be of no help, how could it be by his daughter's doing that his friend would return to the service? Perhaps in some personal capacity therefore, appointed to the admiral's suite, but still on the half-pay? Not that he could put it so directly. 'Can you hope for a sea commission?'

Peto shook his head. 'Port admiral.'

'Ah. That is fitting.'

'Hervey, my leg's no impediment to command at sea – though an admiralty board would likely say otherwise. Nelson managed well enough with one arm. But one thing at a time: port admiral would see me up.'

'I am all admiration.'

Peto laughed. 'Meanwhile I am commodore of the Blakeney lifeboat!'

Hervey smiled. 'An honorary position, I trust?'

'I give them my advice freely.'

'I can imagine . . . I am just so very, very glad to see you so well.'

'Then tomorrow I'll show you *how* well. I'll show you my commodore's command. Two boats – one lately acquired. And we'll go by way of Holkham. You must see the house . . . and the forcing gardens. There're glasshouses and a hypocaust you'd scarcely conceive of – fruit the long year round!'

'I should like that very much. And in truth, I've yet to see the northernmost part of the county, and it's as well that I do.'

'Capital! Now, see here: I must go and bathe my legs in brine – my daily immersion – and then we'll assemble for dinner at eight. I've asked Tom Innes and his wife to dine with us – my nearest neighbour of any account. You'll recall my speaking of him – fellow midshipman in the West Indies. He too's beached, though not for long, I expect. And the parson – decent sort. Your cornet seems a very good sort of man too; I look forward to his acquaintance more.'

Hervey nodded. He was sure the acquaintance would be agreeable; and in turn that St Alban would enjoy the company of Rebecca Codrington. He had served him so well these past weeks that he deserved the contemplation of one as attractive as she, and, in return, he trusted, the attention of a pair of fine eyes.

They dined in the 'Marble Parlour', a room of such exquisite gilding and veining that Hervey had to beg indulgence at first, so distracted was he by it. But it was not so large as to spoil the intimacy of the little party, an assemblage got up in his honour but also for conviviality. Captain Thomas Innes, of whom Hervey had indeed heard his friend speak more than once, seemed cast in the same mould of Norfolk naval men as Peto himself, and spoke loudly and plainly. His wife wore a permanent expression of contentment, and as 'matron of honour' spoke graciously and with a deal of wisdom, which implied that she had not rested solely in the county when her husband had been at sea. The rector of New Houghton was agreeable enough: no great scholar, and his sermons therefore (Hervey supposed) inclined to be long; but he did know a good deal about rotation and (to Hervey's surprise) threshing machines – and spoke with evident affection for his 'Norfolk Horns', having no truck with the recent fashion for putting them to Southdown rams. Rebecca Codrington herself was got up very fetchingly and *à la mode*, her hair arranged elaborately with a white esprit, the Apollo's knot fastened by a diamond (or perhaps it was marcasite) comb, and her dress a light-blue *gaze de Paris* over a satin slip, the skirt very wide, such as he had not seen much, trimmed with blue velvet flowers, the bodice cut low but becomingly, and set off by two strings of pearls. He was always attentive to the appearance of 'the sex'; even so, he found hers notably arresting, and was certain that St Alban would do so too.

Peto sat at the head of the table, with Mrs Innes on his right and Hervey on his left, and then, opposite each other, Rebecca and St Alban, with Thomas Innes and the rector keeping the further chairs.

The conversation was at once lively and general. Rebecca Codrington spoke charmingly, he thought, with a poise and assurance beyond her years. Plainly Cornet St Alban thought so too; yet beyond her natural courtesy she seemed to show him no special attention, her eyes returning the while to their host. And Hervey began to notice – or thought he noticed – that, indeed, Mrs Innes treated with her as if she were the hostess (though as the dutiful wife of an officer with ambition still, perhaps she thought it prudent to defer to a daughter of a vice admiral . . .). Yet he supposed that *someone* must act as mistress of the house, and since Rebecca Codrington was here – perhaps even at the behest of the Cholmondeleys for this very purpose – it was only fitting that she did so. And as if to confirm that supposition, after their excellent dinner of preserved pheasant (how much of that estimable bird he had eaten since coming to the county, even so late in the season!) and ices, it was Rebecca who rose to withdraw, and Mrs Innes who followed. And throughout, Peto showed a contentment that was rare in any man, let alone in one who had so recently been parted from the sea, the love of his life – and, indeed, from the woman who had at first pledged to being the second love.

They stayed perhaps overlong with the port, but Captain Innes was intent on a complicated story about Peto's prowess with the gun in the forests of Darien, which in turn prompted a lengthy reminiscence – not entirely without bearing on their 'Darien expedition' (and certainly not dull) – on the relative attractions of each of the Windward Islands, of which there seemed to be principally five (after a dispute as to whether Dominica was not more correctly in the Leewards), and then the many smaller islands of the Grenadines, all of which too seemed to have their distinctive charms, so as to make Hervey quite envious of their acquaintance with those parts, and only wondering if Fairbrother, were he here, might trump them all with some tale of those other Indies.

And so, as they rejoined the ladies, Peto felt that some apology was due, which he made with great enthusiasm, bringing the sweetest of smiles from Rebecca, and from Mrs Innes the assurance that she knew from many years' familiarity with the Windwards – if only anecdotally – that their charms were too many to be lightly dealt with. But cards had been promised, and cards they therefore played, though the hour was late (the rectory was only a short walk, and the Inneses lived barely three miles away).

It was half past midnight when the guests left, and Rebecca too – and in turn St Alban – leaving the two friends together in Peto's parlour for one last glass of his own excellent brandy.

'What a capital evening, Hervey. I never enjoyed myself more.'

He said it as if he truly meant it. Hervey wondered, for he had always had a very clear understanding of his friend's notion of pleasure, and it certainly did not consist in dinner parties and cards. A good dinner in his cabin with a few of his officers was all he'd craved – a simple 'Welsh venison' pudding, with redcurrant jelly and cussy sauce (how well he recalled those evenings aboard *Nisus*, and his own nescience: 'Know you not that prime eight-tooth mutton – wether mutton – fuddled and rubbed with allspice and claret, can be ate with as much satisfaction as the King's own fallow deer?'). And yet here was no man dwelling in, or even much conscious of, his disappointment in love and war – the loss of his affianced and the loss of his command; but rather a man at peace.

And, laying aside the loss of an arm – his right arm – and the mauling of a leg, his old friend had never looked better. The livid scar across the forehead was no more now than a line of character, of experience. His hair was full and brown, and his form that of a lieutenant, not a captain ashore and given to indulgence. His eyes were bright and his mind was active. Indeed, he himself felt poorly in Peto's light.

'Yon parson's a good man, Hervey, 'case you didn't have opportunity to form the opinion for yourself. Visited me every day when I was first come here. And he can preach a soul-stirring sermon.'

Hervey helped himself to more brandy, and gave his friend a challenging smile. 'I recall you were not very partial to the claims of the church.'

Peto smiled back benignly. 'No man who goes to sea is mindless of his Maker, Hervey. Rather had I found that it was His ministers who were too often mindless. But that's now in the past. I declare I'm as observant a congregant as ever my father would have wished.'

Hervey wondered if that were not also in part Rebecca Codrington's doing, for he imagined that she like many a young lady brought up 'well' (and here he held in his mind a momentary image of Kezia at divine worship) was ardent in her faith. But he would not say so.

'And Tom Innes – oh, what hours we've had here recalling simpler times!'

'I can well see your attachment to Houghton.'

'I'll bide my time here – Cholmondeley insists on it; says it keeps the house warm when he's away so much. Excellent young man, excellent – and then when . . . when things are opportune, I'll move into my house. I'm having it much pulled about, mind. We might drive there on our way to Holkham.'

And before Hervey could make any reply, his friend, as if summoned by the bell at the hand of the bosun's mate, got up with remarkable haste and pronounced himself ready for his bed. 'Forgive me, Hervey: I don't tire as a rule, but nor have I been more animated in months by the prospect of what beckons tomorrow – Holkham and Blakeney. Believe me, we shall see such things!'

'Indeed,' said Hervey simply, moved by the manifest delight. 'Indeed.'

XIV

CROSSING THE BAR

Next day

'The wind's got up strong,' said Peto, announcing himself to the breakfast party. 'Backed five points since last light – north nor-east, and freshening by the minute. Near gale by the midday, I'll warrant.'

'Good morning, Peto – or do I say "Beaufort"?' replied Hervey drily but with a distinct smile. 'Shall we have more snow?'

'The glass is falling.'

Hervey took it to mean that snow could be expected. 'That does not interfere with our plans?'

'Not in the least,' replied Peto emphatically, 'though perhaps we might set out sooner – and take the tour of the house here tomorrow instead.'

Hervey nodded.

'And St Alban – you'll not mind bringing the horses back from Holkham?'

'Not in the least, Sir Laughton.'

'Coke's people'll give us horses as far as Blakeney, then we'll hire to Fakenham and a man from here can bring a change to meet us.'

'Admirable,' said Hervey, helping himself to more coffee. 'What is it from Holkham to Blakeney – ten miles?'

'Ten exactly, and twenty thence back here. Pity that Coke's away – parliament and all, but his housekeeper will show us the place. Such marvels.'

The weather being so inauspicious, they took the precaution of a particularly hearty breakfast, and the ham was then wrapped for the excursion.

Corporal Wakefield brought the regimental chariot into the arcade just before nine, and Rebecca Codrington saw them off with smiles and words of envy – and a good deal of solicitude for her 'patient'. Hervey was again much taken by her frankness. She evidently took pleasure, too, in nursing his old friend. Such a restoration of body and mind there had been; and he was sure that Peto spoke only the truth when he attributed it to her ministration – though without uncommon fortitude on his part, no amount of admirable nursing could have wrought such a change.

The Houghton horses – four of them – were fine roadsters, and with one of the Houghton grooms as guide Wakefield took them in a good trot the seven miles to South Creake – Peto's father's old parish. Here they inspected the improvements being made to what had once been the glebe house, which *Commander* Peto had bought some years before but then neglected willingly to be at sea, but which was now to become the worthy seat of Captain – perhaps even Rear Admiral – Sir Laughton Peto.

There was snow on the ground here still, making it difficult for Hervey to appreciate fully the foundations for the new wing, and although there was no sign of masons and bricklayers outside, there were carpenters within. He knew nothing of these things, but thought it unlikely that the work would be complete before the autumn – if, indeed, the winter. Nor could he fail to appreciate how painful such a visit was for his old friend, who ought by rights to be showing him the house in which his sister was to be installed as mistress. He knew he must say something.

They did not tarry, however.

'Deuced fine bricks, those,' said Peto as they got under way again. 'Better than Houghton's even – *much*.'

'So I observed,' replied Hervey, if not entirely truthfully, thinking instead how best to broach the matter of Elizabeth.

'Those carpenters – best in Norfolk. I know a thing or two about carpentry.'

'Indeed.'

'You observed that oak?'

'I did.'

'From the old *Acis*, broken up at Yarmouth last year.'

Hervey could not but indulge his old friend's enthusiasm for the detail of his building, especially when it was so intimately connected with his late profession – indeed, his soon-to-be-resumed profession (pray that it would be so). Yet he could not avoid mention of Elizabeth for ever . . .

'And stored at Houghton is some of the best Baltic pine you'll ever see – bought at Linn from a Bremen trader.'

'Peto, I—'

'Nothing shall be too good for her.'

Hervey thought he'd misheard – or perhaps the house, as his ship, was feminine.

'Good for *her*?'

'Indeed.'

'I'm sorry, I don't follow. For whom?'

'Miss Codrington, of course. We shall be wed late this year.'

Hervey's jaw dropped. 'Wed? This year?'

'She wished to be wed at once, but I believed it right to wait till she's eighteen.'

'But . . .'

Peto continued blithely, yet well knowing what must be the multitude of his friend's thoughts. 'You see, it was she who knelt beside me that day on the orlop – and before me, the other mangled souls brought below . . . Aren't you going to congratulate me?'

'Why, I . . . Yes, of course. I heartily congratulate you.'

'I suppose you think the disparity of age somewhat extreme? But it was the same with the Duke of York – I mean the Stuart, James – when he took the Italian girl at fifteen, and he forty, and by all accounts they were unconscionably happy. And he a sailor, too.'

Hervey was at a loss for words. 'I . . .'

'Certainly it's greater than with your own good wife, but not excessively. And, you know, the Turk may have taken my right arm, but he didn't unman me.'

Hervey felt the blow to his stomach as surely as if it had been real. In what melancholy contrast did his own situation stand with his friend's new-found and wholly deserved content – and yet here was Peto supposing it was his equal. There was nothing more he could say.

Holkham, ten miles distant, was a most welcome diversion. Peto had talked for an hour about his bride-to-be, his house, his prospects; his happiness seemed to know no bounds – and Hervey felt meanly for his own envy of it.

And then as they turned off the road onto the long, straight avenue towards the house, the voice became suddenly confiding. 'My dear Hervey, I've spoken of myself incessantly since your coming to Houghton. I've not once asked how things are with you, and I hope you'll not think ill of me for it, for I fancied you'd speak when the time came.'

Hervey was uneasy. Had his friend some intimation of how things were between him and Kezia? But how might he have? He himself was hardly aware of how things truly stood. Perhaps he had in mind his command? 'Well, I . . .'

'No matter,' said Peto, waving his hand airily. 'When the time comes.'

'Of course . . . of course.'

They passed peacefully between the gatekeeper's lodges, though Hervey felt the stomach pangs still.

'Now, what think you of this!' demanded his old friend, signalling a determined change of tack.

Hervey was only too pleased to conform. He gazed out of the window again, observing the straightest avenue of trees he'd ever seen – though all bending exceedingly – and the horses leaning hard into the climb. 'It is very fine, I grant you. And Mr Coke appears to have found the highest hill in Norfolk – or perhaps had it made.'

'Wait till you have the prospect from the top – see yon high obelisk?'

He did.

'From there you'll have the fairest view of house and sea. There's nothing it's like!'

And Hervey would soon agree. On a fine day of a summer there could be no more pleasing thing than to walk up to this place and survey the builder's and the gardener's art, and, beyond, that of Nature – God's: *For in six days the Lord made heaven and earth, the sea, and all that in them is* – though on this lion day of March the sea, distant as it was, looked angry, and the sky ominous.

Then down the hill they went, into the wind. A precautious coachman would have taken it at a walk, with the brake on perhaps, fearful of the coming gale, but Corporal Wakefield kept the four in a trot – better to make them work than risk the wind taking hold, like oars pulling to gain steerage in a fast stream – until finally, in the lee of the house, he could slow to a walk and make his approach at a proper, respectful speed.

The housekeeper was waiting with coffee and madeira. She seemed to know Peto well – perhaps from long years, for she was evidently a Norfolk woman and Hervey knew they kept their own society in this part of the county – and showed no wonder at his coming, or made remark as to his condition, so that he concluded that his friend was indeed much about the place, and much at home in being so.

They began their tour with a *coup d'éclat* – the marble hall, 'Though it is chiefly of pink alabaster, from Derbyshire,' explained

223

Mrs Gedge. 'And it was modelled by Mr William Kent on a Roman basilica.'

Hervey nodded. The likeness to the dome of the Pantheon was most striking.

'The hall is more than fifty feet from floor to the ceiling,' she continued, 'and atop the stairs, which are of true marble, is the peristyle of Ionic columns.'

She was very practised as *cicerone*, he noted, and plainly delighting in her task.

'The colonnade is copied from that of the Temple of Fortuna Virilis in Rome, and supports the coffered ceiling, which is inspired by the Pantheon.'

He was greatly pleased by this evidence of his own artistic appreciation, which as a rule his sister was all too ready to deride. He was about to ask Peto if he could recall their visit to the Pantheon ten years before, but remembered that Elizabeth had been with them too, and so thought better of it.

Up the white marble steps they walked (Peto with quite remarkable ease), to even more intimations of Rome: 'In the niches of the peristyle are statues of classical deities' – all familiar to him: Apollo, Flora, Bacchus, Isis, Aphrodite, Hermes; but the saint . . . Susanna perhaps? Or Felicity or Perpetua – one of the Roman martyrs, plainly; and a nude youth of the sort that abounded on the Capitoline. How these Whigs loved to imagine themselves as classicals!

And on through the *piano nobile* – the saloon, the statue gallery (whose pieces were clad for much warmer climes, or not at all, though Mrs Gedge showed no concern), the long library, the dining room . . . Paintings, furniture, sculpture of every sort, the bounty of the Grand Tour brought back to the northern shore of the county of the Iceni – they who had once burned the Romans out of Colchester, St Albans and even London.

An hour they walked and looked and questioned and remarked, and Hervey began truly to imagine how his friend could be content in the mere proximity of such a place as this, even in a house 'good only for a curate' – if extended to more gentlemanlike proportions . . .

But for Peto himself, even in the midst of Palladian splendour and the Green State Bedroom, came the call of the sea. 'We must sheer away,' he pronounced suddenly, recalling Hervey from his close contemplation of a particularly vivid oil of *Jupiter Caressing Juno*. 'We must see Blakeney with daylight aplenty – the harbour there, my new boat, the church and all. But before we go, the great wall of the kitchen garden – I would have you see that. I would wish your opinion.'

Hervey counted himself no greater gardener than he was a builder, but was perfectly content to humour his friend. They therefore gave thanks, and generous coin, to Mrs Gedge, and went by way of the servants' hall to the gardens.

'See! See!' cried Peto, as they rounded the corner.

But Hervey was at a loss to perceive anything but a wall – admittedly a very high wall, higher perhaps than he'd seen. 'What is it that I'm to look for?'

'*There*, Hervey! Mark that edifice.'

He looked at the object of his friend's enthusiasm with some puzzlement. 'As serviceable a wall as ever I saw.'

'Ah, but not merely a wall,' said Peto, warming to his subject ever more keenly. 'In the summer a veritable cornucopia – pears, apples, succulents of all sorts. You mark its thickness?'

Hervey was perhaps used to seeing a wall as first and foremost an obstacle to surmount – to breach, preferably, or to scale. Peto's, or rather, Holkham's, was a full twenty feet – as high as those at Badajoz (what an escalade that had been), and at Bhurtpore, whose breach he'd climbed through when the sappers had done their job of tunnelling and exploding. But a wall for *fruit* . . .

'It is a wall of walls, I grant you. Enough to make Joshua himself tremble.'

'You see, Hervey, were we to come here in spring there would be half a dozen and more columns of smoke, like so many engines

225

getting up steam – like Chatham yard. All from the stoves fitted to the wall as soon as the first fruits appear, just like an antique Roman floor, to keep them from the frosts. And this wall I shall build in my own garden, or rather, a smaller of its type – a frigate to a first-rate. And Miss Codrington shall have fruit as early and often as any in this fair county!'

Hervey smiled. His old friend's fervour was that of a man half his years – the fervour he himself could still, occasionally, recall. Was it apt, engendered by a fascination with a girl less than half his age ('fascination' was, no doubt, unfair; 'gratitude', perhaps)? Who should say? Was it transient? Who *could* say?

'Miss Rebecca Codrington is the most fortunate of young ladies.'

'And I of men, Hervey.'

Peto had no ship, perhaps no true prospect of a port-admiralcy either – just a folio of builder's plans, and, of course, the devotion of a fine woman (yes, she might be called 'woman', to judge by her mind and air), and the wish to please her in so delightful a way. Contentment enough. More than enough. What strange things could be wrought by shot and shell.

'Not so pretty as on a summer's day, I grant you,' said the contented captain as they bowled along with fresh horses; 'but infinitely more diverting. A gale such as this – and, mark my words, a gale it is – will be driving some curious shipping for haven at Blakeney.'

'Because it is blowing onshore?'

'Exactly so. The harbour's the best on the coast, a good retreat in a heavy sea. She'll take vessels of four or five hundred tons – and the easiest to find on account of the church. You can see it as far as the Dudgeon light, eight leagues off.'

'But in this weather may it be seen so clearly?'

'No, a master who has his book of sailing directions – and there should be none without – can set his course at the light south sou'west half-south till he sees the tower, and then if he brings it to bear sou'west by south can run in that direction till the buoys. There's a hillock half a mile to sou'ward of the harbour which you can see a full three leagues off: if he keeps the church open to the north-west of it half a cable's length he'll be carried to the outer buoy.'

'Well,' said Hervey, in a voice of some awe, 'I've little idea of what you speak, but it sounds most scientific.'

Peto waved his hand as if to say that was but half the story. 'Blakeney's a bar harbour, you see, and though she's buoyed the sands shift. A stranger'll be disinclined to try, though in a strong gale it'll always be prudent to run for it rather than hazard being driven on shore. They hoist a flag on the church as a signal when you may run for it if the boats can't be got off – the pilot boats – and there'll be a full nine feet over the bar.'

'And there'll be ships running for harbour in this weather?'

'Indeed – unless they're big enough to stand well out in the first place. It's the coasters from the Tyne chiefly that come across from the Humber and don't have the sea space to round the point at Cromer. Even the steamers.'

'How fascinating,' said Hervey, and meaning it. 'I hadn't quite appreciated the full hazard of a lee shore. But what is a ship of five hundred tons?'

'*Nisus* was a thousand.'

'Ah.'

'*Nisus* could stand out to sea in any weather. A frigate'll weather a hurricane.'

'And your boat?'

'*Boats*, Hervey: we have two, for the time being at least – an old Lukin unimmergible that's done us well for nigh on twenty years, but Cromer's lately bought a new and bigger boat, and we've taken their old one, a most seaworthy Greathead. Ten oars and broad-beamed – she can take off a dozen comfortably.'

'Greathead?'

'The builder, South Shields man.'

Hervey would have shown an interest in his friend's new 'command' come what may, but the matter – like any touching on innovations among men of action – was genuinely intriguing. 'What is it that makes the boat so serviceable, besides her broad beam?'

'Do you know the Norway yawl?'

Hervey had to admit he didn't.

'The Greathead's built along the same lines – curved keel, but rising even more fore and aft, so even when she's inundated amidships a good third at either end's out of the water, so she can still make headway without foundering. An' she's steered by an oar not a rudder, so she can be rowed either direction, and the curve makes her easy to steer about her centre, a God-send when you're trying to take off crew from a wreck.'

'And she was first at Cromer?'

'Aye, but they've now a bigger boat. They have to reach further out than Blakeney.'

Peto's regard for the new Blakeney boat proved extensive – her sides cased in cork four-inch thick, copper plating securing the fenders, seven hundredweight unladen – so much buoyancy, such superiority over the former craft . . .

Hervey took careful note, such as he could, and on that coasting road, with the horses' ears pricked to the coming force and noise, with Corporal Wakefield bent so much in the saddle that his cheek brushed the leader's mane, and Peto thrilling to the elements that had given *Nisus* and then *Prince Rupert* their power and their glory, he began to smile. The sea air, even as tempestuous as this, was so evident a tonic that all Miss Rebecca Codrington – Lady Peto as would be – need do for the perfect happiness of her adoring captain was to eat the fruit of his forcing wall and to accompany him on a daily drive to pay homage to Neptune. Admiralcy was not essential to his old friend's self-esteem and contentment. Not for him the ambition that drove the lonelier man. Only the companionship – the love – of a good woman, to reciprocate and increase, and in a place the spirit was at ease: *Happy the man, whose wish and care / A few paternal acres bound, / Content to breathe his native air / In his own ground . . .*

Boom!

Peto started, like an old hunter to the horn. 'Maroons!'

The lookout's urgent summons – even above the wind. Then again, like a thunder-crack.

'A ship in trouble?'

'For certain! Two rockets to summon the Blakeney crew.' He leaned out of the window. 'Corporal, make haste, if you will!'

Wakefield let slip the rein, and kicked. They'd just crossed the Stiffkey, not three miles to the town, and he'd hardly worked the Holkham pair at all. Now he could really ask of them – if not a canter on a road he didn't know, and one so rutted, but a flying trot, almost as good as.

And how they flew! In ten minutes he was turning onto the harbour road.

Peto could hardly contain himself. 'Damme, all this time and I've never yet seen a boat put out!'

Hervey counted himself fortunate indeed.

'There! There she is. 'Pon my word, she was got away sharply.'

The Blakeney boat was stationed at the furthest point of the sand spit that enclosed the harbour, with some sort of runway that got her into the water without horsepower. There was a perpetual look-out from a cottage on the sandbank (sand spit, all but) with a watch three miles east and west, at whose signal the Blakeney fishermen would rush to their boats and thence to the point of the spit to man the Greathead. There'd been an unpleasant business of late, Peto said, though before his time, when the boatmen had been laggardly, wanting to stay their hand till a master actually called for salvage, when they could claim their nine-tenths (one master, seeing the boat so close, had decided to risk running the bar, and afterwards claimed he'd only asked for pilotage). 'But I put a stop to all of that, for it's but a short step to wrecking.'

Wakefield pulled up on the hard, and Peto was half out in an instant, grabbing a hand-hold for the roof.

'Have a care!' cried Hervey, hastening to help.

But Peto was atop the chaise in no time, glass in hand, nimble as the cripple at Bethesda.

'Can you see the distress?' called Hervey (there was no safe space for two of them).

'I see her tops . . . two – no, she's beam-on: *three* masts! What the devil's she doing putting in?'

'Is she too big?' shouted Hervey, for he'd seen the flag on the church tower.

'The point is she's big enough to stand out to sea,' bellowed Peto. 'She must've sprung a leak or some such.' He began clambering down.

'Shall we drive to the bank?'

'Can't – not with the tide in. Besides, there's no use watching. If she's in such trouble as to run for it and miss the bar they'll need to take off crew and all and pretty quick. And if she's as many passengers as she's built for . . .'

He beckoned furiously to the watching men on the harbour wall. 'Come on, you landlubbers! Look lively!'

'What do you intend?' Hervey was still shouting, the wind relentless.

'To get yonder boat into the water!'

Hervey saw a tarpaulin thirty yards away, supposing it was the Lukin coble.

The half-dozen men, two of them little more than boys, broke into a sort of double – as if they couldn't help themselves, for all their quarrelsome independence.

'Now, my good lads,' began Peto, with a look that *won* as much as commanded, 'we must get our old boat in the water and be ready to take off the crew and all from the new one, for they'll have to make more than one rescue if yon barque's sailing full-laden.'

No one questioned his right to call on them – Hervey supposed they must know exactly who he was – but the sheer force of his command and assurance seemed effortlessly to propel them to the task. In no time at all the tarpaulin was unlashed and the rollers laid out.

'Good men! Capital!'

There were only a dozen yards to run to the water, but the boat was no seven-hundredweight, and even Hervey saw they wouldn't shift it by their own muscle alone.

Peto was ahead of him. 'Corporal, will you lend your horsepower?'

'Aye, sir!'

They sprang into action like ostlers to a mail coach. Hervey helped unhitch the traces and run the two in tandem to the front of the coble. One of the 'volunteers' had got the hauling ropes ready, which Wakefield hitched to the wheeler's collar, while Hervey struggled to steady the leader.

'Now then, listen to me,' rasped Wakefield to the volunteers, so uncharacteristically assertive that Hervey looked twice. 'You pull on those ropes to take up the slack – right? And then I'll lead these on to take the strain – right? And you'll keep on the ropes till we're in the water an' I tells you to let go – right? And no noise. I don't want them being started behind.'

They all nodded eagerly. Had Wakefield been in uniform he couldn't have made a greater impression.

But who was to man the oars?

Now it was Peto's turn. 'Hold hard for the moment, if you will, Corporal. Now, well done, lads, well done. Now, when we're in the water, who's coming with me?'

Hervey winced. *With* him? Surely he didn't intend . . .

'Yes, my lads, I'll be in yon boat. I've commanded many a one in my time – as well y'know. We needn't go beyond the bar – safe water, just a bit of a pull against the wind. Now, who's with me?'

It seemed that most of them were. Whether because of the compelling power of Sir Laughton Peto's celebrity and disposition, or the prospect of a share in the salvage, Hervey couldn't suppose. It mattered not at that moment.

'Capital! Now, as her bow begins to lift, all hands aboard!' He turned to Wakefield. 'Ready?'

'Aye, sir.'

'Then haul away!'

She moved easily – thank God – and the horses were no more shy of the water than the road. Wakefield and then Hervey pulled themselves astride as they splashed into the breakers.

Ten yards, the beach gently shelving, water now up to the belly – and the bows lifting. In scrambled the coble's scratch crew, ten of the liveliest – and Peto.

'Haul me up, my lads! Let loose the ropes!'

'Turn 'em about, Colonel!' shouted Wakefield as the lines fell clear.

Hervey brought the leader round clear of the traces, the wheeler following with Wakefield still up, and quietly, then edged alongside the coble until he could lunge aboard – with much cursing as he caught his knee on the gunwale.

Wakefield was making to follow.

'Get back, man! See to the horses!'

But he took no notice, sliding into the boat on his stomach. 'Sorry, Colonel. If Sar'nt Acton were with you I could.'

Hervey gritted his teeth. He'd given an order – or thought he had – and Wakefield had ignored it. Yet how could he upbraid a man for claiming his duty lay with the harder course?

'They'll be right enough, Colonel. They'll stand quiet.'

But Hervey was already distracting himself with an oar, trying to slide it into the rowlock.

'Now, see here,' Peto hailed. 'There are life-preservers in the sternsheets.'

Landlubbers he may have called them, but more than one was looking handy. Out came the cork vests, and then, one by one, out went the oars.

Once he'd got the likeliest of his lads to fit the rudder – 'I appoint you bos'n!' – he settled in the sternsheets and took charge of the pulling. 'Give way together!' and then 'Pick up the stroke!' and 'Cheerly now!'

Hervey shook his head and smiled to himself: truly his friend was in his element. They might be pulling for a man-o'-war rather than a Tyne barque.

Yet Blakeney harbour was no little place, no mouth-of-the-river and breakwater affair, but a good mile and a half of shallow bay bounded by a line of sandbanks. 'The Frisians in miniature', Peto had called them. At low water much of it became salt marsh, gouged its full length wide and lazily by the Glaven stream, and marked at its western limit (for the purposes of pilotage) by the Stiffkey, which met with the Glaven at the harbour entrance; that entrance, at least, which was passable to more than a smack.

The sea was nothing compared with what was running beyond the sandbank, but at its widest there was half a mile of water between bank and shore, and the swell was enough to persuade Peto to make straight into the wind for the sand's lee, and then due west, hoping at the turn to have the wind in their favour.

It was hard pulling, a good while before they could do aught but keep the stroke – and a quarter of an hour's hard labour (Hervey threw off the cork vest and his coat, so heavy was the work) until they found the slacker water.

Peto put the rudder to port. The coble answered west as handily as a jolly boat. 'Pick up the stroke now!'

And it *was* a deal easier, oars now entering the water cleanly rather than battering against the swell. And the wind had veered just a point too, so it helped them make headway rather than hindered.

But it was a full twenty minutes still before they reached the harbour mouth, with the tide now on the ebb and a quickening current to work against the wind.

'Keep the stroke!'

The Blakeney Greathead, stationed at the furthest end of the sandbank, near the lookout, and so ready to put into open water in minutes, was already coming off the wreck with a full lading – a dozen of the barque's passengers, some women and children.

Peto stood up – heaven knew how, for Hervey didn't – and began signalling with his arm. What intelligence, what orders, it conveyed was beyond his landsman-friend, but evidently not the coxswain of the Greathead, for Hervey saw the boat turning directly for them.

'We'll bring ours alongside and take off her trade,' called Peto hoarsely, the wind now shrill rather than mere roar. 'Blakeney men never turn back!'

It made sense, for the Greathead was an altogether bigger boat, with more freeboard; if there were others to take off from the barque it were better she do it, for beyond the bar the sea was tall, the breakers pounding the dunes like a siege battery, and the swell so heavy as to lose her from sight in the troughs.

Peto now brought the coble about to head into the stream, knowing that presently the current would be stronger than the wind, the tide running out fast, and ordered oars to pull just that bit lighter – just enough to hold her steady so the Greathead could come up on his starboard with the more sea room.

And indeed they held her very steady for a good few minutes, while the Greathead rose and plunged towards the less lively water of the harbour mouth, and then running in fast.

'Starboard side, boat oars!'

It was lubberly, but it was done.

'Steady now!'

And then the Greathead was coming alongside, larboard oars boated and hands ready with ropes to lash the two together.

'A dozen more to take off, Sir Laughton – crew mainly,' boomed the coxswain.

The boats locked fore and aft.

'Good man, Dauncey! Let's get these across sharp.'

Helping hands got the orphans of the storm into the coble, Peto and his bosun bidding them crouch low so as not to hinder the oars.

Hervey was too preoccupied with the unfamiliar contents of his hands to take in much (an oar was a deal more refractory than the nappiest trooper's reins) but the face of rescued humanity was compelling – innocents plucked from the watery jaws of death . . .

But then he saw Peto on his feet once more (how, he couldn't tell, for the motion of the boat was enough to upset the ablest-bodied), shouting orders, beckoning, pointing, just as he supposed at Navarino – master of men and the wooden world; magnificent! What privilege it was to call him *friend* . . .

The Greathead heaved suddenly and slammed against the coble. *Crack!*

The starboard oar closest the stern for some reason trailed, snapped above the blade. The loom swung round with the kick of a mule and pitched its handler into Peto, who fell sideways, grabbing for the gunwale but missing as the boat lunged on the swell and pulled the coble with it. Over the side he went – and all in a split second.

Hervey was up in an instant, but Wakefield was first, diving without a thought or a glance. He went in after him, just ahead of one of the Blakeney men, leaping rather than diving, not trusting to his reach. His head went under, his heart seemed to stop; it was an age before he broke surface. And it was all he could do to stay there. There was nothing but the sea whichever way he looked – great walls of it. His boots were leaden.

And then a cork vest washed over the swell, and he grabbed it, and it was now just a bit easier to keep his head above water . . . but still he couldn't see the coble – nothing but the great grey walls. Where was Peto? Where was Wakefield? If he couldn't see which way to strike, would he be taken by the tide? Had he passed out with the sudden immersion, been minutes asleep? Had he – had *they* – been taken, swept out, beyond the bar, beyond sight?

The cold was already in his marrow. It was now assailing his head.

Would the end come this way – with not a soul to see?

But then, like the stage scrim suddenly lit and the players revealed, he bobbed over the swell. There ten yards away was the coble and the Greathead, still lashed, and hands leaning out to others. And he roared at himself to crawl through the water, which seemed to resist all his efforts, refusing him all progress, trying even to pull him below . . . until, without sensation of movement, without rhyme or reason, there were suddenly helping hands to grasp.

'Peto? Peto?' he gasped, not hearing his own words.

'Hold hard, sir!'

He couldn't hear. He couldn't see. But he knew somehow he was saved – though the Greathead was gone back to the wreck and the coble was making fast for the landing before his senses were restored, and the dread that he alone was spared was so happily dismissed.

A good moon favoured them home from Blakeney. Hervey had thought it best to put up at the White Horse where the sodden party had taken refuge, not least for the recovery of Corporal Wakefield, by whose endeavour Peto was rescued; but with a change of clothes and half an hour before a good blaze that admirable NCO had insisted he was more than able to ride post – by no means an easy road too – and he brought the White Horse's liveries to Houghton in a little over three hours without once using the whip. Even after reaching the house he would not quit till the grooms had rubbed down the geldings, thatched and rugged them up, given them hay, and then, half an hour later, when their breathing was regular once more and the sweating done, a warm mash. Only then would he take a hot bath – a thing so rare as to defy his memory of the last time, but which Hervey insisted on – and then a mutton pie the like of which he would say he had never known, and the best stout porter this side of Bow. And Hervey would tell Johnson (whose relief at seeing the overdue party was most marked) to procure somehow – anyhow – a third stripe for him, and to have it sewn on his tunic by morning.

And when he himself had at last gone to Peto's parlour, close to eleven, where there was a spread to delight the better part of a troop, and warmed himself with the best burgundy that Lord Cholmondeley's cellars could render, and sent away St Alban, who was even yet in dismay that his colonel had been in peril of his life and he had not been at hand to assist the gallant Wakefield, and listened patiently to Johnson's strictures ('A man who's survived shot 'n' shell and the edge of the sword, the point of the spear and all the diabolical creeping things and climates of foreign parts, and he risks his all on a Norfolk beach; the hero of actions too numerous to recall, and now at long last commanding His Majesty's 6th Light Dragoons, and he puts to sea in a boat that a midshipman might command . . .'), he sank into a low armchair to contemplate the restorative properties of a good fire, and the thorough revitalization of his old friend.

Rebecca Codrington now came, woken, Hervey supposed, by the late return, and bidding them both not to rise went to her hero of Navarino (and now Blakeney), and showed him every tenderness. And while Hervey felt a moisture in his eyes – *such* compassion for his old friend she showed, and such a gladness he had in Peto's transfiguration – he knew it also to be self-pitying. It was perverse to think thus, unworthy, unmanly, but in two days he'd seen more of contentment than he could rightly digest. Indeed, he unnerved himself by its contemplation. He must with all speed end this bitter-sweet stay, return to duty, immerse himself in its every detail whether of moment or not. Peto, he knew, would protest, as would Rebecca, but tomorrow he would start back for Hounslow.

XV

WHITHER FLED LAMIA

Walden Park, Hertfordshire, three days later

The last time he'd come to Walden had been a year ago – a little more. It had been a cold coming then, too, on account of the weather, the snow lying deep – and of the reception. He'd arrived without notice (but then, why should he send notice to a wife?) and presented unpalatable news of a foreign posting (Lord Hill had offered him command of a battalion of his own regiment, in Gibraltar). Unpalatable, that is, to Kezia; for Hervey, in despair of getting command of his own regiment, which was under sentence of reduction, had been keen to accept what he saw as his best chance of advancement. And then he'd left hurriedly next morning after an express arrived saying his mission to the Levant was to begin sooner than expected. It was hardly the recipe for reunion – restitution, indeed, for Kezia had taken herself back to her people (and their marriage only the summer before). Perhaps it was not so unreasonable that she did so. He'd made no plans for their own establishment, so much depending on his prospects; and in any case he'd had to return to the Cape, to the temporary assignment with the Mounted Rifles. But he'd hoped there might be a beginning, not least for the sake of Georgiana. The honeymoon had not been as he'd wished; without question. The month and more that was customary had given way to but a few days – all that could be spared – and Kezia beset the while by sick headaches. The courtship had been too hurried, perhaps, and his motives uncertain. Widower marrying widow, each having a child – there was inevitably more than a touch of convenience in such a match. That he'd been powerfully attracted to her there was no doubt; whether she to him was altogether unclear. These matters, he understood, had a way of resolving themselves in the 'mutual society' (as the Prayer Book had it) that followed. But prospect of mutual society there had not been, and at their last meeting Kezia had been at pains for that state to continue. Yet for his part there'd been no choice but to take himself off; when first they'd married his place had been at the Cape, with his troop and the Rifles, and then again, last year, in the Levant; but in both cases he'd desired – expected – no more than *physical* separation (indeed, there'd been nothing to prevent Kezia's coming with him to either place). There was no call in either sense – none that he could fathom – for the sudden distance between them. They had not, it was true, been conventionally affectionate lovers during their courtship, but things had happened quickly, and the place and circumstances had never been auspicious. And then although he'd not intended it, while in the Levant he'd somehow steeled his heart to the situation, if not entirely successfully, as of late the dark nights of the spirit testified. Seeing Peto in his pre-connubial bliss, however, had unexpectedly turned his mind to the cause of reconciliation. Indeed, to pass King's Walden on his return to Hounslow without a call would have been an act of defiance that any Christian should denounce as sinful.

His arrival caused some consternation. Kezia's people were not at home, and the house (Walden Park was a considerable place) was shuttered and shrouded and in the care of what he would have called a depot party, the principal servants having gone to London with Sir Delaval Rumsey and his wife. But the sound of the piano told him that Kezia herself was here, and its abrupt ending that she had been alerted to his presence. A little while later – not long enough for her to have retired first, nor quickly enough for her to have come at once – she appeared in swaddling clothes and shawl (the house was unconscionably cold), and with the air of a convalescent being dutifully hospitable to a well-wisher of limited acquaintance.

'Matthew,' she said simply.

He had not spent the journey from Houghton to Walden without thinking what might be their manner of greeting. He had resolved, come what may, to embrace her in the manner a husband ought.

But he could not. Whether because of something within, or Kezia's manner, it mattered not, for the effect was the same.

'I am on my way to Hounslow.'

She did not ask from where, or why. He had not *come* from Hounslow, evidently, and so his call was accidental.

'You were in the Levant.'

But he'd not been for some months, and he'd not told her so, or even written (much, at least), or sent her presents, or brought with him any now.

'I was.'

He *had* intended writing. He'd wanted to write to ask her to come to Hounslow, to be his wife – to be a wife to his position indeed. There was a handsome house to take, and good servants she might engage (he was not without a little money now). And ample space for her piano, the piano that he himself had bought her – for a wedding present. But he hadn't written. Worse, he'd not come to see her – not until now, *en route* . . .

'So . . .' she said, expecting more of him.

But he was at a loss for words.

They stood at twice arm's length from each other, in the middle of the great hall, and she made no move – no bidding to a fire, no mention of refreshment.

He made himself speak. 'You are well, I trust.'

She raised an eyebrow. 'As you see.'

But he didn't see – couldn't see, for she gave not the least thing away. Her complexion was fine enough – as it ever was – but there was nothing in her eyes that told him any more. Perhaps she was a little sparer though . . .

'And how was Herr Mendelssohn?'

She looked almost astonished.

'You said you were to play before him when he came to London. I trust he did?'

He'd learned of it when last he'd visited. It was one of the reasons she couldn't come with him to the Cape.

'He did. I played before him at Mr Hickford's Room.'

He didn't know how this room stood in the estimation of those who knew about these things, but supposed that if Herr Mendelssohn (about whom he *had* heard) patronized it then it must be of some repute.

'Brava!' he tried.

'He paid me very handsome compliments.'

He shifted a little, and glanced about for a servant he might ask a favour of – anything – but saw none. 'Might we speak a little more . . . where it is a little warmer?'

They went to her drawing room. The fire was low. He hesitated, for it was not his house, but reached for a log.

'Please don't trouble on my account, Matthew. I cannot tarry long, for I have calls to make.'

He hesitated again. She'd practically given him his *congé*. He placed the log on the fire, but just the one.

'How is Allegra?'

'She is well.'

'I thought I might . . .'

'She is not here. She is with her governess.'

He shivered. It must go hard with a child, a daughter especially, to be in the charge of a governess, and not yet – what? – four years? And half an orphan. He himself had known a nursemaid until ten (and his governess, when she came, was the finest of women), but a mother also who was much about . . .

'Might we – might I – have some coffee? It's so deucedly cold. The carriage warmer failed this morning.'

Kezia tugged the bell-pull.

'I sent my driver on to the King's Head. We needed in any case to change horses.'

A maid answered, one he didn't recognize. The footmen must all be with Sir Delaval in London, he supposed. She brought him coffee at once, however, and by no means poor. She must have made it in expectation of the bell – and then wondered perhaps why she'd had to wait so long for it to ring. He was still standing when she returned, for Kezia remained on her feet. Indeed they stood like cousins new met – conscious of a connection, but little else.

Once she was gone and his cup was in his hand (though Kezia took none) he braced himself to what he'd been turning over in his mind since Houghton. 'Kezia, I have come to ask – to beg, indeed – that you join me in Hounslow. You will have every convenience. I am now commanding the Sixth, as you will know, and—'

'No, Matthew, I did not know. The last we spoke you were of a mind to go to Gibraltar – and before that to Canada.'

'Yes, but that was . . . well, hastily done, though for the best. The regiment was to have disbanded, to all intents and purposes, but then the decision was overturned.'

'I see. But I cannot in any event come to Hounslow.'

He winced. He'd not expected so outright a rejection – not, at least, with so little explanation. With no explanation indeed. 'May I enquire why?'

Kezia pulled her shawl about her closer. 'I cannot come, Matthew – Hounslow: I cannot.'

Cannot. 'Can't means won't and won't means guardroom' – that was the saying, was it not? But this wasn't the barrack square or the riding school. In her wedding vows she'd promised to obey, yet . . .

'Kezia,' he said softly, almost tenderly: 'Why cannot you come? Am I to be nothing to you? Nor you to me?'

She clutched her shawl tighter. 'I cannot express myself differently, Matthew. I cannot be with you . . . at Hounslow.'

The hesitation was just enough to suggest the difficulty lay with the place – the proximity, perhaps, to the regiment. Could it be – it occurred to him for the first time – that such proximity would remind her too much, too painfully, of her late husband?

'If not Hounslow, then somewhere else – Richmond perhaps. Worsley is there, with his new wife.'

She shook her head. 'It is out of the question, Matthew. It cannot be . . . And now I beg you would excuse me, for I've calls to make. It was very ill done – your coming without warning.'

'Warning?'

She didn't answer.

She gathered up her skirts and shawl, her eyes anywhere but his, shaking her head repeatedly and speaking of 'refreshment' – that Sarah would bring him soup, or meats if he wished, or whatever he willed. But on no account must she delay further. And she fled. There was no way other to describe her leaving.

He walked from the house without farewells, and with not a backward look. There was scarcely point: he knew he'd never see it again.

XVI

WITHOUT DUE PROCESS

Hounslow, next day

'Good morning, Colonel. Your express arrived yesterday. I sent word to the Horse Guards at once that you would be returned today. I fancy we may have word by this evening.'

'Thank you, Malet. I'm minded to report to Lord Hill as soon as may be.'

He seemed . . . distant.

'Did you find things so very amiss in Norfolk, Colonel?'

'On the contrary. Matters are very much in hand, if somewhat too *extempore*. It only requires but a modest outlay to put things on a sound footing. And since it was Lord Hill's wish that I report in person, I feel obliged to do so at once.'

Coffee was brought by one of the sable twins. 'Thank you, Abdel,' said Hervey absently.

'Please, Colonel, it is Hassan.'

Malet bridled.

But Hervey merely looked at him, as if summoned back to the place and moment – and laughed. 'You must either wear different coloured feathers in the turban, or else both answer to . . . *Karim*.'

Hassan appeared to be contemplating the options.

'Away with you, Moor!' Malet clapped his hands, pasha-like, scarcely able to suppress the smile.

'Yes, master,' said Hassan, bowing and trying unsuccessfully to suppress his own amusement.

'What do you fancy Lord Hill would make of the state of discipline in the regiment?' said Hervey when he was gone, diverted by the image of the seraglio and placing Norfolk – or rather, Hertfordshire – behind him.

'That it is sufficient and enlightened, Colonel. Besides, they are not subject to the Mutiny Act and the King's Regulations.'

'Quite.' But then his countenance changed again. 'Collins is, though. How are matters in that regard?'

'I'm afraid there's no change, Colonel. The evidence has now been rendered in writing. I have taken advice – indeed I went to see Sir William Beckett.'

Hervey was impressed – an audience of the Judge Advocate General . . . 'And he received you?'

'He's married to a cousin of mine.'

Hervey nodded. In this game of soldiers-in-peace it was well to have officers with connections – everywhere. 'And his advice?'

'That you yourself have the power to dismiss the charge summarily, if brought, but that in that case Kennett would at once make application for redress of grievance, which would take the matter out of your hands. You know already, of course, Colonel, that you do not have the summary powers to find Collins guilty and then to award punishment. Sir William is of the opinion – without prejudice, he pointed out, for he had not considered the written evidence – that to dismiss the charge summarily would be tanta-mount to impugning the honour of an officer, and that Kennett would therefore have no course but to make such an application. However, and this he believed might be argued to advantage, the charge of assault would turn on the principle of . . .' (Malet looked at the notes in his order book) '*actus non facit reum nisi mens sit rea*, which means—'

'That without intent there can be no culpability. I heard much of it after the affair at the gunpowder mills.'

'Indeed, Colonel. And counsel for the defence's submission would be that Collins intended no assault but merely to avert the commission of a felony.'

'But that is precisely what Collins has said from the outset, and which I have no reason to doubt. Wherefore should I not summarily dismiss the charge?'

'Sir William is of the opinion that an application for redress of grievance would not redound well to your – that is, the regiment's – reputation.'

Hervey blinked. 'I trust that care for my reputation would not inhibit me from choosing the right course.'

'No, Colonel, by no means. Sir William spoke of its being a case of prudential judgement, but I confess I'm at a loss to find any instruction in that. And Sir William said only that it was the attribute of seniority.'

Prudential judgement once more. Hervey sighed. Prudence demanded three things: to take counsel for the means of securing the virtuous end, and then to judge soundly the fitness of those means; and, finally, to command their employment.

Command. That at least was his business. And in the end it was all it came down to – his willingness and ability to exercise command . . . wisely.

But evasion was not to be counted the same as the exercise of wisdom. 'Has Kennett formally – in writing – laid charges?'

'In his evidence, yes, but no charge has yet been framed according to the proper formulary . . . I mean, that I have not drawn up a charge sheet.'

It was what Hervey had wanted – masterly inactivity. But it could not be prolonged indefinitely. 'Then have it so framed and I shall consider it.'

'With a view to remanding him for court martial?'

'That would be one of the two options open to me.'

'Colonel, the other option is, with respect—'

Hervey stayed him with a hand. 'Other business, if you please.'

Malet looked uncomfortable, his commanding officer seemingly set on a course that could only lead to . . . 'Colonel, if I may . . . I believe there is a strong feeling – I will say no more – that Kennett should be obliged to withdraw his accusation by the threat or actual application of force.'

Hervey raised an eyebrow. The 'African option' – a horsewhip, by his own hand . . . 'I trust you dealt with it appropriately?'

'Colonel, a matter such as this, were we on more active duty, could – and might best be – settled, shall we say, summarily out-of-orderly-room, but in our situation here it would not tend to good order and discipline. It would make for all sorts of mischief – faction, notably.'

'You're very wise, Malet. And I've been careful not to say "Will no one rid me of this troublesome priest?"'

'Quite.'

'Then there the matter will rest for the time being. Other business?'

Malet brightened a little. 'Well, though I'm not sure this will be to your liking, we're now to send *three* troops to Brussels. The King will not now go, and will send instead one of the household or a minister – and therefore no heavies.'

Hervey confounded him by brightening very much indeed. 'Splendid news! Though how the Horse Guards suppose they can spare three troops is rather beyond me, but that's of no matter. I shall myself command.'

'You will go to Brussels, Colonel?'

Had it been but two troops, the usages of the service would require him to form a squadron under command of the senior of the two captains. Three troops, however, required an officer in overall command, and whereas he might have sent the major, were he at duty, there was no alternative – it might be argued – to taking command in person. 'I shall. Indeed I shall have to.'

'You might recall the major a month early from his furlough.'

Hervey smiled. 'And he might very well not receive the recall!'

'Or make the senior captain local major.'

'That would be . . . unseemly.'

Malet now returned the smile in full measure. 'You would rather Brussels in June than Hounslow.'

'Quite so, especially as all I should have to share the barracks with is two troops at most. And perhaps at "more active duty", as you put it, a solution to the Collins business might ensue.'

Malet looked anxious again.

Hervey held a hand up. 'I sport, Malet. Have no fear.'

'Very well, Colonel. Do I take it that one of the other two troops shall be Worsley's? And the other?'

'Tyrwhitt's.'

Malet nodded, but with a frown. 'I doubt it will be under Tyrwhitt's command, though. I regret to have to tell you that he's to be arraigned in Dublin in May.'

This was surprising news, but – Hervey would admit, if only to himself – not unwelcome, for Tyrwhitt's presence either in Hounslow or Brussels would be something of an embarrassment. 'Indeed? Is he to return before then? He's not remanded in arrest?'

'There was communication only yesterday that the terms of his bail require him to remain in Ireland.'

'Beyond the Pale?' He chided himself; he hadn't meant to make so disparaging a remark.

Malet shook his head despairingly. 'There was by all accounts a deal of rancour at mess last night. Several knew the lady in question and have a high regard for her.'

It seemed to Hervey that the mess had rancour enough – no mess was ever entirely free of it – and the sooner the officers were put to the mill the better. 'Well, on *this* case we can bring nothing to bear, so I'm content that Mordaunt shall take D Troop to Brussels.'

'Very well, Colonel.'

'Oh, did I say? I gave Wakefield field promotion. Do you think you might calculate when the rank might be made substantive?'

'You didn't say, Colonel, but I did hear of it from Mr Rennie.' He smiled wryly. News of Wakefield's third stripe had passed from guardhouse to orderly room quicker than had the chaise. 'For what conspicuous service was this reward?'

'I shall tell you . . .'

The rest of orderly room and office was completed with despatch and even some pleasure (for defaulters had been few), so that at one o'clock they were able to mess with the half-dozen or so officers remaining in barracks, an agreeable hour in which Hervey learned a good deal of what had occurred in the world, the bachelor's world at least, during his Norfolk sojourn – the fiery destruction of the Lyceum theatre; the progress of the bill for Lord Ellenborough's divorce (though the details of non-cohabitation and Lady Ellenborough's pregnancy did not go comfortably with him); the London protocols on the sovereignty of Greece, with much sentiment for Lord Byron, which he thought so much nonsense (and said so: 'The sovereignty proceeded from Codrington's guns at Navarino, not Byron's pen'); the speech by Lord Blandford in the House of Commons on the 'venality of the close and decayed boroughs', on which even St Alban was moved to keep silence; and then, as if to complete the explosive formula of women, politics and religion, 'apropos Rennell' that no less a person than a son of Lord Spencer, a clergyman, had 'renounced the errors of Protestantism in a Popish chapel in Leicester', intend-ing to become a minister there – and all the consequence of 'Emancipation', which the duke had 'so imprudently let come to pass'.

Yet all was conducted without heat or acrimony – no recourse to pistols, nor even invective. Was this the true temper of the age, he wondered – unless the lady in question was known to one of them (which was always the possibility, of course – as with Tyrwhitt)? It augured well if it were. In some regiments, such was the inflammatory potential of politics and 'the sex' that their

colonel made them inadmissible subjects. The Sixth had its blackguards – mercifully few – but he had every right, he believed, to
consider the regiment to be the equal of any (except in the extreme
of wealth) and the superior of most. The nation was fortunate
indeed to have so many younger sons possessing learning and activity, and that so many of them found their way into the army. And
yet in reputation, of course, so much depended on appearance –
which he knew perfectly was why Malet had been at such pains to
press him over his dealing with Kennett. He, however, was more
than conscious of the necessity of 'appearance', not least his own.
Indeed, it was beginning to preoccupy him.

'I'm glad you're returned,' said Fairbrother, matter of fact, throwing an afternoon log on the fire; 'I found myself in want of leisure.
I never did so much in my life.'

'Not all on my account, I trust,' said Hervey.

'Those were merely the most agreeable, though my time with
General Gifford hasn't been without profit too.'

'How so?'

'Let me tell you at dinner, for there's much to tell – not least that
I've found you the most excellent charger on account of him, and
at no very great expense; well, not greatly more than the figure you
gave me.'

Hervey looked at him warily. 'How much more?'

Fairbrother put on a show of pensiveness. '"The kingdom of
heaven is like unto a cavalryman, seeking goodly horses: who, when
he had found one horse of great price, went and sold all that he had,
and bought it."'

Hervey smiled. 'But the man of the gospel who bought the *pearl*
of great price was a merchant, who intended turning a profit. I
merely have need of a horse that looks and flies like Whistlejacket,
but at a tenth of his price.'

'That indeed was my remit.'

'And the answer to my question?'

'The price has not been settled. I'll tell you more anon.'

'Very well. Tell me of Wiltshire, meanwhile.'

He did. They sat for an hour and more as Fairbrother regaled him with the universal happiness he had found in that corner of England, which even Cobbett's pen described as 'singularly bright and beautiful' (though he had spoiled the effect by, to Hervey's mind, the unwarranted assertion that it was 'not very easy for the eyes of man to discover labouring people more miserable'). His sister, it seemed, was in the bloom of newly wedded bliss, his father was suffused with delight at a canonry which not only promised comfort but also vindication of his churchmanship and even recognition of his modest scholarship (his monograph on Laudian Decorum being now in its third printing), and even his mother's perpetual anxieties appeared allayed; the *Rittmeister-baron* was, said Fairbrother, as full of good cheer as any man he'd known; and Georgiana . . . well, there was a most accomplished young lady who, at twelve, was not in the least inferior in conversation to any of the opposite sex.

To Hervey it was consolation. He did not know yet when he himself might visit. Moreover, he had no idea when he might reunite himself permanently with his daughter, as had been so much the intention when he'd taken a wife. But there were greater evils than this, were there not . . . ?

'I am so much delighted to hear it all,' he said peacefully.

Fairbrother caught something in the tone nevertheless. 'But something's amiss with you, evidently.'

Hervey did not at first respond. As a rule he would not admit to being in the least discomfited by anything so closely connected as his family, so much so that his friend had once said to him that he wondered why a man kept the company of another if he were not to share any thoughts with him but that might be shared with a casual acquaintance at the table of the United Service (he had once trespassed on forbidden ground, his friend's determination to marry Kezia; and the penalty had been disagreeable).

'I fancy it's the situation of Georgiana,' he suggested, knowing that it was probably not.

Hervey woke, but without the resentment that Fairbrother was half expecting. 'Georgiana – no, well . . . yes. But it's nothing I can apply myself to at the moment.'

'Well then?'

Hervey shook his head. 'You know, I've waited on the command of the Sixth for as long as I've thought myself equal to it . . .'

Fairbrother smiled to himself, supposing that moment to be not long after Cornet Hervey had joined his first troop. Yet he couldn't quite believe that his friend was thus preoccupied. He knew he'd called at Walden. Was he going to speak of it?

'And I'd thought that the power of command would permit me . . .'

Hervey fell silent, and Fairbrother sought to give form to his friend's thoughts – or what his friend would wish to believe were his thoughts (Walden he must leave to his own good time). '*Urbem lateritiam invenit, marmoream reliquit.*'*

Hervey laughed. 'How you flatter me! But I would say that Rome was a fine city before, that Augustus only added to it. So in that sense I accept your flattery.'

'Recall also that Augustus was forty years emperor. You have but a fraction of that.'

'Indeed.' But Hervey shook his head, and then cut to the point. 'Collins will be court-martialled. There's nothing I can do – nothing I can do in law – to prevent it.'

Fairbrother sighed. 'You don't think you're in want of dispassion in this?'

'Call it what you will. I've known Collins since the Peninsula. And in Canada . . .'

Fairbrother knew about Canada (Johnson had told him), when the Shawanese had left Armstrong for dead, and Henrietta as good

* 'He found a city of bricks and left a city of marble.'

252

as, and Collins had tracked them for days, beaten them at their own game, on their own ground, and put a noose round the neck of every one of them. And Henrietta's year's mind fell at this time. It must go hard with his friend yet.

'Of course,' he said, simply.

Silence.

'I'll engage the best counsel,' declared Hervey suddenly. 'Money shall be no object. Malet's already been to see the Judge Advocate General.'

Fairbrother shook his head. 'Then there will be much law but no guarantee of justice. I do say we would have disposed of these things better in the King's Africans.'

Hervey was still elsewhere. 'What?'

'No matter – a peccant notion.'

'What is?'

'It's of no account. I spoke without thinking.'

'It's a habit of yours, which I find most congenial.'

'Then it shall ever be so. But now that I do come to think of it, I have only lately remembered that it is Saturday and I have an engagement in Covent Garden.'

'What? It has been Saturday since first you rose this morning. How now do you remember an engagement? We're to talk of matters at dinner, I'd thought. I've not told you yet of Norfolk.'

'No, but Johnson has. By the bye, he says the word in barracks is that a man who rides with you comes back on his shield or else with another stripe.'

Hervey frowned. Barracks banter – a most perilous thing to acquire a taste for (tasty as it might be). Poor Agar, brave Acton, and now Wakefield – was that how the doyens of the canteen saw it? But his friend had evidently made convivial arrangements . . . 'Well, let me not keep you from your theatre. I hear, by the way, the Lyceum's burned down.'

'I was never much fond of opera, there being none to hear in my salad days. But a good song . . . '

'Sung by a fair singer . . . '

'Fair or dark.'

Hervey smiled. 'See, I'll come with you – as far as the United Service, for there are things I can do. We can take horses from the livery here. A canter's a cure for every evil. How is General Gifford, indeed – other than of a mind to sell a horse?'

'Quite well,' replied Fairbrother, guardedly. 'He's removed to his house. Why?'

'I . . . I thought I might visit with him . . . tomorrow . . . To thank him.'

It was a little before six, an awkward hour to call, but not impossible. He ought perhaps to have gone to the United Service first, changed into fresh clothes and taken a hackney to Holland Park, but paying an unexpected call at this time was in any case most unlikely to find anyone at home, and then all he would have done was waste time and expense.

He sprang clear of the saddle, endeavouring to keep his coat clean (the gelding had sweated), took up the reins and pulled on the doorbell.

'Colonel Hervey, sir,' said the footman in evident – and delighted – surprise.

'Good evening, George. Is her ladyship at home?'

The elder and longest-serving of Kat's footmen bowed. 'I will see, Colonel. I shall send a groom at once for your horse.'

A stable lad came running, and then the footman returned. 'Her ladyship asks if you will wait in her sitting room, Colonel.'

He sighed with relief. 'Thank you; I shall.'

It had been many months since he'd waited in Kat's sitting room – a year, at least, or was it two? (He didn't want to calculate; it was unseemly.) A fire burned, there were many candles; it was all pleasingly unaltered (and so much warmer, in every sense, than Walden). He stood before the chimneypiece and tried to compose himself appropriately. They had been lovers, and there was issue from that love, which Kat had contrived, evidently with success, to pass off otherwise – heir to Lieutenant-General Sir Peregrine Greville, lieutenant-governor of Alderney and Sark, a man so high on the gradation list as to be by rights pensionable, but whom the authorities, for reasons best known to them, found convenient to keep on the full-pay. Hervey was not proud of his falseness – indeed he was not – but Sir Peregrine was evidently content with his situation (in his ignorance, that is). He appeared to like London not very much, while liking a good deal the fishing for which his appointment provided ample time; and he found that neither his duties as commandant of what had once been the foremost garrison 'gainst the French, nor those as member in the Tory interest for the 'close and decayed' parliamentary borough of St Felix (consisting of three houses and seven voters, most of the borough having long fallen into the sea), brought him thence more than two or three times a year. In these circumstances, and the difference in their age, it had to be unsurprising that Kat had found the society of men such as Hervey both agreeable and ready; and for his part, inasmuch as he dare think about it, Hervey absolved himself with the notion that he took nothing from the lieutenant-general, for the lieutenant-general availeth himself not.

'Matthew.'

He turned.

Kat was not dressed for the theatre, evidently, or a levee; he supposed therefore she could give him her time – a double relief.

And the sight of her was exactly as it had always been. Even without jewels and ornaments she lit up the room as surely as she had at Windsor. She kissed him and then sat, indicating the chair adjacent.

'I'm sorry I sent you no word. I returned from Norfolk only yesterday.'

'Then I'm honoured, for you must have come at once – before, even, you had discharged all your duties . . . But no, you would never have been able to forgo duty.'

She said it so sweetly and with such a pleasant smile that he could not find her teasing (no matter that it was with an edge) in the least discomfiting.

'How is Captain Peto? You saw him, I suppose?'

'I did, and found him quite remarkably well – thanks, I may say, to your good offices.'

Kat shook her head ever so slightly. 'It was nothing. George Cholmondeley was at once amenable – what was it, now, eighteen months ago? I saw him only lately, and he said that Captain Peto was greatly restored and in excellent spirits. He has a most devoted nurse, I understand.'

Hervey supposed she knew of matters precisely – she had a way with these things – but didn't wish to explore it. The waters were too deep. 'Admirable, admirable.'

'Shall you have a little supper with me?'

'I . . . had not . . . I thank you, yes.'

She pulled the bell, and the footman came. 'Colonel Hervey will take supper this evening, George. There is no one else, is there?'

'No, m'lady.'

'Very well.'

'M'lady.'

'You have no establishment to return to at Hounslow then,' she asked – suggested – when George was gone.

'I . . . well, that is . . . for the moment, at least, we put up at the Berkeley Arms at Cranford. We – that is – Fairbrother and I. He did me great service, you know, in Bulgaria last year – and before that, of course, at the Cape.'

'And you are to take a house soon? The Hol'nesses' perhaps?'

'I . . . I think not, for the moment . . . There is much to be about. The Low Countries . . .'

He supposed she knew the situation at Hounslow as precisely as she did that at Houghton, for she was a patroness of Almack's: *All on the magic list depends / Fame, fortune, fashion, lovers, friends*. And their business was everybody's.

'But lonely, it must be,' (she said solicitously) 'the exercise of command, without one to share its trials and tribulations – and, of course, its delights.'

'You speak as one with experience.' He regretted saying it. It was unkind, for it was true. But it was as near as he intended acknowledging her enquiry.

'But I entered upon my contract knowingly, my eyes wide open, Matthew, and Sir Peregrine likewise.'

He said nothing.

'You, however, entered upon yours honourably. I do not say that I did otherwise, for mine was not "taken in hand, unadvisedly, lightly, or wantonly", as the Church cautions, and most definitely not to satisfy "carnal lusts and appetites"; but it was not, I freely admit, for the causes for which matrimony was supposedly ordained, except perhaps in the extreme of the meaning of "help and comfort in prosperity".'

Her recall of the Prayer Book was quite exact. Indeed, he found her quite reverent for once – almost earnest.

'But you, Matthew – you wished, did you not, in all sincerity, to embrace those causes?'

'Kat, I . . .'

'And, as I understand it, those causes are now denied you.'

But how did she understand it? By whose word? Was it, in any case, true that the causes were denied him? And how had he exerted himself in those causes? And were not these early days, still?

What nonsense! He deluded himself; had he not walked from Walden Park knowing he would never return?

'Matthew, I make no judgements, I merely speak as I find. And I find you . . . if not unhappy, then less happy than you have a right to be. And in being less than rightfully happy, others about you must be less so.'

This, however, was a proposition he could find no warrant for in his own experience. He was sure of it. He had always been able to leave behind whatever melancholy beset him as soon as the trumpet sounded.

And yet he owed her more than simply pretending now, as they spoke, that indeed he heard the trumpet. They had for too long been one flesh.

'Kat, I . . .'

She smiled compassionately as his words petered out. 'There is so much to speak of, Matthew.' She laid a hand on his reassuringly. 'And there is time this evening.'

*

In Rules, which had now become quite his favourite place to entertain his growing circle of Garden acquaintances, Fairbrother was dining too, and with not one but two pairs of fine eyes. And so charmingly and wittily attentive he was to them that neither lady could have noticed how from time to time he glanced about the room, and to one, empty, table in particular – a table which of late had become the property, so to speak, of a considerable swell; a table commanding the room – the *street*, for to gaze within by any window would be to see this *table d'honneur* beyond any other. Indeed each Saturday since his friend had left for Norfolk, and several other evenings also, Fairbrother had observed at that table the noisy consumption of champagne and the exaltation of its provider. He was, indeed, a little disappointed that it remained so quiet this night, but was consoled by the thought that it was kept for the arrival of the generous pockets. Meanwhile he'd bought champagne himself, for he'd come a little late, and his ladies were already seated. He arrived, however, with nosegays of spring violets, explaining that he had gone to the flower market and been detained speaking with two of the porters – 'excellent fellows' whom he had met on several occasions – and that he trusted the posies would explain his discourtesy, and the wine make up for it. And they replied that they'd made nothing of it, for the *maître d'hôtel* had told them that he had come in earlier to reserve especially this table before going in search of flowers. So their dinner was as agreeable as on previous evenings, with Fairbrother now all attention – so agreeable indeed that they did not notice the arrival of the swell at the *table d'honneur* an hour or so later.

'Ladies, would you permit me to leave you for a moment, so that I may have words of business with one who is lately come?'

How could they refuse him? Especially when he had beckoned the waiter to bring them more champagne.

He left them to the popping of the cork, and slipped outside unobserved, the curtains by the door as good as the tabs and legs that masked the wings on the stage that his charming companions had not long quit that evening.

'Ronald?'

A man of broad shoulders and few teeth emerged from the pool of darkness that was the entrance to Bull-inn Court. 'Aye, sir.'

'And Billy?'

Ronald indicated that Billy was in the shadows behind him.

Fairbrother beckoned them to follow.

They crossed the street and stopped short of one of the windows a little way along (Rules was as well-lit outside as in). Fairbrother took a look and then bid his accomplice do the same.

'See, the table I pointed to you earlier – the man with the yellow neckcloth?'

'I see 'im, sir.'

'Sure of it?'

'Never surer, sir. Never forget a face.'

They withdrew along the street, back into the shadows.

'Very well. Use what threats and devices you will, but no bones broken, no bruises to see.'

'Don't you worry, sir.'

'Then here's the sovereign, and the other to follow when your powers of persuasion have proved effective.'

'Aye, sir. You can depend on it.'

'I bid you good night then, Ronald. I'll leave with my guests presently. You, I'm afraid, will have a rather longer wait.'

259

'Don't you be worrying about us, sir. We waits all night anyway, us porters. That's the Garden.'

Fairbrother shook Ronald's hand, and Billy's, and made back for the door of Rules, content now in his stratagem. 'Condemned battalion' his Royal Africans may have been, but their ways weren't always inferior. Less law, maybe; but more justice – unquestionably.

Next morning, having bathed and changed clothes, Hervey called on Lord George Irvine after church. He had not thought to do so at first, but a most agreeable development of the evening before made it no longer necessary to call on General Gifford.

It had been a most uncertain plan in any case, but the only one he could conceive of that avoided felony. He had no scruple regarding such a felony, only a concern not to implicate others – not least because it would compromise his own integrity in command. 'Will no one rid me of this troublesome priest?' – it was all, indeed, that he need have said, and Collins's – his – problems would have been at an end. Except that, actions having consequences for ill as well as for good, who knew what would happen after the riddance? And so he had resolved on action by his own hand, intending to call on General Gifford and explain the situation, asking his advice – it was not unheard of for an officer to ask counsel of a senior; and in the course of their conversation, though he had no very clear idea how, he might suggest that Lieutenant Kennett be appointed to his staff, with the free promotion that such an appointment would carry. On condition, of course – as Gifford himself would have to make plain – that all proceedings with respect to Collins were dropped; for it would not do for an aide-de-camp at the Horse Guards to be embroiled in an affair that might excite the public interest (such a reason was surely plausible?). He had hoped that he would not at any point have to allude to the circumstances in which his friend Fairbrother had discovered the wounded general, but had been perfectly prepared to do so.

But all this was now unnecessary. He would be spared – the general too – the indelicacy of such an interview. Kat had insisted she would arrange matters. He had not thought at first to speak of it, but she herself had raised the 'terrible affair of Bobby Gifford' (she knew him well – of course). And Hervey had told her of the connection with Fairbrother, and then as the evening wore on the story of Kennett and Collins, and so much more (how good it was to be able to speak freely), and somehow the plan had been revealed, and Kat had said, 'But Matthew, Bobby is such a dear man. Were I to tell him all this he would at once do as I ask. You must permit me. I can call tomorrow. It will be the easiest thing. Believe me.'

And all he'd been able to say, for such was the hour and his relief that here was Collins's deliverance – and his own (for who knew how Gifford might react to his implied threats) – was that she was the very finest of women, her goodness to him knew no bounds, and he was ever in her debt.

PART TWO

THE COCKPIT OF CHRISTENDOM

For the Netherlands have been for many years, as one may say, the very cockpit of Christendom, the school of arms and rendezvous of all adventurous spirits and cadets . . .

> *James Howell, clerk in the diplomatic service,*
> Instructions for Foreign Travel (*1642*)

THE ARTICLES OF LONDON

1. The union shall be intimate and complete, so that the two countries shall form but one State, to be governed by the Fundamental Law already established in Holland, which by mutual consent shall be modified according to the circumstances.

2. There shall be no change in those Articles of the Fundamental Law which secure to all religious cults equal protection and privileges, and guarantee the admissibility of all citizens, whatever be their religious creed, to public offices and dignities.

3. The Belgian provinces shall be in a fitting manner represented in the States-General, whose sittings in time of peace shall be held by turns in a Dutch and a Belgian town.

4. All the inhabitants of the Netherlands thus having equal constitutional rights, they shall have equal claim to all commercial and other rights, of which their circumstances allow, without any hindrance or obstruction being imposed on any to the profit of others.

5. Immediately after the union the provinces and towns of Belgium shall be admitted to the commerce and navigation of the colonies of Holland upon the same footing as the Dutch provinces and towns.

6. The debts contracted on the one side by the Dutch, and on the other side by the Belgian provinces, shall be charged to the public chest of the Netherlands.

7. The expenses required for the building and maintenance of the frontier

fortresses of the new State shall be borne by the public chest as serving the security and independence of the whole nation.

8. The cost of the making and upkeep of the dykes shall be at the charge of the districts more directly interested, except in the case of an extraordinary disaster.

The Eight Articles of London,
also known as the London Protocol of 21 June 1814,
homologated by the Final Act of the Congress of Vienna
on 9 June 1815

XVII

A CLOSE RUN THING

Waterloo, 18 June 1830

'Show me a man's horse and I will tell you what sort of man he is!' said Fairbrother triumphantly.

Hervey acknowledged, ruefully. Jessye was long gone – Jessye the 'covert hack', as his richer fellow cornets had called her, fit only to ride to the meet, not to hunt. But she'd carried him the better part of the battle that day, when Nero had fallen to French shell (and he with him – and escaping a *coup de grâce* by the closest of shaves), and not once had he wished for another.

'Handsome is as handsome does.'

'As you have often said,' replied Fairbrother, with a knowing smile.

But Ajax – or 'Greater' Ajax as Hervey insisted – was indeed a handsome horse: liver-chestnut, sixteen hands, seven-eighths bred (with Cleveland for strength), rising nine and gelded as a yearling, he possessed every quality required of the battle charger of a commanding officer of light dragoons. And although Hervey had paid a good deal more for him than he'd hoped, the price was a good deal less than General Gifford would have got in Leicestershire. And Dolly, a nice-looking bay mare bought from his new brother-in-law, the baron, served him very well as second charger. Both had done the seventy miles from Ostend without casting a shoe. The beautiful grey Orlov, however, which Princess Lieven had sent him, remained in the care of the riding-master at Hounslow, for he'd not yet discerned whether he might keep him. An inkstand was one thing, but a stallion of that quality . . .

What a coming they'd had of it compared with before – fifteen years before – when they'd had to push the horses overboard to swim for the beach. This time they'd sailed from the very heart of London, the new St Katharine Docks, and in steamers, bringing them on the tide and with a fair wind to the Belgic coast in just twelve hours, every trooper able to disembark by gangway like a foot passenger. It pleased him greatly to watch the regiment – *his* regiment – assemble with all the regularity that had eluded that first hasty reinforcement, when Bonaparte had slipped his leash on Elba, crossed to the mainland of France and marched to Paris gathering his followers as he went. *Les Cent Jours*, the prefect of Paris had called it – 'the Hundred Days', from the time the Great Disturber reinstalled himself in the Tuileries to the time of his surrender to the captain of HMS *Bellerophon*, 'Billy Ruffian' to her tars. *Waterloo* (so strange a name, yet as English now as *Agincourt*): the battle that had stopped Bonaparte in his tracks, wherever those tracks were meant to be leading (it was most uncertain – and, in truth, probably to nowhere); the battle to end all battles. With what memories he might now conjure, and the soldier's rhyme – *Were you at Waterloo? / I have been at Waterloo. / 'Tis no matter what you do / If you were at Waterloo.*

Malet rode up and saluted. 'Colonel, a galloper from the crown prince's suite. There's delay in their leaving Brussels. The parade's now to be at two o'clock.'

Hervey took out his watch – an hour and a half to wait. 'Very well; the regiment to dismount and loosen girths.'

These things were not uncommon. An hour or so's ease would do no harm – would be welcome indeed, though the day was by no means as hot as it had been fifteen years ago.

'Have the Prussians arrived yet?' he asked, hardly able to contain his mirth.

'I understand so, Colonel.'

'Then I'll go and see them.'

The Netherlanders were already on the field – a regiment of cavalry which at a distance looked much like his own. He could see that they were already messing. He supposed that they themselves would have the canteen waggons brought up sooner or later – Mr Lincoln would make the arrangements in due season. He congratulated himself again on making a regiment of it rather than a detachment. He fancied that his report from Norfolk had disposed the Horse Guards to be generous when he demanded the extra shipping.

And generous they were certainly being, for at first they'd said the horses were to be had from the Belgics, but he'd argued that it would scarcely be to the prestige of Great Britain and the House of Hanover to send a demounted regiment of cavalry (nor, indeed, much of a compliment to their royal colonel-in-chief), and the King had been of that opinion too when somehow (and it was as well that these things were privy) he'd learned of the proposed economy. And then once it had become known that a regiment of cavalry was to be sent to the United Kingdom of the Netherlands, the foreign secretary, Lord Aberdeen, had asked that their stay might be prolonged to take part in the summer manoeuvres, for the French and Prussians had been invited to send regiments too, and he thought it no bad thing that 'we might keep watch on what Talleyrand and the King of Prussia are up to'. And so Hervey had found himself in the office of yet another minister of the Crown, being entrusted with the 'safeguard of what we gained at Vienna' – though in truth his lordship's words were so Delphic that he wondered if anyone in the Foreign department truly knew what was in the mind of anyone else.

'Let us go and pay our compliments to the Prussians,' he said to Fairbrother as Malet turned away. 'And I'll show you the place we stood for most of the day waiting for them.'

His original design had been to ride the whole of the battlefield with the regiment the day before, and he had engaged as guide an officer – an expert in survey and topographical drawing – whom Lord Hill had commissioned to make a model of the battle (for the French had such a one at Les Invalides), but a thunderstorm even worse than that which had soaked them in 1815 kept all in their billets, and it had been only that morning that they had been able to see the field, but from atop the ridge of Mont St Jean; they would ride the rest tomorrow.

Hervey cursed again. 'That damned mound!'

A hill perfectly regular, unnatural, and not at all in keeping with the country around, stood now in the middle of the battlefield (that part of it where the day had been decided); and atop it a huge bronze lion, its front paw upon a sphere, signifying victory – the *Butte du Lion.*

'Well, I fancy it'll afford a fine view at least,' said Fairbrother, inclined to regard monuments as the privilege of the victor.

'I wonder if they consulted the duke before piling up so much earth.'

'You don't think that would have been to elevate him to a status inconsistent with protocol?' replied Fairbrother, with a hint of mischief. 'A king need hardly ask leave to pile up earth in his own realm.'

'Well it's a deuced mountain in such a place. An arch would have been enough – and in the village rather than where the fighting was.'

'And a statue of the duke atop – the "Arch-Duke"?'

'Don't try me. Besides, here he's Prince of Waterloo.'

'I didn't know that.'

Hervey smiled ironically. 'You should make careful study of these things.'

'Come, you know I don't make light of the battle.'

'Of course.'

'And, you know,' continued Fairbrother, now more solemnly, 'it's shrewd of the king – the Dutch king – to build such a monument, for otherwise it's only the duke's battle, or Blücher's, which hardly serves to fortify his dominion over the Belgics. And if the place of that mound is where the crown prince shed blood – he did shed blood, did he not? – then it's a sort of hallowing.'

Hervey frowned.

Fairbrother knew why. 'Oh, I know it's all nonsense if you care to examine it as would a scientific, but that's not the way with these people, is it? We've seen for ourselves how wary they are still. This has been the cockpit of Europe for three hundred years, has it not? I fancy William is ever mindful of that.'

'Indeed I suppose he must be. You yourself are ever thoughtful in these matters.'

'Perhaps only because I have the time.'

'Ha! *Time* – the only supply that Bonaparte refused his generals.'

'He was not always wrong.'

'Now you *do* try me!'

They trotted on in amused silence until coming on the Prussians beyond the crossroads above La Haye Sainte – three squadrons of the 'Death's Head Hussars'. They'd messed together in the week before (and woken next morning with, said the wags, heads like death), and so Hervey was able to pass the time of day with their colonel without formality, though he was a Prussian of decidedly less warmth than old Prince Blücher, before saying he wanted to show his friend the left-most extent of the line at Mont St Jean 'before you came to our relief that day'.

Calculated flattery, but harmless, he reckoned. And, indeed, whatever now the recollections of that day – the duke's own recollections, he'd heard tell – the coming of the Prussians hadn't been a moment too soon.

And so after a rather formal acceptance of schnapps, talk of 'La Belle Alliance' and more saluting, they took their leave.

'You know,' said Fairbrother, as they kicked into a trot and put confidential distance between them and the 'Death Heads', 'for my own part I count this adventure worthwhile purely to meet the Prussian. What a singular race.'

'Better an ally than an enemy, I should hazard,' said Hervey. 'By the bye, I think yon *oberst* was perplexed by your appearance.'

'My complexion or my coat?'

'I've no notion what he makes of your complexion, only your coat.'

'As I've said before, to wear a captain's coat would confuse matters. And a black one was good enough for the duke that day.'

'I can't deny it, but . . .' His thoughts were interrupted by the sudden appearance of rooftops. 'Now, see there.'

They pulled up half a mile on, opposite the hamlets of Papelotte and La Haye a few hundred yards across the valley to the right. Hervey pointed.

'The left flank?'

'I think it was here exactly. We'd come up in column from the other side of the crossroads – there were so many men that morning, and so few marks to go by – and I recall how we executed a very smart turn from column into line – really, it was as if on parade – and we came to a halt on this slope facing across the valley with the sun on our faces. My troop was in the second line forming the support to "B", and Edward Lankester called me forward and asked if I supposed this was where the duke intended.'

'Because you'd ridden with the duke on his exploration.'

'Just so.' Hervey had a moment's recollection of Lankester, the finest of men, who would have become Kezia's brother-in-law had he lived; and of his brother, Ivo, killed at the head of the regiment too, ten years on – men whose boots he now filled . . . 'And I pointed out the scattering of farms below us – mark the roofs yonder, just as they were – where he'd placed the Nassauers. And the farm at La Haye Sainte below the crossroads, over on the right – which you may just see if you stand in your stirrups: he'd garrisoned it with some of the German Legion and the Rifles. We can't see the château at Hougoumont from here, for it's a mile beyond the farm – you saw its roof when we rode the ridge this morning: he put four companies of the Guards there. And, here, look . . .' (he took out the sketch map from that day, which he'd made after the ride with the duke and preserved all these years in an oilskin): 'there's nothing to our east but the Forest of Ohain, and then a couple of leagues or so beyond the forest were the Prussians.'

Fairbrother shook his head. '*Bliss was it in that dawn to be alive!* Oh, to have been with you instead of that fort at Goree!'

Hervey looked grave. 'I'm so very glad you were not, for had you been there you might well not have been here now. Edmonds, Lankester . . . so many good fellows were struck down.'

For once his friend was moved to silence.

Hervey sighed. 'But it's all in the past. So very much in the past. And so much has been in the years since . . . Come, we must get back for our prince – indeed, our princess.'

The landau came on at a good trot with two outriders in Saxon green astride well-matched greys, the same as the coach-horses, four of them – high-stepping, active still after their dozen miles from the outskirts of Brussels where the Princess Augusta had taken up residence for the celebrations.

Hervey stood with Malet and the regimental serjeant-major at the end of the double line of dragoons drawn up for inspection, behind them their chargers, grooms, orderlies and covermen waiting. Two grooms stood in advance with a handsome little Trakehner, got up with a side-saddle (one of Monsieur Pellier's new design, with a balance strap and second pommel, the 'leaping head') over a regimental shabracque with the colonel's Bath star atop the crown sewn onto the points. Princess Augusta was to ride with her regiment over the field of Waterloo – at its head, indeed – and Hervey had been determined that she did so duly mounted. Malet had therefore toured the liveries until he found a gelding that looked the part and was schooled to the Pellier saddle, and a second for the lady-in-waiting, and Mr Lincoln had engaged seamstresses and wire-workers in Brussels to make the saddle-cloth.

The carriage pulled up, footmen alike in Saxon green slipping down gracefully to open the door.

Hervey and party saluted – and did so in some astonishment, for Princess Augusta wore tunic and shako. How she'd got them, and the Sixth's crossbelt, all exactly *comme il faut*, he couldn't imagine. 'Good afternoon, Your Highness,' he said, smiling with the compliment she paid them.

The princess touched the peak of her shako with her riding whip, evidently instructed in the easy ways of a colonel of cavalry.

The party was quite transfixed. Indeed Hervey struggled to recollect himself. The Princess Augusta was a strikingly handsome woman, in her late twenties, Kezia's age, her features angular and her complexion dark for one whose ancestors must have trounced the Romans in the Teutoburgerwald. In court dress, when they'd all been presented in Brussels a few days before, she had dazzled; now, in riding skirt and regimentals, she was truly arresting. Once before had he seen hair gathered up inside a shako – Henrietta's, when she'd visited him secretly in the night, when the Sixth had been on a scheme in . . .

'I am sorry to have kept you waiting, Colonel Hervey, but the prince had affairs of state this morning, evidently.'

'It was no hardship, ma'am.'

She greeted Malet and the serjeant-major. Her lady-in-waiting curtsied.

Grooms brought the Trakehners forward, and mounting blocks. Hervey and his party were quick into the saddle – protocol demanded they be mounted before the colonel – and quickly formed column of twos for the inspection.

The princess was all ease and appreciative nods as she rode along the ranks – no Prussian stiffness, no Saxon chill. What an adornment the Sixth had got themselves. In these days of retrenchment still, a word in the King's ear might be the saving of a troop if it came to further economies; and from such as the Princess Augusta, a word that could scarcely be resisted . . .

Up and down the ranks, until Hervey had presented every officer and serjeant-major – she smiling the while, looking each man in the eye, a little Augustan stardust sprinkled on every dragoon, so that the meanest-bred thought himself superior, and the most hardened that he might yet have a soul.

Armstrong above all, perhaps, had never looked more the part. Every piece of his metal glinted, and his leather shone like washed coal, or else was blanco'd like new-dug chalk, his aspect the personification of hard-won experience and loyalty unto death.

And Collins, too – in his rightful place, with his troop, his character unblemished, his authority undiminished. What a business it had all been. But it mattered not, now, the charges withdrawn. Kat had been as good as her word – evidently; what a deal he owed her . . . in so many ways.

But for the meantime he would mutter simply 'prudential judgement', and put it all from his mind, as he would too the question of who would replace Mr Rennie . . .

The crown prince's party was approaching. They made back quickly for the front.

It was a pleasingly modest cortège, observed Hervey – all mounted (no carriages), half a dozen equerries and orderlies, and a lance escort of the same number.

'Leave to carry on, ma'am?'

As he said it he thought he ought to have expressed himself fully rather than in the abridged terms of the parade ground. However, she smiled and bowed. If she hadn't any notion of what precisely he was saying, she could reasonably suppose that he himself had.

He saluted, reined about, trotted front and centre, and drew his sword – the signal that he now took personal command of the parade.

While the inspection had been taking place, the other two

regiments had come up into line. The Sixth were drawn up on the right, with the Dutch *4 Regement Lichte Dragonder* in the centre, and the Prussian *Leib-Husaren-Regiment 1* on the left, the direction from which they'd arrived on the field at the eleventh hour of that close-run day in 1815. The crown prince slowed his charger to a walk as he came to the Hussars, and having served with the Prussians as a cadet proceeded along their front rank with all his famous affability. Then came his *Dragonder*, with familiar nods and as many smiles, and then to the Sixth.

'Light Dragoons, Pres-e-e-ent . . . Arms!'

Hervey let the words carry towards the prince's party, the cautionary 'Light Dragoons' the privilege of the commanding officer alone. Then, reining left, put his charger into a trot to pay compliments at the junction with the Dutch.

'Good afternoon, Colonel Hervey,' said the prince, his accent guttural but not pronounced, returning the sword-salute with his hand. 'It is a fine thing to see your regiment again after so long.'

Hervey recovered his sword and returned the prince's warm smile ('Slender Billy' might still answer to the name, sitting tall and long in the saddle – Hervey's own age, but a major general before he was twenty-one). 'It is a fine thing to be here again, sir.'

They rode along the front rank, the prince nodding approvingly, with 'good afternoons' here and there to officers and dragoons alike. It was, after all, a day simply to ride over old ground, to mark the decade and a half since that day – a decade and a half of peace indeed, for Waterloo had confirmed Vienna, and Vienna had put an end to war.

'Fine men, Colonel Hervey; fine horses too,' said the prince. 'I am so very gratified that His Majesty King George has seen fit to send them.'

Hervey bowed.

'And so we shall now take a little gallop across the field, and yours shall be the directing regiment, Colonel. Our *objectif* is La Belle Alliance.'

The right was not always the directing regiment, and Hervey took it as a further compliment: 'Sir,' he replied, saluting as the crown prince and his party dispersed to their various posts.

La Belle Alliance: was there ever a more aptly named rendezvous? – the inn on the Charleroi road where the duke had shaken hands with Prince Blücher after the battle. 'Alte Vorwärts' had little French, and the duke no German, so '*Lieber kamerad*' and '*Quelle affaire*' was all they could manage.

And how well did Hervey recall the inn's shelter that night, when he'd recovered the body of Serjeant Strange, wrapped it in a velvet curtain – *blue* velvet, the colour that in life had clothed him – lain down in the same room and slept, exhausted, oblivious of all without . . .

'Colonel Hervey?'

He woke. 'Ma'am?'

'You will permit me to ride with you?'

Hervey tried not to look dismayed. 'Ma'am, I . . . But of course. It is your regiment indeed.'

And if she were to be thrown, and her regiment ride over her . . . Better not to think on it. 'Ma'am, I would have my covering serjeant check the girth.'

Serjeant Acton sprang from the saddle as the princess held up her skirt, and knew at once he'd face a deal of ribaldry at mess that night. He tightened the straps – and then those of the countess's saddle – with singular despatch.

'Thank you, Serjeant,' said the princess, as Acton remounted; and then, to Hervey, 'It is a most fine thing to have a regiment of cavalry keeping watch.'

There was a blush to her face – and, he feared, to his too. He cleared his throat and spoke as blithely as he could – the first thing that entered his head: 'We kept watch most of that day, the battle, ma'am, over on the left flank, until we were called to the centre towards the middle of the afternoon – to about where we stand now, as I recall, though there was a great deal of smoke. I think, however, that we shall ride the very ground over which we charged at the last and sent the French reeling. It was very well judged. The Duke of Wellington caught them just so.'

As he finished he saw with relief the prince take off his hat and with a great flourish wave it in the direction of 'the French': 'The whole line will advance!'

The royal trumpeter sounded 'Walk-March'.

'Exactly as the duke did it,' said Hervey to the princess as they billowed forward. 'The very words and gesture, when we knew it must all be done, the French finished.'

'Then what a day this is too,' she said. 'I never thought to see.'

'Ma'am.' But Hervey's eyes were already on the prince, for he had to regulate the advance. He must trust to the princess to keep up, or else to Acton to rescue her if she didn't.

The first hundred yards let the brigade find its natural spacing, and then the prince's trumpeter blew 'Trot'. The line began elongating, as it always did, though Hervey kept the axis exactly parallel with the prince's, so that the Dutch were pushed even more to the left, and there was a deal of swearing until the Prussians gave ground – just as any field day.

He'd already decided to regulate the pace as well as the direction and dressing (the prince could check his own if he got too far in front), for it wasn't the day for a melee, and he held the Sixth in a short trot as they went down the slope to the sunken lane that had unhorsed so many of Bonaparte's cavalry, in turn forcing the Prussians to come back to a walk temporarily to avoid the shame of outrunning the directing flank. He saw and couldn't help but smile, for they'd now have a devil of a scramble to cross the ditch, fall behind and then have to catch up – with even more swearing.

The princess gave her gelding its head – in and then out of the lane in two easy bounds, with a short step between. Hervey saw – and she his admiring look. He glanced back to see the countess take the lane with the same ease. He need have no worries.

Indeed he could now take his ease: the lane was the only test between the ridge and the inn. Any horse could stumble in a rabbit hole, but there was nothing to check a regiment's worth.

He glanced behind again – the Sixth were in good order – and then left. The Dutch and the Germans appeared to have come to terms, but the prince was pulling ahead, so he extended the trot.

And then the trumpeter sounded 'Gallop'.

With no enemy to charge and no shot and shell to discompose them, the line was better behaved than many he'd ridden, but he was determined nevertheless to keep them in his check. Up the slope beyond Hougoumont they raced, the Prussians pulling ahead until he held out his sabre very emphatically and they began to conform. How much rye grass they trod down he'd no idea, but nothing he supposed to that day – and corn. It had concealed many a man, and all who fell.

Hoofs pounded – joyous noise! – and now they were half-way to La Belle Alliance, where they'd come on the battery, and he'd led the squadrons straight at the big 12-pounders that had tormented the duke's line all day – '*les belles filles de l'empereur*'. The gunners had no fight left in them – they ought to have been able to get off a round of grape, but instead they raced for their horses or cowered under the guns. And the Sixth had fallen on them with rare savagery, the drivers – boys, some of them – crying as the sabres cut, dragoons standing in the stirrups for extra force in the downswing. No one who didn't raise his hands was spared, and some who did found it too late.

The princess galloped on his right. She sat so prettily and with such assurance – with courage, indeed, the pace now fast and the ground unknown. His dragoons would be able to see, too; it would do them no harm to admire their colonel-in-chief.

And now La Belle Alliance was just a furlong ahead – the moment to give point. But the prince had said he wouldn't risk a charge: he wanted the battle to claim no more men or horses.

But the Prussians were once more forcing the pace, and Hervey cursed them roundly below his breath. Out went his sword again, and he glowered at their *oberst* – had *he* ever led a charge in battle? Till at last the deuced man checked his gallop, and in turn brought his hussars back into line.

They were well drilled – of that no doubt – and Hervey could scarcely damn their eyes for long. They rode admirably. He looked forward to their manoeuvres together in the weeks to come – if only they'd admit that Frederick the Great was long dead.

He'd done his duty, though – and more – bringing them up in such order that they might charge now as a brigade, tight enough to break a whole division. But it was the prince's now to take them left or right of the cluster of buildings about L'Alliance, and to wherever beyond – to practise the rally perhaps, or pursuit?

Instead the prince thrust his sword high and his trumpeter blew 'Halt'.

The Sixth checked at once and without repeats, for every man and horse knew the call – C, G, octave C. In fifty yards Hervey had them back in a trot, and halted in another ten. He'd lost not a single bolter – as good as the best field day, and better than most (how right to insist they brought their own troopers).

But the Prussians, unused to the Dutch-English calls, nor their *oberst* evidently to the rules of the game, were slower, and had begun overrunning the prince before getting back in-hand (in truth, 'Halt' was a movable feast, as Hervey always called it: all depended on where it began).

'*Nach Paris, Herr Oberst?*' the crown prince teased, bringing enthusiastic calls from the hussars.

The princess's face was all exhilaration. 'Colonel Hervey, your regiment – *c'est magnifique!*'

Hervey coloured. Perhaps it was the French, and the accent from beyond the Rhine. 'Ma'am, it is *your* regiment. I wish only that you were seeing every man of it on parade.'

'Then I hope I shall have opportunity to do so, in England.'

Hervey answered as he knew would Lord George Irvine. 'Ma'am, you must be welcome at any time.'

An aide-de-camp cantered over. 'Sir, His Royal Highness invites you to take refreshment with him, and your regiment also.'

A princely refreshment too. Behind the inn were picketing lines in the welcome shade of orchards and plantations, and on long rows of canopied tables a cold feast the like of which no dragoon believed he had ever been treated to. Beef, ham, chicken, sausage, pickles, bread of all sorts, cake, brandied fruit, all *ad libitum*, and with plates and forks and knives so that they dined like gentlemen – and drank the local *saison* from Delft tankards specially made which the prince wished every man to take with him; Rennie and the troop serjeant-majors keeping watch on the taps the while, for although the beer was weak, the thirsts were strong. That the Prussians and the Dutch were not so fastidious was their business.

At the crown prince's table, under a white canopy decorated with emblems of the house of Orange-Nassau, Prussian eagles and the Union flag, a dozen sat with easy conviviality – the princess on his right, the object of all attention. Hervey marked, and not for the first time, how the presence of but a single woman (the countess too was at table, on his right, though mute) so completely changed the tone. Not that the conversation was any more elevated (although French had a way of sounding so) but that all seemed to frame their remarks with a desire for the lady's favour. He marked that he himself felt proprietorial – Princess Augusta was *his* colonel-in-chief after all – becoming restive at the accomplishment of the *oberst*, who seemed to extract the readiest smiles from her (must Prussia lord it over every German *staat*?).

So that when towards the end of the *déjeuner* the princess asked their host where they were all to go now, and the *oberst* said without waiting on the prince, '*Nach Paris! Tod dem französisch!*'* he could not force a smile until courtesy to his host (who laughed heartily) demanded he did.

* 'To Paris! Death to the French!'

'To *Brussels*, I think,' said the prince, bringing the mirth under regulation, and then adding to it: 'To the Duchess of Richmond's ball!'

Hervey laughed. It was a good joke, if rather at the expense of the Duke of Wellington.

'Were you there, Colonel Hervey?'

'No, sir, I was not. I was a mere cornet, I'm afraid.'

'Well, I myself left before supper!'

More laughter.

'But this time, I think we may have our supper and dancing without so rude an interruption!'

There was to be a soirée that evening, and tomorrow a grand ball, and a week of drawing rooms and levees, and then field days and schemes of manoeuvre and reviews. It was not to be a summer of idleness.

An aide-de-camp came to the table and bent to speak in the prince's ear.

The prince looked surprised. 'But first, and, I must declare, unexpectedly, the crown princess arrives,' he said, rising. 'I will present you all, gentlemen, and then we shall proceed to the place where the Prince of Waterloo – your Duke of Wellington' (nodding to Hervey) 'made his headquarters for the night, and pay our respects to my former commander-in-chief before returning to the city, where I hope to have the pleasure of your company again at nine.'

Hervey moved to Princess Augusta's side as the crown prince bowed and asked her leave to greet his consort.

'How apropos that they meet in the middle of a battlefield,' she said, sotto voce, when he'd stepped away, 'for they fight like dogs and cats.'

So confidential an aside, and something of a giggle, quite took him aback.

'Brussels is not St Petersburg,' she continued; 'It must be *sehr provinzlerisch*, though she prefers it to Amsterdam.' (The crown princess was the tenth child of Paul, Emperor and Autocrat of All the Russias.)

Would Princess Augusta salute, then, being in uniform, or would she curtsy? He decided it impertinent to ask – for all that she herself had begun it. Besides, these were deep waters: Saxony and Russia had fought on opposing sides so often – as, indeed, had the Dutch (and, for that matter, Prussia). Only the Austrians, he thought, had remained true. Thank God he was an Englishman! Never had England wavered (well, perhaps that wretched Peace of Amiens – 'a peace that every man must be glad of, but that no man could be proud of' – but not for long; not even a year). He might not have rank beyond the crown he wore on his shoulder, but in this of all places he counted himself inferior to none.

They gathered to be presented, but Princess Augusta took herself off to where the carriage halted, wishing to assert her independence – or status perhaps. Hervey smiled to himself as she kept her shako on and saluted rather than bend the knee. Was that why she'd worn uniform today? How clever if she had.

The crown prince guided his consort towards them, all smiles again to her own very formal air. Indeed Hervey thought she brought a distinctly northern chill to the heat of the field.

The crown prince beckoned him forward. 'Colonel Hervey, of His Britannic Majesty's Sixth Light Dragoons,' he said in French.

Hervey, scabbard in his left hand, saluted and looked her straight in the eye. '*Je suis honoré, votre altesse royale.*'

He had earlier toyed with '*impériale*', the honour due her as a daughter of the Russian emperor, but Malet's intelligence had previously suggested that '*impériale*' was a contentious form in the Dutch court.

Princess Anna Paulowna, as she was known less formally, held out a hand. The gesture was unexpected; nevertheless, Hervey was quick to remove his glove to kiss it.

'I am glad to see that ribbon at your neck, Colonel.' (He wore the yellow-edged, red silk of the Order of St Anna, presented to him in Bulgaria.) 'I am informed of your service with our army.'

'Our army' was a revealing locution, and, strictly, he had not served with but had been observing with . . . 'I was most fortunate, Your Highness.'

'You are acquainted with Princess Lieven, I understand, Colonel.'

He managed (he thought) to hide a look of uneasiness. 'Yes, ma'am. I made her acquaintance last year before going to the Levant.'

'And how is the princess?'

'When I saw her last, ma'am, she was exceedingly well.'

He was pleased with himself: he'd answered truthfully but without any indication of how recently they'd met (and thereby frequency) – for intrigue seemed endemic in ladies of St Petersburg.

The crown princess was a year or two his younger, perhaps. She was not what his subalterns would call a beauty, if nevertheless a fine subject for the brush. Her eyes were cold – or, in truth perhaps, sad: she could never have known her father, murdered in his own palace when she was but an infant, and her brothers and sisters were strewn across the courts of Europe like so many stallions and brood mares; and for what cause she and her husband fought 'like dogs and cats' (Princess Augusta's transposition was endearing) he could hardly suppose, and therefore could not judge.

But here Anna Paulowna was dignity personified. Why she'd driven from Brussels so unexpectedly, only to drive back again with her husband, he couldn't guess; but he supposed '*la cour a ses raisons*' (the pun pleased him).

But why had she spoken of Princess Lieven? What correspondence, and when, could there have been between the two, and to what purpose? He had never wished for the sort of 'society soldiery' beloved of so many who put on the King's coat, but it seemed he could not now shake it off.

The audience was over in a quarter of an hour. Anna Paulowna began taking her leave – and rather regally. Princess Augusta gave Hervey a look that could have been 'knowing', and there seemed a moment's confusion as to whether the crown prince would accompany his consort in the carriage or ride with 'his' commanding officers. It was settled that he would ride as far as the duke's old headquarters and there transfer to the royal landau, the second carriage proceeding empty as far as Waterloo.

'You see, her French is so much superior to his,' said Princess Augusta behind her glove. 'If he had the princess's command of the language and she his affability, then Wallonia might love, rather than scorn them.'

Hervey, while obliged, glanced at the Dutch officers, whose hearing (and French) might not have been so hard as to miss her meaning; but all seemed peaceful. 'Is the scorn so marked, ma'am? Nothing was said of it in London.'

She merely raised her eyebrows.

The chargers were brought up, and the lance escort took post to front and rear of the carriages. The crown prince bid Augusta ride with him, Hervey too, and the procession set off along the Chaussée de Charleroi to the three cheers of eight hundred cavalrymen.

Malet, Serjeant Acton and Hervey's trumpeter fell in close on his heels.

'They did well today, the regiment,' he said, beckoning the adjutant alongside as they began to trot.

'D Troop especially well, Colonel, I thought.'

'Especially D, yes. You'll make much of Prickett, then.'

'I shall, Colonel. I saw Mr Rennie nod approvingly to him. Rare praise.'

'Indeed. And I'll breakfast with Mordaunt tomorrow. I find it hard to say "Tyrwhitt's Troop" any longer.'

'I too. We should know the worst before the month's out.'

Hervey wasn't sure what the worst was, for acquittal wouldn't save Tyrwhitt from a charge of scandalous conduct, by all accounts (the reports in the Dublin papers were not propitious). And prison would mean cashiering, a lengthy business. One way or another, D Troop would have no captain for months more. But he'd said they wouldn't speak of it until word came . . .

And so the conversation changed to recollections of the battle as they rode the same path the duke himself had ridden that evening, when old Prince Blücher had said he would take up the pursuit, and the army had lain down exhausted and slept where it found itself when 'Retreat' sounded. The duke had returned to his head-quarters at the inn to write his despatch, said Hervey (as he learned later from one of the aides-de-camp), eaten some supper with his staff – those whom shot and shell had not carried off – and after putting down his pen in the early hours told his physician to bring him the casualty list at first light so that he might attach it. Sir Alexander Gordon, brother of the man who was now the foreign secretary ('I first met him at Corunna,' said Hervey), lay mortally wounded in the duke's own camp-bed, so instead he'd lain down in an upstairs room, wrapped in his cloak. 'But for the roof over his head, which was a needless shelter that night, he slept exactly as every one of the army that night – and the sleep of the victor, close-run that it was.'

He wondered if there'd been witnesses to that return, as there were now to theirs, though strangely few and rather sullen-looking. Or had they all fled, fearful of what the pounding meant – from midday till evening – and the steady procession of carts full of the wounded? What had the face of victory looked like to those vil-lagers who'd remained? *Nothing except a battle lost can be half so melancholy as a battle won*? Had they even recognized the victory? Except that one thing was certain: there were no *able-bodied* soldiers of the duke's making their way along that road – and, more was the point, no Frenchmen . . .

'*Alors! Vite! Au secours!*'

It happened in an instant. Of a sudden. Two haycarts – middle of the street. Crown prince one side, lance guard the other.

Shots – half a dozen. Where from?

Something like a cannonball – bigger – hurtled from an upstairs window, fuse burning furiously.

The prince froze.

Hervey dug in his spurs. Ajax leapt to the royal side.

He grabbed the prince's reins and pulled with all the strength of man and horse through the gap between waggon and wall.

Acton was hard on his heels, then Malet hauling Princess Augusta's reins.

Into a side-street. Seconds – ten, no more.

The prince came to, jerking his horse round. 'The princess!'

Hervey knew, but there were cruel priorities – 'No, sir!'

Acton barred the way.

Besides, a landau was as safe a place as any.

And the escort wasn't idle. The rearguard were pushing their way up the chaussée. The advance guard, in the frustration of being cut off the other side of the waggons, were tilting at every door and window.

But between the carriages stood Rennie – the oak in the gale – fuse in hand, foot on the roundshot, like the lion atop the Butte.

Malet saw him, having slipped Augusta's reins and doubled back to do what he supposed would be bloody. He swung round again and spurred hard.

'The bomb's safe, Colonel! And the princess.'

The crown prince looked dazed.

Hervey glanced at Princess Augusta. She looked helpless, for all the dragoon uniform – the face of a girl, no longer *eine Adlige*, a noble (though why should it be otherwise? *Noblesse* was not everything). For the moment, the soldiers called the tune.

And it wasn't done yet. But the captain of the escort had broken through into the little side-street, so now the crown prince was theirs once more.

Hervey didn't ask leave, just saluted and made back into the chaussée. 'Stay with the princess,' he shouted to Malet, as Acton cut in behind him.

'Sir, I—'

Too late.

He weaved past the first carriage, seeing the serjeant-major. 'Mr Rennie! What do you do there?'

'Awaiting orders, Colonel,' he replied coolly. 'I've told these Dutchmen to get those waggons out of the way. I thought it best to stay with the ladies until somebody remembers they're here.'

Hervey shook his head. Rennie's composure, disdainful of events – though the stock-in-trade of a serjeant-major – was something to behold. 'Where are the orderlies?'

'I sent them to the crossing further back, Colonel, to make sure nobody was going to come on us from the rear. The Dutch've hared off yonder,' (he pointed to the side-street to the right, where the waggons had come from) 'but I reckon the shots were from the left. Colonel.'

Hervey hadn't been able to tell; and he'd seen no balls strike. 'I'll look for myself. Would you stay with the carriages, please.'

'Colonel.'

He put Ajax into a trot up the side-street, reaching the far end without seeing a soul.

Not surprising. What now – search every house? Put a cordon round the entire village; let not a man out or in until it was done?

But it was not his country. He'd done his duty. The rest must be for the authorities.

'Sar'nt Acton, I think we babble; the scent's bad.'

'Aye, Colonel.'

Then Acton cocked his head. 'See there, Colonel – the window above the blue door.'

'A face. Yes. But what of it?'

'There were two, and one vanished when I looked up.'

'Mm.'

'Why would one vanish when the other was bold enough not to, Colonel?'

'Why indeed? Civilians, Sar'nt Acton.'

'Take a look, Colonel?'

It would be better if they were three: one to hold the horses and two to search the house. And if they had powder . . . 'At the door only. Give me your reins.'

Hervey smiled to himself as he took them – colonel covering coverman.

Acton sheathed his sword and knuckled the door. An old woman in a shawl appeared. He saluted. 'Mamselle, voulez-vous,' (he pointed inside) 'take lookee?'

'*Bor! Allemands!*'

She slammed the door.

'She thinks we're Dutch – or Germans,' said Hervey, looking up again at the window. 'We'd better—'

Crack!

A shot – rear of the cottages.

Acton drew his sabre and ran to the corner. Further up lancers were already hauling men into the street.

The blue door burst open and a man dashed out, then another.

Hervey loosed Acton's trooper and spurred at them, drawing his sword.

One fell under Ajax's hoofs and the other to the flat of his blade.

Lancers sped towards him.

A man jumped from a window, stumbled and cowered as he saw them.

Down came the nearest point and took him in the shoulder, pitching him like a rag doll under the feet of those behind – a bloody bundle, twitching for a few seconds more, and then lifeless.

Hervey winced, putting Ajax between his two and the maddened lancers.

Acton doubled back, grabbing his trooper's reins and scrambling into the saddle.

The lancers swerved only at the last, Hervey thrusting his sabre out to the 'Guard'.

He had no Dutch, but bellowed nevertheless – until one of their cornets appeared.

'For pity's sake, the men are fallen! My prisoners! They'll answer to me!'

XVIII

A WATERLOO DESPATCH

Next day

Caserne de la Garde Civile,
Brussels.
19 June 1830.

To The Commander in Chief,
Horse Guards.

My Lord,
*I have the honour to report that yesterday, on the fifteenth
anniversary of the victory at Waterloo, His Royal Highness the
Crown Prince of Orange-Nassau at the head of a brigade consisting
of His own Fourth Regiment of Light Dragoons, the Prussian First
Regiment of Hussars of the Guard, and His Majesty's Sixth Light
Dragoons made a chevachie over the field of battle. His Majesty's
regiment was accompanied by their Colonel in Chief, Her Royal
Highness The Princess Augusta of Saxe-Coburg-Gotha. Afterwards
His Royal Highness entertained the entire brigade to luncheon in
the curtilage of the Inn of La Belle Alliance. I have the further
honour to report that the bearing and conduct of His Majesty's
troops were throughout of the highest order and received the praise*

of His Royal Highness.

   I have to report, however, a most untoward event. By this time the Royal party had been joined by Her Royal Highness the Crown Princess, and later retired to the village of Waterloo for the purposes of visiting the former headquarters of the Duke of Wellington. As the party, to which HRH The Princess Augusta and myself were attached, were passing along the main street there followed a disturbance which, though quickly subdued, might have led to loss of life on the part of the royal assemblage, for shots were fired and a bomb was thrown at the carriage procession, which was rendered harmless by the prompt action of the Regimental Serjeant-Major of HM's 6th LD, whose conduct I commend most particularly to Your Lordship's attention. Several of those thought to be responsible were apprehended and are now being questioned by the authorities.

   This is the first manifestation of violent hostility witnessed by any of His Majesty's troops, though the blue of our uniforms gives rise to confusion with the Dutch (or even the Prussians) and has been the occasion for some disdain towards us, though when the truth of our nationality is discovered it has been followed at once by the most cordial expressions.

   I attach a schedule of our complete undertakings to date, and will, of course, keep Your Lordship informed routinely of our progress, and at once of any further untoward events.

   I have the Honour to remain Your Lordship's obedient servant,

Matthew Hervey,

Lt-Colonel Commanding

HM's 6th Light Dragoons

Reports of the affair at Waterloo were not to be had in any of the newspapers in Brussels, however, which caused him some surprise – puzzlement indeed. On the other hand, events in Paris were the cause of the greatest speculation in every edition. It appeared that in March the chamber of deputies had addressed a motion of no confidence in the king and his prime minister, Jules de Polignac (whom the Pope had made 'Prince'), and in reply the king had dissolved the *parlement*. The government was promptly defeated in the elections that followed, but Charles *dix, roi de France et de Navarre*, was not deterred. He had already dissolved the Garde Nationale – the Marquis de Lafayette's famed militia (in truth, the Paris mob under nominal regulation) – and it seemed, said many, that *le roi* now wished to take the country back to the days before the fall of the Bastille.

Hervey supposed – and Fairbrother was convinced – that the authorities in Brussels had suppressed the news of the attack on the crown prince (not least the confusion of the escort, which Fairbrother had witnessed from the rear of the column). Yet why, he couldn't fathom: such news would surely tend to increase the standing of the prince, for fear of 'the mob', and indeed of revolution, was surely not confined to the respectable citizens of England. Did suppression of the news therefore indicate that there was more general unrest? That the authorities feared the affair at Waterloo, were it to become known, would stir up further strife? He certainly knew of the trouble two years ago, when the Liberal and Catholic parties formed an alliance to demand equal rights for the people of the southern provinces, both the Dutch-speaking Flemings and the French-speaking Walloons, and that it had gone badly with the Protestants, Holland. For some of the Belgics, he understood, such rights meant self-government, even independence; and for the ultra-Liberals, incorporation with France again. But that was all past. And although Brussels, it was said, was unusually full of Frenchmen, many of whom seemed bent on abuse of the Dutch king, he had seen no cause for alarm. And all the celebrations of the anniversary had proceeded without incident save for the 'untoward event' at Waterloo – even the levee that evening, the crown prince being determined to pass off the affair as if it were nothing more than the action of a few hot-heads.

*

The field days and reviews continued as planned (the Princess Augusta continuing to show the closest interest) until, on the last day of the month, Brussels learned of the death of King George. At once the Sixth returned to barracks and adopted the formalities of court mourning, which Hervey had to contrive until the supplement to the *London Gazette* of 28 June arrived with precise instructions:

> His Majesty does not require that the Officers of the Army should wear any other mourning, with their uniforms, on the present melancholy occasion, than black crape over the ornamental part of the cap or hat, the sword knot, and on the left arm, with the following exceptions, viz.

> Officers on duty are to wear black gloves, black crape over the ornamental part of the cap or hat, the sword knot, and on the left arm; the sash covered with black crape; black gorget ribband; and a black crape scarf over the right shoulder.

> The drums are to be covered with black, and black crape is to be hung from the pike of the colour staff of infantry, and from the standard staff and trumpets of cavalry.

And it had kept Mr Lincoln's tailors busy for days, and Mr Rennie and his serjeant-majors at dismounted drill with arms reversed and the slow march. The late King was indeed to be much mourned by the regiment – by order (and Hervey himself, who, besides of late having some feeling of pity for him in his state of dereliction, saw his own patronage at once removed).

'Shall I read you this from *The Times*, got this morning – and at some expense, I may say?'

Hervey had just come from orderly room, where Malet and the sar'nt-major were finalizing matters to mark the royal obsequies. Fairbrother sat by the open window of his comfortable suite in the

Hôtel de Brabant, in which he'd installed himself on return from Paris the day before. The hotel stood in a corner of the Grande Place – to the Flemings, the Grote Markt, but lately the law had been amended to allow French to be an 'official language' in the Flemish provinces (and anyway, Brussels stood outside Flanders proper).

'If it is not too long, for I'm fair famished.'

'The late King's obituary – a good length, as you might suppose, but most unfavourable. This you should hear: "There never was an individual less regretted by his fellow creatures than this deceased King. What eye has wept for him? What heart has heaved one throb of unmercenary sorrow? If he ever had a friend – a devoted friend in any rank of life – we protest that the name of him or her never reached us." Well, what say you to that? Would that the Paris papers had such licence to print what they wished.'

Hervey grimaced. 'I think it lacking somewhat, were it to be the last word on him. Does it say more?'

'A great deal, but in essence no – it is universally abominating, I would say. And parliament's to be dissolved.'

'That is the custom, but I foresee little change there,' said Hervey, looking out into the *Place* and thinking it a fine thing that in England kings and parliaments might change with so little consequence to good order – and, yes, to military discipline. 'Let us go out into this pleasant square and eat, and you may tell me what you found in Paris – of the situation, I mean.'

'Very well.'

'I've brought you black, by the way.' He handed his friend a crape band. 'Lincoln has bought more lace these last few days than a dozen milliners in a whole year. I've decided that every dragoon shall wear it, on his arm. I thought it a proper show as we're abroad.'

Fairbrother said he thought it proper too.

They chose an estaminet in the shade, and a table outside. A waiter brought jugs of red wine, carbonated water, bread and a dish of *charcuterie*.

'So, tell me of Paris,' said Hervey, beginning at once on a *pied de porc*, which he trusted was not inconsistent with wearing black crape.

'I'll spare you the details of my itinerary, but I must say that I never saw a place so full of good things and yet with so feverish a disposition, and which I judge to be its habitual state. When I had coffee of a morning, no matter where, the talk was all of *la politique*, and then the same again *à déjeuner . . . et puis à diner la même chose*. And all so *en fait* that I couldn't fathom if the tumult were any more than it was, say, a year ago, or if it were some great increase on account of the king's doings. I questioned one or two – well, rather a few in point of fact – and they were all of a mind that "*les Bourbons sont finis*".'

'Did you hear tell of another Bonaparte?' asked Hervey warily.

Fairbrother raised his eyebrows. 'I heard much of "*Égalité*" – Louis Égalité.'

'Ah, the wandering prince.'

'Explain?'

'You know he is an *Orléans*?'

'I do.'

'After his father, Philippe, was guillotined – it was he who'd taken the name "Égalité" in the revolution – he fled abroad and fetched up in all sorts of places. Peto told me how his first ship – long before his joining – had stopped an American frigate in the Gulf of Mexico with Prince Louis and his two brothers aboard, and taken them off and put in to Havana, to where they were bound anyway. And they went thence to Canada, I believe, and not long afterwards to England, where he stayed until Bonaparte was sent south. He even proposed marriage to Princess Elizabeth, I understand.'

'Well, in the coach coming back here I'd more time to discuss the prince with his countrymen, and there seems no doubt that if kings were elected, it would be he on the throne and not his cousin.'

'Mm.'

'You sound uncertain.'

'Choosing kings? A doubtful game.'

'Not without precedent. Or are you a Jacobite?'

Hervey frowned. 'Tricky. My father maintains he would've been a non-juror. But the House of Hanover is hallowed by time.'

'And we have a fine new king now.'

Hervey smiled. 'Indeed we do.' He raised his glass. 'To His Majesty.'

Fairbrother raised his. 'The King! And no one hearing us will know which we toast – that at Windsor or Het Loo.'

'Quite so,' said Hervey, smiling the more. 'Just as they can't fathom my blue coat – the Walloons take me for Dutch, and the Flemings for German. Well, in a month or so, if I've heard right, we'll all be in red, and that will settle the matter.'

'But not I, most assuredly,' said Fairbrother. He poured more wine and sliced into a black pudding. 'By the bye, what news of the Waterloo prisoners?'

Hervey glanced left and right. There was no one in earshot, but he lowered his voice nevertheless. 'Those we took appear to be innocent – or rather, common felons. They thought us policemen and bolted. The bomb was by all accounts a crude device, though had it exploded it would have had effect. The authorities are, as they say, pursuing their inquiries. I should add that the crown prince is to present the sar'nt-major with a gold medal, but without public ceremony. The whole affair's been kept very quiet, though how long it will remain so I shouldn't care to say.'

'A rum business.'

'I went to see General Bylandt, the military governor of Brabant. He commanded a brigade at Waterloo. He says the separatists are arming, and becoming bolder, of which the affair on the eighteenth is evidence. Especially about Liège and Charleroi, where there's much industry – coal and iron and the like. The *agitateurs* there want thorough independence.'

'And what did he think were their chances?'

'He thinks it depends on what happens in France. But his chief fear is that in any general tumult the French will occupy the southern provinces, and he'd be powerless to resist, and that the government – the government in The Hague – would then call on the Congress powers to restore the kingdom, since it was they who created it. But would they answer?'

'Would they?'

Hervey shrugged. 'Bylandt knows no more than I. The Prussians might. Another hundred miles or so of border with France can't be a happy prospect for them. The Austrians? Perhaps. The Russians? I think they have their hands full with the Poles at present. Us? We hadn't the troops to send to Portugal three years ago to stop a little fighting between two brothers. If France has designs, now'd be a good time to throw the dice.'

'And did your General Bylandt say what action he proposed?'

'I asked what he'd do in the event of serious disturbance, and he just shook his head.'

Fairbrother inclined his in the way he did to show his detachment. 'Then it would seem that King William in Amsterdam needs to find a commander who's made of sterner stuff. And without delay.'

Hervey raised an eyebrow. 'What you must bear in mind with Bylandt, who by no means lacks courage with the sword – he fought hard at Quatre Bras and was carried from the field at Waterloo – is that his father was court-martialled for surrendering Breda to the French.'

Fairbrother smiled a shade sardonically. 'The sins of the fathers ... And is this haunted gloom descending on his command generally?'

'Well, it doesn't appear to have dampened festivities. There've been fêtes every day this past week. Our men have been taking their ease very agreeably. The troops disperse tomorrow for drill, though, and then come together again with the Dutch at the end of the month, and then back here again in the first week of August for the exhibition, which, I might add, is looking very fine – such clever building. And then the illumination for the king's birthday on the twenty-fourth, which the king himself is attending.'

'I ought perhaps to have stayed in Paris longer.'

'Not at all. I've no wish to sit on the captains' shoulders for a fortnight while they drill. I thought we might see Antwerp – and Louvain.'

'Capital.' Fairbrother took another slice of black pudding. 'I have to say, changing the subject, that food is very different in Paris.'

'So I recall.'

'I liked it.'

'I was never very partial.'

'One of the *restaurateurs* said to me, "In France there is one religion and fifty sauces, but you English" – I tried to explain, but he'd not heard of Jamaica – "you English have fifty religions and but one sauce!" He thought it prodigiously funny.'

Hervey sighed. 'It loses something, perhaps, in its frequent repetition.'

Fairbrother looked disappointed. 'You will admit, however, that Paris is a most civilized place.'

'If you like sauces . . . And French civilization always appears to me accompanied by so much blood and destruction. They are most immoderate. The Grande Place here – you know they reduced it to a pile of rubble?'

'When?'

'But a century ago – well, a little more, but close enough.'

Fairbrother frowned. 'And they're still reviled for it?'

'They brought up artillery and pounded it for days, set fire to the city. Libraries, archives, *objets d'art* – all gone. Half the city lost, they say. As bad as the Prussians. Though, I grant you, clever with sauce.'

Fairbrother looked at him warily. 'I suppose that if you *were* at Waterloo it is not so easy to forget.'

Hervey's eyes narrowed. 'No, it is not. Nor the years that preceded it.'

XIX

LES TROIS GLORIEUSES

Brussels, 30 July 1830

He arrived half an hour before the meeting. Long experience told him his time would never be wasted, for the conference would always be clearer for having pondered the maps which the staff had been consulting, comparing them with his own. Besides, there were always useful confidences to be picked up from friends in whatever headquarters, or those who thought it to their advantage. Not that he expected this to be a meeting like any other he'd attended. To begin with, he'd little idea why he'd been summoned; and, secondly, he had no Dutch.

Gendarmes saluted as he and Malet got down from the landau at the entrance to the baroque house in the Place Royale that was the seat of the civil governor of Brabant, Baron Hyacinthe van der Fosse. Inside he was greeted in flawless English by one of the crown prince's aides-de-camp, whom he'd come to know – and like – in the two months since arriving in Brussels.

'Captain Bentinck, a relief to see you,' he said, holding out a hand, which seemed to be the manner of greeting no matter what the time or circumstances. 'There will be one at least with whom I can speak, and understand. Is the crown prince to come?'

'No, Colonel, but you are here at his request, and I am here therefore to assist you.'

'Very well.'

Bentinck and Malet exchanged greetings. They had known each other many summers; there'd been many a Bentinck at Eton.

'Perhaps you will tell me what is the purpose of the meeting?' asked Hervey as they began the staircase to the *piano nobile*.

'You are aware of events in Paris, Colonel?'

'I am, but, of course, I do not know precisely of what I'm *not* aware. I take it, if the governor has convened a council, that there's a great deal more than is to be had in *Le Figaro* – though that's bad enough.'

'Of course. But it is a council concerned with precaution, Colonel. For your information – not, I think, for your action.'

That would be for him to judge, thought Hervey; but he liked Bentinck – how could he not like one of that name? He would keep his counsel.

'Is the prince in Brussels?'

'No, Colonel, he has gone to Antwerp this morning early, but he returns tonight or tomorrow morning.'

He wondered what was the significance of Antwerp, but if Bentinck knew the answer he would likely as not feel unable to give it, and so he decided not to ask. Depending on what he heard this morning, he could always seek an audience first thing tomorrow.

Bentinck showed them into a large, mirrored state room where a dozen officials – half of them in uniform (including General Bylandt, and General Wauthier, commandant of the city) – were standing drinking coffee. A conference table was spread with newspapers and maps. A tallish, spare, intense-looking man of about sixty detached himself from the assembly and advanced on them proprietorially.

'Colonel Hervey I may presume?' Again, the English was flaw-less. 'Van der Fosse.'

They both bowed.

'It is very good of you to come – and at such notice.'

Hervey nodded. 'At your service, Baron.'

'You know Generals Bylandt and Wauthier, I believe?'

The two nodded, their smiles ready enough – if perhaps less easy than he'd seen before.

'And General Aberson, of the Gendarmerie.'

Aberson and Hervey bowed formally, for they'd not met.

'And Mynheer Kuyff, the chief of police in the city.'

They bowed in turn.

He was brought coffee, while Malet introduced himself to the staff officers and junior officials.

The half-hour passed quickly, not least because Mynheer Kuyff, whose English was as good as his excellent French, wished to know what Hervey made of the incident at Waterloo – was it well planned, well executed &c?

Six or seven others arrived, and then the man for whom they'd evidently been waiting – the secretary to the minister of justice in The Hague.

Baron van der Fosse called the meeting to the table, placing Hervey close on his right.

There was none whose hand he'd shaken or with whom he'd exchanged bows that answered to a name other than Dutch, or, he supposed, Flemish (supposing indeed that he knew the difference – or even that there *was* a difference). Did every French-speaking noble or official of the old Spanish Netherlands eschew public life? There again, if public life required Dutch, it would be hardly surprising. He wondered how he himself would fare this morning.

Baron van der Fosse allayed his concern. '*Colonel Hervey, si vous voulez, nous pouvons conduire cette réunion en français.*'

Hervey said he would be glad of it.

'*Alors . . .*'

He began with a résumé of the events leading to the 'violent convulsions' which had so taken the authorities in Paris by surprise.

The deteriorating relations between the king and his *parlement* had, he said, led to the signing, this last Sunday, of a number of ordinances suspending the liberty of the press – which, he added, had been of late months particularly insolent – and dissolving the chamber of deputies and instituting a number of measures that would materially reduce the representation of the people. 'These measures,' he added, 'we are all familiar with from many years' battle with the *ancien régime.*'

Heads nodded and there were evidently stern words of Dutch.

He continued, and in a tone of even greater distaste. 'It seems the *Bourse* at once suspended all loans, and in consequence the owners shuttered their factories and threw out the workers unceremoniously – so that there was on the street a sudden disaffected army of *sans-culottes*. Some of the newspapers at once complied with the ordinance, ceasing publication altogether, I understand, but others would not, and on Monday the police seized all the newspapers at one of the presses, at which the crowd began jeering "*À bas les Bourbons!*"'

There was more muttering: whatever the aversion to *sans-culottes*, the Bourbons were no heroes to Dutch Protestants.

'A journalist of *Le National* wrote the following day' (he picked up a cutting from the papers before him): '"France falls back into revolution by the act of the government itself. The legal regime is now interrupted, that of *force* has begun. In the situation in which we are now placed obedience has ceased to be a duty. It is for France to judge how far its own resistance ought to extend."'

There was consternation.

The baron continued. 'This morning I received a copy of a despatch from the minister in Paris, who writes that later in the afternoon of Monday troops of the garrison and of the Garde Royale were posted with artillery outside the Tuileries, the Place Vendôme and Place de la Bastille, and patrols were ordered throughout the city to secure the gun shops, though no special measures were taken to protect either the arms depots or powder factories. But in the evening a prodigious violence erupted, and before the night was out there were more than twenty killed, and some soldiers.'

He put down the despatch and reminded his audience that Paris lay two hundred miles (*'trente myriamètres'*) from Brussels, and that their information, even post haste, would always be two days behind events. 'And therefore, gentlemen, I wish this council to convene each morning at the same time until the tumult in Paris has died down. I have sent to The Hague for instructions, but in the meantime we shall proceed with plans for the visit of the king.'

There was a murmur of surprise at this, and speculation on the outcome of the Paris tumult, and then Mynheer Kuyff spoke of the investigation of the Waterloo outrage, believing it not impossible that agents of the French were in some way connected, operating among the colliers of the Borinage, though the others received this with some scepticism. The secretary from The Hague, whose ministry of justice had the primary responsibility for assimilation of the southern provinces, said nothing throughout but made copious notes.

As the meeting adjourned, Hervey asked the baron what he wished him to do. 'Only to be in attendance at these councils, Colonel, as the representative of His Britannic Majesty's government.'

Hervey blinked. He had no such authority. He might not even have the competence, though he knew perfectly well that Castlereagh's had been a signature to the Articles of London, by which the United Kingdom of the Netherlands had been created, and that as one of the 'Great Powers' Britain might be appealed to in the event of anything disturbing the settled peace of the Congress of Vienna. It was no good his saying that he'd no authority *de jure* when he was *de facto* the senior of His Majesty's servants in Brussels (the nearest consul, indeed, was in Antwerp). His first course must be to communicate with Sir Charles Bagot, the ambassador at The Hague.

This he went straight to the barracks of the Garde Civile and did.

He then assembled the captains and regimental staff and explained the situation in Paris and the concerns of the authorities in Brussels. The regiment was, he said, to carry on in all respects as before, except that safeguarding of firearms was to be given special attention.

Quietly, afterwards, he told Malet and Mr Rennie that he wanted ball-cartridge ready for general issue, and that the picket was to have ten rounds each under lock and key in the guardhouse.

The council at the Place Royale next morning, Saturday, had graver news. Fighting in Paris had continued a second day, and the authorities had used cannon; but this time the 'whiff of grapeshot' that had made Bonaparte's name, putting down the royalist counter-revolution, had had no effect. Indeed, many of the troops in the line battalions had deserted, said Baron van der Fosse. But Mynheer Kuyff reported that his informers had detected no signs of increased disaffection in the city, or the province in general, and so with the encouragement of the military officers, the baron said he was not minded to take any additional measures. Bylandt alone said that he was considering doubling all sentries. And the meeting adjourned until the morrow.

By Sunday, however, the news was truly alarming. Paris, by all accounts, was in the hands of the *révoltés*, Baron van der Fosse told them – barricades throughout the city, and the king 'cowering at Saint-Cloud'. The *tricolore* flew everywhere. 'The Tuileries have been sacked,' he said despairingly, as if final affirmation of the overthrow of all that stood for order. And then, shaking his head as though he could scarce believe what he read, 'A man wearing a ball dress belonging to the duchesse de Berry, with feathers and flowers in his hair, was observed at a palace window crying: "*Je reçois! Je reçois!*"'

Hervey suppressed a smile, for besides the absurdity of the image he couldn't fathom why the baron thought that any words of a man dressed in the duchesse de Berry's ball dress could be in the slightest degree edifying, least of all that he was 'at home'.

But the baron's report was not over: 'And, gentlemen, the Hôtel de Ville is in the hands of the mob.'

Hervey swallowed. The silence at the table was profound.

And then General Bylandt said quietly, '*C'est fini.*'

It was. Next day the king – and the dauphin, in whose favour Charles had tried to abdicate – renounced their rights to the throne and fled for England. But instead of Charles's grandson, the duc de Bordeaux, taking the throne, the provisional government invited the duc d'Orléans – Louis Philippe – to rule as a constitutional monarch, 'King of the French', just as Fairbrother had foretold.

Word reached Brussels on the fourth. That evening the news-papers were full of speculation, if little fact, and for several days it seemed a matter of mere curiosity in the coffee shops. One king had been replaced by another – *et alors*? Except that, as Hervey pointed out to General Bylandt at the council still meeting daily, a Dutch 'king' had replaced the crowned head of England a century and a half before, and the last rising in support of the deposed line had been over fifty years later. Would the supporters of 'Henri Cinque' a dozen years from now, when the infant was come of age, try to reclaim the throne by force? But Bylandt countered that a good constitution would not be overthrown: 'For why would anyone shed blood merely to replace one king with another? The world has been enlightened since the days of the Stuarts.'

Hervey acknowledged that the *ancien régime* – Bourbon or Stuart – was gone, 'But with all due respect, I believe your king should be on his guard, or at least his ministers, for I understand that Polignac as well as Charles has had to flee. And all in so short a time – "three glorious days", as the papers have it.'

But the good general said something about trusting to the innate wisdom of the Dutch, and the need to thwart the opponents of enlightenment in the southern provinces – the 'Catholic party of reaction' – and, in any case, he declared, the characteristic peaceableness of the people of the south stood in contrast with the propensity to violence of the French. 'The cockpit of Europe, Colonel, as well you know we are called, was the place of combat only of *foreign* fighting birds.'

It was true; but, suggested Hervey: 'Caesar said the Belgae were the bravest of the three tribes of Gaul.'

Bylandt had read Caesar too. 'And do you recall to what he ascribed that quality?'

Hervey did – and very perfectly, for in the classical remove at Shrewsbury his attention had been fixed firmly on the Legions. '*Minimeque ad eos mercatores saepe commeant atque ea quae ad effeminandos animos . . .*'

'Exactly so, Colonel Hervey – "being furthest from the civilized parts, the merchants least frequently resorted to them, and the Belgae did not therefore import those things which tended to effeminate the soul". Two thousand years of history has not been without its effect, however. Look about you now: the Belgae are a veritable nation of merchants!'

'Did not Bonaparte say something of the same of England?'

Bylandt shook his head. 'My dear Colonel, I believe I may assure you: today's Belgae will not trouble King William as once they troubled Caesar.'

XX

A NIGHT AT THE OPERA

19 August 1830

As his carriage drew up at Princess Augusta's villa, Hervey was still pondering on the letter from The Hague. It was dated 15 August, and acknowledged his report of 30 July, but without reference to the delay in replying, saying simply that the ambassador had no greater knowledge of the state of affairs in Paris than would he in Brussels, but that the Dutch government – in particular the minister of justice – had no declared concerns. 'I spoke with Mynheer van Maanen this morning – the minister of justice at The Hague – and he is of the opinion that if there be any implication at all it will be to the benefit of the unified Kingdom, for the Catholic party in the southern provinces will be suspicious of the new King of the French, and will therefore tend to moderation. His Majesty intends proceeding to Brussels next week, in accordance with the plans laid some months ago.'

Sir Charles Bagot was a diplomat of wide experience, not long returned from St Petersburg. Hervey had met him in Canada, a dozen years before, when as minister plenipotentiary he had been sent to settle a number of vexations that remained in the wake of the War of 1812. Lady Mary Bagot, the Duke of Wellington's niece, had accompanied him. Indeed, she had stood proxy for Lady Camilla Cavendish at the baptism of Georgiana. He had had no connection with them since, but the 'sad circumstances' of Canada (as his family were wont to call the death of Henrietta) must, he presumed, have made his name known to the ambassador, and he supposed therefore that the absence of any instruction to stand aloof from affairs in Brussels was an implicit expression of confidence. Fairbrother had cautioned him against such an assumption, on account of an affair he recalled in Jamaica, when the judgment in the high court had gone ill against the magistrates in Ocho Rios: '*Delegata potestas non potest delegari*' – even if the ambassador were minded to delegate his powers, he had no authority in law to do so. But Hervey had countered that he did not seek powers, merely the freedom to act. If His Britannic Majesty's government sent him and his regiment to Brussels to be their representative, he must surely have the authority to represent them in the way they would wish to be represented? The regiment was to form part of the Dutch king's procession, as a gesture of enduring friendship; they would therefore be unable to escape the consequences of any violent demonstration, and must take due precautions. And the situation in Brussels (and indeed the surrounding country, according to the troop captains) was still, to his mind, uneasy – even if the mood of Baron van der Fosse's daily councils had grown steadily more sanguine. Until that morning's.

Hervey had called on the princess regularly in the past month. He felt it his duty to apprise her, as colonel-in-chief, of all that he knew for as long as she remained in the city and her guidon therefore – both figuratively and in fact – uncased. Besides, her company was both easy and stimulating: she received him with little formality and he could speak with her in German (enjoying, indeed, her occasional corrections), although as a rule she spoke in English.

This morning he was admitted as usual by her butler, an elderly and rather stiff old family servant, but a faithful one who had once worn the green of a Saxon jaeger before being discharged, wounded, after Jena – and so had escaped the awkward shift of Saxony's allegiance to Bonaparte. Though Hervey was always able to extract a few words from him, he could never manage more than a look of resigned approval. However, Serjeant Acton reported that he was always most hospitably attended to in the servants' hall, and that he thought Herr Amsel (he was always punctilious about honouring him with 'Herr') had once made an appreciative remark about the Duke of Wellington – though he couldn't of course be sure. This morning, as he showed him to the drawing room, Herr Amsel simply muttered '*Frankreich*,' and shook his head.

Hervey bowed as he entered, and took his usual seat. 'Amsel seems discomposed today, ma'am.'

'He has been reading the *Augsburger Allgemeine Zeitung* – the only German newspaper that seems readily to be had in Brussels.'

'Forgive me, ma'am: does that newspaper have pronounced opinions?'

'The Bavarians, Colonel, owe much to the French – or rather, to Bonaparte.'

Hervey thought he understood, but trying to fathom the mind of 'Alte Amsel', who had evidently formed a strong distaste for the French – or, strictly, France – in the last twenty-four hours, was perhaps too ambitious. 'I suppose if the events in Paris may have consequences here, they may elsewhere too – in Germany maybe. That is his reasoning?'

'It is. And it is also mine.'

Pleased though he was to have solved the riddle, it seemed the princess was not minded to discuss it. 'What is the news from London?' she asked abruptly.

Hervey had no news. But while what happened in Paris might have echoes beyond the Rhine, the Channel was another matter. 'I know of no ill effects, ma'am. Nor would I expect any.'

The princess shook her head. 'I do not make myself clear. I refer to the elections of parliament.'

'Of course—'

A footman appeared with coffee, which interrupted his thoughts for the moment. On the death of the King, parliament had been dissolved – on 24 July – and a new parliament summoned to meet on 14 September. The first contest at the polls had been held on 29 July, and the last was due on 1 September. Such reports as he had – by way of *The Times*, the *London Gazette* and letters from Wiltshire – were not auspicious.

He measured his words carefully. 'I think that the duke may not be making the gains he supposed. The reports of unrest in the country districts, too, are troubling. As here, the harvest has been poor. Yet I would have imagined such disturbances to favour the duke's cause rather than that of the radicals. I cannot believe he will be unseated. The country has too high a regard for him.'

And having given his opinion so decidedly, and the princess replying that she could only hope he was right, 'for otherwise it will be to remove the wisest of counsels from the Concert of Europe', he passed to a summary of what he'd learned at that morning's council. 'There have been inscriptions on the walls in the lesser streets for some weeks – "Down with Van Maanen . . . Death to the Dutch" – but these have now begun to appear in streets closer to the Place Royale, and leaflets were found last night.'

He handed her one: *Le 23 Août, Feu d'Artifice; le 24 Août, Anniversaire du Roi; le 25 Août, Révolution!*

The princess seemed unmoved. 'And what do the authorities make of this?'

'There was some dismay this morning, and I think for the first time. Kuyff, the policeman, was particularly concerned, and thought it best to cancel the fireworks and the illumination for the king's birthday. Baron van der Fosse agreed, but the decision will be taken only on the twenty-second, after the king has arrived, and on account of unfavourable weather.'

The princess raised her eyebrows. 'And do we take it that it is not because of the superior divinings of weather available to the

311

authorities that they are able to say it shall be wet four days hence? This present rain has the nature of a passing shower.'

'I should have said *ostensibly* on account of the weather.'

'*Ostensibly?*'

'*Angeblich.*'

'*Ach, so.*'

'It does seem a risky venture, ma'am. In three days' time it may very well be dry, in which case . . .'

'Quite. But the king is still to come.'

'Indeed.'

'Well, if he is to see the exhibition, which he must, the authorities will not wish to close that, and nor the theatres. I hope not, for I have taken a box at the Opera on the twenty-fifth.'

'Nothing was said about closing the theatres, ma'am.'

'Good. And you are invited, Colonel, and four of your officers, for I have taken an adjacent box, and afterwards shall give a supper party.'

The opera: Hervey tried hard to sound appreciative (he'd been to too many to be diverted by the prospect). 'I thank you, ma'am. Might I enquire which is the opera?'

She bowed, suggesting his enquiry was very proper. '*Masaniello.*'

Hervey frowned a little. 'It is not one with which I am acquainted.'

'*Masaniello, ou la Muette de Portici.*'

He shook his head.

'No, nor I, for it is new . . . by Monsieur Auber. And Nourrit is to sing.'

Hervey had heard of neither Auber nor Nourrit, but thought it ungracious to admit it (and he had no wish to appear *der Philister*). 'Ah.'

'I say it is new; it was new but two years ago, though it has not been performed since. But it is thought most highly of.'

'Then I look forward to hearing it, ma'am. Do you know what is its subject? Who is Masaniello, and this *stumme Italienerin*?'

312

'Ah, of that I do know – and you too, I would think. Tommaso Aniello led a rebellion against the Spanish in Naples, two centuries ago. *La muette* is his sister. She has been ill used by the son of the Spanish viceroy, though I am uncertain if this is true, or whether a . . . *Verfeinerung*? – '

'*Refinement . . . elaboration.*'

'*Ja* – an elaboration of the librettist's.'

Hervey had never supposed that what he saw on stage – especially if sung – bore much relation to reality; it was, after all, for the entertainment of the paying public. 'I fancy a play in Brussels about a revolt against a foreign occupier would see a full house?'

'Indeed so,' said the princess, solemnly. 'And because it has been proscribed in the Netherlands since it was first performed in Paris – and is only lately allowed.'

'Better, perhaps, that people have the opportunity to weep into their handkerchiefs than paint on walls. But, *la muette* – if she is dumb – she can hardly have much to sing, can she?'

The princess frowned. 'You do not make fun of me, do you, Colonel?'

Hervey smiled. 'No, ma'am, I do not! The enquiry is most genuine, if perhaps – I admit it – lacking in understanding of these things.'

'*Du bist ein schlicht Dragoner?*' she teased.

Schlicht – simple; what a cover for sins . . .

'I *simply* do my duty – yes, ma'am.'

The princess smiled, as if to say she'd had her satisfaction.

'Well, Colonel, I may tell you that the part of the *muette* is taken by a dancer, who will be Mademoiselle Noblet of the Ballet de l'Opéra de Paris.'

Hervey confessed himself in awe of her knowledge, and doubly enlivened by the prospect, for he'd never before seen a dancer of the Ballet de l'Opéra – indeed, of any ballet.

She smiled again. 'I am pleased therefore to be an agent of *Aufklärung*, Colonel.'

Hervey nodded, for it was a clever pun: a Saxon dragoon would say *Aufklärung* to describe his efforts to find the enemy, and a Heidelberg philosopher for 'Enlightenment'. What a colonel-in-chief the regiment had got themselves: the look to turn any head, and then to engage the cleverest of them.

They talked of the arrangements for the king's visit, and where she would ride in the procession, and other matters of business, so that it was a full hour later that he took his leave, saying he would call at the same time tomorrow after Baron van der Fosse's next council. He wished perhaps that she'd asked him to stay and lunch, for he'd come to enjoy their safe and easy intimacy, and he'd not yet had occasion to speak of his sister and new brother-in-law. Except that her colonelcy was not made for his enjoyment. He must remind himself, he knew full well, that the princess was *freundlich, nicht freundin* . . . friendly, not a friend.

Amsel showed him out, now muttering about '*der alte Feind*' (the old enemy).

The rest of the day he spent with Malet, for papers had arrived from Hounslow and there were matters needing prompt attention. A headline in the Dublin press on proceedings against Tyrwhitt in the Court of Common Pleas was first to command his attention: *A man might have a wife in each of the three kingdoms although polygamy be not permitted*. It was the sort of clever remark to be expected of an Irish journalist, he supposed, as were the ironic references to 'the 6th Light Dragoons, a regiment which flatters itself as one in which good breeding is the first requisite of an officer'. The report was altogether unedifying.

'I regret having to show it you first, Colonel.'

'It makes no matter, I suppose, first or last – except perhaps you'll leave me with a *bon mouche*?'

'There are some letters of appreciation, yes.' Malet picked up one of the sealed papers he'd placed on one side. 'But these are marked for your personal attention.'

'Open them if you would; I've no objection.'

The first bore the stamp of the regimental agents. Malet broke the seal and read.

"'Pon my word, we're delivered, Colonel. Tyrwhitt's made application for the half-pay ... It seems he applied in May.'

Hervey said nothing for the moment. A letter from Tyrwhitt personally would have been the customary courtesy.

'Greenwood says it'll be gazetted on 15 September.'

Hervey nodded. 'Then we're excessively fortunate.'

Indeed he was, for much that Mordaunt held the reins with increasing sureness, the tribulations of its captain could not but have their corrosive effect on the pride (and therefore discipline) of his troop. Now he would be able to let Mordaunt take proper command; if, that is, the lieutenant had the means to 'pay the difference' – buy the captaincy; and he wondered if he might make an exceptional case to the Horse Guards, that in effect Mordaunt succeeded to command 'in the field', as if 'by death'. And yet Malet was by seniority entitled to the purchase ...

Malet opened the next letter.

'From the Board of Ordnance ... begging to inform you that the half-yearly returns were found satisfactory.'

'Mm ...'

Then Hervey recollected himself – 'Tyrwhitt's captaincy: you are Mordaunt's senior – I trust you'd be content to pay the difference?'

'On the same terms as F Troop, Colonel – titular?'

'No, I could hardly ask that. To take proper command.' It would be disagreeable in the extreme to lose an adjutant who understood his mind so well, but ...

Malet looked thoughtful. 'Colonel, I'm greatly obliged to you. May I have a day or so to think on it?'

Hervey was happily surprised by the hesitation, though he didn't suppose further reflection would lead Malet to turn down the offer. He most certainly had the means.

'You may have as much time as you will.'

'Thank you.'

'Perhaps, though, we should make it our intention meanwhile to determine who's to be sar'nt-major. I fear the time has come.'

'I await your instructions, Colonel.'

'Mm . . . I must ask Mr Rennie for his decided opinion. I only hesitate to do so in case I must contradict him.'

Malet smiled.

'And you've had no reports whatever of there being any falling off in Collins's standing these past months – no increase in indiscipline and the like?'

'None whatsoever, Colonel.'

'No, he appears to me only to have risen in stature. What a most curious business was Kennett's retreat.'

'Curious indeed, Colonel.'

'Weeks he'd had to ponder on his judgement, yet without show-ing the faintest glimmer of doubt – remorse – that Collins might have been acting in good faith, and therefore to ruin an NCO of his seniority and service over something that could not with certainty be established . . . contrary to natural justice.'

'Certainly no argument of mine could convince him.'

'And then, just as you are in the very act of framing the charges, and Collins under notice for arraignment, he writes from London saying he felt no longer that he could offer evidence – as if he were no longer able to attend a ball or some such.'

'Quite. Though I understand he'd felt indisposed for some days.'

Hervey was reassured that Kat's stratagem – in truth *his* stratagem, subtly adapted – was evidently not common knowledge. 'And then – how Fortune bestows her favours on the unworthy – he's appointed to General Gifford's staff.'

And the devil of it, he was certain, having now seen the actual papers, was that Kennett must have written withdrawing his accusations before Gifford could make the offer – before Kat's artifice could have had its effect. Before, indeed, she might even have been able to *speak* with Gifford. What, therefore, had induced

Kennett to change his mind (he was sure it was not conscience)? But it was perilous on several accounts to make enquiry – especially merely to satisfy curiosity. *And the Lord rooted them out of their land in anger, and in wrath, and in great indignation, and cast them into another land*: had the subalterns themselves rooted out Kennett?

There were times – even if in public he always maintained the opposite – that it were better the lieutenant-colonel did not know certain things: *The secret things belong unto the Lord our God.* For to know – and to know therefore that others knew – meant that action must be taken.

Meanwhile he had an infinitely more important choice to make – Collins or Armstrong (and perhaps even a new adjutant). But more immediately was the king's visit – and those handbills: *Le 23 Août, Feu d'Artifice; le 24 Août, Anniversaire du Roi; le 25 Août, Révolution!*

In the event the visit of the king passed off quietly – even well. Not only were there no affronts to his dignity, let alone any violent disturbance, William – 'Wilhelm', 'Willem', 'Guillaume', or however the varied citizens of Brussels wished to call him – accompanied by both sons, was cheered on his progress to the exhibition. It was the greatest pity, said Baron van der Fosse, when the council met on the twenty-third, that the king had allowed himself to take fright of shadows, cancel the fireworks and illuminations, and hurry back to The Hague to mark his birthday there and not in Brussels. A longer stay in the capital of the southern provinces could only have strengthened the ties with those of the north.

And yet shadows there undoubtedly were. In fact in the days that followed they multiplied – the slogans on the walls, the handbills, the intemperate articles in the press, the public meetings, the jeering of officials and troops ... At the meeting on the twenty-fifth the baron said he couldn't reconcile it with the spirit he'd observed during the royal progress, and urged further precaution. General

Bylandt said that he'd issued orders for his men not to show themselves in public places for the time being, and General Wauthier that he'd withdrawn the guards at the various palaces and state offices to within their walls. General Aberson informed them that he'd doubled the strength of the gendarmerie patrols, and Mynheer Kuyff that his spies were giving him troubling but contradictory reports: there were labourers come into Brussels from the country in want of work, and these were receiving doles to keep them in the city to add numbers to the demonstrations being planned for the opportune moment. Why the king's visit had passed so quietly he was uncertain, but there was no doubting the disaffection. 'I put it down to last year's harvest being all but exhausted, and this year's promising even worse.' The baron asked what was to be done about the opera that evening: would it be an occasion for speeches and declarations? To which Mynheer Kuyff replied that he had men in the audience who would give the names of any who took such liberties, and they would be arrested the following morning. General Aberson said that his gendarmes would be present as usual, and that he saw no more reason to close the theatre than there had been to cancel the fireworks and illuminations, 'Otherwise we shall for ever be at the mercy of *la foule.*'

Hervey told them that he and four of his officers were to attend the opera with the Princess Augusta, at which General Aberson became uneasy. She had not asked for any special measures to be taken regarding her safety, he said. Hervey explained that it was of the nature of a private visit, and as there was no guard upon her villa – nor on that of any other foreign dignitary that he was aware of – she had probably not seen it necessary to ask the authorities for such measures. She would, in any case, have the services of five officers of her own regiment.

'Do you intend going in uniform, armed, Colonel?' asked Aberson.

'I dislike going about in uniform *unarmed*, General,' replied

Hervey, in as conciliatory a manner as he could. 'A sword to an officer is as his hat or gloves, as you yourself will own.'

'It has the merit of being recognizable, I suppose,' agreed Aberson.

But the baron looked troubled. 'It would be unedifying if she were recognized and subject to insult. Can you not persuade her to stay her attendance, Colonel?'

Hervey raised his eyebrows, as if to say that some things were beyond his powers – or his better judgement. 'Yours would be a more persuasive voice, sir.'

But the governor of Brabant evidently thought not. 'I . . . I think that on balance it is better to make no interference with Her Highness's plans.'

The meeting closed with an air of distinct uneasiness. The threat to the peace was construed from a perceived *atmosphere* rather than any solid evidence of intent. The precautionary measures therefore seemed feeble. Hervey decided he would put his own barracks on alert that night, and double the picket. As for the opera, it sounded as though things might be lively, and enjoyable for once therefore. Except that there was the dignity of his colonel-in-chief to take account of.

Le Théâtre Royal de la Monnaie was a building in the classical style, raised but a dozen years in the middle of a newly made square where once the royal mint had stood, whence its name. It had been Bonaparte's idea to build something altogether grander than he'd found, but there had been other calls on the public purse, and it was not until the union with the northern provinces that work began.

Hervey, his three troop leaders and the adjutant, with Serjeant Acton, stood on the steps of the Monnaie's vast portico admiring its eight soaring Ionic columns, the very expression of permanence. The sun had set and the lamps in the square made a pretty picture. All about them, the buzz of opera-goers promised that here, this evening, would be a performance of distinction, the steady procession of carriages bringing more and yet more of the *qualité* of Brussels to this most 'French' of the city's institutions.

'There is evidently no other place to be this night,' said Hervey, finding that even putting his back against a column gave no refuge from the jostling. Before the first performance of *Messiah*, in Dublin, the posters had begged 'Gentlemen are particularly requested not to wear swords' and that ladies should appear 'without Hoops, as it will greatly increase the Charity by making room for more company.' Hoops, he knew, were not quite *la mode* – not, at least, those of Herr Handel's day – but he trusted the princess would not choose them this evening. He'd certainly not considered leaving behind his sword, despite the doubts.

A little while later, the arrival timed fashionably, for the performance was not long due to start, her carriage hove into the square. There were no outriders, but two footmen in evening livery stood between the springs.

Hervey and his party, still with some difficulty even as the curtain bells began ringing, moved to the foot of the steps to welcome her.

An appreciative knot of onlookers applauded as she alighted. Her cloak – cream silk, edged in pink – was very full, and her hair was gathered up in a Grecian plume. She gave her hand to each of the officers (and the countess, dressed not dissimilarly but without plume, likewise), and then with effortless grace the footmen began leading the party to the boxes, the press of people parting like the sea before Moses.

There was champagne waiting, and they toasted the King's health.

In a few minutes they were called to attention by applause for the conductor, and boisterous cheering in the pit, and took their seats expectantly. When the overture began, with its dramatic flourish, the cheering erupted again, only subsiding with the 'Neapolitan' tune that followed – but resuming with each return of the dramatic theme and its elaboration, so that when the overture came to an end after the better part of ten minutes the greater part of the audience was in a frenzy of cheering, stamping and singing – though with what words Hervey couldn't fully discern. And it had to be reprised to satisfy the relentless calls of '*Une autre!*'

It was, he couldn't deny, full of good tunes, and very lively – his foot tapped willingly – but the opera was two hours long, and repetitions would sorely test his devotion to duty. 'Monsieur Auber evidently knows how to please an audience, ma'am,' he said, and hardly needing to whisper.

'He is very fine, Colonel Hervey,' said the princess, lowering her opera glasses, 'though not of the same order as Herr Weber.'

Hervey smiled. He did not know Herr Weber, but to be German was – naturally – to be *per se* the superior musician. But she said it with such sweetness that he could scarcely hold it against her.

He was saved from reply by the curtain, however, which rose to reveal, his card told him, the garden of the palace of the duc d'Arcos. A party of Spanish soldiers marched on stage, and at once there was booing. Hervey thought he might enjoy the evening after all.

Act One continued noisy, the audience very volubly expressing its dislike of the viceroy's son, who, apparently having seduced *la muette* of the title, Masaniello's sister, was to marry a Spanish princess.

The first interval was not long, and taken in the boxes rather than attempting a promenade. Princess Augusta gave her favourable opinion of the singing. Hervey said that it was as fine as any he'd heard in Rome when she pressed him for his estimation, though he then had to admit, when she asked him to elaborate, that he couldn't quite remember what was the opera he'd seen.

Act Two began more peacefully, on the seashore, the stage filling with a chorus of Neapolitan fishermen sorting their catch, mending nets and the like, and some pleasing singing, and then Fenella, *la muette*, appeared, and danced a little – and very charmingly, Hervey thought – and seemed to be telling the fishermen somehow what had befallen her, the seduction, her imprisonment by the viceroy, and her escape, which did not go at all well with the more vocal of the audience (as well as with those the composer had presumably intended – the chorus). Masaniello then arrived, to encouraging cheers from the pit, and as he learned of his sister's ill-use by the viceroy's son, the mood turned dark. A duet began, not unlike the Marseillaise, sung by Masaniello and his friend Pietro, a call to arms which enlivened the audience a little more, and then suddenly, at the words '*Amour sacré de la patrie*', both pit and boxes alike were convulsed with the loudest cheering.

'*Amour sacré de la patrie, rends-nous l'audace et la fierté; à mon pays je dois la vie. Il me devra sa liberté.*'* – The words came clearly even in the tumult, and as the fishermen swore perdition to the enemy there was a thunderous ovation which continued long after the fall of the curtain.

They remained in the boxes for the second interval, for Serjeant Acton reported there was a rather fevered crush in the promenade.

The start of Act Three was delayed by an altercation between General Aberson's gendarmes and some of the most vocal of the pit, who had begun waving the Brabant *tricolore* – red, yellow, black – but a merry scene in the market place soon quietened tempers. But then the viceroy's own police tried to arrest *la muette* (for a reason Hervey couldn't entirely follow), which appeared to be the spark for a general revolt in Naples – and more uproar in the pit.

The hour was late, and Hervey was becoming uneasy, but the princess showed no inclination to curtail her enjoyment (the singing was unquestionably fine), and so he endured Act Four with reasonable equanimity, though the further complications of the plot – Naples in uproar and the viceroy's son a fugitive, whom *la muette* for some reason now wished to save (the curious ways of women . . .) – he found trying (as well as the uproar on

---

* 'Sacred love of the fatherland, give us courage and pride; to my country I owe my life. It will owe me its liberty.'

stage that was increasingly echoed throughout the theatre, even the boxes). But the house was truly elated when finally the city magistrate presented Masaniello with the royal crown and proclaimed him king of Naples, with cheering for several minutes after the curtain.

It was beyond the supper hour when the last act began – another gathering of fishermen, in which one of Masaniello's friends revealed that he'd given him poison (perhaps, reckoned Hervey, to punish him for accepting the crown – though this, he'd thought, had been what *les pêcheurs* had wanted). But then another of his compatriots rushed on stage to tell of a fresh column of Spanish soldiers approaching, with the viceroy's son at their head, and the crowd began entreating Masaniello to take command of them once more. A battle followed, quite lifelike compared with some he'd seen, complete with an eruption of Vesuvius (with more smoke and flame than he thought entirely prudent with so full a house) – but then Masaniello was cut down while saving the life of the Spanish princess (though Hervey wasn't sure why she was even there), and *la muette*, discovering that her brother was dead, threw herself from a belvedere, and the Spanish retook the city.

Hervey breathed a sigh of relief as the curtain came down.

Serjeant Acton appeared as the cheering and curtain calls mounted, his jaw set firm. Hervey moved to the back of the box to ask what was wrong.

'Riot, Colonel. All hell let loose. The princess's men've gone to get the carriage but I don't reckon they'll be able to. I don't think any of the carriages'll be able to get into the square, let alone through it.'

Hervey thought for a moment. 'Tell the adjutant. I don't suppose there's another door we can leave by? All the others will be thinking the same, mind. It may be safest to stay here, but it's too great a crowd for my liking . . . We're six, and the ladies – it ought to be possible to make our way tight through the square. Where *is* the carriage?'

'In the littler square two streets off, Colonel – with a lot of others.'

'Very well, we'll make for there. You will lead.'

'Colonel.'

He turned and told the princess.

She remained serene, though the countess looked troubled.

'Have no fear, ma'am. It's not the business we had at Waterloo. There's no one being hunted – just an uncouth sort of rabble.'

Besides, five officers and a serjeant of light dragoons was an ample escort.

Nevertheless their progress down the grand staircase and out into the portico was a slow affair, with much jostling, pushing and elbowing – and unconscionably noisy.

But outside was noisier yet – and impossible to make out what was the commotion. Riot it certainly was, but against what or whom he couldn't tell.

For the moment, however, he had but the one intent – to get the princess to her carriage. He motioned to Acton to lead on.

They edged along the inner wall of the portico until they could use the last of the columns as a rallying-point. Acton glanced back at Hervey for the 'off', and then with a few sharp words parted a knot of anxious patrons atop the steps to slip into the square, followed by the tight ring of blue protecting their charges.

It was doubly dark after the limelight of the theatre, and the crowd wasn't that of the pit; they were menacing rather than merely rowdy. Hervey was glad of his sword, but prayed he wouldn't have need in a press so tight.

Now came shots – at least, reports of some kind, fireworks per- haps; he couldn't tell. The mood turned violent.

Flames began to lick at one of the buildings across the square.

Suddenly a dozen roughs brandishing clubs were barring their way.

'*Kut-Hollander!*' one of them spat.

Acton's robust English reply only confirmed their misidentification.

'*Sales Hollandais! Allez-vous faire foutre!*'

Hervey grimaced. Drunk – the roughs that Kuyff had spoken of no doubt, paid to do mischief. Where *were* his police, and the gendarmes?

'*Nous sommes Anglais!*' he barked.

They didn't hear, or didn't want to. '*Kut-Hollander! Moffen!*'

Then they rushed them.

Acton had his sabre out in a split second. Two of the roughs lunged but a cut to the wrist stopped one club. The other swung heavily but Acton sidestepped and sliced into the man's upper arm. His yelp carried even above the tumult.

Hervey and the rest drew sabres and gave point.

The drink was powerful, though. The roughs weren't deterred.

More now loomed.

Acton ran at them, choosing his man, felling him in a bloody heap with a flash of cuts.

Fell one, frighten twenty. A good rule.

But not all had seen it. Hervey was suddenly having to parry.

And no longer clubs. Swords came from somewhere.

Malet leapt forward as one of them charged, went to guard, deflected the blade and followed through with a looping cut that almost severed the arm.

Hervey pulled the princess to him with his left arm, parried a cutlass and put his point into a throat.

The other sabres were no less active.

Yet more came on, like savages.

The fight was unequal in skill, but numbers might yet tell . . .

Hervey held the princess tight. She made not a sound.

Parry, thrust, parry, cut – a dozen bloody bundles soon lay still or writhing on the cobbles.

He prayed she wouldn't faint.

What sense to add more?

But more came at them, and they fell as bloodily, and not a single blade touching the party.

Until just as suddenly they were gone.

'The carriage, Acton!'

Hervey loosed his grip to take the princess by the arm. She was shaken. No doubt of it.

'Come, ma'am, it's done.'

They hastened for the nearest side-street, the others following at his heels, Malet facing rear in case of another rush.

But they made it without check, slipped into its eerily empty haven and hastened into the next and beyond to the place where the carriages were parked.

The princess's footmen had out their staves, ready, though the *cul* was still empty. Even by the dull light of the coach lamps her ordeal was evident. '*Ihre Hoheit!*'

'*Denken sie sich nichts dabei, Clemens.*'

Hervey realized he still had hold of her arm, and loosed it awkwardly. '*Entschuldigung, Hoheit.*'

She said nothing, but turned to the countess. 'Are you well, Beatrix?'

'I am well, Your Highness.'

Hervey spoke to the coachman. 'We can't go out towards the square. Can you turn the carriage, or must we unhitch?'

The coachman said he could.

'Then turn at once . . . Whose is behind?'

'*Es ist zu mieten, Herr Oberst.*'

A carriage for hire two streets from a riot – as lucky as it was singular.

'Worsley, Vanneck, Mordaunt – take the hackney behind, will you. Follow us to the princess's.'

'Colonel.'

'Sar'nt Acton, take the footboard.'

'Colonel.'

'Malet, come with me in the princess's carriage.'

'Might it not be safer to get an escort from the barracks, Colonel?'

'I fancy the road to the villa's a good deal quieter than to the barracks, but we'll only know when we begin.'

Shooting – if that it was – increased. And an orange glow lighting the sky.

'Come, then, gentlemen,' called Hervey breezily, not least for the ladies' benefit. 'We may have to forgo our supper, but we'll not be without honour!'

XXI

THE ARTICLES OF LONDON

Next day

Hervey sat with his troop leaders and staff at the dining table in the officers' house to contemplate the events of the night – and, indeed, of the morning. He and Malet had stayed at Princess Augusta's villa until a cornet's escort, a dozen dragoons, arrived just before dawn to mount guard. The drive back to barracks had been a dismal business – the streets full of the debris of riot, and not a few bodies, though whether these had given up the ghost or lay merely to rise again when the effects of drink had worn off was impossible to tell without descending from the carriage; and Hervey felt no cause for that.

'Well, gentlemen, I meet with Baron van der Fosse and his watch committee in an hour, and I trust they'll have a more complete account of matters, but there's little doubt that – for the time being at least – the authorities have a very imperfect control of the city. I shall have to make a deposition respecting the events of last night, and our actions, but to whom at present it is by no means clear. Mr Lincoln, how do the arrangements stand for our return to England?'

The quartermaster said that three steamers were engaged for the fifth of next month – ten days' time – and that if there were any delay there would be a penalty applied, which, he presumed, the War Office would accept as a contingent charge; but, of course, the delay could not be indefinite since the ships would have other contracts to honour, and it might then not be possible to engage any other steamer for some time, and the regiment would have to trust to sail.

'The intention is to march for Ostend on the second, Colonel,' said Malet.

It was seventy miles on a good, straight, and for the most part flat, road. They could do it in two days, not three, if it came to a pinch, but stragglers mightn't make it (as ever, much would depend on the farriers).

'Might it not be better to quit the city sooner, in the circumstances, Colonel?' asked Vanneck.

Hervey nodded. 'Yes, but I've a mind the English here will look to us for safety if this trouble isn't quickly brought to an end.'

'We can't be cooped up here till the second, Colonel,' said Worsley.

'No, I've no intention of being cooped up, but just what's prudent I can't say until I've consulted with Fosse – and, of course, General Bylandt, under whose orders we are still placed, though that was for the purpose of ceremonial. In the meantime it will be best to exercise horses at dawn. There seems to be some aversion to first light when it comes to rioting.'

They all nodded: it was the best they could make of things. Hervey called for more coffee, they discussed the situation at large, and the regiment's interior economy, for another half an hour, and then he left for the daily meeting at the Place Royale.

The governor of Brabant's house was now strongly picketed by gendarmes and regular troops. The Place Royale itself was not without the detritus of disorder – window glass, uprooted cobblestones – but evidently the appearance at some stage of so many men-at-arms had deflected the rioters to other parts, and the house was untouched. Inside, the mood was sombre, and, thought Hervey, the gathering council lacked any appearance of resolve. The baron called them to order without the usual formalities or pleasantries and asked the chief of police for his report.

It was a grim reckoning. The disturbances had, it seemed, begun in the Place de la Monnaie (which Hervey could well believe), and a crowd had gone thence to the offices of *The National*, the leading 'Dutch' paper, which was popularly presumed to be the mouthpiece of Van Maanen, broken every window and door, and destroyed the printing presses. Another crowd had gone to the house of Count Libri-Bagnano, one of the king's most intimate advisers, in the Rue de la Madeleine and put it to the torch. Only the outer walls remained. A number of gun-smiths' shops had been broken into and their contents carried away. Several small patrols of police and gendarmes had been surrounded and compelled to surrender. More than fifty people were reported dead. The French *tricolore* was flying from many buildings, and that of Brabant.

General Bylandt especially looked uncomfortable. His confident predictions had been proved wrong, and his want of strong precautionary measures – not least the movement of troops closer to the city – had allowed a disturbance to grow into something far worse. General Aberson, who'd evidently slept little, said he'd ordered his gendarmes to withdraw from the streets after dark this evening: he didn't have enough to patrol in the necessary strength, and felt their presence on the streets in daylight would make a greater impression.

Baron van der Fosse asked General Wauthier if he could make troops available for the support of the gendarmerie, but Wauthier said it was all he could do to guarantee the security of the royal palace and Hôtel de Ville. The baron then applied to Bylandt, who demurred, saying that while he acknowledged there'd been too few troops available last night, any augmentation in the city now would be highly inflammatory, and that he needed to refer matters to The Hague: if the trouble grew so great that it could only be subdued by the use of troops, reinforcements must be sent from the north so as to make the intervention overwhelming. But he was of a mind, yet, that the disturbances were likely to die down of their own accord, when the rougher sort had had their fill of drink and glass, and that it should remain meanwhile a police matter.

There was sense in this, thought Hervey – intervening with overwhelming force – but only if there were no overall increase in violence meanwhile, for it would be vastly more difficult to restore order at that stage. Indeed, his words with the Berkshire sheriff came back to him: 'Temporization on such occasions might be said to be a dangerous and even cruel policy.' And, in truth, 'a stitch in time' was likely as not a good saying here as at home; as their own, albeit bloody, action had demonstrated last night . . .

'May I speak, Baron?' he asked, judging his moment carefully, when the others at the table seemed to have reached a sort of *impasse*.

Baron van der Fosse gave him leave, and Hervey explained his thoughts, ending with a strong appeal to promptitude. 'I fear that those I saw last night are capable of even greater mischief. There was murder in their eyes.'

Yet Bylandt would not be moved – except to enquire whether Hervey would place his own regiment at his disposal, to which he replied that he would, but that he must of course send notice at once of his having done so to the ambassador in The Hague, at the risk of his orders then being countermanded. Bylandt thanked him and said that he understood perfectly, but showed no sign of any great determination to take up the offer.

Kuyff, the chief of police, added that he believed the events of last night to be the work of considerable organization, by no means spontaneous, and therefore likely to be repeated. So far no leader had declared himself or stated any demands, but the tenor of the demonstrations, leaving aside the 'mercenaries', the roughs from the Borinage, and the usual criminal opportunism, had been in the separatist cause – autonomy, independence even. Tonight, he said, would either be wholly quiet – the 'political' point having been made by last evening's violence – or else more violent still.

A considerable silence followed, and then Baron van der Fosse brought the council to a close, saying that when they reassembled tomorrow they would have a far clearer idea of what it was they faced, and the actions to be taken, but meanwhile that he hoped General Bylandt would send for more troops and muster all that were immediately available and place them on alert.

Hervey left in some dismay. Laying aside all questions of justification (in truth he'd formed some sympathy for the Walloons, whom the Dutch seemed to consider not so much different as inferior), he abhorred *la foule, de menigte*, the mob. Was it necessary to look further than Paris thirty years ago, and now, it seemed, once more? He went back to the *Caserne* hardly speaking a word to Malet, sat down at once to write to the ambassador, then changed into plain clothes, put the letter in his pocket and took himself off to see at first hand how things stood.

Rarely, he imagined, did personal reconnaissance prove its worth greater than now. In the space of two hours he came to conclude that the authorities faced a problem that would only get worse. The streets were full of people with ribbons – red, white and blue, or else red, yellow and black, the colours of the first Brabant revolution forty years before. On street corners and in the public squares were armed pickets at bonfires kept burning high despite the August heat. Others were handing out leaflets with calls for the Dutch to leave the country. And up and down the main thoroughfares bands of Borains, many in the clothes of the coalface, ranged ominously, with the look of 'wait until dark'. Serjeant Acton said he'd take his pick of them for a 'forlorn hope', but wouldn't want to have to disperse them with just the flat of the sword. Hervey agreed. He had a high regard for men who hewed coal, for besides aught else, Armstrong himself was from that stock. But they won their coal under regulation; heaven only knew what *unregulated* men from the infernal regions were capable of.

He then sought out Fairbrother in his rooms in the Grande Place, and found him in unusually solemn mood. He too had had his evening rudely curtailed, having been dining with an old acquaintance of his father's near the Place Royale when the noise of breaking glass had put the *patron* in a fright, and he'd closed up hastily.

Hervey had a particular favour to ask, one that he might trust to any of his officers, but which he could trust to his good friend even better – not least for his capacity for robust advocacy. He explained all that had gone before – the opera and then this morning's meeting – and asked if he would take a letter to Sir Charles Bagot in The Hague. It was necessary that someone from the embassy come at once to Brussels.

Fairbrother, far from deeming it granting a favour, accepted the errand at once with gratitude, for he confessed he was becoming bored. And in view of the urgent necessity of bringing some plenipotentiary of His Majesty to Brussels, he declined the offer of a carriage and said he would ride post instead. It was, by all accounts, about a hundred miles, but there would be numerous ferries to engage, and a carriage would take him twice as long. If the post-houses were alert and the roads well signed, he could, he believed, if he set off at once, make The Hague by midday tomorrow.

Hervey was much relieved. 'I've thought long since the meeting this morning. I've no notion why Bylandt's so supine, nor indeed Baron van der Fosse, who, I believe, is in a position to overrule him, or at least appeal to The Hague to do so, but two possibilities occur to me – that they act in good faith but wholly mistakenly, or else they're in sympathy with the cause of the separatists. With which I'm not concerned, only to the extent that they let in the French, either by invitation or neglect.'

'I confess I've been expecting to see them any day now.'

'Quite. Now, I've said nothing of it in the letter, for seen from so distant a place as The Hague the situation may look different, the view all too sanguine, but I've resolved to take the regiment to observe the border – tomorrow or the day after. Those damned French *tricolores* – an invitation to the dance.'

Fairbrother looked wary. 'Is that entirely wise? On whose authority?'

Hervey nodded. His friend's question was entirely apt. 'Not whose authority, but by *what* authority.'

'Explain?'

'Before we left Hounslow I asked Malet to get a copy of the "Articles of London", for it seemed only courtesy that I was acquainted with them – little knowing of course that they would become of such moment. The first of them – there are eight – which the Congress at Vienna took into its treaty, is of the essence, and unequivocal: "The union shall be intimate and complete, so that the two countries shall form but one state". And I must tell you, Fairbrother, that that day fifteen years ago, at Waterloo, a good many Englishmen, many friends of mine, fell astride the road to Brussels to keep the French – Bonaparte – out of here. And if all that's to be set aside now, what purpose was served that day? If there's no one else in Brabant who can or will place the interests of His Majesty – His *Britannic* Majesty – foremost in their actions in the coming days, then I for one will not shrink from doing so.'

That night General Wauthier's troops remained inactive, guarded by the walls of the buildings they were meant to be guarding. And Bylandt, despite the parting request of the provincial governor at the morning's meeting, moved no others to his support, so that by dawn on the twenty-seventh Brussels had the appearance of a city occupied by a hostile force – 'hostile' rather than 'liberating' because the destruction of property, a good deal of it belonging to private citizens, was so widespread. Only by private enterprise indeed would the destruction be checked once daylight came, when the remnants of the Garde Civile were taken in hand by Baron D'Hoogvoort, one of the city's more active magistrates, and joined by an impromptu militia of tradesmen and those of property who feared not only for their lives but for their livelihoods.

But though the violence abated, its true purpose revealed itself: the Brabant *tricolore*, its horizontal stripes even more striking than those of the French, now flew everywhere, and royal insignia on those buildings not guarded by troops were torn down.

Meanwhile, news – reliable or not – that reinforcements from Ghent were marching on the city brought a deputation to Bylandt, threatening that no troops would be allowed to enter the city without the utmost resistance. Bylandt at once sought out Baron van der Fosse, who summoned General Wauthier. But the city commandant protested that it was all he could do to guard himself, and that he could spare not a man from the defences of the royal palace to act against the *agitateurs*. Bylandt therefore agreed to have the reinforcements halt, and to keep his own troops in their encampment at Vilvoorde, ten miles north, until he received orders from The Hague.

The concession, whether prudent or not, at once emboldened the agitators in deeds and words alike. The press gave free vent to emotion, the *Catholique* of Ghent thundering:

> There is no salvation for the throne, but in an ample concession of our rights. The essential points to be accorded are royal inviolability and ministerial responsibility; the dismissal of Van Maanen; liberty of education and the press; a diminution of taxation . . . in short, justice and liberty in all and for all, in strict conformity with the fundamental law.

The *Coursier des Pays Bas* was perhaps more circumspect regarding actual independence, but was nevertheless uncompromising in its demands, including the dismissal of Van Maanen, and adamant The Hague must act to save the union:

> We repeat that we are neither in a state of insurrection nor revolution; all we want is a mitigation of the grievances we have so long endured, and some guarantees for a better future.

And some of the gentry of the uprising, believing themselves now to be masters of events, sought to dress the violence in more humble clothes. Next day, the twenty-eighth, a rally at the Hôtel de Ville appointed a deputation of five, led by Alexandre de Gendebien, a prominent lawyer from Mons, and the comte de Mérode, to bear to the king a loyal address setting out these grievances, and asking respectfully for their removal.

Meanwhile, having learned that morning from several *émigrés* that the new government in Paris intended sending troops to Wallonia 'to protect their French-speaking cousins', Hervey set out for the border with two troops.

XXII

NE PLUS ULTRA

Later

There were conventions for choosing which troop. If it were a
detached command, the senior captain's had the privilege. But in
leaving D Troop in Brussels as a depot Hervey broke no rules –
since in strict law Tyrwhitt was still captain; nor, indeed, did he discompose either Vanneck or Worsley, for the prospect of getting out
of the city and seeing a little action, albeit, he assured (warned)
them, peaceable, was more than enough to entice them. Besides,
although they would be under his direct command, they would, he
explained, range so widely as to be in effect quite independent.
Indeed, though he did not tell them (hardly needing to), he had
chosen their troops for that very reason. In Vanneck and Worsley
he had captains on whom he could rely – rely absolutely. And this
would be a game in which a card played ill could cost them dearly
– life, limb, reputation; perhaps even the safety of the realm.

At least, that was how Hervey saw it. And so did Vanneck and
Worsley, for when he told them his intention to go and look for the
French they said it was the finest thing, if the greatest hazard.
Afterwards they speculated on what in the circumstances they
themselves would have done, but determined only that while as

captains, even of cavalry, they would probably be spared the fate of Admiral Byng, shot for a seeming want of zeal to close with the enemy – '*pour encourager les autres*' – perhaps a lieutenant-colonel would not be. There again, Admiral Codrington had hardly been feted for his determination to close with the Turks at Navarino.

There was another reason, too, for choosing Vanneck and Worsley – their serjeant-majors. Armstrong and Collins had faced the French on too many occasions to be either overawed or over-excited, and this was an undertaking that needed the strongest of resolution and the coolest of heads.

In truth, the only decision that had required much consideration was whether he should leave the quartermaster and regimental serjeant-major in Brussels. He concluded that, to begin with at least, Lincoln should come with him, for the business of provision-ing was his, and in that regard Mordaunt's troop was well provided for; while the question of shipping home was in these circumstances secondary. As for Mr Rennie, it would have been an affront to remain where there was but one troop, even though matters in Brussels would have benefited greatly from his judgement, which Hervey would have found reassuring. Moreover, was there ever a cooler head than that which had defused the bomb at the wheels of the crown princess's carriage? His place was at the frontier.

The march south took them across *two* battlefields – Waterloo and Malplaquet. It seemed more than a little portentous. Both those great contests had been towards the same purpose as theirs now – to keep the French out of the Low Countries. Of Waterloo every dragoon was now an authority to varying degrees, but Malplaquet, a century before, needed instruction in the saddle. There, England's other great captain, the Duke of Marlborough, had defeated Marshal Villars and the following month retaken the great fortress of Mons. Yet he had suffered such losses – it was perhaps the bloodiest battle in all of that bloody century – that Villars wrote to the French king, 'If it please God to give your majesty's enemies another such victory, they are ruined.' And Marlborough had received no letter of thanks afterwards from the Queen, as he had for his other victories. While the field of Waterloo was therefore somehow an inspiration to ride across, that of Malplaquet was a warning. And Hervey was most conscious of it.

They had kept the baggage to a minimum – tentage, five days' rations, cooking pots and twelve hundredweight of corn per troop. There would be green fodder enough – it had been a good summer for grass – and last year's hay would not be too hard to come by perhaps, but bread and meat were already short, as well they knew from the half-starved beggars who'd been filling the streets of Brussels. They had three days' supply of salt pork and dried peas, but he knew full well they wouldn't be able to remain in the field long unless Lincoln were able to buy more. He certainly had the means: the imprest account saw to that, though doubtless there'd be questions to answer on return to Hounslow. Hervey reckoned they could subsist for a fortnight, at most; but, then, if the French were to make a move it would surely be sooner than later, before reinforcements from the northern provinces could be sent into Wallonia. And they'd be imprudent to do so without some reconnaissance, some probing of the border, for they couldn't risk a clash of arms with the Dutch. No, a fortnight should be enough.

It was on this supposition therefore that he laid out his design to the captains on the first night – in the Château de Seneffe, seat of the Depestre family, whose wealth had come from contracts with the Austrian army in the century before, and who were perfectly happy to increase it with billeting money (and, indeed, for Lincoln to settle contracts for a good deal of fresh meat, flour and potatoes). It was a chance choosing, but one that did Hervey's reputation for resource and luck no ill at all.

'Gentlemen,' he began, presiding at the head of a vast dining table on which the captains had spread their maps, and the regimental staff their order books; 'I shall take you now into my complete confidence, for it is only right that you understand that this enterprise is not without peril – not so much to life and limb but to our good name – and that we play for high stakes.'

Peril, high stakes . . . what cavalryman worth his salt did not thrill to such words? Ears pricked like a seasoned hunter's to the sound of the horn. Even the surgeon, who thought his lot was ever to administer pills, sat up at the words, despite the assertion that the threat was not to life and limb.

'You are as aware as I of the tumultuous state of affairs in Brussels. Its local consequences we cannot foretell; nor do they concern us at this time. If, however, the French take this opportunity to make mischief then the consequences for England must be great and apparent.'

Vanneck and Worsley nodded readily. They knew their history as well as any man: the hostile shore was ever a concern, the Scheldt, the barrel of the gun.

But what might two troops of light dragoons accomplish?

'Gentlemen, it is possible – *possible*, mind – that if the French come they will do so in great strength and sweep all before them. That, however, might be tantamount to a hostile act – invasion, indeed; which of course it would be, no matter how it were to advantage dressed – protection of their French-speaking cousins and such like. So it seems to me to be at least as possible – and, I would claim, more probable – that if they come they will do so guardedly. And if, finding no troops barring their way, they then advance boldly and so disperse themselves about the Walloon provinces, the Dutch would have a nigh impossible task to eject them. I am yet to discover what Dutch troops – I should say Dutch-Belgic – there are to bar the way, but I have it on some authority that those that there are in Wallonia keep only the old barrier fortresses – those of principal interest to us being at Ath, Mons and Charleroi – and have none about the country but gendarmes. But since by my reckoning the French would not wish to appear to be making war on the Dutch, they would not invest those places but seek to slip by them.'

Again Vanneck and Worsley nodded. The logic was unassailable. But Worsley was examining his map with close attention, and looking increasingly uneasy.

Hervey sensed why. 'Is it possible for a French force of any size to slip between the barrier forts thus? Let me answer in this way. We crossed the field of Malplaquet today, that bloody place where Marlborough lost . . . what – twenty thousand? But only two years later, as you'll recall, he slipped through the lines of "Ne Plus Ultra" during the night and the French found themselves out-manoeuvred – out-generalled.'

Worsley smiled, conceding the point.

'However, gentlemen, the French must not slip through *our* lines of "Ne Plus Ultra".'*

And to stay the obvious protests he raised a hand.

'I'm perfectly aware that two troops of light dragoons hardly constitute "lines" worthy of the name, but our advantage compared with those of Marlborough's day is that our lines are not fixed. We may place them where we have a mind to once we've discovered the French route of advance. It's possible they may cross the border in numerous places: there are good reasons for doing so. But such a dispersal would not necessarily be to their advantage, for if they are opposed in one part and their other columns continue, unknowing, the scheme therefore takes on the nature of invasion again – which, if my original supposition is correct, they would not wish. So I'm persuaded that their course will be to advance via the single best route, and that route is that which Bonaparte himself took fifteen years ago – the road down which we have ridden this day. Or else that which he also took to attack the Prussians, to the east towards Charleroi. Captain Worsley, the Mons road shall be yours, and Captain Vanneck, that from Jeumont.'

The captains examined their maps again. The distance between

* 'Not further beyond', the supposed inscription on the Pillars of Hercules at the Straits of Gibraltar warning ships against passage west.

the crossing points on the border was about eight miles – too far to be of mutual assistance, not so very different from those tumultuous days in 1815.

'As I have said, I believe the best interests of the French would be served by a single avenue of advance. As soon as that avenue is detected I shall withdraw the other troop to the support of that astride the advance. However, eight miles – an hour and a half to bring a troop to the support of the other: it would be close run. I intend therefore to scout the fortress at Maubeuge, which is the obvious *point d'appui*, to gain the earliest indication of which road they'll take.'

The captains looked reassured – except that Maubeuge stood square in French territory.

'Now, the manner of your barring the way: it is to be without violence. I mean, not a shot nor a blade is to touch a single cuirassier, lancer or whatever manner of cavalryman is sent. Draw swords – certainly; warning shots if necessary. I leave it to you to devise what drill you may – and for the night also, for it's not impossible that they should try to pass in darkness; and I'll talk with you of it when you see the ground tomorrow. We want no "untoward event", no Navarino' (the proximity of opposing forces had a momentum of its own, just as in that unfortunate battle): 'if they offer violence the game's up: it's then invasion, and there's nothing for it but to melt before them, as at a field day. We'll have done all that's reasonably in our power to do.'

Vanneck and Worsley nodded once more. There need be no sacrifice – not a single dragoon – *if*, unlike at Navarino, cool heads prevailed.

'Now, there's much for you to ponder, but one last detail, and as we've ridden across the battlefields of the two greatest exponents of exploring, let me quote the first duke, that nothing can be done without good and early intelligence. Cornets St Alban and Jenkinson shall therefore be detached for the purpose of exploring Maubeuge. In plain clothes, of course.'

The adjutant looked distinctly uneasy.

'Mr Malet?'

'Colonel, I was merely wondering if it might be more . . . with respect, prudent, to keep Jenkinson within his troop. If he were to be taken, detained, captured, or whatever it were, the nephew of the late prime minister . . .'

Hervey smiled just perceptibly. 'It is for that reason that I choose him.'

Silence. There could be no clearer statement of their leader's steely earnest.

And Hervey was aware of it. Just occasionally it was necessary to impress upon even the best of men what a business theirs was.

But if soldiery were, in the end, a business of some heat, it did not follow that it should be grim. His smile became wry: 'Jenkinson's safety is assured. He and St Alban can play the part of two English *milords* on their grand tour. The only hazard is that the late prime minister's nephew – "BA Oxon" – will think himself too strongly into the part: I fancy there's enough at Maubeuge to keep an *army* of antiquarians absorbed for days.'

Worsley smiled. 'A whole regiment might pass unremarked if he were wrestling with some inscription.'

Vanneck shook his head. 'But St Alban would not miss a crowd, and the chance to lecture them on Reform.'

There was knowing laughter. Hervey had pulled off the trick to a T.

Next morning they paraded before first light. In the circumstances it was as well to lose no more time than need be, but there was anyway something to being under arms at dawn that set the blood coursing – the shiver of anticipation. They'd had months of ease; the pace must now change.

The plan was simple enough. The captains would ride to the border, present their compliments to the gendarmes and the customs officials, and explain that they were come to keep watch but would

otherwise not disturb their work. They would then make a reconnaissance of the country just short of the crossing to determine the
best place to take post, and then, when their troops joined them,
rehearse their own designs for the interception of, as Hervey put it,
the *incursores*. Only then would the 'milords' proceed into France
(indeed it would not do for them to appear at too early an hour,
being 'gentlemen of leisure').

Hervey and his party rode ahead. It was the most perfect of
mornings, the air new-scrubbed but warm, mist hanging over the
streams, birds in full throat, late in the year though it was, the fields
lush green and the cattle content, or else stubbled, with poppy and
cornflower in the balks, and here and there an early gleaner, or a
wisp of smoke from a cottage hearth; a country still at rest. It was
a good time to be making tracks, on foot to begin with and then in
a mile or so, the horses warmed to the work, into the saddle and a
steady trot. A dozen or so miles west and it would not have been so
bucolic – Mons, and, beyond, the Borinage, the infernal dominion
of the coal pits. He ought perhaps to see it, if only to know what
those places in England looked like.

Twenty-five miles. Four hours and without mishap, so that it was
not yet nine when they rode up to the customs post on the Rue des
Trieux, two leagues north of Maubeuge, the Marquis de Vauban's
great fortress, and Hervey made his introductions to the startled
douaniers and the *caporal* of gendarmes.

Having first taken them for Dutch – and been courteous – once
persuaded their visitors were English, the guardians of the crossing
became positively friendly. Coffee and genever was produced. And
useful intelligence, too. The French, they said, had begun sending a
patrol – half a dozen lancers, as far as they could make out – to
their own *douanerie* a hundred yards down the road, morning and
evening. They'd not done this before. They'd spend a quarter of an
hour at the post, wave in a comradely manner to them – and they
themselves would return the greeting – and then turn back in the
direction of Maubeuge.

'*Et c'est tout à fait?*' asked Hervey, wondering if there were not some other revealing detail.

'*Oui, mon colonel* – it is indeed all.'

It could mean anything – perhaps that the French here knew of the tumult in Brussels and were on the lookout for some sign of its spreading . . .

He drank his coffee, accepted more, and a second glass of genever, bought some of the bread and pork dripping which an enterprising *épouse du fermier* brought from a cottage near by, and then explained that a troop of sixty or so *dragons légers* would soon be arriving. It was to do with the anniversary of Waterloo, he said (not untruthfully), at which the guardians of the post looked perfectly content, and the farmer's wife delighted. And having thanked them all profoundly and shaken hands, he set off to follow the line of cairns and posts that marked the border to where Vanneck's troop would in time be stationing themselves, just north of Jeumont – and where, indeed, but for any enterprising wife, the encounter with the second party of gendarmes and *douaniers* was exactly like that with the first.

Both troops reached their picket posts towards ten, their baggage an hour later. Hervey had said they couldn't expect billets: the maps suggested these parts were not much built over, and besides, the very appearance of military tentage ought to serve as a signal – a check – to the French.

By midday the videttes were posted, Cornets Jenkinson and St Alban were making their way incognito and unhindered to Maubeuge (dressed, indeed, as if for Paris), and at one o'clock Vanneck and Worsley met with Hervey at the rendezvous near the Bois d'Avau between the two crossings to arrange the system of signals and gallopers that might unite them at the proper moment. In this, the ground certainly favoured them, the country flat or at most gently rolling, and the best going short of Newmarket that a galloper could reasonably wish for. Malet made the contact arrangements: a corporal's relay from each troop by day (Hervey thought the risk of mishap at night too great); and the trumpet-major had both captains' trumpeters rehearse the ancillary calls. Then Hervey went to each picket in turn and spent half an hour reviewing the preparations. By three o'clock the campfires were lit and the beef boiling.

Towards four, Jenkinson and St Alban returned. They had ridden across country as instructed to evade the gendarmerie, to the cross-roads midway between Jeumont and Merbes-le-Château, where Hervey intended planting his pennon – and where with two order-lies Corporal Johnson had supervised the erection of a gaily striped maiden's marquee, with table, chairs and washstand, while Mr Lincoln's men put up more conventional canvas for the rest of the party.

Hervey arrived in good spirits, having found the pickets in exemplary order. 'Well,' he said, surveying the regency stripes, 'if the King of France himself comes we shall not feel inferior.'

Johnson mumbled something appreciative, glad that there was no enquiry as to the marquee's provenance (it was an ill riot that blew no good).

'The scouts are returned, Colonel,' said Malet, thinking it best to divert attention from the obvious question (Mr Rennie could be relied on to deal with things in due course – prudentially).

The cornets, taking their ease under a chestnut tree, had been roused by Serjeant Acton and were hurrying over. They looked at the same time grave and yet accomplished.

'Good afternoon, gentlemen,' replied Hervey to their salutations. 'I perceive you have something to report.'

'Yes, Colonel – indeed so,' said Jenkinson.

He bid them sit at the table, and Johnson brought coffee in the campaign china.

'You had no trouble passing to and from Maubeuge, evidently?'

'None at all, Colonel,' replied Jenkinson, claiming seniority. 'We rode into the town unchecked, made a circumnavigation of the entire fortress and its environs and then took our refreshment in the grand square, where we were soon engaged in conversation with a party of officers of the garrison, who were most hospitable.'

'Carry on.'

'Colonel, it is exactly as you surmised: there is a regiment of cuirassiers come into the town under orders to conduct a "cavalcade", as they called it. They are to ride towards Mons to see what is the reply of the garrison and the people, and if favourable then towards Charleroi. We asked if they were to be followed at once by greater numbers, but they were uncertain; however they did believe that theirs was the only such expedition.'

'Mm. "Cavalcade" – a somewhat picturesque choice.' He looked at St Alban. 'Their exact word?'

'Yes, Colonel.'

'Mm.' It was gratifying to have such 'good and early intelligence'; even if, by its very nature, incomplete. He pressed his exploring officers nevertheless for any detail that might reveal something more to advantage: what would be the day and time of the cavalcade; in what strength; would the two of them be able to re-enter Maubeuge if necessary?

St Alban revealed the most profitable line of further exploration. 'Colonel, Jenkinson and I discussed between us – as best we could at the table with the French officers – whether it were better to reveal that there was an English regiment barring their way, for it seemed we might accomplish your purpose without the two coming into proximity, but we concluded that this would be too perilous: the French might then devise some scheme of testing the regiment, whereas if they were to come across it unexpectedly, the initiative would remain with us.'

Hervey thought for a moment. The idea had its attractions – and, indeed, there was evidently still time to do it – but he too concluded that to surrender surprise would be a mistake. 'One more thing: the *douaniers* on the Mons road spoke of lancers coming to the crossing morning and evening of late, yet you spoke only of cuirassiers.'

'We saw no sign of lancers, Colonel.'

Hervey nodded. 'Very well; it's perhaps of little import . . . But I shall want you to return to Maubeuge, take rooms somewhere and observe. I want early warning of this cavalcade. By early I mean at least an hour by day – to give time to get the horses under saddle and the troops into line, which means that you yourselves must be at an instant's readiness.'

'Colonel.'

He rose. 'You have done well, gentlemen. I look to you to do the same tomorrow – or whenever it may be.'

At about five next morning as the headquarter party went quietly about its business of the new day, with the smell of bacon, and birdsong and the rhythmic munching of oats to complete the impression of pastoral peace, Fairbrother rode into the encampment. Hervey was sipping coffee (Corporal Johnson had brought him tea at first light, with voluble recollections of doing so on the morning of Waterloo, and how much more agreeable it was today – 'no rain, no Frenchies'). He rose and greeted his good friend warily, for although he was ever glad to see him, the fleetest of postboys could not have made The Hague and back so soon.

'The greatest of good fortune,' Fairbrother reported: 'I learned at one of the post-houses that the ambassador was at Breda; and so he was, and received me at once, for he'd heard of the disturbances, and he read your letter with close attention.'

Johnson brought coffee and a bowl of hot water, Fairbrother being covered in the dust of the road.

'He questioned me closely on the events of the twenty-fifth and the reaction of the authorities, and said he must return at once to The Hague to see the king, but would send the secretary of the embassy to Brussels – Cartwright, his name. He much approved of your decision to come here.'

He took several gulps of coffee, piping hot though it was.

Hervey nodded. 'He approves the decision. Well, that is something indeed. He offered no directive, I take it?'

Fairbrother shook his head. 'Carte blanche, I would think. His words were that from his observations in Canada and what he had read of the Cape, there was no one in whom he would have greater confidence.'

Obliged though he was, Hervey merely inclined his head. As a rule he cared not much for the approval of someone who'd never worn the King's coat, but Sir Charles Bagot was no place-man. 'Capital,' he said quietly.

Fairbrother poured himself more coffee. 'I thought it might be pleasing.'

Hervey now quickened. 'Now hear, I've good intelligence from Maubeuge. I believe we may see the French this day— But I forget myself: Breda's, what, a hundred miles? You'll have slept little. There's a pleasant swimming pool in the stream yonder, which I bathed in just before you came.' He pointed to the spinney the other side of the crossroads. 'And you may avail yourself of my bed.'

Fairbrother confessed he'd lain for three hours at a post-house by Brussels, but reckoned that unless he could sleep for twelve it were better that he stayed on his feet – especially with the prospect of a little action. 'I'll take myself off to bathe, and then beg a little breakfast of you.'

While he did, Hervey took up his pen to write a second despatch to London – which this time he was able to do with all the assurance of approval. Though not, of course, with licence to make actual war.

An hour later, Fairbrother, shaved and shampooed, his coat sponged by Johnson and his boots blacked by one of the orderlies, returned to the table with renewed vigour and joined in a fortifying breakfast of eggs and bacon.

Malet joined them too, fresh from his inspection of the corporals' relays. 'They were posted by a quarter past four, Colonel, and keen as a razor – Denny and Walton.'

'Then I hope the French won't keep us waiting. I've a mind to send scouts down the road, in case St Alban and Jenkinson miss them, but it would be a deuced tricky thing to have them discovered.'

'Both captains will be sharp on the lookout, Colonel.'

'Indeed,' said Hervey, lapsing into thought.

Fairbrother eyed him, cautiously. 'Do you want me to scout, in my plain coat?'

Hervey shook his head. 'No, I'd something else in mind. You said that Bagot was not in the least anxious about what I proposed?'

'On the contrary. As I told you, he spoke of the imperative necessity to keep the French out of the Netherlands. Though not, I'm sure, by force of arms.'

'Mm.'

He thought a little longer.

'Malet, instruct the sar'nt-major, if you please, to issue Captain Vanneck's troop with ten rounds of ball-cartridge.'

'Colonel?'

'Ten rounds. Each troop has five already, do they not? Worsley's won't need more. And I would have a man take him orders, which I'll write presently. If it is "imperative necessity" to keep out the French, then we may have to make more than a mere demonstration.'

Fairbrother made to protest, but Hervey stayed him.

Malet rose and went to find the serjeant-major.

Fairbrother, his plate now clean, pushed it aside and spoke firmly. 'Hervey, a show of force is one thing . . .'

Hervey nodded, gravely. 'I know, but if the French *aren't* over-awed by show, how can we *not* apply that force? If we call their bluff, then who will censure us? And if it comes to war with France, then what moment to anyone will be the action of two troops at its commencement?'

'Two troops of cavalry?'

'If that is all His Majesty can place in the path of the French, then so be it.'

'Remember Codrington. Battle came out of nothing but proximity, and then out of that battle war between Russia and the Turk. You yourself have said it.'

'Yes, and I said it again when I gave my design to Vanneck and Worsley; but I don't think it an entirely apt comparison. The Turks were not attempting to force a passage; they were at anchor. We cannot let Navarino haunt our every decision. Peto lately told me of a far more fitting *memento*: his hero, Hoste, at Lissa signalling "Remember Nelson". And so I *shall*.'

'Noble sentiment.'

'But quite why we must look to naval officers for example . . . Nevertheless, be assured that I shall indeed remember Codrington, most certainly, and Nelson – and Byng.'

Fairbrother studied his friend intently. No one had ever stirred him to exertion as he. No one else he had known displayed such simple certainty in King and Country, nor yet a purblind loyalty, nor an incapacity to see corruption and absurdity, just an unshakeable faith that in his England there reposed the best of all worlds – on balance, in sum, for better or worse, *ceteris paribus*; and in consequence where duty lay (in which lay also the true glory). It was, indeed, the very motto which his family had borne for generations, *Quo officium ducit* – where duty leads. What he himself would not give to have such faith! But being not a true believer (not yet, at any rate), he would follow like some seeker after truth; for what, otherwise, should detain a gentleman? He had, in former times, taken his pleasure in Dionysian proportions; it did not last beyond the next sunrise. His true pleasure now lay in the company of this man, and, yes, in the company of those who answered to him. What *was* this mystery?

'Fairbrother?'

'What? I—'

'You seemed to be elsewhere. Corporal Johnson asked if there was anything more?'

He looked at his host, and his host's most admirable corporal; and he smiled.

'Might I have more bacon? It really is most unconscionably good.'

An hour later, the bacon finished, the meditation over, the despatch for London given to an orderly for the post at Mons, Vanneck's orders written and delivered, and the ball-cartridge issued to his troop, Hervey was ready to take to the saddle to make an inspection of the pickets. Johnson, insisting on his true position as 'groom of the charger' rather than – as the wags in the canteen had it – of the close-stool, brought up Ajax and Dolly.

'Captain Fairbrother will accompany us, Corp'l Johnson.'

Johnson turned to the dragoon leading Dolly. 'Go and fetch that bay of the adjutant's, will you, Toddy.'

Hervey sighed. But there was little point telling Johnson that 'Toddy' was 'Pickering' on parade (except to save him from the ordeal that would follow if the sar'nt-major heard); it had taken all his powers of persuasion to get him to *wear* the rank.

'Mr Malet's already said as 'e could 'ave 'im, Colonel.'

'Most generous.'

'Might I have a sword?' asked Fairbrother awkwardly, addressing the request to no one in particular. 'I would feel so deucedly undressed otherwise.'

'It'll 'ave one on t'saddle, sir,' replied Johnson.

Hervey sighed again. Johnson had lapsed into the enunciation that so confounded him when first he'd become his groom (he could never fathom why it came and went as it did). But what things they'd seen in their time; what triumphs and disasters. And always the flat vowels and want of aspirates – revealing so little, and imper-turbable. Had they spoken thus when Ivanhoe ranged 'In that pleasant district of merry England which is watered by the river

Don . . .'? Except that, by Johnson's own account, its pleasantness was now much diminished. That morning at Waterloo – he could never forget it – Johnson's hand shook his shoulder, though but a touch was needed to wake him (the instincts of five years' campaigning) . . . Besides, the rain had allowed no more than a fitful sleep, and it had been near midnight when he'd at last lain down . . . The hand, and 'tea, sir' . . . How *had* he found a fire to brew it on such a night? Not one officer in a dozen could have been woken that way. Yet in Spain no one had wanted him . . . a refugee of the coal-pit, difficult to understand – no, just plain difficult. The canvas of his valise had kept out the worst of the downpour, but he'd crawled into it already soaked to the skin – and he'd shivered as he took the tea: 'Couldn't get no brandy or nothin',' Johnson had said. 'A German 'ad some snaps but 'e wanted gold for it – gold!' Flat vowels, want of aspirates – defiant badge of a man who would remain his own no matter what. What memories bound them. *Were you at Waterloo? / I have been at Waterloo. / 'Tis no matter what you do / If you were at Waterloo* . . .

'Colonel?'

'What?' he said absently.

'I said look yonder.'

He turned. 'Great heavens.'

They came on at the trot. Everywhere, dragoons braced.

He brought his hand up sharply to the salute. 'Good morning, Your Highness.'

Behind the princess, Lieutenant Mordaunt bore the look of a man who knew he had a difficult explanation before him – though Hervey might guess it, for he'd placed him in command of the colonel-in-chief's safety.

'Good morning, Colonel Hervey,' she said, with the most winning of smiles, so that he almost began thinking himself pleased she'd come.

'I was not, of course, expecting you, ma'am.'

'I was not expecting you to leave Brussels, Colonel.'

353

She had made her point. He ought to have told her himself, but time had been pressing, and . . .

'I'm about to inspect the pickets. May we offer refreshment?'

She shook her head. 'We have no desire to make ourselves a burden. We put up last evening at the Abbaye du Bélian, not ten miles from here, and breakfasted well.'

He helped her from the saddle (at least she didn't wear uniform). 'The Trakehner you rode at Waterloo, ma'am?'

'Indeed. Mr Mordaunt was most attentive in finding her.'

Hervey glanced at the attentive Mordaunt, who looked ever more awkward.

'Admirable. Exactly as should be. Thank you, Mordaunt.' He added a smile, albeit wry.

'Colonel.'

'Then let me tell you what we've learned here, and what we're about, ma'am,' he said, indicating the table outside his tent, where he could spread a map (that was, assuming her to be acquainted with maps).

But his intention was stayed: 'Colonel, yonder,' snapped Johnson, never overawed by an occasion.

Hervey turned, irritated – an interruption too many. 'What—'

The exploring officers – one of them.

'Ma'am, forgive me—' he said tersely.

An orderly took the sweat-covered reins as Cornet Jenkinson jumped from the saddle.

'Colonel, they're on the march. Two squadrons – two hundred horse. We watched them parading and move off. None went east, only north. St Alban's gone straight to alert Captain Worsley.'

Good thinking; what they'd lost in time, perhaps, they'd gained in assurance that he could withdraw Vanneck's troop at once – save for a vidette, just in case. 'Mr Malet, have Vanneck's troop come up to Worsley's immediately.'

'Colonel!'

'What were the French – lancers?'

'No, Colonel. Cuirassiers only.'

'In haste, or . . .'

'With much ceremony, Colonel.'

'Good. We may have a little time then. And they a surprise, by the sound of things.'

He turned to the princess, who'd come forward to hear.

'Ma'am, I must fly.'

'I shall follow, Colonel.'

His look was pained. 'Ma'am, may I request – with all due respect – that you remain here?'

She smiled again, as winningly as before.

There wasn't time to argue. 'Very well, I'll tell you all as we gallop.'

A quarter of an hour, cutting (riskily) across the salient of French soil west of the Bois d'Avau, over stubble fields, here and there a stream, and a hedge or two – a spirited, fortifying gallop in-hand, the princess keeping up with ease, relishing the pace indeed, choosing her own line at the hurdles, skirts no impediment (nor to her lady-in-waiting) . . . They beat the French to the ground by five minutes.

'Halloo, Worsley!'

B Troop's captain was standing in the saddle, middle of his line, peering through the binocular telescope he'd bought in Brussels.

Hervey cantered to his side.

'Colonel, good morning. Movement in the trees yonder.' He nodded towards the clump of oaks next the French *douanerie*.

Hervey took out his spyglass. 'Yes, movement . . . I think – horses?'

'Horses, assuredly – and cuirasses. Scouts, maybe?'

'Or council of war, perhaps? They see us clearly, I trust. I wonder what they make of such a reception party.' He lowered his glass. 'Now, mark you: I've sent for Vanneck's troop, and they have fifteen rounds ball. If the French come on hard I may have you withdraw and give them a volley or two – in the air to begin with, but if necessary . . .'

Worsley looked uneasy – a departure from the orders of last evening.

'But I want no more, still, than a determined, barring action by you – no edge or point, mind.'

He looked assured again. 'No, Colonel. We've drilled exactly to your last order.'

'Good man.'

Only now did he see the princess, halted at the end of the front rank. 'Your Highness,' he said, saluting. 'I beg pardon.'

She pressed forward. 'Captain Worsley, what a week it has been!' – and the same disarming smile.

He looked at Hervey for enlightenment, but received only a raised eyebrow.

Malet came galloping, and the serjeant-major. 'Vanneck'll be here in ten minutes, Colonel. Kenny's bringing them short by the Bois.'

'Thank you. Would you escort the colonel-in-chief to the spinney to the rear. There will be a fine view.' He turned to the princess. 'Ma'am?'

She held her smile but was too astute to challenge an order once given.

Five minutes, and the column trotted three abreast from the line of oaks to the chaussée six hundred yards ahead, breastplates glinting.

Hervey put his telescope back in its saddle-case. 'What a sight to behold, Worsley. I never thought to see again French cavalry advance on me.'

At Waterloo they'd come on in line, at the charge; but the day before, when Wellington's own cavalry had covered the withdrawal of his weary infantry from Quatre Bras, they'd watched them come on thus – and ever so gingerly, not at all wanting to close for a fight. At muster that morning his troop leader, Edward Lankester, had ridden along the front of the first squadron, exchanging words with his dragoons for all the world like the owner of some well-run estate hailing his contented tenants: 'I'm sorry, First Squadron – no breakfast, no rum, no Frenchmen, but I think we'll have all of them aplenty and in good time, if not in that order!' Oh, the laughter, and Lankester's good-hearted riposte: 'It could be worse, though!' And a voice from the ranks: 'How's that, sir?', and Lankester's 'Well, it could be raining!' – and half an hour later it was.

But this was too fine a morning for rain – not a cloud, not a breath of moving air. A good day for powder.

He looked left and right. B Troop was admirably posted. He wouldn't do as Lankester. It was Worsley's troop; he wouldn't steal his thunder.

He turned and saw Serjeant-Major Collins in his place, behind the rear rank, and centre. He'd have been just as content with Vanneck's troop, and Armstrong, but it was especially good to see Collins. What a loss to his country he would have been – and all for the sake of a lieutenant's spleen . . .

Malet returned. 'I've told Mordaunt he's to seize hold of the princess's reins if necessary, Colonel.'

Hervey nodded. 'What a deuced fine thing, though, that she chooses to come.'

'Colonel?'

'Nothing.'

'Ah,' said Worsley, taking up the contact on his own reins suddenly. 'Here we go!'

The column had stopped. A few seconds later they began deploying into line.

'How many do you make it, Malet?'

The adjutant was already scribbling in his notebook. He looked up for a moment or two. 'They're fronting fifty, Colonel, two lines.' He took out his telescope and studied closer. 'And the same again beyond. Two squadrons, evidently.' He wrote down the details and the time. It was his to keep the regiment's diary – and who knew what evidence might be needed if . . .

'I think so too,' said Hervey, and with some relief, for it meant the column hadn't divided.

They watched in silence as the lines formed and dressed – and then the trumpet call: *En Avant*.

There was not a sound from the troop but the grinding of bits, the odd snort and stamping foot (the flies, curse them) and the creak of leather.

Four hundred yards – a walk still, and in perfect line.

Three hundred – the same.

Two hundred . . .

'With permission, Colonel?'

'Carry on.'

Worsley drew his sabre and put his weight into the stirrups. 'Troop will draw swords. Dra-a-aw . . . *swords*!'

Metal on metal – eighty sabres rasping from the scabbard – the sound of grim resolve, fortifying him that drew it and unnerving him that heard it drawn.

Sound carried in that still, warm air.

The squadrons halted . . . and drew swords.

Hervey no longer shivered at metal on metal. But the rest . . . For many it was the first time.

He'd said to expect as much. This was a game for cool heads and calculation.

Vanneck's troop came over the crest with the momentum of a whole brigade. Hervey saw the French commander trying to take in what lay before him.

Then the advance resumed. Walk-march . . . trot . . .

So many men – two hundred, four lines, an overlap, a great weight in the press of horses: he'd need Vanneck's to bolster Worsley's, yet be able to extricate them to form a firing line if . . .

'I shall take post with the supports now, Captain Worsley. A resolute front, mind.'

Worsley saluted with his sword. 'You may count on it, Colonel.'

He knew he could. But these things were better said – if only for the benefit of those on whom Worsley in turn depended.

He reined left and trotted to where Vanneck had halted and drawn up his troop, fifty yards to the rear on rising ground, with Acton at his heels, and Fairbrother, Johnson and the little knot of others who formed his suite.

Vanneck had anticipated his orders. The troop was already dividing into three to cover Worsley's flanks while keeping a few carbines for support.

'Nicely done, Captain Vanneck.'

'Thank heavens we set aside Dundas this last month.'

Hervey nodded. 'No doubt he has his uses, but not today for sure.'

And this was the dangerous time. If the French broke into a gallop they'd be unstoppable without shot or counter-charge. All Worsley could then do – and he'd have to judge it to the second – was go threes-about and wheel left or right at a pace.

They stumbled into a short canter. It was still a peril.

Hervey grimaced: was it bluff?

Worsley swallowed hard, but stood his ground.

At a hundred yards they fell back to a trot, then halted suddenly.

An officer rode forward and called to them in what sounded like Dutch.

Worsley answered with the authority of his broad acres, wearying of their blue being taken for a foreign coat. '*Pas Hollandais, monsieur; nous sommes Anglais!*'

One of his corporals lofted the Union flag which they'd carried in the parades in Brussels.

It hung limply in the still air.

The spokesman conferred with his colonel, who shook his head vigorously. '*Anglais? Pas possible,*' he said, in a voice that carried clearly. '*C'est une ruse de guerre!*'

He turned and said something to his adjutant.

And then abuse erupted the length of the French line: 'Cheeseheads! Marsh-frogs! Clog-feet!'

Hervey angered. '*Rosbifs*, yes,' he said, gathering his reins and spurring forward, 'but I'm damned if I'll be called aught else.'

B Troop sat impassively, aided by growls from Collins.

'Stand fast, Worsley, while I go and speak with that fellow,' Hervey called.

But their colonel was in no mood for parley. He waved his sword: '*En avant!*'

The line billowed forward.

Hervey cursed, reined about and cantered for the support line. Once, he'd tried to make some Portuguese troops look like the King's infantry, in red coats, and the ruse had failed. Now he couldn't persuade a Frenchman that he wasn't a 'clog-foot'!

It was up to Worsley – and Vanneck if it came to carbines.

The trot was in-hand, but they'd still barge the line, for although Worsley wasn't in open order, he wasn't knee-to-knee either (he hadn't the numbers).

Hervey gave Vanneck the look that said 'ready yourself.'

But it was Worsley's moment. 'Quarters left!'

Round swung every troop horse, just as in the park at Windsor. There were now no gaps – and the line not a fraction shorter.

'Good work, B Troop,' said Hervey beneath his breath.

The French checked, stumbled for the most part to a walk and collided with them with no more force than a boat coming along-side in a light swell.

Now the mounted ruck. Cursing, swearing – every sort of imprecation – arms, elbows, knees, boots, pushing, shoving, kick-ing, gouging.

But sabres both sides stayed shouldered.

'Now Vanneck, if you please: the flanks,' called Hervey.

No words of command, just signals with the sabre. Twenty dragoons with a cornet peeled off from both ends of Vanneck's line to extend Worsley's.

'Nicely done,' said Hervey beneath his breath again. They might be at a field day.

And then, like the challenging stag which, knowing the contest to be uneven, breaks from the lock of antlers, he saw the colonel of cuirassiers turn about and ride rear. It could not be long now . . .

'I do believe Worsley's outwitted them!'

Malet heard. 'And see, Colonel – how Collins steadies them.'

He was trotting the line with no more agitation than before an inspection.

Would Armstrong? Or would it be fists by now?

Perhaps it was just a matter of time, for no recall was sounded, and the push of troopers was becoming like the old push of pikes. If one side wouldn't yield, it must come to blows . . .

The curses increased, mutually unintelligible, but plain enough.

And then a Frenchman lashed out with his sword arm.

St Alban parried.

All that clashed were sword hilts.

But his coverman, furious at the affront, lunged with his knuckle.

Others followed.

Then sabres clashed.

Collins was there in an instant: 'Swords up, damn you! Up!'

He drove between the two locked blades.

'Up, I say!' thrusting his sabre between them.

Another – instinct, or evil? – cut at his sword arm.

Blades flashed left and right.

A dragoon fell. Two cuirassiers followed.

Blades the length of the line now.

Rennie weighed in from nowhere with all the authority of his rank, somehow transcending the barrier of noise and language.

Both sides reeled momentarily.

Their colonel bore down. '*Arrête!*'

NCOs berated their own, on both sides.

The brawl petered out.

Hervey galloped into the melee and all but seized the colonel's

361

reins. '*Vous avez blessé des soldats du Roi d'Angleterre!*'

The lines fell still – a sullen, glowering stand-off.

The colonel seemed only now to comprehend. He saw the black crape. He looked dazed.

'For whom are you in mourning, *monsieur*?'

His accent was more of the street than the château.

'For His late Majesty, King George,' barked Hervey.

Confusion overcame him. 'You are, then, English?'

Hervey spoke his precisest French. 'I am the commanding officer of His Majesty King William's Sixth Light Dragoons, and under the terms of the Final Act of the Congress of Vienna I am authorized to prevent the invasion of the sovereign territory of the Kingdom of the Netherlands.'

Bluff it might be called; audacity certainly – magnificent audacity. Either way, there could be no more words. *Ne plus ultra*.

The colonel sheathed his sword.

Hervey merely recovered his.

And, oh, the irony. In life the old King could do nothing but put on uniform and play the game of soldiers, while in death he could turn back a regiment of cuirassiers. Hervey grew tall in the saddle and demanded he yield.

The colonel cleared his throat. '*Monsieur le commandant*, I am commanded to make no war on an ally. My orders are only to secure the safety of the people of these parts.'

Hervey bowed. 'They are in no danger, *monsieur*, as you might presume from the presence of His Majesty's troops.'

The colonel, his aspect still one of daze, shook his head. 'In that case I shall withdraw at once to Maubeuge to consult with my superiors.'

Hervey nodded. 'I understand, *monsieur*. But please make plain to your superiors that English troops shall remain here to secure the safety not only of the people but of the Kingdom of the Netherlands.'

The colonel, humbled like the challenging stag that had not the potency, though it might one day, withdrew warily. Hervey had not been inclined to melt at the word 'ally' and to part on fraternal terms, for one of his dragoons was unhorsed. It was no occasion for civility.

When the French had quit the field, he turned to the bloody consequences of his audacious victory. The surgeon had set up post at the spinney, where Hervey found Princess Augusta kneeling next to the dragoon, whose leg was broken and bleeding, and a corporal whose nose was split so badly that blood had turned his tunic facings red, the countess trying to staunch the flow with pieces of her petticoat, while the princess used hers to bind the dragoon's legs together.

But Milne and his orderlies were cutting away urgently at another coat, which was blood-soaked beyond recognition – like their aprons.

'Who . . . *Collins*?'

'Artery, Hervey . . . If I can't get a clamp to it . . .'

Hervey shuddered. He'd seen men die in minutes for want of a tuppenny clamp.

Collins lay still, his eyes misted.

'It's bad,' whispered Milne. 'It'll have to come off. Only way to get at the artery. He's cut to the bone.'

The right arm.

An arm was an arm, but a sword arm . . .

Hervey grasped him by the shoulder. 'All your skill and science, Milne. All of it. Save that arm.'

'Colonel, it will need all my skill and more to save his life.'

Hervey blanched. 'Then save his life first, Milne – and *then* the arm.'

XXIII

UNDER AUTHORITY

Caserne de la Garde Civile, Brussels, 21 September 1830

Hervey put down the letter, shaking his head. '*Thou art my battle axe and weapons of war: for with thee will I break in pieces the nations, and with thee will I destroy kingdoms.*'

'Joshua?' asked Fairbrother, laying aside his book.

'Jeremiah. None more apt.'

The day before, the separatists had disarmed the Garde Civile, stormed the Hôtel de Ville and declared a provisional government. Gone was the Committee of Public Safety – dread title, Jacobin (and soon there'd be a Robespierre, no doubt), yet a force for moderation nonetheless – and in its place a fierce tribe of Belgae who'd treat with The Hague as their forebears had with Rome. He could feel no great triumph.

'Well, if the Kingdom of the Netherlands is to be destroyed, it will be on better terms for your address. Two troops of light dragoons, and Monsieur Talleyrand is confounded!'

'If only Bylandt had shown more resolve, or perhaps I . . .'

Fairbrother shook his head. 'A tide in the affairs of men, Hervey. Think not on it. The affair at the border was a far greater imperative. I don't believe that even you know quite *how* brilliant an affair: you judged the place and the method to perfection. And I trust that Windsor shall hear of it.'

'I trust that Windsor shall hear of *Collins*.'

Fairbrother sighed. 'Nothing is ever without cost. You and I know that.'

'I would not stand here now had he not been my coverman at Toulouse.'

'I know it.'

'Toulouse, and many a time before. But Toulouse especially – in the very last hours of the war, indeed.'

They'd just taken a battery, and a Frenchman had sprung from beneath a gun and thrust a spontoon in his thigh. Collins had leapt from his horse and launched so ferocious an assault that the man had no time to parry, and the sword cleaved his skull in two. Blood had bubbled like a spring for a full minute where he lay twitching.

If only he'd been able to do the same for Collins in that needless melee . . .

'He was a man for whom duty was all,' said Fairbrother consolingly. 'It's unwise, is it not, to count the cost too . . . particularly? Else we'd never hazard anything.'

Hervey nodded. Had it come to carbines they'd be counting a good deal more. 'I must do all in my power to see him settled well.'

Fairbrother answered brightly. 'Others have prospered with but a single arm; and he's resourceful.'

'Indeed.'

'And no man lost his life.'

'God be thanked.'

Fairbrother's brow furrowed. 'I think you yourself may take a little of the thanks too.'

Hervey inclined his head as if to acknowledge, for every man of the Sixth was saying the same, said Johnson.

'And you have the acclamation of the ambassador. And I'll warrant there'll be a ribbon in it.'

'You know, I trust, that I do nothing for acclamation and ribbons.'

'Hervey, I was not with you at Toulouse or Waterloo, or any number of places you've drawn your sword – great's the pity – but you will grant that we've seen *some* action together!'

Hervey conceded with a nod, but said nothing other than 'Luck went with me.' Anyway, it was time to be done with dark thoughts.

'Who is the letter from? What exactly does it say?' asked Fairbrother.

'The secretary of the embassy. And it conveys in writing what he said in person yesterday – expressions of gratitude et cetera. And he attaches a copy of the ambassador's last letter to London.'

He handed it to him:

From His Excellency Sir Charles Bagot, His Majesty's Ambassador Extraordinary and Plenipotentiary at the Court of the Netherlands,

To The Rt. Hon. The Earl of Aberdeen, Sec. of State Foreign Dept.

The Hague, September 7, 1830

My Lord,
The Baron Verstolk has just read to me a despatch, which is forwarded this evening to Monsieur de Falck, and which will be equally addressed to-morrow to His Netherland Majesty's Ministers at Vienna, St Petersburgh and Berlin, upon the subject of the modifications which it may become necessary to make in the Loi Fondamentale, under the project of a separate administration of the two great divisions of this kingdom, and of the manner in which such modifications may be thought to affect the objects and stipulations of the Powers, parties to the eight Articles of the Treaty of London.

This despatch directs M. de Falck, and the King's Ministers at the above-mentioned Courts, to request, that in the event of discussions becoming necessary upon this latter point, instructions may be sent to me, and to the Austrian, Russian, and Prussian Ministers at The Hague, to enter into conference upon the subject, with the

Plenipotentiary who may be appointed by His Netherland Majesty
for that purpose.
   I have the honour &c,
      Charles Bagot.

Fairbrother gave it back with a look that said these were indeed momentous events.

But it hardly needed a letter – certainly not one written a fortnight ago – to tell them they were amidst history in the making. Or rather, had returned to the midst of history-making, for events had moved rapidly while they'd been out of the city. News of the riot the night of the opera had reached The Hague on the 27th, and the Prince of Orange, evidently, had urged the king to accept the resignation of the justice minister and to take a conciliatory stand with the southern provinces, but he'd refused flatly either to dismiss Van Maanen or treat with the rebels. However, he did give the prince permission to return to Brussels with a 'mission of enquiry', and agree to receive a deputation from Brussels, while ordering more troops south – and when the prince reached Vilvoorde, just outside the city, he sent an aide-de-camp to Baron D'Hoogvoort, the magistrate, one of the few men (in Hervey's view) to be acting with both calmness and determination, to bring him to a conference there. But the news of the gathering troops whipped Brussels into a frenzy, and at the conference D'Hoogvoort urged the prince not to bring them to the city, for the separatists threatened to oppose them '*à outrance*', to the limit, and to come instead with just his personal suite under his (D'Hoogvoort's) own protection.

And, indeed, the prince did make his entry thus, on 1 September, the streets lined with the Garde Civile. As he had no authority to concede anything, however, after three days he returned to Vilvoorde. Meanwhile, the king had received the Brussels delegation at The Hague, but said he would not treat with any while a pistol was at his head. Instead he issued a proclamation, which no sooner was it posted on the walls in Brussels than it was torn down, and the unrest spread wide and fast thereafter. Five hundred armed men from Liège alone marched on the capital, and others from Louvain, Jemappes, and Wavre. And, like the fiends of legend rising from the nether regions, the miners of the Borinage *en masse* quit their world below ground to join them, so that Brussels filled with men as revolutionary as any Paris mob. Reform was then no longer the cry, only independence.

And so, last night, all order had been overthrown, and the provisional government proclaimed. It was well that the regiment was leaving.

'I'm sorry we shan't see what becomes of it all, though,' said Fairbrother, jauntily. 'I never saw a full-blown revolution before.'

Hervey shrugged. 'You may stay if you wish. You are not under orders. For myself I believe we have done all we can here, and it's better that we return to England as soon as may be. As soon as Ostend is able to arrange matters.'

'And a "Protestant wind" if there's no steam.'

Hervey smiled at last. 'Indeed. But the wind always changes, if you have the patience.'

Fairbrother wondered, though, for there was more to it than a happy return. A fair wind would speed them to England, but his friend also to the emptiness of the matrimonial bed. He'd put his tribulations behind him when they'd crossed the Channel hither, yet once returned to England ... *Heaven send the prince a better companion.*

He shut away the thought. 'And you have the question of Mr Rennie's successor decided, at least.'

Perhaps it was the talk of winds that made him tactless – ill ones that blew no good &c. He checked himself.

'I meant no hurt. I know what a business it's been.'

Hervey shook his head. 'I've escaped the choice. I'd no right to.'

Fairbrother frowned. 'Put it from your mind. Either man would have made an admirable sar'nt-major. And it doesn't diminish

Armstrong's appointment, your not having made the choice.'

Hervey brightened somewhat. 'I know it. You are quite right, as ever. Well, almost ever.'

'I am at your service.'

Hervey knew him to be – and looked thoughtful again. 'Tell me something; it has puzzled me. When I told you that Kennett had withdrawn his allegations against Collins, you showed no surprise.'

'Why should it have been surprising? You told me General Gifford had offered him a captaincy.'

'But I told you he'd withdrawn before I myself knew of the offer.'

Fairbrother looked faintly uncomfortable, if only momentarily. 'I don't recall.'

'Mm. *Ex Africa semper aliquid novi . . .*'

He smiled. 'I have left the Africans behind me.'

'And they you?'

Fairbrother shrugged. 'You mean "blood will out"?'

Now Hervey smiled. 'I mean that I wondered if the ways of the Africans – the *Royal* Africans – commended themselves to colder climes.'

Fairbrother shook his head. 'Thou speakest in riddles.'

'Mm.' But he was sure his meaning was clear nevertheless.

'By the bye – and of this I'm certain – the exact quote from Pliny runs *Semper aliquid novi Africam adferre*. And it's a Greek proverb he quotes.'*

'Then I happily stand corrected, and will enquire no more.' He leaned forward to take a look at his friend's reading. 'What is your book?'

'It is called *Pride and Prejudice*.'

Hervey knew of it. Henrietta had once pressed it on him, though he'd never taken it up. 'You're still intent on closer acquaintance with society then?'

'And on human nature.'

---

* 'Africa always brings something new.'

'And you find it instructive?'

'And entertaining.'

'Are there military men in it? Does Miss Austen – it is Miss Austen, isn't it? – draw them faithfully?'

'Only Militia.'

'Ah.'

'But you would find it . . . Well, let us say there is much to recommend it.' Though he doubted his friend would ever begin on such a book, and certainly never finish it.

There was a knock at the door, and Johnson came in.

'Mr Lincoln'd like to 'ave a word, Colonel.'

Fairbrother rose. 'I shall repair to my quarters. I think by now my baggage will have been brought from the Grande Place.'

Hervey nodded. 'You will join us all at dinner, I trust.'

'Thank you; I shall. But I would come with you first to see Collins.'

'By all means.'

He left and the quartermaster came in.

'I'm sorry to disturb you, Colonel, but word has just come from Ostend that the shipping is arranged for Friday – steamers. We can march out of here tomorrow. I've arranged to hand the barracks to the commandant at midday, though with things as they are I shan't be surprised if I have to lock up and leave the keys at Ostend.'

Hervey raised an eyebrow. 'Indeed. And Sar'nt-Major Collins?'

'I've got him a *dormeuse*.'

'Excellent. I'm about to go and see him. I think it best that he travels with the colonel-in-chief's guard after she takes leave of them tomorrow?'

'That is the adjutant's intention, Colonel.'

The princess and her suite were to set out at dawn. He would take his own leave when he saw Collins.

'Very well.'

Lincoln hesitated.

'Is there anything more?'

'Colonel, I had intended waiting until we returned to Hounslow, but I believe it better to inform you now. I shall be sending in my papers presently. Mrs Lincoln and I are to purchase a small hotel at Brighton.'

Hervey was dumbstruck. Lincoln had been a part of the regiment since the day he'd joined. His attestation papers had long since been conveniently lost . . .

He rose and looked at him directly, hoping the curious anxiety that assailed him did not show. 'Mr Lincoln, I'm truly sorry to hear this, although of course I sincerely wish you well at Brighton. Is there nothing I can say to change your mind? You are . . . so much the regiment.'

Lincoln shook his head. 'No, Colonel, there's nothing. My mind is quite made up. But thank you for the sentiment. It goes without saying, I hope, that I much regret I shall be leaving during your command, but I cannot stay at duty for ever, and it's best that I go before my time than after it.'

Hervey smiled, and held out his hand. 'Admirably put, Mr Lincoln. And I thank you for that sentiment too . . . Your establishment in Brighton will surely become the most comfortable and efficient on the south coast.'

The quartermaster allowed himself a rare smile by return. 'Thank you, Colonel. And . . .' (he cleared his throat) 'if young Pearce is to make his way in the army, it's better that his father-in-law is no longer a presence.'

'I trust that is *not* a consideration in your decision.'

'No, not a consideration – more a happy consequence. And he ought, in any case, to exchange into another regiment. It would be for the best.'

One in which his wife, for all her beauty and accomplishments, would not be known as the daughter of a quartermaster? Hervey shook his head, though he would not discuss it now. Lincoln had quite enough to concern himself with. 'It may be as well, but these

371

things need not be hurried. And we need have no farewells now. There'll be time and place – mark my words!'

Lincoln took his leave, the lump in his throat not entirely concealed. Johnson reappeared.

'A postboy's just come from Ostend, Colonel.'

'An express?'

'No, 'e was carrying two bags.'

That much was a relief. The last thing he wanted was any change of plan. It was bound to be out of date.

'Would you bring me some coffee, please. And I'd have you come with me when I go to see Sar'nt-Major Collins.'

'Colonel.'

When Fairbrother returned, booted and spurred for the ride to Princess Augusta's, he found his friend in noble spirits.

'Something evidently pleases you. The postboy brought you good news too?'

'Too?'

'A considerable remittance from Jamaica, and a doubling of my allowance. You see before you a single man in possession of a good fortune. I must thereby be in want of a wife.'

'Of what are you speaking? Want of a wife?'

Fairbrother smiled. 'You really ought to read Miss Austen, you know. She has the keenest sense. Her book – it begins with that proposition, and how when such a man comes into a neighbour-hood every mother of an eligible daughter at once has designs on him.'

'And that's what it's about, is it – the marriage mart?'

'That and a great deal else. But I shan't sport with you on the question. I merely wished to share with you my satisfaction. What is *your* good news?'

Hervey handed him a letter. 'Read this – from John Howard.'

The Horse Guards,
September 16, 1830.

My dear Hervey,
I write in haste to catch the King's Messenger leaving this evening for
The Hague via Ostend and Antwerp. Yesterday the French
ambassador had an audience of Lord Aberdeen and expressed his
deepest regrets in regard to the untoward events of 30 Ultimo, over
which the Foreign Secretary had made the most vigorous protest, and
assured His Lordship that His Majesty the King of the French (as
Louis Philippe is to be known) has no intention of interfering in the
affairs of the Kingdom of the Netherlands. Lord Aberdeen
communicated to Lord Hill his appreciation of the services rendered
by the troops in Belgium, and having read the latest despatch of Sir
Charles Bagot, Lord Hill this morning, in council with his Military
Secretary and the Adjutant-General, directed that you should receive
a Colonel's Brevet. It will be gazetted as of today.
*   I send you my heartiest congratulations, and best wishes for yr safe*
return,
*   Ever yr good friend,*
*   John Howard.*

'Well, my heartiest congratulations, too. And did I not foretell as much?'

'Did you?'

'At Hounslow, I seem to recall.'

Hervey nodded, smiling a little sheepishly. 'Now I think of it, I do recall something of the sort.'

'Well, we'd better be making for the princess's, ought we not? You'll tell her of it, of course?'

'I . . . I don't think it quite proper. Not until it's gazetted.'

'But you must, Hervey. She'll take inordinate delight in it.'

'Inordinate?'

Fairbrother shook his head. 'Perhaps I should have said "prodigious".'

*

'What's a brevet again, Captain Fairbrother, sir?' asked Johnson, who was standing remarkably erect and NCO-like in the princess's little ante-room, while in the library, which served as Collins's convalescing-ward, Hervey waited for the surgeon to re-dress the wound.

Fairbrother was standing at the window observing the increasingly purposeful swallows. The swifts had been gone these three weeks: it would not be many days now before the skies would suddenly empty – and then another northern winter could not be far behind (and he shivered at the thought).

'A brevet? It's a sort of courtesy rank, temporary, but in the expectation that it will be made substantive in due course.'

'I know Colonel 'Ervey 'as 'ad one once before, but I don't remember why.'

'The thing is, Corporal Johnson, the brevet gives a man the rank in the army but not in the regiment, so Colonel Hervey will be able to continue in command while his seniority as a colonel in the army is preserved.'

'Well, that's nice, sir.'

'Indeed – the very reason, I suppose, that the commander-in-chief has bestowed it. And so if the regiment were to be brigaded at any time, the brevet would give him seniority over the other lieutenant-colonels – unless any of them had a brevet gazetted earlier – and so he would command the brigade.'

Johnson was much awed.

Meanwhile in the library, the surgeon was pronouncing himself satisfied. The amputation, for all that it had been done *in extremis*, had been without complication, and the wound was healing well.

'Thanks to your skill, Mr Milne, and the sar'nt-major's constitution,' said Hervey.

'Aye, Colonel – that and chloride of soda.'

Hervey had no idea of what he spoke, but Milne had much impressed him as a scientific sort of practitioner. 'It sounds foul-tasting, but evidently efficacious.'

'Why, man, if ye were to drink it ye'd be beyond all hope o' my medicine. It's a disinfectant.'

'I stand corrected.'

Corrected, but not enlightened. However, he had not come to advance his chirological knowledge.

'I'll see the sar'nt-major in private now, if that's in order, Mr Milne.'

'Indeed it is, Colonel. He's fit to travel, and to undergo punishment.'

The surgeon's humour could be a little arch, but Hervey found he could live with it, especially after so definitive a demonstration of his skill.

Milne gathered up the appurtenances of his profession, made what passed for a click of heels, and withdrew, leaving him alone with 'the patient'.

'Well, Sar'nt-Major, I'm most excessively pleased to find you in this way.'

Collins, propped up with enormous cushions in a bed the like of which he'd rarely seen, let alone slept in, smiled encouragingly. 'Another month of this and I'd be ruined, Colonel. That countess's the best of nurses, though you'd never think it to look at her.'

Hervey nodded. She could assume the look of the Teuton. 'I know what you mean.'

'Well, at this rate in another week I'll be handing in my sword to Mr Lincoln's stores – *left*-handing in, that is.'

Hervey could smile but a little at the drollness. 'I see no cause for that.'

But Collins shook his head; there was no precedent he knew of for an invalid at regimental duty.

'And, you know, Colonel, that I'll be leaving the regiment arsy versy?'

Hervey looked mystified.

'Well, I mean, when a man joins the Sixth, ten to one he can't write, and when he leaves, ten to one he can. Whereas I *could* write when I joined!'

Hervey laughed with him, before sitting in the chair next to the bed and putting his forage cap on the counterpane.

'There's no cause for you to leave.'

Collins shook his head again. 'A serjeant-major with no sword arm, Colonel?'

'There are other positions.'

He shook his head again. 'Colonel, I can't even ride roughs with just one hand.'

'No, not that. I want you to be quartermaster.'

Collins looked at him, disbelieving.

'Mr Lincoln is to send in his papers. And as I'm sure you're aware, Mr Rennie is to have a commission in the Royals.'

Collins was still astonished. 'I suppose I could learn to write left-handed soon enough.'

'And have a clerk do the most of it.'

Silence.

And then Collins nodded, slowly. 'Thank you, Colonel. Thank you very much. I'd always hoped one day . . .'

'Well, it's come somewhat early. And despite the circumstances, I'm very glad of it.'

With a little awkwardness, they managed to shake hands.

Hervey's leave-taking of the colonel-in-chief was not a prolonged affair, but he took much satisfaction in it – pleasure indeed. She received him in a little south-facing drawing room, her writing case open on a table by the window, and the produce of evidently some hours' correspondence sealed and waiting for her footman.

'I have written to Lord George Irvine in the most appreciative terms, Colonel Hervey, for all the courtesy you have shown me.'

'The honour was sufficient, ma'am, but I thank you nevertheless.'

'And not merely courtesy, but your protection. I am well aware that I put myself in harm's way.'

'And the regiment is all admiration for it, ma'am.'

'But I placed you and your regiment in harm's way too thereby.'

'It is the occupation of a soldier, ma'am, no more.'

She smiled as if to say she could not agree but would not pursue it.

Nor did she, and for a quarter of an hour they spoke instead of the present state of the country (and of her own), as well as of more agreeable matters.

There was no undue formality. There never had been, but the events of the last month had made for a particular easiness. It was hard to think of her as his junior in years – by, what, ten, twelve? Her composure was that of a woman twice her age, and her resolution – her courage – the equal of any. What a prize, indeed, had the regiment obtained.

When she had satisfied him that her return to Schloss Ehrenburg was all arranged with perfect safety, she rose and went to her writing table.

'Colonel Hervey, I should like to present you with this expression of appreciation.'

She handed him a green leather case the size of her palm.

'Ma'am, I'm . . .'

It was not unusual for such an expression to be given, but he found it awkward nevertheless.

She looked away as he opened it.

He expected a medallion of some sort – the usual appreciation. But it was a miniature, and a very fine one. It caught her likeness – her appeal – very exactly.

'Ma'am, I'm honoured. I . . . shall place it in a position of prominence . . . in the regiment.'

'Where you will, Colonel Hervey,' she replied softly.

She walked with him to the villa's entrance, where Fairbrother and Johnson were waiting with the horses.

Fairbrother observed the look upon the face of his good friend. He'd seen it from time to time in others; he'd once known it himself. What the attention of a pair of fine eyes could bring . . .

And soon a fair wind, and steam, would be taking him back to – what? – 'the mutual society, help, and comfort, that the one ought to have of the other'?

Ought – but not.

And, of course, his friend would put on that precious mantle again, that mask – the mask of command – and sally on: *For I am a man under authority, having soldiers under me . . .*

Though in truth was it not more 'the mask of night', that else would make a man blanch (*'Thou know'st the mask of night is on my face, Else would a maiden blush'*) . . .

He sighed, and looked away.

'A single man, good fortune . . . and want of a wife.'

'What's that, sir?' asked Johnson.

'Oh, nothing, nothing,' said Fairbrother airily.

Then adding below his breath, 'but in truth – *everything.*'

HISTORICAL AFTERNOTE

'With thee will I break in pieces the nations.'
The Book of the Prophet Jeremiah

Two days after Hervey took his fictional leave of the Princess Augusta, Dutch troops led by King William's second son, Prince Frederik, occupied Brussels, at a stroke uniting the hitherto disparate Belgian uprising. Street fighting followed, some of it bloody, and during the night of 26–27 September the Dutch beat a retreat. The committee of the various insurgent factions now transformed itself into a provisional government and on 4 October declared independence. The revolt, which had hitherto been largely confined to the Walloon districts, spread rapidly throughout Flanders. Garrison after garrison surrendered, regiments from the southern provinces going over to the provisional government. The remnants of the Dutch forces retired into Antwerp, and with yet more bloodshed, embittering the Flemings as much as the fighting in Brussels had embittered the Walloons. King William appealed to the signatories of the Articles of London to restore the situation.*

* Bylandt was blamed, and recalled on 24 November. He subsequently published several pamphlets protesting his 'innocence', but never again held active command, retiring from the service in 1840, though he was promoted to lieutenant-general in 1843 after the crown prince had succeeded to the throne, largely in recognition of his service at Waterloo.

Representatives of the signatory powers – Austria, Prussia, Russia and Great Britain (together with France) – met in London on 4 November, the timing opportune. Not only were Austria and Russia preoccupied with their own internal difficulties (the Polish revolt in particular, and unrest throughout Germany), but a change of government in Britain brought a new foreign secretary, Lord Palmerston, sympathetic to the Belgian cause. The Tories had won the general election following the death of George IV, but in November the Duke of Wellington, having refused to support reform of the House of Commons, was defeated on a motion to examine the accounts of the Civil List (in effect a vote of no confidence), the Tories themselves dividing, and resigned. A minority Whig government was formed under Earl Grey, to which Palmerston defected. And to The Hague's dismay, under Palmerston's influence the representatives of the signatory powers refused to back the Dutch king, instead imposing an armistice and declaring that their intervention would be confined to negotiating a settlement on the basis of Belgian independence. Palmerston's concern, besides any natural sympathy for the Belgians, was to check French ambitions, not least to keep the Scheldt estuary and Belgian coast out of potentially hostile hands (Talleyrand, the French plenipotentiary, had made a beguiling proposal to carve Belgium into three parts – Antwerp and the coast to be a British protectorate, the eastern part to be annexed by Prussia, and the lion's share to be reincorporated with France). While the plenipotentiaries were deliberating, the provisional government in Brussels resolved that their new state should be a constitutional monarchy and that the (Dutch) house of Orange-Nassau should be forever excluded from the throne, a committee being duly appointed to draw up a constitution.

On 20 January 1831 the plenipotentiaries issued a protocol defining the conditions of separation. Holland was to retain her old boundaries of 1790, and Belgium was to have the remainder of the territory assigned to the kingdom of the Netherlands in 1815. However, Luxemburg, hitherto a part of the southern provinces of the United Kingdom of the Netherlands, was excluded from the settlement. The new Belgian state was to be perpetually neutral, and its integrity and inviolability guaranteed by all and each of the signatory powers. The provisional government took objection to these and other conditions, as well as proposals as to the choice of monarch; proposals that prompted the Dutch king to give his assent in the hope of winning the plenipotentiaries' support for the candidature of the Prince of Orange.

It was a forlorn hope. Palmerston strongly favoured Prince Leopold of Saxe-Coburg, the uncle of Princess (later Queen) Victoria, who had been living in England since the death of his wife. The other powers raised no objection, and Brussels agreed, electing him king on 4 June. But the Dutch king rejected the overall proposals (known as the XVIII Articles), announcing his intention 'to throw his army into the balance with a view to obtaining more equitable terms of separation'.

The Dutch army, once one of the most effective in Europe, had been humiliated by the rebels' easy successes and was bent on restoring its reputation. On 2 August, the Prince of Orange, at the head of 30,000 picked men and a formidable force of artillery, crossed the frontier. The Belgians – the army of the Scheldt and the army of the Meuse – were taken by surprise. The army of the Meuse fell back in disarray on Liège, while that of the Scheldt was also forced to beat a rapid retreat towards Brussels. Leopold now took personal command, and although the Dutch worsted the army of the Meuse at Louvain they did not press on to the capital. On hearing that a French army had entered Belgium at Leopold's invitation, the Prince of Orange rapidly concluded an armistice (brokered by the British minister in Brussels, Sir Robert Adair), recrossing the border into Holland on 20 August (though the garrison at Antwerp remained), whereupon the French too recrossed into France.

The 'Ten Days' Campaign' had gained its purpose, however: when the London conference reassembled the plenipotentiaries revised the Articles more favourably towards The Hague. The northwestern (Walloon) portion of Luxemburg was assigned to

Belgium, but a considerable portion of Belgian Limburg was ceded to the Dutch, giving them command of both banks of the Meuse from Maastricht to the Gelderland frontier.

Although the new Articles created profound dissatisfaction in both Belgium and Holland, King Leopold, by threatening to abdicate, managed to secure acceptance in Brussels, and on 15 November 1831 the treaty was signed in London by the five great powers and by the Belgian envoy, solemnly recognizing Belgium as an independent state whose perpetual neutrality and inviolability was guaranteed by the signatories.

Still King William would not assent, objecting in particular to the proposed regulations regarding navigation of the Scheldt, and he refused to evacuate Antwerp. Throughout the spring and summer of 1832 *notes verbales* flew between London and The Hague. The conference did its utmost to find some accommodation but ultimately had to resort to the threat of coercion. Although Austria, Prussia and Russia declined to take any direct part, they approved the use of force as a last resort by Britain and France, who on 22 October concluded a convention for joint action. Notice was given to The Hague to withdraw all troops before 13 November on pain of blockade of Dutch ports, an embargo on Dutch ships in the allies' harbours, and armed action against the garrisons remaining in Belgian territory. William immediately refused.

The allies acted promptly, an Anglo-French squadron at once sailing to blockade Dutch ports and the mouth of the Scheldt; and in response to an appeal from the Belgian government a French army of 60,000 men again crossed the Belgian frontier, and laid siege to Antwerp.

The siege lasted a month, the Dutch capitulating just before Christmas, though Rear-Admiral Koopman burned his twelve gunboats rather than surrender them. The blockade and embargo continued, however, until the Dutch gave way and evacuated all troops from the former southern provinces. By the Convention of London, signed on 21 May 1833, William undertook to commit no acts of hostility against Belgium while a definitive peace treaty was concluded. Negotiations dragged on for several years, however, principally over the question of Luxemburg, but Dutch opinion gradually swung towards conciliation, not least because of the expense of keeping the army on a war footing. On 19 April 1839 Baron Dedel signed the treaty on behalf of the Dutch king.

It was by this Treaty of London, which in 1914 the German chancellor, Theobald von Bethmann Hollweg, dismissed as 'a scrap of paper', that Britain went to war upon the invasion of Belgium by German troops.

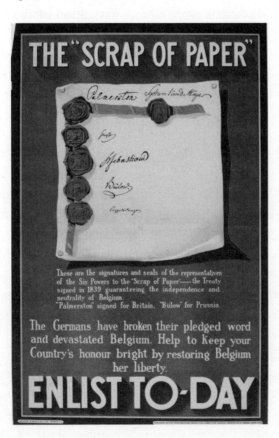

MATTHEW PAULINUS HERVEY

BORN: 1791, second son of the Reverend
Thomas Hervey, Vicar of Horningsham
in Wiltshire, and of Mrs. Hervey; one
sister, Elizabeth.

EDUCATED: Shrewsbury School (praepostor)

MARRIED: 1817 to Lady Henrietta
Lindsay, ward of the Marquess of Bath
(deceased 1818). 1828 to Lady
Lankester, widow of Lieutenant~Colonel
Sir Ivo Lankester, Bart, lately
commanding 6th Light Dragoons.

CHILDREN: a daughter, Georgiana,
born 1818.

MILITARY HISTORY:

1808: commissioned cornet by purchase in His Majesty's 6th Light
   Dragoons (Princess Caroline's Own).

1809~14: served Portugal and Spain; evacuated with army at
   ✕ Corunna, 1809, returned with regiment to Lisbon that year:
   Present at numerous battles and actions including
   ✕ Talavera, ✕ Badajoz, ✕ Salamanca, ✕ Vitoria.

1814: present at ✕ Toulouse; wounded. Lieutenant.

1814~15: served Ireland, present at ✕ Waterloo, and in Paris
   with army of occupation.

1815: Additional ADC to the Duke of Wellington (acting captain);
   despatched for special duty in Bengal.

1816: saw service against Pindarees and Nizam of Hyderabad's
   forces; returned to regimental duty. Brevet captain; brevet
   major.

1818: saw service in Canada; briefly seconded to US forces, Michigan
   Territory; resigned commission.

1819: reinstated, 6th Light Dragoons; captain.

1820~26: served Bengal; saw active service in ✕ Ava (wounded
   severely); present at ✕ Siege of Bhurtpore; brevet major.

1826~27: detached service in Portugal.

1827: in temporary command of 6th Light Dragoons, major;
   in command of detachment of 6th Light Dragoons at the
   Cape Colony; seconded to raise Corps of Cape Mounted
   Rifles; acting lieutenant~colonel; ✕ Umtata River;
   wounded.

1828: home leave.

1828: service in Natal and Zululand.

1829: attached to Russian army in the Balkans for
   observation in the war with Turkey.